Venus Love Trap

JESSICA SHERRY

Published by Jessica Sherry
Copyright © 2026 by Jessica Sherry
jessicasherry.com

All rights reserved.

No part of this book may be reproduced in any form or by any electronic or mechanical means, including information storage and retrieval systems, without written permission from the author, except for the use of brief quotations in a book review. Please note that no part of this book may be used or reproduced in any manner for the purpose of training artificial intelligence technologies or systems.

This story, all names, characters, and incidents portrayed in this book are fictional. No identification with actual persons (living or deceased), places, and buildings is intended or should be inferred.

ISBN: 979-8-9944349-0-1 (print)
ISBN: 979-8-9887254-9-7 (ebook)

Book Cover Design by Ink & Laurel
Printed/Published in the United States of America

Author's Note

Dear Reader,

Thank you for picking up *Venus Love Trap*! Before you begin Venus and Henry's roller-coaster love story, please note that it features realistic, wounded characters and sensitive subject matter that may upset some readers. If you'd rather not know any spoilers, ignore the following paragraph and skip to chapter one with my thanks for reading.

For those who prefer to know, this book deals with the following complex topics: mentions of suicide of a family member (no on-page descriptions); mental health representation; anxiety; grief; moments of impulsivity and situational harm related to an ADHD diagnosis; loss of a relative (not a parent); bullying; moderate sexual content; and profanity.

Please know that I did my best to handle these topics with respect and sensitivity. Thank you for reading.

Big Hugs,

Jessica Sherry

*To the difficult, the different, the damaged, the imperfect, the weird, the bullied, the misunderstood—all brave defenders of the extraordinary.
You're all sunflowers.*

And to Jenny, who said, "Have you been to the carnivorous garden?"

1. I Miss You - Blink-182 (Henry's song)
2. Kings and Queens - Ava Max (Diner song)
3. Breakfast - Dove Cameron
4. Vodka Cranberry - Conan Gray (Venus's song)
5. The Man Who Can't Be Moved - The Script
6. Love Lost - Mac Miller
7. Roses - Jenna Raine
8. Down Bad - Taylor Swift
9. So Good - Halsey
10. Sweet Emotion - Aerosmith
11. Still Into You - Paramore
12. Casual - Chappell Roan
13. Lonely People - Tiny Little Houses
14. Pretty Slowly - Benson Boone
15. Love Bites - Def Leppard
16. Sweet Heat Lightning - Gregory Alan Isakov
17. Wish You Were Here - Pink Floyd
18. Run - Harrison Storm
19. i am not who i was - Chance Peña
20. Stay - Gracie Adams
21. Love Looks Pretty On You - Nessa Barrett
22. Everything Has Changed - Ed Sheeran and Taylor Swift (Henry & Venus's song)

23. Before You Leave Me - Alex Warren
24. Everywhere, Everything - Noah Kahan, Gracie Adams

Listen on Spotify

https://open.spotify.com/playlist/63zcxxNBOIet5q4USpmqCT

CHAPTER 1

Henry

"HAVE you ever missed someone *and* never wanted to see them again?"

My words escape in a beleaguered breath—not uncommon for an asthmatic. But emotion makes it worse, adding heaviness that steals room in my already tight lungs.

My business consultant, Marnie, and I are on the second-floor rooftop balcony of my late uncle's curiosity museum, discussing plans for its renovation and reopening—a plan that she's just proposed would include a carnivorous garden installed by the local expert on Venus flytraps, Dr. Richard Blake. The mere mention of the Blake family or even carnivorous plants brings up thoughts about Venus Blake—thoughts I'd rather leave in the past.

I can't believe it's been ten years.

"Missed someone *and* never wanted to see them again?" Marnie's head tilts thoughtfully. "Yes, my mother."

My hand slips into my pocket for my inhaler while I nod, not surprised that she relates to such an off-the-wall comment. It's only our third meeting, but Marnie's one of those people who just *gets it*. I love people like her. Positive, uplifting, empathetic, insightful.

Even so, she's the professional helping me reinvent the curiosity museum—not my therapist. I shouldn't be talking about this. I feel exposed, like the time Ruby Mack pantsed me on the bus in elementary school, sending everyone into hysterics over my Batman underwear.

Yes, my bully in elementary school was a girl—I have no shame in admitting it.

That dark day ended my themed underwear phase. It's been black boxer briefs since. Some traumas are forever.

Marnie shifts against the balcony overlooking the Cape Fear River, her red hair flying in the breeze, as she opens up about her mother. "I needed her, and she wasn't there, over and over. It made me angry. I never wanted to see her again and swore that if she showed up, I wouldn't give her another chance—very unlike me."

My bitterness isn't like *me*, either. I've been told I'm the quintessential nice guy. I teach over a hundred middle schoolers every day without complaint—I love getting to know my students and the challenge of bringing the past alive for them. I arrive early, stay late, and my door is always open. I'm a habitual people-pleaser.

Case in point—I'm taking over my late uncle's campy, failure of a curiosity museum, despite being a history teacher, finishing my master's, and knowing nothing about running a business, because that's what *he* wanted. It's what I want, too—I'd love for people to get excited about local history the way I do. Like Uncle Jay did. My negativity over Venus feels unnatural, toxic even, like cigarette smoke invading my lungs and squeezing my already winded chest.

"After a while, though, that sharp pain became a dull ache, subsiding into hurt," she says. "*I was hurt*. But I still loved her—why else would it hurt so much? So, when she came back into my life, I could've been angry and told her she'd lost her chance. But seeing her again, I didn't want that. I wanted my mom back."

"Did you get her?"

Her smile grows. "Better. I got the mom I always wanted. A little sister, too."

"*Happily-ever-afters aren't real*," Venus said one rainy day after finishing *The Princess Bride*—one of many old movies in Mom's collection. We were ten, and I'd been slowly introducing her to movies and sitcoms. Her father didn't allow TV in their house. "*When you've read every book, then we can discuss a television*," he used to tell her and her sister, Ivy.

"*Love is a social construct designed for cohabitation and procreation. There's no need to romanticize the survival of the species*," she continued. "*But I enjoyed the shrieking eels and the poison game. Inconceivable.*"

Her awkward, throaty laugh echoes faintly in my ears. I barely remember it now.

"I'm glad for you, Marnie," I sigh. "But reconciliation isn't always possible... or wanted."

Nearby, her art consultant and sister-in-law, Marigold, busily sketches the rooftop space with a charcoal pencil on her worn notebook. Her artistic focus reminds me of Venus, too, as if I can't stop seeing her everywhere now that Marnie brought up the Blake family.

"I get it," Marnie says finally, "but hanging on to anger only hurts *me*. So, I let it go. The first step to a second chance is being open to it. It has to happen at the right time, too. Letting her back in came easier because I felt safe enough to do it."

"Why is that?" I ask.

"I'd just fallen in love with my soulmate. Anything feels possible when you're with the right person... and that's especially true when you come through something together that *feels* impossible, like me and Grady did." Her blue eyes gloss with tears when she goes on. "He crashed into me on my wedding day—the worst meet-cute ever! The wedding flopped. So did the groom, eventually. But that day turned out to be my luckiest. Grady saved my life, took care of me when no one else would, and showed me what love and family truly meant." She glances over at Marigold with a gentle smile. "It doesn't matter what we had to go through to get to each other—I wouldn't change a thing."

Marigold peeks up from her notebook with a rare grin as she eyes her sister-in-law, and I feel the love between them.

Marnie swipes under her eyes and abruptly asks, "Are you seeing anyone?"

"I don't date." The words sound almost snippy—another thing not like me. But Marnie's too friendly and personable to deflect. I'm a helpless oyster, and her questions might as well be a knife, edging me open and twisting until I crack.

I don't discuss Venus Blake if I can help it. Even among my oldest friends, she rarely comes up anymore—not that I have many *old* friends. It strikes me funny how so many friendships end up like expired trends, everything one minute, and nonexistent the next.

The same happened with Venus and me.

Even so, when I consider our twelve-year relationship, I can't deny that she gave me the best parts of my childhood. She taught me to explore, get dirty, ask questions, and stand up for myself. I wouldn't be myself without her. How do you regret someone who changed your life for the better? Still, a bad ending wrecks twelve good years like they were flimsy under the sudden weight of it. It bears down on me even now, especially since I never got answers.

Still, I tell my son, Olly, about our adventures from childhood, as if I can't help but keep our history alive and hand those stories down for safekeeping. I didn't set out to include Venus in his upbringing. One night, he asked me to tell him a story, and the only good ones I had included her.

Marnie laughs at my anti-dating declaration. "Yeah, that's what my husband used to say, too. Tell me, why are you keeping yourself away from some lucky lady, huh? And don't say Olly—he already spilled the beans that his mom dates. Why don't you?"

"My soulmate doesn't want me. I don't want her, either. There's no coming back from that. And settling for anything else is... unfair... to everyone involved."

This I know firsthand. I tried so hard to fall in love with Olly's mom, Carly. I wanted us to be a family. But forcing myself to love her didn't work. Neither did living together. In the end, I made us both miserable by being disingenuous, and that wasn't *me* either. But I hope Marnie doesn't press for more information. I don't want to explain to this sunny newlywed that happy endings don't always happen.

"Sometimes, being alone is better."

Marnie closes her gaping mouth at my declaration and shakes her head vigorously. "Having been alone, I don't believe that... but I understand the inclination. Besides, how can she be your soulmate if she doesn't want you?"

This prompts an easy smile as I remember all the reasons. "She just... is."

Marnie's blue eyes widen softly. "In that case... there's always hope, Henry. *Always*."

Her giddy grin is gone, replaced with a sternness that *almost* makes me believe her. But what Venus did to me and the silence that followed confirms what I already know—there's no hope for us. I wonder now if there ever was. Giving my heart to a woman who didn't believe in love was a reckless mistake that I won't make again.

"I appreciate your optimism, Marnie, but no, there isn't. I'm ready to put my hopes in this place, though."

She snorts. "Nice redirect. Henry Greene, you might be a bigger project than this place!"

"That's probably true, but fixing me isn't part of our deal."

"Well, no pressure about the garden. Dr. Blake will understand. It's okay to back out."

A deep sigh and the calming river views break through my tension. "Um, no. The carnivorous garden is a great idea. I'm being oversensitive."

"Then, we'll do it?"

"Sure. I've always liked Dr. Blake, and Venus wouldn't care about a little garden like this. She's too busy saving the world. Besides, she hated those plants, despite being named after them."

"Geez, hating the plant you're named after must be frustrating," she says.

"She prefers to say she's named after the Roman goddess. I mean, she *preferred*. Who knows anymore?" Not knowing tightens my chest, prompting another puff from my inhaler. My lungs burn, but open, taking in the warm spring air. "Enough about that. I'm starting to feel excited about my inheritance, finally. The Weird But True Wilmington Museum will be incredible—a real tourist destination."

"And a local favorite," she quips, finger raised. "The response on social media has been overwhelmingly positive. Everyone's excited to see this place turned around."

"Given its rocky history, that surprises me."

She laughs. "Well, your uncle had a flair for the unusual."

"I still have nightmares about the time he tried to turn it into a serpentarium. His python, Harry, escaped while he had guests here. It wouldn't surprise me if Harry lives in the walls."

"Was that before or after he tried those haunted lock-ins?"

"After... though a snake writhing in the walls may've given his customers proof of paranormal activity," I say. "I think they were mostly disappointed."

"The, um, mirror maze was a decent idea," she offers.

"Oh, yeah, until a mirror got whacked with someone's cane, shattering everywhere. It's a wonder he didn't get sued for that... or the gator that got out," I say.

Marnie chuckles. "Yes, the escaped gator story made the paper, though I'm sure Greta just walked to the river and dove in. She's probably living her best life now."

I shake my head. "He never should've tried live animals."

"He was brave—I have to give him that. The laser light shows could've worked," Marnie says.

"If only he'd stayed away from pyrotechnics. It's a wonder the place didn't burn down."

She giggles. "Maybe this place is luckier than we think."

"Let's hope," I say. "He wasn't the best businessman, but he was a great guy. I hope I do his legacy justice."

"You will. How are you and your family coping?" she asks softly.

"We're... doing our best. Thanks for asking." I breathe out, still stuck in a sordid reality, where the man I loved and admired took his life in this very building, where so many of his plans and hopes fizzled and died. "I love him and miss him. But I'm pissed at him, actually. Pissed that he couldn't talk to us."

Marnie nods. "Sometimes it's hard to talk to the ones we love most."

I smirk. "Easier to talk to a friendly stranger?"

"We started as strangers, but now we're friends," she says. "I'm here whenever you need to talk, Henry."

"Thanks, Marnie."

She scribbles on a page torn out from her vintage Trapper Keeper notebook. "I'm giving you homework. Start thinking about the design and clues for the escape room—local lore and history. And a memorial to Jay—his service, favorite music, anything that he loved. We'll put it at the entrance, so it's the first thing anyone sees. We want him remembered for his life, not his death."

"That's what I want, too," I say, slipping her list into my pocket.

"I've lined up an excellent contractor for the project. We'll meet Dot here on Monday. I'll give Dr. Blake the go-ahead for the garden. Marigold will work on the signs and the exterior mural. This ugly duckling is about to become a swan."

I laugh at the bounce in her step as she says it. "I have no doubt."

Through the second-floor balcony's access door, we take the red-carpeted staircase down to the main museum—a dusty, dark hodgepodge of serial killer displays, movie memorabilia, and diverse oddities from voodoo dolls to shrunken heads. The six-foot, glass-enclosed witch from the recent blockbuster film, *Hunter The Return*, looms eerily in the corner, her decrepit visage facing the wall, so as not to scare Olly.

Or me, if I'm honest.

I wince at the towering witch. "I haven't gotten used to the witch yet. It was one of the last things Uncle Jay acquired, but I don't know about keeping it."

"Let's devote one room to scarier items with a warning for parents," she suggests. "Marigold can create some signs for us."

Marigold scribbles into her notebook, her eyes barely visible under the brim of her bucket hat.

"That's a good solution. The corner storage room would work. That way, Olly and I don't jump every time we walk in the door," I say.

"I don't care for it, either," Marigold says, not looking up.

Marnie takes notes, smirking. "People love movie memorabilia, and that's one thing that keeps Wilmington weird, right? That's a good place for the Fort Fisher Mermaid, too. It's a bit creepy. I'll make some adjustments to the design and send you a revised layout."

Our meeting ends, and once they leave, I check my watch. I have half an hour before Carly returns with Olly, and my day switches to his first-grade homework, dinner, and prepping for my classes tomorrow. The end of the year is always an overwhelming rush for teachers to get things done. With 115 eighth graders taking their exams this week, I need to have their last-minute reviews ready.

Still, I need a break. Reaching for my keys on the counter in the foyer, I notice the hand-carved blue jay figurine my uncle kept by the cash register for good luck. It's on its side, wobbling slightly.

Did I knock it over?

I set it upright, pat its head, and leave.

Two blocks over, I enter the Queens and Dreams Diner—me and Olly's favorite place outside the museum. Growing up, Jay would take me here for burgers, shakes, and music on the jukebox he salvaged and restored for DeeDee, the owner.

"My favorite history buff," DeeDee greets me, her red lips turned up in a smile almost as wide as the polka-dotted dress that swishes with her every move. "Just one today, Henry?"

"Um, how about a booth? Carly'll be here soon with Olly."

She seats me near the window and engages in light chitchat. *How are you? How's school? How's Olly?* But my answers come in short sentences, as if that's all I can muster.

Finally, her penciled brow perches high on her forehead. "What's wrong? You don't seem yourself today."

"Um, wrestling with some old ghosts," I answer simply.

She nods, her bright brown eyes glancing toward the jukebox as if she's thinking about Uncle Jay.

"Jay, yes, but I don't mean him. This girl I knew. Venus. Not that I want to talk about her. Sorry for unloading my drama on you. I'll have my usual."

"Never apologize for drama," she says, waving her hands in the air, motioning toward her restaurant, which is *all* drama, from the neon lights, the red vinyl booths and barstools, to the exquisitely dressed drag queens waiting on tables and manning the long counter. Her red lips widen again as she assesses me. "Besides, I know about Venus. Jay and I were friends, remember? Missing him has probably made you miss her, too."

"Yeah, something like that."

With a gentle squeeze on my shoulder, she says, "I get it... I'll get your order started and prep Olly's double-decker grilled cheese."

"And a strawberry milkshake for Carly? She loves those," I say.

"Absolutely. I'll put it in a to-go cup, in case she's in a hurry."

"Thanks, DeeDee."

Sunshine through the window catches on my glasses, drawing my attention outside to the concrete grays and rusty bricks of downtown, the flow of foot traffic, and the stream of cars, but none of it distracts me.

It's impossible not to think of Venus now that I've started. Not that I've ever stopped.

I wonder where she is and if she ever thinks about me.

CHAPTER 2
Venus

"WHO'S HENRY?" Dr. Miner holds up my worn, overfull field journal, which contains illustrations and notes from the last several months. I've documented my experiences in nature since my father gave me a black-and-white composition notebook in kindergarten, the cover of which bore the words "FIELD JOURNAL" in bold letters. *"Keep records of what you see and discover,"* he said.

So, I have.

Perched sea birds, cresting whales, and fields of sea kelp adorn the most recent pages, as we are on a ship—*The Poseidon*, to be exact, a NOAA research vessel currently six nautical miles off the coast of San Pedro Bay, California, where we will soon dock at the Port of Los Angeles.

"That's private," I say, reaching for the journal. She pulls away, flipping it open.

"These illustrations are quite detailed." Her eyes soften but only a little. I detect amusement, edged with critical annoyance, her common expression when talking to me. "If not somewhat rustic. Have you ever considered publication? There's a market for material like this, particularly in education or coffee table books."

I gape at the suggestion. My journals are scientific, not decorative.

"You'd have to stop addressing your field notes to Henry, of course," she adds dryly.

My shoulders slump as if weighted. I haven't *always* addressed them to Henry. Only since I've been without him. *Has it been ten years?* My therapist, Dr. Broderick, claims that my journals provide an imaginary connection, a poor substitute for the life I could've had if I'd made a different choice. She calls it my surrogate boyfriend. I disagree. Sometimes, a journal is just a journal.

I address them to Henry simply because I miss him.

I straighten in the seat across from her desk. "That seems counterintuitive to my mission as an environmental scientist. It's a waste of trees, energy, resources, space—"

"The world needs books, Venus." Her brown eyes roll behind her reading glasses. "And there's more to life than field work and research."

My eyes narrow. Her remark seems paradoxical, considering that I've spent the last decade by her side conducting *her* fieldwork and research.

"Who's Henry?" she asks again. "I vaguely remember your father mentioning—"

"No one. He's... no one."

Her small office feels stuffy and uncomfortably confined, especially with this interrogation. It's highly unusual for Dr. Miner to examine my private property or make personal comments. Our ten-year relationship has been mutually beneficial and blissfully impersonal. At my request, my father entrusted me to her care at eighteen. She has mentored me through my higher education and provided the hands-on experience for my profession.

But I wouldn't call us friends.

Dr. Miner is an esteemed and ambitious scientist. I've learned a great deal from her, but the best lesson she's modeled for me is how to be alone. She is comfortably numb, and I've tried to be more like her every single day.

Even so, it feels jarring that she doesn't know about Henry, as if I've left a blank space on the vital paperwork needed for this arrangement. I know about *her* people. I glance at the photos lining the shelf behind her —a prepubescent male with braces holding a violin, a teenager in a cheerleading uniform, and a middle-aged man wearing a blue suit and a half-hearted smile, like he's at a funeral. Dr. Miner's son, Allan, daughter, Sophie, and husband Brian—names I know because she mentions them. Significant others *should* be mentioned in long-standing relationships, even one as impersonal as ours.

She should know about Henry—my most significant *other*, if the impact he had, *still has*, on my life, and the frequency of thought I give him are considerations in such a title. Anyone who knows me beyond a passing acquaintance should, even if our relationship no longer exists beyond a journal he'll never see.

"Thank you for the safe return of my property," I say, holding out my hand. She passes it to me.

"That's not the only reason I called this meeting."

"Then, why have you summoned me?"

"Venus, you will not continue on this project after we arrive at port," she says in a long exhale.

"Explanation, please?"

"Your lab work and research notes are thorough and insightful. And your idea to combine okra polymers with sundew polymers for a stickier resin was truly inspired. That one adjustment has advanced our research into the safe extraction of microplastics by months, at least."

"Thank you," I say weakly. "Then, why—"

"It's your behavior." She interlocks her fingers on the desk. "You're difficult with the other team members..."

An internal cringe envelopes me, hearing that word. *Difficult*—of course, it's *that* word.

"... You disregard the buddy system on dives..."

Only to explore where others refuse to go.

"And there's Julio and Quinn." She huffs.

"I was abundantly clear with each of them *before* intercourse that there'd be no attachments or relationships—sex only. They agreed to my terms."

"You were seeing them at the same time. They felt threatened by each other."

I shake my head vehemently. "No, not at the same time—weeks apart. Regardless, I'm not responsible for their actions."

"You inspired a fellow researcher and the ship's navigator to have a bar fight—you're to blame on *some* level, even if they misunderstood your intentions or wanted more from you unfairly... But that's not the main issue. It's your *other* behaviors that concern me."

She doesn't need to elaborate, but she does, like my infractions require an audible acknowledgement. My occasional vodka nights, when drinking too much renders me useless the next day. My spontaneous ocean dives, which raise, frankly, irrational fears in the ship's crew. My refusal to stay below deck during storms. When I feel trapped or caught up in emotions, my impulses overrule my reason, driving me to these necessary escapes—it doesn't feel like a choice. It's a necessity, freeing me, if only temporarily.

Like what's building right now. I don't want to be here, closed in. Dismissed. Unwanted. With Henry's name still lingering in the air. My body clenches, and my fingers curl tightly around the wooden armrest.

Henry once compared my emotional surges to summer storms. They build slowly, without much notice, but happen all at once, fiercely and unpredictably. It's a heaviness around me, *in me*, as if I take on the dropping barometric pressure before a storm and can't find relief until it's released. Henry understood, didn't judge, and would hold me tightly until those feelings left me—a vise that only he could unwind. I haven't felt similar comfort since the last time he held me, in the greenhouse.

I can't find that release in my cubbyhole of a room. Or in this office. Or on this ship.

Not in the arms of strangers, either.

I hug my journal tightly to my chest, desperate to clutch something, to hold on. To feel the pressure.

But again, I think of Henry.

"If you're not in the lab or your notebook or exploring a forest somewhere, you seem lost," she says.

I like getting lost. On busy city streets. In wild countrysides. In untamed meadows, rugged moors, and dense woods. I like venturing off the trail.

Getting lost has not only earned me my beautiful freedom but also my most outstanding scientific credit to date. I discovered a new species of plant—a flowering fern that I named *Henricus filicis*, Henry fern, because its long, spry leaves reminded me of his long legs and spindly arms, and its brown flower blossomed from the ends like Henry's always-unruly hair.

Besides, I owe him a fern, at least.

The irony is that had I been looking for it, I never would've found it. I happened upon the discovery in my off-hours—a cosmic joke considering that I've committed myself to doing scientific grunt work that should lead to incredible discoveries, but rarely does.

My fingernails cut into my palms as I practice the breathing technique Dr. Broderick taught me. "What about the Nat Geo project?"

She's pushed our team for years, hoping for that assignment, and

I've worked diligently to help her get it, counting on the unspoken promise that she'd take me with her.

"Venus, our partnership is ending," she says, her voice stern and slow, "but I've arranged a temporary position for you."

"What temporary position?"

"Teaching summer school, a special topics course on…" She shuffles the papers on her desk. "The Rare Plants of North Carolina, at UNCW—"

"That's my father's school, my father's class. Is he unwell?" I sit up, nearly falling off the chair.

"He's fine. He's taking a much-deserved sabbatical, albeit on very short notice. You'd know this if you kept in touch regularly. When he informed me of his intention, I reached out to them and recommended you."

"I should've been consulted. I'm not a teacher, and I hate classrooms."

"You have a doctorate—you're qualified. Besides, he'll provide all relevant materials. What could be easier than subbing for him on a topic in which you are just as knowledgeable? It's only for the summer, Venus."

"Let's pretend it's always summer for us." Henry's voice wafts into my memory, but it's faded, like I can't quite remember how he sounds.

"I don't want to do this." I fidget with my bracelets and rings as my anxiety builds. "There must be something else. Anything else."

"You have no permanent residence or current offers. You have nowhere else to go. It'll be good for you to be on solid ground for a while, see your family," she points out. "Don't you miss them?"

"Do you miss *your* family?"

Her scowl tells me that I've overstepped. "Venus, I *talk* to my family. You've all but *abandoned* yours."

The word stings. My brain misfires as I attempt to launch a counter-argument and overloads with things I miss—Ivy's often-annoying cheerfulness, my father's slow *hmmm* whenever he considers something, the earthy warmth of the greenhouse, and the memories it holds.

I recall our quiet evenings—Dad in his favorite leather chair, Ivy and I on the couch, usually under a shared blanket, all of us reading while classic rock played on the record player. Dad would put the kettle on, and the air would fill with fragrances from his homegrown teas. I once loved those lazy evenings, those times when I didn't feel trapped.

Or perhaps I'm idealizing those memories in their long absence. The immense pressure to escape began in that house. That's where I discovered how little I belonged and what a burden I could be. I haven't been home since the Christmas before last. The longer I'm away, the harder it is to go back.

"Missing them is irrelevant," I say, pushing those feelings aside. "I shouldn't be fired because of a few minor instances. My impulsivity problem is under control and managed with professional care." I'm flooded with memories of school and the numerous times I made the same argument, only to fail to persuade my teachers or the administration.

"Idiosyncrasies are one thing. Swan-diving off the ship is a risk to you and anyone who might jump in to save you—"

"I didn't need saving. I just needed… to reset. The boat was anchored."

"You're a liability, Venus. A distraction. And this isn't a debate."

My father's voice whispers through my internal monologue. *"Best accept what you cannot change, Venus,"* and still I wonder how that can be true.

"Go home, Venus," Dr. Miner says sternly, forcing my attention back on her. "Take some time. Do a good job with your father's class, and I'll provide a positive reference for your next project."

A reference from Dr. Miner would secure me any research position I want. Without it, I'd lose my credibility, given that I've spent a decade under her tutelage.

"Does my father know?" I ask, my voice as weak as my limited options.

Her wry smile spreads. "It was his idea."

Outside on the starboard deck, I adjust my head scarf to keep my long blonde hair out of my eyes. I say blonde, but on closer inspection, my hair is at least a dozen different shades of gold, pale yellow, and light brown. I read a book once that likened one's natural hair to the uniqueness of a fingerprint.

DNA, fingerprints, hair color, *difficulties*. How can we be so unique and so utterly inconsequential?

Inconsequential… that's what I am to Henry now. I imagine he doesn't think of me at all anymore.

But that's what I wanted.

The wild, full-bodied thunk when my body pierces the water's surface disrupts my thought cycle. I push deeper into the darkness, the pressure surrounding me like a cold blanket until it relaxes my thoughts and calms the unwanted energy surging inside of me. My boots are heavy with water, dragging me lower, but I kick up strongly—I'm an expert swimmer. I made sure, *after*. The muffled sounds of yelling swirl over my head—the captain won't be happy. But what does it matter? In a few days, we'll be at port, and they'll be rid of me, as they want.

As they all want.

CHAPTER 3
Venus

I KEEP my exact arrival home a mystery, leaving room for diversions and excuses to get lost along the way. But tired and resigned, I don't divert. I make all of my necessary flights and arrange a ride from the airport.

The driver drops me off in the small parking lot that borders our property. We live on a public nature preserve dedicated to carnivorous plants. We have a private driveway—a dirt lane that curves through the tall pines—but it's easier for strangers to navigate the paved lot. With no cars occupying any of the ten spaces, I assume Blake's Carnivorous Garden is blissfully vacant until I spot two bikes lying carelessly on their sides at the mouth of the footpath.

I heft my overstuffed backpack and roll my suitcase behind me on the pebbled path that cuts through the pine grove, gazing at the informative placards that mark the journey. No need to read them—I have them memorized.

The Venus flytrap can only be found within a 100-mile radius of Wilmington, North Carolina.

Venus flytraps can go without eating for 1-2 months. They eat bugs and even frogs!

When digestion is complete, 5 to 12 days later, the trap reopens, and the insect's exoskeleton falls out.

Venus flytrap leaves eat 3 or fewer insects in their lives before turning black, dying, and being replaced by a new leaf.

The trigger hairs of a Venus flytrap are sensitive enough to tell the difference between signals from living prey and non-prey, like raindrops or fallen leaves.

Please do not touch the plants.

Once, Henry and I covered the signs with drawings of oversized flytraps with exaggerated fangs, biting off limbs of park guests and spitting out the bones, with a final sign that read: *Enter at your own risk.*

Dad wasn't pleased, though he said the artwork was quite commendable.

The distant sound of children playing pulls my attention to the property that borders ours. Over the moss banks lining the path, through the chained link fence, and across a patchy, sandy lawn lies the elementary school that Henry, Ivy, and I attended. The side closest to us is the cafeteria, a brown brick box with small, awkward windows that barely opened and never caught a breeze.

If inside those walls again, I'd likely find the same round, red seats that Henry and I occupied for most of second grade—the year we became friends. I still remember him plopping down in front of me with his carefully packed Batman lunch box in one hand and his inhaler in the other.

"What are you doing?" I asked.

He pushed up his glasses with his nail-bitten fingertip. "Eating lunch."

"Why are you eating lunch *here*?" I clarified. I'd known Henry as a classmate, but we hadn't interacted willingly until a few days prior, when I assisted him with directions, and later, with a bully named Ruby Mack. I enjoyed our brief encounter and fighting an injustice, of course, but I didn't expect more to come of it. I didn't have friends.

My question confused him until another classmate threw a banana peel over his head and onto my turkey and cheese sandwich, yelling, "Bomb's away! Watch out for banana bombs, lice head!"

Laughter ensued. I rolled my eyes.

"What's lice?" Henry asked.

Rolling the peel into a paper towel to take home for compost, I explained, "*Phthiraptera*—a parasitic insect that lives in hair follicles and causes severe itching and discomfort."

"You talk funny."

"I'm aware," I said. "They're itchy bugs that live in hair."

"So, lice aren't nice?" he asked with a grin as he tried to punch his straw through his juice box.

"They're creatures trying to survive this world, like the rest of us." I reached for his juice box to assist. "I don't have them, if you're wondering."

He handed it over with a shrug and a smile. "Maybe he does since he knows about 'em."

Amused, I returned his successfully punctured beverage. "He might start calling you a lice head if you sit with me."

"I don't care. Uncle Jay told me that many great people in history were bullied," he informed.

I was skeptical. "Name four."

"George Washington, Albert Einstein, Rosa Parks, and Michael Phelps. He's an Olympic swimmer," he said with impressive quickness.

My brow quirked. "Name two more."

"Teddy Roosevelt—he had asthma, like me—and Michael Jordan. He's the greatest basketball player ever, and he's from here," he said with excitement.

Rarely did someone offer me information I didn't already know, especially so willingly. "That's unusual to know."

"I like knowing unusual things." He shrugged. "Besides, I've been called worse."

He brushed off the concern and remained in his seat. Much later, I learned the truth in his words. His father, Dale, ridiculed him for not being "tough enough" because of his small stature and his asthma. All the while, Dale worsened Henry's condition by smoking in the house. My understanding of a *normal family* was limited then—still is—but such a lack of consideration felt cruel.

"What do you know about anything, you damn orphan?" Dale's voice echoes.

Though I'm not an orphan, I didn't argue.

"Unconventional" is the term most frequently used to describe my family. My father, Dr. Richard Blake, demonstrated his expertise in carnivorous plants in his early twenties, resolving the long-standing debate over how the Venus flytrap triggers its trap. He concluded that an electric current produced in the plant's cells mechanized the leaves—a veritable *shock* in the scientific community.

I enjoy wordplay.

He authored the definitive work on the subject and several books since, while becoming a tenured professor at the University of North Carolina Wilmington.

He purchased land in midtown, where a pre-existing bog the size of a football field provides a natural habitat for his beloved carnivorous family. He built an A-frame house with extensive gardens and a greenhouse. Then, looking up from his microscope one contemplative afternoon, he decided to start a family. That he had no relationship or any desire for one didn't deter him from his quest. Through lawyers, he found a surrogate—an Icelandic woman, hoping to finance her education and remain anonymous to the infant she delivered. Soon, my father had his firstborn. Me.

"*The Venus flytrap is challenging to grow, somewhat intimidating, strangely beautiful, and refuses to sit idly by waiting for sustenance,*" my father told me once when I complained about my name, "*just like you, Venus.*"

I should have argued that he assigned me the name before he knew me. Even now, I wish to debate him—did I become like the plant or is the plant like me? At the time, I asked, "*Does that mean the dead parts of me will turn black and fall off, too?*"

I was four.

He laughed.

But that's what happened. My capacity to love and be loved has dried up and fallen away. My chest constricts with the thought—*the absence*—but it could be the heaviness of my backpack.

Ivy entered our family when I was two through another surrogate, an Italian woman named Marta, who wanted to give someone else a family and needed the money to help her own. She stipulated her desire to maintain correspondence with her biological daughter. The letters and packages started when Ivy was in preschool and haven't stopped, even though Ivy is an adult, a registered nurse, and lives on her own in a townhouse.

A mother through correspondence is better than being called *motherless*. Their connection grew exponentially once Ivy had a phone. She texted and called Marta often, anytime she needed to talk, and Marta would drop everything to explain French braids, eyeliner, boy troubles, gelato, or whatever Ivy wondered about at the moment.

I didn't have that, exactly. But I had Henry's mom, Maggie. *Sometimes.*

The cobbled path toward home first spits me out onto the observation bridge overlooking the bog. The land is recessed, a sandy pit of low-nutrient soil that's perfect for carnivorous plants. Tall, slender pitcher plants in green, burgundy, and purple stretch out across the landscape like children raising their hands in a classroom. Lower, sticky sundews tangle like thick cobwebs. And lower still, lie mossy patches of Venus flytraps. The distinctive plants are difficult to see this early in the season and are smaller than people expect.

People *expect* monsters.

They aren't, though. They're misunderstood, which is arguably the best commonality between my namesake and me. Now, they cower. Their eerie, fanged marginal spikes pricking from their leaves, open and waiting, are the size of fingertips.

A dog barks, bringing my attention to the far right, where a middle-aged couple wearing bike helmets traverses the paver-marked paths in a slumped hunt.

Beyond the low-lying pit of sunken plants lies home. We affectionately call it the fairy house, as do most people—a trend that started when Ivy and I were in elementary school. Having never found evidence of fairies, I cannot verify their existence. But an A-frame house is unusual for the area, especially one nestled into the trees and surrounded by gardens. At night, with the interior lights on and string lights twinkling in the gardens, it looks rather ethereal—like the house and grounds exude their own bioluminescence, only ours is a warm light rather than a cold one, like at sea. Dad constructed the greenhouse from old windows, including a gorgeous stained-glass circle rescued from an old church. There, the light isn't just golden, but a twinkling rainbow of greens, ambers, and purples. It's understandable why people might associate it with mythical woodland creatures and their luminescent fairy dust. Growing up, Ivy and I resisted the fairy label, but as we got older, we came to embrace it, realizing it was another unchangeable view not worth fighting. In high school, Ivy and I posted a sign in the front yard—*Don't piss off the fairies!* I chuckle at the sight of it in the distance, glad Dad hasn't taken it down.

Perhaps it'll be good to be home.

I hop down from the decking to the garden, my suitcase thumping against the wooden planks and banging onto a cement paver. I beeline for the other side, head lowered to watch my step.

"Excuse me!" the woman calls, speedwalking toward me. "Excuse me!"

Her second declaration forces me to stop, as I imagine Dad imploring me not to be rude.

"Excuse me," she says, softer this time as they hurry over. "We're trying to find the Venus flytraps, but we're having trouble. Has something happened to them?"

My heavy backpack nearly knocks me over when I lean down to the moss near my hiking boots and point to the tiny plants nestled into the underbrush.

"They're so small," she muses.

"I'll get a stick. Let's see if we can get it to—"

"No! Don't. Instigating the trap expends an exorbitant amount of energy for them," I say. "Doing so could mean they go hungry. You'll hurt the plant."

He scoffs and shakes his head. "I'm sure it's fine."

My narrowed, stern gaze diminishes his easy-going smile.

"We'll behave," the woman promises, as her dog lifts his leg and pees against a tuft of pitcher plants.

My grip strangles the suitcase handle as I leave them without another word. Engaging them further might lead me to do something regrettable, like calling them *eco-hostiles* or peeing on their discarded bikes to mark *my* territory.

Humans are the worst invasive species.

Across the garden, I climb the short embankment, pass our sign, and roll over the small dirt lane. The absence of my father's ancient Land Rover tells me he must be out. It's a Friday afternoon, and he could be anywhere—in his office at the university or the lab, meeting with colleagues, in a swamp hunting for more specimens, or playing chess with strangers at Greenfield Park. He has diverse interests.

Movement catches my eye on the extended deck, where a man I don't recognize waters the potted plants and flower boxes along the railing. He twirls around as if dancing to an inaudible tune, swishing the floral smock he wears and splashing water from his purple watering can. What looks like a paperback sticks out from the rear pocket of his worn blue jeans. His gray hair is kept away from his face by a red bandana, endearing me to him. I am rarely without a scarf tied to my head or dangling from my hair, as I find them useful and convenient, especially in the field. With a spin and flick of his hips, his eyes land on me, and he goes still.

Is he Dad's housekeeper? Renter? Is he trespassing?

His long face flashes into an unnaturally wide smile. It stretches all the way to his ears and eyes. "Venus! You're here!"

He plops the watering can down, claps his hands, and nearly tumbles down the deck stairs. For a moment, I fear he might embrace me. Instead, he takes my suitcase and eases the heavy backpack off my shoulders, swinging it around his. "It's absolutely thrilling to meet you. We wondered when you might get in."

"Who are you?"

He waves a hand in the air. His fingernails are painted neon green. "Oh, forgive me. Richard told me he hadn't mentioned me yet. You must be completely confused. I'm Christie. Ed Christie, but I go by Christie."

He extends his hand while balancing my bags and leading me up the deck stairs. I engage in a light handshake and ask again, "Who are you? And how do you identify?"

His broad shoulders lower as he beams with appreciation. "What a thoughtful question. I'm gender non-conforming. My pronoun is he, but they is fine, too." He takes a steeling breath. "I'm your father's partner."

I stop on the top step and stare at him quizzically. "Partner? Business, academic, bridge? Could you be more specific?"

"Romantic," he says with a smile before opening the front door to usher me inside.

"But my father doesn't have romantic partners," I say, utterly confused now.

"Believe me, it surprised us both," he beams. "But the heart wants what the heart wants, as they say."

I resist the urge to argue that the heart is an organ that pumps blood through our bodies—it doesn't have wants, so to speak. But something tells me the conversation would be futile. "Is he here?"

"He's grocery shopping for tonight's dinner. Don't worry. I gave him a specific list, so he doesn't wander aimlessly. You know how he is."

"Um, I do." The fact that my father wanders in grocery stores feels like intimate knowledge, strengthening Christie's claim of a romantic partnership. Still, this information stumps me.

Christie rolls my suitcase to a stop in the open living room. He sets my bag down beside it, takes a deep breath, and rests his hands on his hips. "It's so perfect that you're here for tonight."

"What's tonight?"

"Ivy's bringing her new beau over to meet your father. I already know Gil. He's a sweet soul—you'll love him," he says. "I'm making lasagna."

Though lasagna sounds wonderful, I feel myself unraveling at his rapid-fire information. My hands fist at my sides as tension fills me. My father has a romantic partner? Ivy has a new boyfriend? They have plans together? Dinner with Ivy, Dad, and two veritable strangers isn't the homecoming I anticipated.

My deadpan expression meets his excited one, and he takes me in, his grin falling into concern. "How about I take your bags upstairs, and when you're ready, you can join me for a cup of tea? Your father's hibiscus honey blend is lovely."

He doesn't wait for an answer, but heaves my luggage upstairs. I follow slowly, taking in the familiarity of home. The buttery wood walls, the faint scent of Dad's teas, and the warm light of his Tiffany-style lamps. It's minimal, but comfortable.

But there are differences besides Christie. I take in the expansive great room with its practical navy blue sectional—one end covered with folded throw blankets because Ivy and I routinely needed them—and my father's worn leather chair. His side table is stacked with books and scientific journals, in which he often appears for commentary. But beside his reading materials are paperbacks featuring couples in varying states of undress, Christie's presumably. A newer leather chair with a matching ottoman has been placed between my father's side table and the fireplace.

Christie must be important to my father to have his own chair.

I head upstairs, noticing that the formerly barren wall is now covered in framed prints. Not just any prints, but my artwork—drawings that I gave to Dad growing up. A baby turtle hiding in the grass behind our house. A squirrel's nest I observed while climbing a tree. A cardinal pecking for worms under a bush.

My artwork often helped me express myself when I couldn't do so otherwise. Only the best drawings from my field journals became gifts, after Henry lit up when I first gave him one, a frog we played with once.

"*Frank the Frog. I love it. I'll keep it always,*" he said—a promise I'm sure he didn't keep.

The absence returns, an ache in my chest. Home sometimes hurts.

"We've made some upgrades," Christie says as I meet him on the landing, "to make it more comfortable. No more twin beds or Ivy's stuffed animals."

I turn the corner into the loft bedroom to find a full-sized bed adorned with plush, hotel-style linens in sage and gray. Soft light from the skylights overhead creates rectangles on the bedding. The large windows bring the outside in, and the glass door leads to an outer deck. A cedar chest has been added, and it holds my old notebooks, probably a hundred filled journals, some bursting at duct-taped seams for the many feathers, leaves, dried flowers, and even the occasional dirt or bark sample I tucked within the pages.

Christie hovers over me, as if gauging my reaction. "Your father wanted them kept safe. It must be fun to see all of your journals in one place."

"Not all," I correct weakly, "but yes. It's very organized."

It's a wonder that he kept them, let alone stored them so carefully. They're messy and rudimentary, but these remnants of my past show skill and promise. Instead of trophies, certificates, and acceptable grades, I had these. Being a so-called genius proved detrimental in school. There, I rarely, if ever, felt smart.

My work desk is clean, as if waiting for me, but the shelves above it are still lined with specimen jars and beakers. The small plant clippings I once propagated are now mature plants. The thick vines of a half-dozen varieties of pothos curl along the shelves and climb the wall, latching onto the wooden surface with their aerial roots. They will soon crest the ceiling if I don't trim it back.

Still, I love plants that go wherever the hell they want.

"I love this room," Christie coos, opening up the balcony doors with a flourish. "It feels like a treehouse."

All I can say is, "Yes, it does."

"I'll let you get settled," he says, with a delicate pat on my shoulder. "When you're ready, come downstairs for tea and nibbles. You must be peckish."

Christie disappears, and I step outside, reveling in the pines and oaks surrounding me. The viney trellis hangs off the balcony's side, latched between the railings and the house, and is where I used to climb down and escape, usually to Henry's house. Sometimes, he climbed up to see me. On closer inspection, I spot a familiar broken slat. Though

Henry was slight in his younger years, by tenth grade, he was taller than me. By our senior year, he'd filled into his six-foot-two frame, his branches thick with muscle and his base broad at the shoulders, like a stick-figure, expanded and broadened with lines and colors that added richness and depth. He was exquisite, and, at eighteen, too substantial for the trellis. The wood split when he climbed up it.

"Meet me in the greenhouse." His words flutter into my thoughts like tired wings.

My fingernails dig into the wood railing as I stare at the overgrown path toward his house. We were back and forth so much then that the trail just appeared underfoot. Now, short grasses fill in what used to be upturned dirt from my boots and his sneakers. His childhood home is a half-mile through the trees to the northwest, a ten-minute walk.

I wonder if he's there. Somehow, I *feel* him there, making the ache inside of me gnaw and throb as it grows. I'm a parasite, desperate to reclaim the sanctity of my host. To feel wanted again. To feel... liked. To feel his arms securely around me, holding me in place.

I survived my so-called education by two conditions: first, that it was best to keep my head low and my mouth shut, though I was not very good at either.

My second was Henry. To this day, he's the only friend I've ever had.

I imagine taking our path, making it worn and clear again, and tapping gently on his bedroom window until he stirs and lets me in, sleepy-eyed but smiling to welcome me.

Like it used to be.

Like nothing happened.

Like we could erase the time between.

Like we could have a second chance.

That unwelcome tension in me grows. The longing to see him is fierce and unrelenting, a lightning bolt of needy energy. *Do it. Just do it.*

But reason steps in, shutting down my impulse. I must accept what I cannot change. I'm still me, and he's still better off without me.

I need to put Henry Greene out of my mind.

Or, at least, do what I always do—tuck his memory into a dim corner where it doesn't hurt quite so much, and only pull it out in the quiet at night, when I'm alone and desperate to feel *something*, even if it's sadness. I've become skilled at deflection and distraction.

Only it's a challenge relying on those skills *here*.

With deep, strengthening breaths, I close my eyes and square my shoulders. I've been at sea, atop mountains, in deep jungles, and in a myriad of dangerous situations, and I've survived them all. I can survive this. I put on my comfortably numb armor and prepare myself to face the family that has gone on without me.

CHAPTER 4
Venus

"VENUS! THEY'RE HERE!" My father's voice bellows from the bottom of the stairs. The front door opens and closes, excited greetings are exchanged, and the unmistakable yap of a dog adds to the chaos.

I've been home only a few hours. I had tea with Christie, assisted my father with the groceries upon his return, unpacked *somewhat*, and showered. I'm rundown from travel and nerves, but I've ticked the necessary boxes.

A dinner with Ivy and her new boyfriend adds tension, as it will take every iota of my remaining energy to be *pleasant*. Ivy's the pleasant one. She's so skilled at it that anyone in her vicinity has to make a concerted effort not to seem awkward and unsociable by comparison.

It's a cosmic irony that we ended up in the same family.

I rush downstairs so as not to be rude.

Ivy looks as lovely and perfect as always. Her brown hair falls like a satin sheet around her shoulders, and her blue irises sparkle under her pristine makeup and thick lashes. She wears sandals that showcase her pink-painted toenails and a form-fitting sundress covered in pastel polka dots that even I find adorable, although dresses, polka dots, and open-toed shoes don't exist in my wardrobe.

The tall man beside her looks equally well-dressed, as do Dad and Christie, each wearing varying shades of chinos and button-down shirts, though Christie's is silky, and he wears a floral scarf as a tie.

A glance at my cut-off jean shorts and *Be Kind to Nature* t-shirt assures me that I'm underdressed, not that I own anything suitable for a dinner party.

"Venus, I love that you're here!" Ivy coos while a dog barks at my feet. She hesitates before lunging for a hug. I allow her embrace, and jasmine perfume tickles my nose. "I'm so excited for you to meet Gil. *Don't be weird.*"

She whispers the last part, and I'm yanked to the past again, when she used to say the same thing whenever her friends came over.

Gil Tripp offers a gentle handshake, smiling affably. "I've heard a lot about you, Venus. Nice ink." With an unsure glance at the others, he adds, "Not that I have ink. Or mind that someone else does. Two of my brothers have tattoos. I've just never… needles, you know."

He releases my hand with a nervous flourish, as if he couldn't tell if he'd shaken it too long. It's nice not to be the only awkward person in the room.

"Those are her design," Dad says, blank-faced, though sounding proud. "Venus is an artist."

"I'm an environmental scientist and botanist," I counter.

His hands go into the pockets of his gray chinos, and he teeters on his feet. "Hmm, you think you're a scientist who dabbles in art. I believe you're an artist, determined to be a scientist. What you should be is an artist *and* a scientist—equally and equally important."

"Are you suggesting that a wall painting is just as important as a scientific discovery that betters people's lives?" I challenge.

"Art betters people's lives, too," Dad returns in his typically calm voice. "The effects may not be as measurable as in the scientific community, but everyone needs beauty and inspiration."

"You surprise me with your vague generalities. A safe and healthy environment is infinitely more important than pretty decorations," I huff, but my heart palpitates when I take in their distressed expressions, as if I've said something wrong. *Did I?* "But…"

They watch me like I'm a ticking bomb, nearing the end of its countdown.

I try to formulate a better response, but it gets tangled up in memories. My father's perpetual mild-manneredness, while a comfort, proved irritating growing up. He *never* got mad—and I don't use absolutes lightly.

Even when I was angry.

Even when I needed him to be angry, too.

In early childhood, before I knew or understood myself, Dad would try, calmly, to explain my hurts to me.

The other kids teased me for my big words, dirty hair, and muddy boots, and called me every variety of the word annoying because *"People often ridicule what they don't understand."*

My teachers didn't like my questions... or couldn't answer them because *"Your questions often fall outside the curriculum and exceed their knowledge set."*

I didn't feel I belonged because *"The intricacies of group dynamics don't favor those who are exceptional."*

Or *difficult*, I'd tack on in my head.

My frustration led to impulses I struggled to control, often failing.

Screaming, at no one in particular, just to give the energy surge somewhere to go.

Stamping my feet.

Fisting my hands.

Pulling my hair.

Running.

Always running. Racing through the woods flickers through my thoughts. In the rain. In the snow. In the heat. Sunlight. Grayness. Darkness. Boots. Bare feet. Socks. Scratches on my arms and legs from whipping through branches. Tripping. Hurting. Panting.

My head shakes, breaking me from the thought cycle. My control increased with age. But my worst moments are most remembered, as if it takes a million positive encounters to cancel out a single negative one. They still expect the worst from me.

Ivy and Dad almost appear to be holding their breaths, awaiting my response. I wonder how Dad and Ivy explained me to their significant others. Evidence suggests that they may have said something like, *"She's smart but difficult."* That's how they've explained me before.

Always with a *but*.

But I understand—I often say the wrong things. I have a lazy, unreliable filter with a low efficacy rate. At least, that's what Dr. Broderick and I have concluded. I sift through years of my therapist's advice for an answer that I hope isn't *weird* or *difficult*. "Your thoughts are intriguing and worth consideration." I tack on a toothy smile for good measure, though it feels incorrect on my face.

Everyone relaxes at once. Well, except for Dad. He maintains his usual composure.

A white and black puppy paws at my leg, demanding attention. I lean over and give it a customary rub behind the ears—I've read that dogs appreciate that.

"That's Buster. He's a Border Collie." Ivy reaches into her bag for a ball and tosses it across the room. The dog races after it, fishtailing across the wood floor. He retrieves the ball dutifully, drops it at her feet, and races around our group, barking.

"Hmm, I do believe we're being herded," Dad says, amused.

Gil presents Dad with a bottle of wine. "Christie said we're having lasagna. I thought a pinot might be a good pairing."

"Ah, excellent." Dad scrutinizes the label, though he's not a wine connoisseur. "A good wine pairs perfectly with good company. I'll get this open."

"I'll help with glasses," Gil says, following him into the small kitchen.

"Okay, girls," Christie coos conspiratorially, "let's hurry outside to the table and dish about how cute and nervous Gil is."

Giggling ensues as they rush through the living room to the glass doors. Buster yaps, trailing behind them. I hesitate, unsure if I want to engage in that conversation.

But when Christie holds the door open and waves me along, I comply. Christie is an excellent conversationalist, as he demonstrated earlier when he "spilled the tea" about his relationship with Dad.

They met several months ago when he and his daughter, Wren, discovered Venus flytraps around a swamp near their home in Seagrove. Interested in preserving the discovery, they emailed the expert for advice. Dad drove out to see for himself.

"He expected a woman. I signed my emails *Christie*, you see," he laughed as he explained, "but he wasn't disappointed at the surprise. We're both single dads with daughters named for something in nature—funny, right? It was an instant connection. It's never too late to find your soulmate."

"Um, if you believe in that sort of thing," I said, though I do. "I'm happy for you both."

"I knew you would be," he grinned. He went on to tell me about Wren, who recently graduated from high school and has gone to Europe. It was his gift to her, funding her travel during her gap year.

"We're meeting her there," he explained after telling me about his planned trip with my father. "The International Horticultural Society's convention in Belgium, followed by a week in Paris, time in Spain, and then backpacking with Wren. It's the trip of a lifetime. But you know all about that—you've been everywhere."

I didn't know what to say to that, so he solicited my help in setting the table for dinner. This involved linen napkins, a rustic, floral tablecloth, silverware, and a vase of wildflowers as a centerpiece. At first, I thought these items were superfluous, more to clean up. But now, I understand how it makes the table more pleasant.

We sit in mismatched chairs at the round table overlooking the garden and woods. It's warm and humid, but Christie, who was an electrical engineer before retiring to be a stay-at-home dad, has made several upgrades to the property, including installing ceiling fans along the underdeck and pergola.

He's also installed an ingenious misting system in the greenhouse that recycles water from our in-house dehumidifiers. He calls it the Misty Christie.

Ivy's full laughter pulls me into the present. She leans closer to Christie. "He tried on four shirts before finally deciding on that one, and they were all the same, just different shades of blue."

They laugh.

"I appreciate a man who dresses up," Christie says. "It's not every day that you meet your love's father. It's a dressy occasion."

"I don't own a dress," I blurt. I run my finger over the long oval of my mood ring, finding some comfort in its smooth surface. "Or dress clothes."

Ivy smiles. "Don't worry about it, Vee. You didn't know about tonight's dinner, either. We understand."

"You're here," Christie smiles. "That's all that matters."

The night passes pleasantly enough, especially once I make myself a Vodka Cranberry from Dad's bar cabinet. I observe their interactions and show customary interest in Gil's job as a software developer, his gaming hobby, and his large family, as well as Christie and Ivy's mutual appreciation of the romance genre. Everyone enjoys Christie's lasagna. Buster settles after seemingly pointless running, wrapping himself into a tight ball under the table.

I long to get up, explore, and be on my own. Prolonged conversation exhausts me. I imagine it's like a muscle that must be exercised daily over time to succeed in a long marathon like this. But I endeavor to see this through, to once more feel a part of the family.

Still, I don't belong. The couples engage in what I can only assume is their typical affection—holding hands, occasional kisses, and constantly leaning in toward each other, as if they're unable to communicate effectively outside of a three-centimeter range. This creates two pockets, one on either side of me at the round table, and highlights my aloneness. I don't say much at dinner, unless asked directly. Keeping my head down and mouth shut prevents *difficulties*.

But once the vodka achieves its numbing effect, impulse takes over, and I blurt the question that's bothered me since learning that my father has succumbed to romantic feelings. "What happened to romantic love being a construct, perpetuated by society, religion, and the need to procreate? Independence showed true strength, you said. Depending on another person to feel complete undervalues our worth and makes us reliant on a fantasy for our happiness. Makes them reliant, too. Romantic love is a *burden*. That's what you told me."

Despite my conversational tone, the table falls silent. A Carolina barn owl hoots overhead, as if citing my faux pas. *People don't like being called hypocrites*, I can hear Dr. Broderick saying. Ivy's obvious irritation strangles me from across the table.

Dad sets down his napkin with a thoughtful, "Hmm. I failed to factor in the soulmate equation and the immense power of a... what do you call it? A meet-cute?"

Laughter roars across the table, and Christie practically falls out of his chair, gushing, "Yes, a meet-cute! You're learning my book terms!"

"Meet-cutes are my favorite," Ivy coos. "Gil and I met over a game board—he let me win. That's how I knew!"

"Seeing you smile mattered more than winning," he grins, slipping his lanky arm around her shoulders.

Flummoxed by Dad's non-answer, I sip my drink and say nothing as stories about how they met and when they *knew* float blissfully across the table.

I knew many times with Henry. Though I didn't understand my feelings then. At the time, it felt sacrilegious, or at least disrespectful, not to put my complete trust in my father's words. His lifestyle and our unique family unit proved his claim against romance to be true.

Even so, Henry was different.

I knew when we first met in second grade. He cut through our property to go home rather than take the bus, and, so surprised to see someone in *my* woods, I fell out of a tree right in front of him.

Or maybe I fell on purpose—my motives are murky now.

He dropped to my side and asked, *"You okay?"* in a tone that suggested genuine concern. Once I assured him I was fine and that falling out of trees happens to me frequently, he laughed and joked, *"That's because people don't belong in trees,"* and I couldn't fault his logic. He helped me up and asked how to get home. I understood his confusion. Things look different in the woods. We talked the entire journey to his house, the longest conversation I'd had with a peer.

I knew *almost* right away that I'd love him if romantic love existed. I couldn't decide without further evidence. At the time, all I knew was that he didn't seem to mind me—not my scientific facts, my lazy filter, or my so-called difficulties. He was curious, insightful, patient, more intelligent than most, and had a smile that favored his left cheek in a delightfully asymmetrical way, like a lopsided ice cream cone—sweet and tempting me to catch it before it fell away.

When that lopsided smile sat across from me at lunch a few days later, my endearment grew into hope.

I *knew* love existed the first time he held me close amid a loud and tumultuous storm as we hovered, scared, in our lean-to. We were eight. He latched onto me when the crack of lightning hit nearby, shaking the ground underneath us. *"I don't like this, Venus,"* he said, voice trembling as his breath tickled my neck. *"It's okay. You're with me. Everything'll be okay,"* I said, pulling him tighter, and feeling, all at once, this beautiful relief, like his touch untied the knots inside me. The tighter he held me, the better I felt, like he was an anchor holding me in place.

When the danger ended, we slowly let go, but he said, *"Thanks, Venus. I, um, didn't mean to be a baby."*

"A baby?" I retorted. *"You're not a baby."*

He shrugged, looking sheepish and bothered. *"My dad calls me that sometimes."* Even thinking about it forced him to use his inhaler.

"He's wrong. You're the bravest, kindest person I know. Everyone gets scared. I was scared. You made me feel… better. Safe, actually."

I meant every word, despite his shock. He had to be the bravest and kindest—he was friends with me. His surprise drifted softly into something like pride, like he couldn't believe himself to be any more than a tagalong on my adventures. *"Me? Really? I, um, didn't think you even liked me all that much. Your face always looks so… bored."*

"Henry, examine the evidence. I wouldn't build a lean-to with anyone I didn't like. Besides, my face doesn't… I don't look…" Struggling to find the

right words, I used my father's. *"I didn't come with as many smiles as other people. However, their rarity makes them more precious. That doesn't mean I'm not smiling on the inside."*

His eyes widened behind his round, rain-specked glasses. *"Are you smiling now?"*

The question made me laugh. *"Yes."*

"Good," he said with a cough.

"You're soaked. Your mom'll be mad. Let's get you home."

But halfway there, he turned to me. *"Venus, whenever you want to feel better... I'm here."*

I took him up on his offer, and *knew* again, the first time I tapped on his bedroom window, desperate for an escape from the trouble I was in at home—I forget the infraction that time. He let me in and held me until the sun rose enough to find my way home again. We were twelve.

And all the times thereafter. I don't think I could pick *one* moment. It was *every* moment.

I went on to climb mountains instead of trees, explore biomes instead of backyards, and try to make a difference, but only because he'd made such a difference to me.

I *knew* the night I told him. *I love you, Henry.* In the greenhouse. That last night.

Soon, darkness falls, and the automatic twinkling lights come on, warming the deck and gardens in a soft glow. I'm reminded of the stars at sea, flickering, and moonlight catching the tips of waves—the warmth and welcome of light. Ivy and Christie coo collectively, as if this doesn't happen daily. But I understand the appeal. It's always been a lovely home, an oasis.

Once the plates are cleared and a tiramisu is served, Dad says, "Congratulations on your discovery."

"Oh, what discovery?" Christie coos.

Before I can explain, Dad says, "*Henricus filicis.* It was in the department's newsletter."

I fidget with my bracelets under the table as the others give me questioning looks.

"The Henry fern," Dad finishes. "Venus discovered a new species, and that's what she named it."

"New species are discovered every day," I say, warding off their commentary. "It's not that surprising for a botanist. Its distinguishing characteristic is that brownish seed balls appear on its fronds, similar to dandelions, that scatter easily into the air. It's prevalent in North Wales."

The stares continue as if I'm not explaining myself well.

"Who's Henry?" Gil asks with a playful smile. I wish we could revert to nervous-Gil, the one who didn't ask pointed questions.

"Venus's best friend, boyfriend, soulmate," Ivy says shortly, leaning closer to him. "Or he once was. Do you plan on seeing him while you're here?"

"No!"

Buster startles at my bark, answering with a determined yap.

Ivy tilts her head, glancing from Dad to me again. "Well, you know—"

"Venus doesn't want to discuss Henry," Dad says suddenly. It's unlike him to interrupt or come to my aid. He fiddles with his napkin, nodding toward my sister. "So, we shouldn't."

Christie follows Dad's lead by explaining the special espresso beans that give his tiramisu its delicious flavor. I retreat inside for a refill on my Vodka Cranberry.

When dinner ends, people linger in the living room over coffee and tea. I thank them all for a lovely evening, as is customary, and wander alone through my father's lush backyard, a maze of herbs, vegetables, greenery, and flowers. But even his upgraded irrigation system and blooming rose bushes around the perimeter fail to keep me from glancing over my shoulder at our old trail.

My impulses should be muffled, like distant voices—I'm on medication and took a second dose this afternoon in preparation for socializing—but they conspire anyway in corners, under my breath.

My fists tighten, and tension grows as I force myself in the opposite direction, toward the greenhouse.

It's illogical to think he's out there, at his childhood home. It's even more illogical to think he'd want to see me, even if he were. If he thinks of me at all, he must hate me.

Hate me.

I push into the greenhouse, sloshing my drink on my hand. I'm greeted by the soft trickle of water moving gently through Dad's carnivorous bog. The twinkling lights outside shine through the greenhouse's recycled window panes and the circular stained-glass window over the door, creating amber and green flecks of light that dance around my boots. It's a heavenly place, warm and full of memories.

Through the tall pitcher plants and low, but ominous flytraps, I make my way to our garden, mine and Henry's—a raised bed in the corner that Dad gave us to do whatever we so desired. Every summer, we planned what we'd grow and harvested everything from cucumbers and tomatoes to blueberries, strawberries, and sunflowers (though the bed was too small to accommodate the giant flowers).

Among the diverse, lush greenery, our bed lies empty and dry.

The door thwacks after Dad wanders in, promptly stuffing his hands in his pockets when he sees me hovering over the dirt pile.

"I told you to use this space," I remind him, "the last time I was here and many times before that."

"Hmm, I didn't need it, but since you're here for the summer, you're welcome to—"

"No, I'm not starting a garden. I'll take care of yours, but that's it."

He nods, edges closer, and tugs a weed from the base of his container plants. He flicks the unwanted invader into a compost bin on his cluttered workstation. "Venus, my remarks about romantic love were taken out of context."

"It doesn't matter," I say, stepping toward the door.

"Wait. Take a breath. Hear me out. Remember what I always say. Listening is loving."

I stop, huff, and face him.

"You were eleven, remember? And frustrated, over your peers' fascinations with boy bands, princess movies, and pop culture-isms that you weren't interested in. You felt left out. I explained why they were drawn to such things to help you understand—hormones, social constructs, and yes, romantic love. Strengthening your independence felt more important than humoring ideas that, frankly, you were too young to entertain. I thought undermining those notions would make you feel better about your situation."

"Make me feel better about being alone, that is," I conclude for him.

"I was wrong. I'm sorry."

"Don't be. It's for the best." I force a weak smile.

"It must be strange for you," he says after a breath, "coming home to all of this change."

"Change is life's most-kept promise. That's what you used to say."

"It's true," he chuckles. "I'm fifty-six years old. Twice in my life, change has rescued me from my dormancy and pushed me, once by design and then by accident, into my best seasons—first, when I became a father, and second, when I found love. I'm sorry I ever called it a burden. Love is freedom, Venus. To be yourself without compromise, to discover your passion, to *belong*. This is what I hope for you."

"I know where I belong—away from here," I say, with numb resignation. "My hope for me is to be an adequate replacement for you and get through this summer as quickly as possible. Goodnight."

I leave him, once again desperate to be alone.

CHAPTER 5

Henry

THE BLAKES' greenhouse door had a very distinctive snap. Too much tension in the coil, Dr. Blake explained once. I almost hear it in the distance, but I know it can't be. Surely, the noise would be muffled by the trees and everything else that's grown wild without our disturbance over the years.

I'm imagining her. Imagining us.

My stepdad Fred and I settle into our after-dinner food comas as we watch Olly play with lackluster excitement over the newest *toy* Mom invented for Olly. She turned an old tackle box into a first aid kit containing the following *fun* items: ointments for sunburn, bug bites, cuts, sore muscles, and rashes; antibacterial wipes; gauze and superhero bandages; small scissors, tweezers, and typed cards explaining what to do for each injury or situation. Her gift is topped off with an exterior card that reads "Olly's Ouchy Kit," featuring a sad, teary face, and is followed by an oversized "9-1-1" so he'll remember.

She also handed him a stuffed bunny with extra-long legs and ears, and said, "Have fun treating Bun-Bun's injuries, Olly. It's good practice."

Mom lives in a state of perpetual worry, and even her *fun* is marred by it.

But I get it. She spent the first half of her adulthood in a terrible marriage to my father, Dale Greene, before courageously ousting the smoker, drinker, and bully from our lives. On top of that, she had me, an asthmatic, chronically ill child who could literally drop dead without his inhaler, and Venus, the wild girl next door, who routinely tested Mom's boundaries. It's no wonder that Mom still lives in a worst-case-scenario mindset.

All the what-ifs overwhelm me too, sometimes.

Even so, watching Olly trying to respectfully enjoy his new toy, though clearly not having any fun, solidifies what I already know—I don't want this for him. He's too young to worry about first-aid kits and sanitizing his hands every five seconds. I want him to be brave and confident, a kid who'll jump into puddles and climb trees, despite the messes and scratches that might come with it. I want him to have a fun, memorable childhood, filled with adventures and cool stories to tell, just like I had because of Venus.

"*I know you think* I'm *brave, Henry, but...* " she said one afternoon after I randomly shared that King Henry VIII had a suit of armor made for his dog, and joked that he could be called Sir Barks-A-Lot. "*Amusing me is a monumental feat, and you do it with ease. I believe that you're exceptionally capable.*"

Those words stayed with me, like she branded them to my soul—*I'm exceptionally capable*. Without those words on mental replay, I doubt I would've had the confidence to be a father.

Mom doted on me, inadvertently making me feel weak.

My father belittled me, reinforcing my insecurities.

Venus busted through my preconceived limitations and made me believe I could do anything. And *she* was right.

"Hey, Olly, why don't you grab my gardening tools from the flower bed?" Fred says, with his charming Southern drawl. "Rough Bun-Bun up a bit, 'til he needs medical care. I got ketchup packets in the junk drawer, if you wanna make it realistic."

Olly perks up and races off.

"Don't run with gardening shears, Olly," I say, hating myself a little for it.

"So, when's the big camping trip?" Fred asks, tilting his beer in my direction.

"Soon. I haven't set a date yet. With everything at the museum and us getting into our new summer routines, I didn't want to overdo it."

"It'll be good for Olly to get his hands dirty and have fun outdoors."

"Good for us both," I say. "Um, are you interested in coming along?"

He chuckles good-naturedly. "I may look feral, but I'm more of an indoor cat, Henry."

It's a remarkably apt analogy—Fred *is* the human version of an alley cat. His old-school mullet hairstyle and beard look scruffy, but somehow work for him. His darkly tanned skin displays colorful tattoos that have faded with age and sun exposure, and his hands and fingernails seem perpetually covered in oil stains and grease, no matter how much he cleans them—the curse of being an auto-mechanic, he says.

He's also one of the nicest, most generous men I've ever met, which hurts his street-cat claim. The day Mom's car broke down outside Fred's Garage on the way to an urgent doctor's appointment for my unyielding cough was serendipitous—Mom's timing belt went out at the right time. Fred dropped everything to take us to my appointment, and has been there for us ever since.

Though I expected he'd turn me down, having another adult for our first camping trip might've tempered my anxiety over it. The camping trip was *my* idea, *my* plan to make some outdoorsy memories with Olly while teaching him not to be afraid.

But *I'm* afraid, and it makes little sense considering all the play groups, sports, day trips, and unusual classes we've done together. Pickleball and medieval cosplay with wooden swords are two recent examples. Olly and I don't shy away from trying new things.

Camping is different, though. I haven't camped since I was a kid, and then, I had Venus. She not only knew every plant, insect, and animal, but she existed fearlessly among them as if in her natural habitat, too. Nothing stopped or slowed her down, except for me. I promised Olly I'd take him on an adventure like the ones in my stories about Vee.

But the supplies sit in a corner of our apartment, tags still on.

I just keep thinking, *what if*. What if he gets stung, bitten, or exposed to something harmful? What if he's scared? What if I have an asthma attack? What if I can't find my inhaler and Olly is left alone, unable to get help? What if I'm weak and frail, just like Dale always claimed?

"Just be Henry. You're brave, kind, and capable, just as you are." Venus's voice slips through my thoughts like raindrops over leaves.

"You've bought all the supplies. You're going to a well-populated public park. You'll be fine, Henry," Fred says, breaking me from my memories.

"Fine about what?" Mom asks, slipping through the sliding glass door with a pitcher of lemonade and cups.

"Campin'," Fred answers.

She rolls her eyes. "As if you don't have enough to worry about. You should put it off until the fall, when it's not as humid, and there are fewer allergens to trigger your asthma. Olly! Lemonade!"

Olly pops up from his spot on the ground, where he's nearly dissected Bun-Bun's left leg and doused the wound in ketchup. He wipes his hands on his shorts, leaving red trails behind.

"Oh, my! What've you gotten into?" Mom cries, zooming in on the stains. "Is that ketchup? What's happened to Bun-Bun?"

"Bar fight," Fred quips with a raspy laugh.

Her mood lightens slightly. She reaches for paper towels and dabs at the stains on his shorts while Olly drinks his weight in lemonade. I predict a sugar rush at bedtime and him having to pee on the ten-minute drive home.

"Baking soda and lemon juice," she tells me when the paper towels don't remove the stains entirely. "Work it into a paste, apply, and let it sit for ten minutes. The enzymes break down the tannins in the tomatoes. Or something." She cocks her head in a thoughtful smile. "Venus taught me that."

"There's a name I haven't heard in a while," Fred says fondly.

Olly pulls the empty cup away from his wet mouth. "Dad's Venus? The one who climbs trees and goes on adventures and picks up snakes and makes treehouses? That Venus?"

Mom sighs. "There's only one, thank goodness."

"Olly, go use the bathroom and wash your hands. We have to go soon," I tell him.

He puts all of his six-year-old might into pushing the door open—I almost get up to help—but it gives, and he races inside.

"You still think about her, don't you?" Fred asks with a tender tone that doesn't match his gruff exterior.

I fixate on the shrubbery lining their property as if I might see the lights from the fairy house through the woods when I already know I can't. "Course I do."

Mom groans. "You talk her up to Olly like she's a superhero—it's not good."

"She's the closest thing to a superhero I've ever known."

"A superhero wouldn't have made you sick with her shenanigans, traipsing through the woods and goading you up trees. Have you forgotten all the cuts, bumps, ticks, rashes, and bruises you came home with, thanks to her? Or the times she got you in trouble at school? I should've put a stop to it early on. If I'd been more attentive, I could've prevented you from nearly dying and at least from having your heart broken—"

"More attentive?" I laugh. "Mom, you tracked me on my phone while I was in class… in elementary school! Wild animal tamers aren't as attentive as you."

Fred laughs good-naturedly. "He's got you there, Mags."

"Besides, Venus never *made* me sick," I defend weakly. "My asthma and allergies did. She encouraged me to do things I never would've done without her. Venus made me strong."

"Is that what you think you're doing for Olly? Telling him about her? You want him jumping off roofs and setting fires?" she counters.

"Venus never jumped off a roof. I mean, not exactly. And the fires were contained. Mostly."

Mom shakes her head and folds her arms. "She hurt you, Henry. Over and over. I don't think you should idolize her to Olly."

"I tell Olly stories, that's all. You told me your stories, like when Uncle Jay taught you to roller skate, oh, and the time he carried you after you sprained your ankle—"

"No more of that," she snaps. "I don't want to talk about this anymore."

"It's okay, Mags," Fred says gently. "Your brother was a great man, worthy of being remembered."

"We're creating a memorial at the museum," I add. "Did you know he saved ticket stubs from every concert, movie, or comedy act he attended? I'm framing them into a collage. If you have any suggestions—"

"No. I don't. I don't want to talk about him." Her words are strained and borderline curt. Still, she folds up her obvious anger and tucks it away behind a barbed-wire smile. "I'll, um, pack up some leftovers, so you don't have to fix lunch tomorrow."

She retreats inside.

I sigh. Fred takes a long swig of his beer. I guzzle lemonade. A dog yaps in the distance.

"She'll get there," he says.

"I'm pissed at him, too. It must be worse for her."

"She feels betrayed that he didn't talk to her. Blames herself. Blames her anxiety. She's gotta go through her grief," he says.

Venus's voice pipes up in my thoughts like a monotone announcement coming over loudspeakers in a store. *"The Kübler-Ross model predicts five stages of grief: denial, anger, bargaining, depression, and acceptance. These can be applied to any loss and don't have to be linear. Where are you in terms of your parents' divorce?"*

I remember smiling and saying, *"Acceptance. I jumped straight to acceptance."*

She grinned because she understood more than most what my father was like. *"Excellent."*

We lost Uncle Jay nearly four months ago, and Mom's stuck on the angry stage. Losing her older brother, especially like that, I can't blame her.

"She's seeing her therapist again," Fred offers. "Maybe you should, too."

"Yeah, maybe." It's not a bad idea, if I can find the time. Therapy has helped multiple times in my life. After Mom divorced Dale, we attended family sessions to help us heal from the abuse. Mom insisted again when I was in college and struggled to get myself together after Venus. I went again when Olly was a toddler, while living with Carly and trying to make our family work.

Now, those dark fingers feel like they have a grip on me again, dragging me to places I shouldn't go. I glance toward the shrubbery wall and towering treeline. A barn owl hoots overhead, and an ominous breeze stirs the trees, bringing tension with it.

I want to duck behind the shrubs, find our path, and make my way to the fairy house. Do something bold to make me brave again. I can find my way, despite the overgrowth and darkness. When we were teenagers, we could walk it blindfolded—we tested each other, taking turns covering our eyes with Venus's scarf. *"We should always be able to get to each other, no matter the conditions."*

Always repeats in my head—Venus was careful in her use of absolutes. We could always reach each other *then*.

The tightness in my chest intensifies as we head home and begin our bedtime routine. Olly insists on a Venus story, instead of choosing a library book from the stack Mom gave us. Too tired to argue, I begin the story of Frank the Bullfrog for the thirtieth time.

"Once upon a time, Venus heard a fellow fourth grader claim that touching frogs causes warts…"

Olly giggles. "Warts."

"Venus didn't like it when people talked badly about others, especially creatures unable to defend themselves. Ever the scientist, she decided the only way to confirm that frogs were not to blame for warts was…"

"An experiment!"

"Right. We were the test subjects, along with an irritated bullfrog I named Frank."

Olly giggles again. "Frank."

"Venus discovered Frank in a drainage ditch and pulled him from the muck, bare-handed, like a trophy. *All hail, Frank, the king of the bullfrogs*," I coo, making my son laugh and snuggle to my side.

"Frank is my favorite frog," he says, sleepily.

"Mine, too. Venus held him for five minutes as he croaked—I timed her. Then, she pushed Frank toward me and said, *'Your turn.'* Well, I wasn't thrilled about holding Frank, as nice as he seemed. Venus could tell that I was reluctant. *'Henry, I will be honest. He's squishy and moist in an unpleasant way, but he's a perfectly gentle creature living his innocent frog life, and he deserves justice. Friends help each other disprove wrongful claims. Please, be brave, for Frank's sake.'* Then Venus smiled, something she didn't often do—it made me warm inside. She had the prettiest smile. It made me forget the risk of warts."

Olly snickers into my shoulder, barely moving this time.

"So, she slowly handed him over," I say, my voice softer. "His long legs flailing, his croaker croaking. He wiggled and squirmed. But I wrapped my hands around him, palms to his belly and fingers around his lumpy, bumpy back. We came face to face—his bulbous black eyes shifting over me, his thin lips seeming to smile, and his, yes, very moist and rather unpleasant body nuzzled against my skin. Holding him worried me at first, but I resisted those thoughts that told me to be scared and realized *I was doing it*. I was holding a bullfrog. And Frank was strangely okay with it, which made me feel okay, too. Brave, for the first time. And Venus smiled like she could see my courage grow. *'You're holding him perfectly, Henry,'* she said, and I felt even prouder. The five minutes blew by, and before I knew it, she said, *'Time's up. We did it.'* She offered to take Frank back for his release, but I wanted to do it. Frank and I connected, you see. We both had a croaking problem, at least. I balanced over the ditch, one leg on each side. Venus thanked Frank for his participation. Then, I set him free into the watery muck."

Olly's body feels heavy beside me, his breathing soft and rhythmic.

"We checked ourselves each day for a week, and we never got warts. Thank goodness, because I wouldn't have wanted to explain that to your grandma. Venus, Frank, and I lived happily ever after. The end," I finish in a whisper.

I hesitate, still and quiet, for a solid three minutes. Then, I inch out from underneath my sleeping son with the skill of a cat burglar making his escape.

But we didn't live happily ever after, I think, as I prepare for tomorrow. Venus would say that happily-ever-afters don't exist in real life. They're a narrative device, invented by writers to create satisfying endings. Otherwise, the story would go on forever, and readers would see the truth—that happily-ever-afters are impossible because no one is happy all the time and nothing is ever perfect.

Back then, I would've argued. I *did* argue, especially after we'd watch classic rom-coms from Mom's collection, only for Venus to bash the ending.

But she wasn't wrong.

CHAPTER 6
Venus

I CAN'T SLEEP in the loft's upgraded guest bed, despite its plush linens and comfortable mattress. By three in the morning, I'm irritated and restless. I tug my boots on, grab my hammock, creep outside, and attach my trustworthy sling of a bed between the weeping willow and crepe myrtle at the back end of Dad's garden.

When my eyes open, the afternoon sun beats down through the branches, heating my face. My head hangs nearly upside down off the side of the hammock, hair grazing the ground, and one leg spills from the other end—I'm barely hanging on.

I hear laughing.

Finding my footing with my untied boots, I see my father and Christie, each carrying a mug at different levels near their faces, watching me like I'm a creature in an exhibit. *This is a rare Venus in her natural habitat. Don't provoke her. She may become... difficult.*

A glance at my watch reveals I've slept twelve hours.

Christie snickers at my clear confusion. "Travel exhaustion. Here, drink this." He hands me a mug, which warms my hands and fills my nose with delicate smells—cinnamon, ginger, and lemon. I inhale deeply, awakening my senses. I've been all over the world, and nothing compares to my father's homemade teas.

"Thank you," I mumble.

"Are you unwell, Venus?" Dad's forehead scrunches with concern.

"I'm fine."

"Was the bed uncomfortable?" he asks.

"You're the first to sleep in it," Christie explains.

"It's not the bed... It's the lack of movement," I say, standing and stretching.

"She has sea legs. She has to get her land legs again," Christie summarizes.

"Ah, it may take time to adjust your equilibrium," Dad agrees. "Come inside. We fixed you a late lunch."

Over tea and grilled cheeses at the small table near the front window, Dad skims the local paper through his reading glasses, occasionally *hmming* or commenting. Meanwhile, Christie giggles and gasps over his paperback. I fetch my journal, perusing pages in my lap so they can't see, while I eat and sip. Despite the addition of Christie, this is how we used to eat our meals—Dad, Ivy, and me. It's oddly comforting —our version of normal.

"Tomorrow morning, I'll take you to the university to get you acclimated," Dad announces softly. "Classes begin Monday at nine."

"Is it too late to make it a virtual class?" I ask.

"Yes. Most students prefer a classroom experience," he says, "with discussions and camaraderie."

Christie's eyes cut to Dad's like they're sharing a secret.

"As the professor, you'll have control," he adds. "You'll enjoy that, I think. It's an entirely different dynamic than you remember from school."

"So, I get to torture students this time?" I say, deadpan.

While Christie snickers, Dad and I share a look that carries an entire conversation.

Hmm, torture seems an exaggeration.

Torture is the intentional infliction of suffering. Not an exaggeration.

No one intended to hurt you, Venus. Some of your teachers might argue that you tortured them.

Scoff. I was a child.

A child, yes, but not always an innocent one.

I stood up for myself.

Knocking others down in the process. Academic showdowns with teachers and conflicts with peers—you didn't make things easy for anyone, least of all yourself.

I didn't realize that making things easy was my responsibility. No one made it easy for me, either.

You insisted on proving that you were the smartest in the room. You didn't give them a chance to love you.

Christie clears his throat with a giggle, breaking our unsaid conversation. But Dad's words from long ago ripple through my thoughts like a rock plunked into a creek. He never knew the whole story—no one did because I didn't tell them. Minimizing the damage felt safer than expounding on it.

Dr. Broderick has since validated my feelings and experiences, and assured me that I was worthy of being heard—then and now. But if nothing changes, what's the point of it?

I recall my first-grade teacher admonishing me for questioning the efficacy of recycling. When I offered suggestions for in-home recycling, she told me to hold my questions until the end of class. She couldn't answer me then either, but instructed me to log my questions and research the answers myself. She curtly refused to let me report my findings to the class the next morning. She wanted my silence, not my contributions.

That made me feel so small.

"She's kidding, Richard," Christie says, "Venus won't torture them. I'm sure."

Dad looks unsure. "Hmm, in my experience, it's better to have a torture-free classroom. It'll make the summer go by quicker."

"Time won't move any faster regardless," I huff.

"We'll discuss the syllabus over milkshakes in the quad," he adds, knowing sweet treats are my weakness, "and have lunch at Roma's. What do you say?"

Though I am a proud omnivore, Roma's Vegan Kitchen is a distinct highlight of my occasional visits.

I feel like I'm being blackmailed.

"There's a new nursery in town. They claim to have epiphytic fertilizers and authentic sphagnum peat moss."

His tone suggests he doesn't believe it, and I concur with his skepticism. Most nurseries cater to hobbyist gardeners, rather than academics and experts who understand the differences between peat moss, natural fertilizers, and truly nutrient-rich soil.

"We could check it out after lunch," he suggests.

"Ah, that sounds like the perfect day!" Christie coos. "A little father-daughter time would be nice."

I nod and ask, "What time should I be ready?"

The next morning, I descend the stairs at 8:25—five minutes earlier than Dad's suggested leave time. He waits for me at the small kitchen table, arms folded and staring into the wood grain, his gaze strangely transfixed as if he might be daydreaming. My journal sits uncomfortably close to him, thankfully closed, though off-center from where I left it. He perks up when I step into the kitchen and smiles with a nod to the door.

"Shall we?"

"We shall," I answer.

His Land Rover rumbles into his assigned space just outside the Environmental Sciences Building. With summer sessions starting on Monday, the campus has entered a brief dormancy. It's a beautiful place, compact and tucked away in a peaceful oasis of trees, ponds, and pathways. Common shrubs, meticulously trimmed, and azalea bushes line our short walk to the building.

Dad takes me to his office first—a cluttered corner room on the top floor overlooking the wide walkway outside that leads to most academic buildings. The musty smell of books mingles delightfully with my father's spiced tea smell, instantly lifting my spirits. He's added a cushioned window seat, a coat rack armed with umbrellas, and more of my artistic gifts, framed and scattered across his overflowing wall of bookshelves. I pick up one of the small images—a luna moth I drew when I was around ten. I remember mixing three different shades of green with a silver acrylic to achieve the right lime-green coloring and moon-like glow. I left it on his bedside table and didn't think anything of it when he didn't mention it.

"They're so accurate that I use them with my students sometimes," he tells me. "Actias luna is a favorite, but students love your flytrap scene the most."

He motions to the framed print perched on his top shelf. I stretch to reach it, and holding it in my hands, I'm overrun with memories. I had long forgotten this painting, even though it's larger than most, and took me a week of concentrated effort to complete it. It's a Venus flytrap, surrounded by moss and shadowed by pitcher plants. Each of its jaw-like traps is in a different stage. One is open wide, its pink interior concave and waiting for its prey. Another has a guest, a fly, tickling its inner triggers to snap at any moment. Another is partially closed, having captured a cricket, but tiny ants are moving through its teeth, too small to keep. Another expels the dried carcass of a tiny frog, done with its meal. Surrounding the active stems are blackened ones because that's what happens once flytraps serve their purpose. They turn black and shrivel and die.

That's how I felt when I made it, like my heart had turned black. This wasn't a project I enjoyed—it came from a place of anger at the world for the way it takes, traps, hurts, uses, and spits us out. And for how small and insignificant we are. How easily we're hurt and how difficult we are to love.

It was the first summer Henry was forbidden to play with me. I broke an unsaid social rule by arguing with Dale about smoking around Henry. Explaining the dangers of secondhand smoke should've been illuminating—not upsetting.

He didn't appreciate it, though. *"I don't want that know-it-all bitch around Henry. Why doesn't he hang out with boys? Normal kids?"* Henry and I overheard him with Maggie. She later overreacted to a minor incident at school, telling me that it'd be best for Henry if I stayed away that summer.

The injustice sparked big feelings and led to negative impulses—destroying our lean-to, racing into storms, uprooting the garden we'd planted—until Dad insisted that I, *"Create rather than destroy."* I endured two weeks of the ban before I calmly demanded a meeting with Maggie to plead my case and beg for her forgiveness. She eventually agreed to supervised visits.

"I threw this away," I say to Dad.

"I rescued it." He tugs it gently from my hands and returns it to the shelf.

My fists clench at my sides. It feels like a violation. "I don't know how I feel about that," I admit, my voice edged with frustration.

"When in doubt, it's best to err on the side of positivity," he advises simply. "I kept it because I liked it, and many others have liked it, too."

He diverts my attention by explaining his grading system, class list, and schedule. We discuss office hours and the material for his lessons, all very basic and straightforward. He hands me a thick file.

"I printed the materials for you," he says. "Feel free to modify or deviate from the plan. Students love a good anecdote."

He takes me to his classroom on the first floor—a lecture hall with stadium seating that seats 150 students during normal semesters. For the Rare Plants class, it'll accommodate twenty-five students.

My tension rises sharply. I can't imagine teaching five, let alone twenty-five.

But the setting is familiar, at least. Ivy and I spent many quiet summer days here in the front corner with books and snacks in hand, while he delivered lessons on pollination and photosynthesis. That I'll be taking his place feels absurd, though I hold the same doctorate as him, with two additional degrees. I hug the thick file to my chest, hoping that physical pressure will alleviate the mental one.

"It helps to imagine that you're teaching one person rather than a crowd. Just picture explaining the concepts to Henry, like you used to," he says.

Imagine myself in a room full of Henrys? I don't think so.

Soon, he ushers me outside for the milkshakes he promised, and we enjoy them on a bench overlooking the turtle pond. My cookies-and-cream shake satisfies me immensely. This was often our reward for staying quiet in his summer classes, one I didn't always earn. Some days, sitting still proved too challenging for me, as if I had ten times more energy than everyone else and could spontaneously combust if I wasn't actively moving.

After an elongated, peaceful silence, Dad asks, "Do you have any regrets, Venus?"

His question stuns me. Thanks to therapy, I know my family fails at effective communication. Dr. Broderick assures me that most families do, but in our case, Ivy overshares, while Dad and I are the opposite. Ivy could talk for hours about absolutely nothing, which makes it easy to lose focus. Dad and I could sit for hours without speaking. The conversations we did have stayed at surface level—plant care, garden ideas, and our thoughts on journal articles or books we'd read. Attempts at real emotional depth felt strained and unnatural, especially since I'd do nearly anything to escape those feelings.

But when I was in trouble at school, our comfortable rules of engagement changed drastically.

Then, our talks were meant to cut straight to the heart of me—a full dissection to analyze my inner workings and determine why I behaved the way I did. Verbalizing my private thoughts and deepest feelings felt forced... *difficult*... given that I'd had little practice.

Only with Henry did I feel comfortable sharing feelings because he so freely shared his with me, but *only* when he asked, and *only* with the knowledge that he wouldn't judge or shame me for it.

"Forgive me for prying," Dad says after a beat, "but I haven't had the opportunity to spend time with you, and I've often wondered."

"I regret my inability to control my impulses and being difficult. Is that what you mean?"

"No, your impulses weren't your fault, and I never viewed you as difficult. You faced challenges I failed to understand—that's one regret I have."

An unsure smile plays at my lips at his declaration. "I appreciate that."

"I want to understand you better now. So, please don't say what you think I want to hear. I mean, genuine regrets, decisions that changed your future for the worse."

"I regret getting Henry into trouble so much, and the times our activities led to his discomfort. I regret not listening to Ivy most of the time."

He chuckles. "We're both guilty of that."

"Beyond that, I don't know how to answer. Most of my decisions have been made for me."

"I never should've let you go," he says after a pause. "That's my deepest regret."

"I wanted to go," I argue, confused. "That's what *I* wanted. Not just wanted, it's what I needed, and it was the first time you listened."

"I always listened," he corrects gently. "I didn't *always* know what to do or how to help you. But that night, you were desperate and hurting —you needed your family. But instead of holding you and assuring you, I gave you permission to run away, and you've been hiding ever since. That's my fault. Perhaps it's too little, too late, but I'm sorry."

Energy surges in me, forcing me to stand and set the milkshake down at my feet, unable to enjoy it. "Is this why you insisted I come back here?"

"I didn't insist," he says, ever-calm. "Dr. Miner called me with her concerns."

"So, you conspired against me, trapped me into this," I finish, hands fisting around the manila folder I still carry. I slap it against the bench beside him, and the breeze flutters it open.

He pauses. "It's not a trap. It's an opportunity. I'd like us to talk more."

Dr. Broderick would be pleased—talking more usually benefits those involved and builds stronger relationships. But already our communication feels like walking a tightrope, and any misstep could send me over the edge. He regrets letting me leave, but he doesn't understand how that one decision saved me. Even worse, his apology makes me feel like I've done everything wrong. A dark tunnel closes around me, swallowing me in suffocating tension.

"Talk more?" I repeat weakly. "Such a conversation will only make us both feel worse. If we talk more, I'll be forced to explain the full extent of the suffering I endured over people who failed to understand me. I survived indignities, mistreatment, and abuse *alone* because I was convinced that it was better that way. If you're determined to entertain regret, regret *that*—not the one decision that finally gave me... a chance."

"Venus, I'm confused. What haven't you told me? I want to help."

"You helped when you sent me away," I say, my hands flexing. "Trust me—it was the right thing."

"I trust you," he says after a beat. "But perhaps you could elaborate further?"

"There's no point. It's done. Over. I don't want to talk about this anymore."

"Venus, I love you, and I want you to be happy." His green eyes lock on mine, and he offers a small smile. He says it like it's easy.

Happy. It's such a vapid word. Simple and biting, yet just vague enough for the masses to toss it around like a delightful beach ball. No—it's more of a dodgeball. Some people have it and slam it into the faces of those who don't.

The tension grows, electrifying through me, making my legs wobble on the tightrope. Needing to do something, I yank the cornflower-blue scarf from my hair and wrap it around my hand, pinching my bracelets and rings into my skin. "I'm not like you and Ivy. Happiness isn't an achievable goal—not for me. I don't belong anywhere with anyone."

"Yes, you do. You did. Once. Don't you ever wish you'd stayed? Wonder what could have been?"

My eyes shut tightly, tears stinging. Henry appears in my thoughts, approaching the fairy house with a big bouquet of white, yellow, and pink daisies, the same flowers I had inked over my heart soon thereafter, always to remember that moment, not that I could forget.

The sweetness and the agony.

My eyes flutter open, and I *see* him. A gasp escapes as my heart rams against my chest. My boots scoot forward but stop against the edge of the bench. I squint as a figure rushes across the street and down the line of academic buildings. A tall, broad frame. Glasses. Brown hair, messy. Hands in his pockets. His purposeful stride. He's too far away—specific features are indeterminable at this distance. He's a blurry stick figure, *resembling* the Henry I imagine. In my distress and irritation, I've conjured him like a ghost through a mental Ouija board.

I refocus on my father. "There's no point to wondering. Look at Ivy. Look at you. I'm sure Henry's… thriving, too. Leaving was best for everyone. Best for me, especially."

Dad opens his mouth to speak, but I can't hear another word about regrets. I don't realize I'm running until I've put acres between us.

CHAPTER 7

Henry

LONG BLONDE HAIR waves in the distance, catching my eye. Across the quad near the turtle pond, a woman stands beside a bench. Loose, almost wild-looking hair surrounds a tall, athletic, and flustered figure. Her hands ball at her sides. *Is that Venus?* She's too far away to confirm it.

But my feet scrape against the concrete, coming to a complete stop. My chest aches with immediate tension, layered with bitterness at the possibility.

Bitterness *and* this nonsensical, agonizing hope. I step toward her, my feet moving before my brain catches up. But I stop suddenly—*why would I go to her?*

Fuck me. I run a hand through my hair. The only thing I *should* want when it comes to Venus is never to see her again. That was her final gift to me—absence.

The woman storms off, her hair like a cape behind her, reminding me of Venus again, but ending my debate. It can't be her, and why should I care, regardless?

I'm late to meet my academic advisor—a meeting she called. What this could be about has me spinning with possibilities—none good.

I check my watch. Five minutes is forgivable, but I'm edging closer to fifteen. I take the stairs two at a time up to the front doors of the education building and race through the halls to Dr. Kwon's office.

"You're late," she says without looking up as I spill into her office.

"Sorry." I plop into the chair in front of her desk. "Busy morning. A student stayed behind after class. Thanks for your patience."

She softens, tapping her hands on a thick folder that I instantly recognize as the teaching portfolio I turned in months ago—one of the final requirements for my specialty in Academically or Intellectually Gifted students, or AIG. Nerves swell in my gut.

"Is there… a problem?" I ask, eyeing the file with my name printed over an image of a wilted sunflower.

Her head tilts with scrutiny before she beams with a salesperson's smile. "Not a problem. An opportunity."

She flips the folder open, revealing red-penned notes covering the front page and colorful tabs peaking out from the rest. She clears her throat. "I have a confession."

"Okay…"

"It's your paper, Henry. I can't stop thinking about it," she says with an anguished sigh. *"The Problem with Sunflowers*…it's just so angsty and beautiful. It's not just that the stories are incredibly well-written; it's how they made me feel. That's why I… well, I passed it along to my agent."

"What? Why?"

"There's a book here, and I want you to write it. So, does my agent. She loved these pages."

I lean back in my chair—this isn't at all what I expected. "I don't understand."

"You spent most of your education with this girl, Buttercup. I love the pseudonym, by the way," she grins.

"It's from one of our favorite movies," I admit.

"I think you've only scratched the surface of your experiences with her. A student with a Mensa-level IQ, an academic upbringing, and learning differences? She's like a perfect storm and a Halley's Comet at the same time," she gushes.

My hand rakes through my hair. "That may be, but—"

"She's so intriguing, Henry," she goes on. "Her notebooks. The dirt always under her nails and the leaves trapped in her hair. How she clearly understood far beyond the course material, yet struggled to maintain a passing average. How despite having an IQ in the top 2% of people worldwide, she was unable to fit the mold of a model student. For that matter, who *is* a model student? Exploring this further, telling the full story, could be amazingly insightful to educators. To yourself. To those with friends and family members like her. To *her* friends and family. Don't you want to finish it?"

"Um, I'd love to offer that sort of insight, but I don't think I can. Writing a fifteen-page paper about her felt like scraping my soul with a melon baller. It's too—"

"*Difficult?*" she asks with a wry smile, using the word I repeated throughout my paper. That's what everyone called Venus. *Difficult.*

"That's not fair."

"Research is finding more and more that learning differences and giftedness go hand-in-hand." Dr. Kwon leans back in her desk chair, folding her arms over her silky blouse. "Is she the reason why you wanted to pursue an AIG specialty?"

A lump catches in my throat. *Is she?* I suddenly feel like a kid—I'm Olly, searching the bedroom for a lost sock only to find it on my foot already. "Um, maybe. I don't know."

She smirks as if she can see my distress over the realization. "So, if you had been her teacher, what would you have done differently?"

"I would've gotten to know her," I answer quickly. It's a question I've asked myself a thousand times. "Then, I would've found a way to relate to her, probably by connecting history to botany and art to engage her more. I would've given her individualized work. I would've let her speak when she had something to say, and I wouldn't have been afraid to say, 'I don't know,' if she asked a question I couldn't answer. For starters…"

My voice trails off in a flood of memories. Whenever Venus huffed over my *"boring history facts,"* I'd regain her interest with something like, *"The USS Constitution is made of Southern Live Oak that was so strong, it earned the nickname Old Ironsides for withstanding enemy fire. And the ship still floats after over 200 years!"* Or I'd explain how family herb gardens helped the war effort in World War II. I still remember the gentle perk of her brow when I said something that interested her, and the spark of pride it inspired.

A smile plays on my lips with the memory. "She deserved better—a better education *and* a better best friend."

"Henry, writing about your experiences could be just as cathartic for you as it would be helpful for others. I've had students like Buttercup. They burn bright and fast, and most of the time, we miss them. Or they fly right over our heads. By telling her story now, perhaps we won't miss the next one."

"I don't want to miss them. I want to help them, but..." I say with a sigh. "I've spent the last decade trying to put her out of my mind."

She taps my paper with a knowing look. "How's that working out for you?"

"Miserably," I admit sheepishly. "It's hard not to think of... Buttercup."

"Then, perhaps this isn't as finished as you want it to be," she reasons, looking partly proud but mildly annoyed.

"I gave Olly that same look this morning when he remembered to wash his hands after using the bathroom, but proceeded to dry them off on his pants," I quip.

She laughs. "Right. Your work isn't done here. Besides, writing about her may help you better understand the past. You should appreciate that, as a history teacher."

"I'll, um, think about it," I say, though I'm already crafting the email to let her down gently. I don't have the time, energy, talent, or mental fortitude to write a book about Venus, let alone reach out to her to ask her permission.

"Take this. Read my notes. See if you're inspired enough to attempt an outline. Fair enough?"

I stand, slinging my messenger bag over my shoulder. "Okay. Thanks, Dr. Kwon."

She holds up a finger. "Oh, wait. I have something for you." She reaches into her desk drawer and pulls out a purple velvet sack. I loosen the strings and reveal a palm-sized shark's tooth with a boomerang-shaped root at the top, indicative of "Megalodon. What an incredible find. Where'd you get it?"

"Granddad wanted you to have it. Found it hooked to his nets ages ago. He included a map to show you the coordinates and a note about its discovery."

"I can't wait to show Olly. His excitement over finds like this has been a great motivator to get the museum reopened," I tell her. "I'd love to display it. We're doing an entire section of coastal treasures. Thank you, and please, thank him for me."

"Knowing people will enjoy it makes him very happy," she smiles.

I return the treasure to its protective case and shove it into my bag. I have other megalodon teeth from Uncle Jay's collection, but none have been found locally. It adds credibility when an artifact isn't purchased online and comes with a personal story.

Dr. Kwon isn't the first to offer me family treasures after learning about my mission to make Weird But True Wilmington an accurate representation of our eclectic community. It thrills me to be an unexpected curator of local history.

The spring humidity hits me as soon as I exit the building. I check my watch. I have thirty minutes to make it back to school before my third block. I glance toward the pond and scan the area for the woman with wild hair, but she's gone.

CHAPTER 8
Venus

THE LAND ROVER squeaks to a stop beside me, earning a long-winded honk from drivers scooting around it. Dad rolls down his window.

"Venus, please, get in. We don't have to talk."

My boots scrape against the concrete, my folded arms drop, and I take a cleansing breath. I shouldn't have left him there, and as the sharp energy rush settles to a gentle current, I feel embarrassed for allowing words and memories to dictate my actions.

I climb into the passenger seat, buckle my seatbelt, and stare out the window as he maneuvers away from the curb. He keeps his promise, saying nothing as he navigates to our next destination.

Roma's is busy, but we're given a small table on the back porch. I tighten and loosen the scarf still tied around my wrist, focusing on the pressure, while my boots tap under the table.

Dad orders sweet tea for us and pushes a bowl of homemade pickles toward me. Then, he distracts me with a game we used to play, where we'd take turns pointing out living things in our natural surroundings using their scientific names.

Taxodium distichum. Bald Cypress.

Tillandsia usneoides. Spanish Moss.

Ardea herodias. Great Blue Heron.

Amused, he spots my discovery over his shoulder.

The tension leaves me, but slowly, like the fronds of a *Henricus filicis* detaching one by one and taking flight on a gentle breeze. This is a game he cannot play with Ivy, as she has never shown interest in plants, only in humans. This makes it *our* game.

We order our meals, and in the silence of waiting, I finally say, "Sorry, Dad."

"Thank you, I accept your apology, and I'm sorry, too," he says. "Ah, *Lonicera sempervirens*." He points to the bank of the lake where white flowers protrude from a tangle of vines. "Remember when you used to sit on the fence post, sucking the nectar from the honeysuckle's flower?"

"I'd do anything for sweets," I smirk. "The yield failed to satisfy, though, considering the effort."

"Remember how nervous Henry was the first time he tried it?"

"Poor inside person." I shake my head. "He feared that the pollen might make his head explode. Though given his medical history and his mother, I don't blame him. He did try one, eventually—a completely nonexplosive event."

Dad chuckles. "Do you still think about him much?"

I untangle the blue scarf from around my hand and retie it in my hair, pulling my long waves into a messy bun. "I try not to."

It's the best answer I'm able to give, but Dad nods in quiet understanding and doesn't push. I need time to consider his remarks—time when I'm not spun up in my energy vortex. Dad seems to understand that about me, almost like he can see when my edges start to fray.

It's what he saw when I begged him to send me away, except it wasn't a vortex that I was in, but a void I couldn't free myself from without his help. He gave in, relenting to my sheer desperation.

I *was* desperate—a feeling I never want again. Desperate to free myself from the education I was *supposed* to receive, from cold shoulders and rolling eyes, from unfair expectations, from feeling trapped. Desperate to free Henry, too.

Still, given the day's events so far, I decide to reach out to Dr. Broderick for an emergency session. I don't enjoy discussing my feelings, but talking to a paid professional and an objective academic makes it easier. I need to regain my footing if I have any chance of surviving this summer.

I *want* to see this through. To live up to Dad's expectations rather than be his disappointment. *For once.* It'll also provide me with the opportunity to alleviate his misguided guilt. Succeeding this summer would reassure him that sending me away at eighteen was best for everyone.

It'll make leaving again easier, too.

After Roma's, we visit the new nursery. Upon seeing epiphytic fertilizers and authentic sphagnum peat moss, as their website claimed, Dad excitedly fills a flatbed cart. Meandering down the rows of perennials, he explains that he's agreed to a small carnivorous garden installation and asks me to help him remember everything he needs. I recite the list from memory, in the order of application. It's not simply dirt in a pot for carnivorous plants.

"I've ordered the raised beds for the mini-bog, a filtration system, and a rain barrel and had them delivered to the site," he says. "I'll have these materials delivered as well. Now, all I need to do is gather the plants."

"I can help with that." Getting my hands dirty again fills me with unexpected excitement.

He smiles across the flatbed. "Sounds lovely."

As he pays and makes delivery arrangements, I wander through the messy clearance racks where wilting and damaged herbs, annuals, and perennials are haphazardly shoved into metal shelves like canned vegetables at the back of a pantry, expired and unwanted. I stumble at a crack in the floor, nudging the rack as I do, and witness a marigold blossom fall off its stem.

The most beautiful part of it, lost in an instant. Losing Henry felt like that.

I imagine these imperfect, broken plants, destined for the garbage, never given the care and space to grow, never belonging anywhere.

Dad finds me at the racks, piling weedy, unsightly plants into a cart. When it's clear that I mean to rescue them all, he helps, grabbing the ones on the highest shelves. I don't leave a single plant behind, though some are probably already dead. They shall have a proper plant funeral, I decide, thinking of our composting bins—we have seven.

We load them into the Land Rover—this messy hodgepodge of mistreated and unwanted plants that make no sense together. It's an impulse buy, for sure, but Dad doesn't judge. Nor does he bring up my adamant refusal to plant a garden while I was here—words as impulsive as this act itself.

Instead, he declares, "The ones with the least expectations usually try the hardest."

At home, it's annoyingly obvious that I've overbought for the small, empty bed normally reserved for Henry and me. But I'll get creative to ensure these unwanted plants have the space they need, somewhere in Dad's perfect, overflowing garden.

Only, the next morning, Dad and Christie wake me with sounds of hammers hitting wood, and I discover that they're constructing a new raised bed along the greenhouse's exterior. Together, we fill the ten-foot bed with composted dirt and natural fertilizers. I don't bother with gardening gloves. The cool, musty dirt feels good between my fingers.

I get lost in the work. Two days pass in planting, pruning, and watering, my skin sun-kissed and my clothes dirty. It's the best I've felt in ages, especially when the plants show hints of revitalization, convincing me that there's hope in even the most unlikely second chances.

On the third night, I sleep for a few hours in the loft bed and come downstairs to a mason jar of wildflowers perched next to my field journal with a note.

V –

Christie and I decided to take an earlier flight. Best of luck!

Love,
Dad

P.S. Please see to the museum's garden installation this afternoon at the following address.

The house is eerily quiet in their absence. I recall Dr. Broderick's most recent advice: *"Find opportunities to connect."* That was after lecturing me for running away from Dad instead of practicing the techniques she taught me. I defended myself as usual. *How can I think straight when I'm not thinking straight?* And Dad's admission of regret made calling up the STOP acronym or any other mindfulness technique feel like being asked to recite the alphabet backwards when the only letters I could conjure were F-U-C-K.

Dr. Broderick got a kick out of that analogy. I like amusing her. But connecting will prove more challenging with no one here.

Folding the note, I notice more handwriting on the back.

My artful and sweet new bestie,

I left my favorite romance novels by my chair for you. It might be nice to read something without footnotes or a bibliography, right? Help yourself to any of my scarves on the hall tree and enjoy the fruit salad I made for you in the fridge.

XO,
Christie

P.S. Maybe have some fun with your sister? I know she misses you.

I groan. I love my sister, but it seems unlikely that she would consider me fun.

Over Christie's fruit salad, which is quite delicious, I read Dad's class notes and revise my resume. I update my necessary profiles, hoping for opportunities to start filling my sparse inbox.

I shower and dress in my usual work clothes: a tank top under jean short overalls paired with high socks and my delightfully worn-in hiking boots. A red scarf with peonies tames my hair into a loose top knot. I stick my gardening gloves in my pocket along with the note and grab the keys from the hook in the kitchen. Behind the wheel of Dad's Land Rover, I twiddle with my bracelets and rub my thumb over my pitch black mood ring.

I should stop calling it a mood ring. It's probably onyx. It's never been any other color than black, not that I care to have my mood detected by a piece of jewelry—that's scientifically unsound.

But if it could reflect my mood, it'd be black anyway. Meeting and communicating with strangers is an unsettling chore. I recheck Dad's note. He hasn't even given me a name.

I huff. Unfortunately, this summer promises a distressing amount of awkward socializing.

"*Let's pretend it's always summer for us.*" Henry's words echo through my thoughts.

Summers belonged to Henry and me. Free from teachers and classmates, we'd spend the day in the woods or on our bikes or, if it were raining, in his basement watching Maggie's old DVDs. Henry insisted that movies were vital to my education, and it was his duty to ensure I watched all the classics. Though they were mostly absurd, they always gave us topics for discussion, and few things delighted me more than all-in-good-fun debates with Henry.

Of all the movies he showed me, the most illogical turned out to be my favorite—*Little Shop of Horrors*. Not only did the story grossly misrepresent Venus flytraps, my bitter namesake, but it did so in *song*.

"*That's* your favorite?" Henry gawked. "What about *A Fish Called Wanda*?"

"Glorified prostitution."

"*Pretty Woman*?"

"Same."

"*Clueless*?"

"A Jane Austen retelling? As if."

"*The Breakfast Club*?"

"Teenagers left unattended during detention? Please."

"*When Harry Met Sally*?"

"Too much talking."

"*50 First Dates*?"

"Statistically speaking, that type of head injury—"

"Fine. What's so great about *Little Shop of Horrors*?"

"Seymour was stuck with a plant he hates, and in trouble for his misguided attempts to help Audrey—I relate," I smirked. "At least I never resorted to murder."

He looked concerned. "And you *wouldn't*, right?"

"Of course, not," I said with less conviction than he wanted.

"The fire ants were drastic enough," he said, and we giggled, thinking about it. The day I helped Henry in the woods, he confided that a classmate named Ruby Mack pantsed him on the bus that morning. He'd been teased all day about his Batman underwear and couldn't bear the thought of a second attack. So, he'd texted his mother that he'd be walking home.

I could relate—not to themed underwear or being pantsed, but to the teasing. A day didn't pass without someone calling me a know-it-all, a weirdo, or a plethora of other demeaning or dismissive words. I was used to being teased; Henry wasn't. Not at school, anyway.

The next day, I covertly released a specimen jar of fire ants down Ruby's backside and into her backpack to suggest she unknowingly brought them from home, and everyone believed it, though it's entirely illogical.

A wiggle turned into uncomfortable scratching until Ruby finally jumped from her seat, did a strange dance, and pulled down her shorts in a desperate attempt to stop the stinging. She did, but not before revealing her Strawberry Shortcake underwear. Hypocrite.

All's fair in love and elementary school.

I know now that my actions were extreme and that causing physical harm is wrong. I feel bad for the fire ants lost to my prank. But my strong sense of justice prevented me from sitting idly by. Friends stand up for each other. And I desperately wanted a friend in Henry.

Now that I think about it, I hope he wasn't my friend out of fear. As I collected the survivors, Henry overheard me whisper in Ruby's ear that next time she messed with Henry, it'd be snakes.

People have an irrational fear of snakes. But that was enough for Ruby to change her ways. And isn't that better for everyone?

The Land Rover rumbles over cobblestone streets along the waterfront as I near my destination. The red brick building strikes a familiar chord, though I can't make out the whole melody. Dad would bring us downtown for visits to the children's museum, the natural history museum—my favorite—and, for historic tours—Henry's favorite.

Maneuvering into a parking space, I huff. I'm not usually like this. Being home has instigated a resurgence of memories I've tried to leave behind—Henry is all around me. I almost *feel* him.

Distracting myself with manual labor is just what I need.

I exit the Land Rover, weave around parked cars, and cross the street. A cargo van sits outside the entrance, advertising *Dot's Home Improvement*. I smirk at the words below the logo: *Woman-Owned & Woman-Run. Ask About Our No Creeps Promise.*

I reach the sidewalk and approach the glass front door, currently propped open by a paint can. I knock anyway and call out, "Hello?"

Inside the small foyer, a wooden blue jay sits on the counter, and again, an eerie feeling washes over me. I recall two men laughing. *Have I been here before?*

"Hello?" I call again.

Three voices answer.

"Yo!"

"Coming!"

"Oh, sorry. Be right there."

A light commotion ensues, and a dark-haired woman wearing a tool belt appears, presumably Dot. Then, a smiling redhead carrying a Trapper Keeper.

"Can we help you?" she asks enthusiastically.

"Painter, plumber, or delivery?" asks Dot.

"Gardener," I say simply, and the redhead's face shifts from chipper to horrified in a blink.

"I'll take care of the door," a voice says, coming up behind them.

I know that voice.

As his name whispers through my thoughts, he appears. Tall, handsome, and utterly destroyed at the sight of me.

Henry.

CHAPTER 9

Henry

I CAN'T BREATHE. Can't think. Can't move.

It's *her*.

Radiant, artsy, messy, *her*.

Overalls and boots, *her*.

Mom's old scarf tied in her hair, *her*.

My grandmother's mood ring—always black—still on her finger, *her*.

Infuriating, *her*.

Heartbreaking, *her*.

Her.

A beat passes that feels like an eternity. Her lips part in a silent plea, while her green eyes widen and glass over with what could be tears. I edge through Dot and Marnie, desperate to be close to her, to touch her, to know that she's real. Only I can't decide what that touch will be—a strong shove out the door or a firm pull into my arms.

Fuck me.

"Henry, breathe," she says. "Breathe."

That's when I realize I'm wheezing. Badly.

"Holy shit, dude," Dot exclaims. "Chill."

"Where's your inhaler?" Marnie asks.

I fumble in my pocket as Dot eases me into a chair. I take a quick inhale, but relief is minimal. My lungs have tightened to the size of raisins, as if she's vacuum-sealed the air right out of me.

"Not... you," I rasp, sounding angrier than I want. "It was not supposed to be you."

"I-I-I didn't know." Her voice trembles with distress. "I'm sorry, Henry. It was a mistake. I won't—it won't—I'm sorry."

Her eyes circle from Dot to Marnie. "I'm sorry," she tells them, too.

Then, she turns and bolts from the building.

"Do I need to call nine-one-one?" Marnie asks, phone poised.

"Hop in the van," Dot counters. "I'll have you at the hospital before you can say *awkwardest reunion ever*."

I hold up my hand in protest. "I'll... be... fine." Another draw on my inhaler slows my breathing and opens my lungs just enough. I need to slow down. To focus. To relax.

But part of me begs to run after her, lungs be damned.

"I apologize, Henry," Marnie says. "Dr. Blake told me *he'd* install the garden. We touched base yesterday when the other supplies arrived—he said nothing about Venus."

"So, that's Venus, huh?" Dot grins. "You must be nursing some serious wounds to hate her that much."

"I don't... hate her."

"He just never wants to see her again," Marnie finishes for me.

Dot peeks out of the open front door. "She's gone, just peeled off in a classic Land Rover."

"I expected her to be more... villainous," Marnie says. "She seemed sad. Definitely surprised. I'd better text Ivy and let her know what happened. Dr. Blake must've arranged this."

Dot laughs. "He parent-trapped you two. Hmm, that's not right. Love-trapped?"

Damn. She probably expected to meet a stranger and install a garden as a favor to her dad. The place looks so different now that I doubt she remembers coming here with me to visit Uncle Jay.

I'm only grateful that Olly already left with Carly and didn't witness this. How would I have explained falling apart over the woman I've only revered in his eyes?

I hate this.

Even worse, I hate what I said. *Not you. It wasn't supposed to be you. Fuck.* Whenever I imagined seeing Venus again and delivering all the words I never got the chance to say, I failed to consider that my faulty body might prevent me from saying much of anything. Questions I should've asked bombard me. Starting with *why*? Why she left? Why she left *me*? Why she made promises she didn't keep?

"So, what's the story with this girl, eh?" Dot asks, grabbing a bag of Cheetos from her pocket.

"She was my best friend," I say, still gasping slightly. "Then, my girlfriend. We were headed to UNC-Chapel Hill together. Then, one night, I saved her life. She saved mine. She told me she loved me, promised me prom. She left the country instead. Ghosted me."

"Yikes, that's rough." Dot tilts the bag in my direction. "Cheeto?"

"No, thanks," I sputter.

"Henry, that's heartbreaking," Marnie frowns. "How could she do that to you?"

"It's what she does. She runs." I take a few more measured breaths before standing up. "I'm going to lie down for a bit."

"Good idea," Marnie says. "Dot and I will keep working on your new display cases."

I leave them for the stairs, desperate to be alone and recover from the shock of her.

But lying on my bed under the ceiling fan, breathing back to normal, I'm restless and upset. There *is* no recovery from Venus. *That's* the problem. There hasn't been before, and there won't be now.

Fuck, she looked beautiful though.

I close my eyes and remember her climbing into my bed when we were eighteen. She'd done that since we were twelve. The deep pressure stimulation of being held relieved her, and I was the only person she felt comfortable enough with to ask. I never minded, even when she sometimes startled me awake or nearly got me in trouble for it.

But that night was different.

She slid into my bed, and I curled up behind her, spooning her as she nestled into me.

"You okay?" I breathed against her neck in a sleepy haze.

She nodded, but I knew better. Senior year was starting, and Venus hated school. Summers were our best times. I wrapped her up, tightening my hold, and she relaxed with deep breaths. With my lips a breath away from her neck, her familiar scent of rosemary and roses, her body so close, my thoughts drifted to how good she felt in my arms. With only my boxers and her jean shorts between us, I grew hard against her. Embarrassed, I rolled onto my back suddenly, mumbling an apology. She wanted my comfort, not *that*.

She twisted to face me, propping her hand under her head. "Don't be sorry. Be reassured that your body functions properly, in this instance, at least."

I guffawed. "Gee, thanks, Vee."

She smirked at my sarcasm, but really, I loved that she joked about my asthma. She made me feel better about it, like it wasn't the anxiety-ridden curse Mom made it out to be.

Now perched on her side, staring at me, she said, "Can I help?"

"What?"

She pointed to my boxers. "Let me help you with that."

My eyes went wide with disbelief. "You want to help with my hard-on?" I clarified, though in hindsight, it shouldn't have surprised me. Venus viewed life through a scientific prism—everything was worthy of exploration and experimentation. Sex shouldn't have been an exception.

Even so, I never expected this.

"It's a natural reaction to having someone of your preferred gender in your private space—a space I'm presently violating," she reasoned. "It's the least I can do—"

"I don't think that's a good idea."

"Why not? We're adults, Henry."

"Yeah, but..." We'd only just celebrated our eighteenth birthdays this summer. With our senior year upon us, we felt like adults still trapped in kid lives. For me, the year ahead would be easy, a formality. For her, it'd be uncomfortable and miserable.

"But what?" she urged.

I sat up, groaning. "You don't believe in love or romance. You don't want to be my girlfriend. You don't want to kiss or hold hands or date. But you want... this?"

"We are *more* than any label or social construct, Henry. What we have is perfect. Stop overthinking it. I want to make you feel comfortable and meet your needs. And I'm... curious."

"Curious?" Moonlight illuminated her face just enough for me to see a sexy smirk coiling on her lips. Still, I sighed. "Take some deep breaths. Think it through."

She did as I asked—after years of friendship, she'd gotten better at listening to me. Trusting me.

A minute later, she smiled triumphantly. "Done."

"Still want to?"

She nodded into my pillow. "If you want to. I've studied the required techniques. If you're willing to let me."

She could've asked me anything, and I would've said yes. She'd already been the first woman I held, my first kiss, and I imagined she would be my first everything.

But it was a risk that would either catapult us into a real *us*, like I wanted, or mess everything up, even our friendship. My desperation for her—all of her—overruled the risk.

"Okay." I laid back down and tried not to be nervous as her hand fell to my chest and went lower. She sat up a little, watching me, and I brushed her cheek, hoping she'd kiss me.

She smiled instead, her hand inching over my stomach, until, "Venus…"

The pure ecstasy of her hand slipping into my boxers caught in my throat—her fingers delicately exploring me, her fingertips gently grazing over my tip.

"It's bigger than average, Henry," she whispered. "And so thick. You must be proud. The average size is—"

"Vee, please."

"Oh, right." She worked me, but clumsily. "We need lubricant."

"Give me your hand," I said, breathy and wanting. She sat up and gave me her free hand. "Not that one. The other one."

Now sitting beside me, she corrected herself and held her hand out to me. I gently gripped her by the wrist and brought her hand to my mouth to lick her palm. A breathy gasp escaped her, eyes widening with intrigue. Her dampened hand made a quick return to my dick, and she sighed in approval.

"Much better," she whispered, edging to my side again, watching me, draping her bare leg over mine.

I slid my hand under her shirt as she curled at my shoulder, my fingers skirting up and down her spine. I imagined her mouth on me, her on top of me, the warmth and excitement of being her first. Of her being my first.

"Tighter," I begged. She nuzzled closer, her face nestled in my neck, and tightened her grip. I felt her watching me, gauging my expression, measuring my pleasure. "It feels so good."

She stayed uncharacteristically quiet as my eyes rolled back in my head before closing. The release felt seismic, and even better, she didn't pull away, letting me spill all over her hand.

"Wow," she said with a breathy smile.

"Wow," I repeated, gasping. I reached for my inhaler. Then, we lay there, curled together, for several minutes, both of us catching our breath.

Soon, she edged out from around me for the bathroom. When we were both clean, we returned to bed, me spooning her, her back comfortably nestled into my chest. I slid my hand to her waist with a gentle squeeze that pulled her against me and buried my face in her long, wavy hair, close to her ear. "Thank you," I whispered softly.

"You're welcome."

"Can I touch *you* now?"

She tensed in my arms. "What?"

"Let me touch you, meet your needs."

"Um, well," she said, voice weak.

"Do you trust me, Vee?"

"Yes," she said without hesitation.

"Would you like me to try? Are you curious?"

"For educational purposes," she said, her voice labored with the idea. "Yes."

I smiled at her ear. "If you want to stop, just tell me."

"Okay," she says. "Go ahead. Please."

She nuzzled against my chest, pressing closer to me. I gently lifted her shirt, my hand slipping to her bare stomach. She gasped, but nodded for me to continue, her breath coming in quick inhales, as my fingers undid her shorts, pushed under the waistband, and into her panties.

"You're so wet," I groaned as my hand glided lower.

"Um, that's a normal physiological reaction—"

"Shhh. Deep breaths. Listen to my voice," I whispered as I explored her. Her breath hitched when I found her clit—she wasn't the only one who had studied. Firm, slow circles with my finger brought a soft moan —a deliciously satisfying sound. "Like that?"

"Yes." Her head leaned back next to mine. "Don't stop."

"I won't. You're so warm. I like you like this." I kissed her neck and nibbled her earlobe. "Does that feel good?"

"Yes, Henry."

"Fuck, I like it when you say my name like that. Say it again, please."

"Henry," she groaned. I was rock-hard again, pressing into her ass as she arched against me. Her breath quivered as she whispered my name again.

"That's it," I coaxed, loving her pleasure, loving that I could do this for her, that she needed me, wanted me this way. "Come all over my hand like I did to you. Let me feel you."

She shifted, pushing against me once more, spreading her thighs, and propping her leg over mine. Opening for me. My hand slid over the full range of her, my fingers dipping inside. I wrapped my free hand around her, cupping her breast over her shirt.

"Ah, Henry, this is better than I…"

"Shhh, just let it happen."

"I…" Her voice shook. She'd never been so freely at my mercy before, never this blissful, never so damn wanton. Her entire body quivered with my touch. I thought her touching me was amazing, but this, this was better.

This was Venus *letting* me love her. Finally.

"Think about me when you come, Venus," I whispered. Those words marked her undoing.

"Henry," she whimpered, convulsing against my hand. When her body relaxed in my arms, I wanted to fucking cheer.

Her body trembled against mine as she came down from her release. I wondered what she was feeling—did it feel the same as mine? That build, the release, the exquisite converging of everything at once. Finally touching her that way made me realize how much I'd always wanted her, even before I understood why.

But then she said the words no one ever wants to hear.

"This… this was a mistake."

She pulled my hand away and wriggled free of my hold altogether.

"What? Why?" I sat up, watching her shift her clothes into place and tug on her rubber boots. "Venus, what's wrong?"

She stopped in a huffing breath. Her hands drifted onto her hips as she formulated words. "This was not the outcome I anticipated."

I let out a nervous chuckle. "That was… the perfect outcome. What outcome did you expect? You know how bodies work."

"That's not what I mean," she said with exasperation. "I. I."

I pulled myself from the blankets to sit at the edge of the bed. "I'm so sorry. Please tell me what I did wrong. I thought you were enjoying it."

Her body softened, her face falling into a pout. "You didn't do anything wrong. You *never* do anything wrong, Henry. You were right. I should've taken more time to think this through, considered all the variables."

"What variables did you fail to account for?"

She sighed. "Feelings, Henry. I would've accounted for feelings."

I gaped. "This is the *result* of *our* feelings, Vee. Not the cause. We never would've done this if we didn't care for each other. You wouldn't climb into my bedroom window night after night if you didn't feel something for me. Right? What's wrong with caring for each other?"

"Nothing," she shook her head, swiping at a tear on her left cheek. "Nothing. And everything."

"Please, don't go," I said, patting the bed beside me. "Stay with me. Talk to me."

Her brow knitted into a creased triangle, the same face she made anytime she worked through a complicated puzzle. "We can't be friends like this."

"You're not my friend anymore?" I said the words slowly, afraid that at any moment, I'd push her over the edge. That she'd run. "I don't follow."

She huffed, nibbling on her fingers.

"Take a few breaths. Help me understand."

"There's nothing to explain," she tried in a scoff. "Only that... the line is crossed, and we can't go back, and we can't move forward, either. We're at an impasse."

"Why can't we move forward?" I asked calmly. I needed her not to bolt. To stay. "I mean, slowly. Together. As a couple?"

She sighed. "That's what I mean, Henry. I'm not the marrying type."

Before I could utter, "Who's talking about marriage?" she was out the window, long blond waves wild behind her as she raced for our path.

I'd known Venus for ten years by then, knew her better than anyone. I knew that when it came to feelings, she preferred flight over fight—emotions made her run.

But that was the first time I understood that her flight tendency even applied to me.

The word *never* reverberated in her wake. *I never do anything wrong.* It hurt that she used an absolute on me. Venus rarely operated in absolutes. She referred to them as verbal traps, intended to declare something that, more than likely, cannot be proven and will, in fact, be disproven in a blink. *Absolutes are abso-don'ts*, she'd say when she felt playful. But this wasn't playful. I *never* do anything wrong.

Then, I did something very wrong.

In the weeks that followed, it felt like Venus had abandoned me. School interactions were met with coldness, and each time I visited or asked to hang out, she'd be politely but sternly busy.

So, when I got drunk for the first time at my friend Brock's place, I did the unthinkable—I told him what happened with Vee.

Then, he told everyone else.

It was a fucking nightmare. I was pissed at myself for betraying her this way, pissed at everyone for repeating it. I imagined her hating me. She should've hated me.

I wanted to apologize. I found her in the greenhouse, amid the trickling bogs, on her knees as she yanked dead weeds from an overgrown flower bed—our bed, which made me feel worse. Her long, dirty blonde hair was tied with a red scarf, one of Mom's hand-me-downs, into a messy bun on her head with strands dangling down on her bare shoulders. She wore garden gloves, rubber boots, crossed at her ankles, and denim overalls. She spotted me out of the corner of her eye when the door thwacked shut behind me. But she didn't react, except with her typical greeting of, "Hello, Henry."

"I need to talk to you. It's important."

She stood, brushed herself off, and put her hands on her hips. "What is it?"

"I told Brock—from school, the basketball team," I clarified, "what happened with us… that night… in my bedroom. I was drunk and, I don't know, still confused about it, I guess. Anyway, he told other people, though I told him not to, and now, a lot of people know. I'm so fucking sorry, Vee. I messed up, and I'm desperately sorry."

"Your apology is unnecessary," she said, sounding unbothered.

"I did something wrong, something awful. I've ruined your… reputation."

She let out a boisterous laugh. Her arms folded over her chest, and her head tilted at me. "Yesterday, one of Ivy's friends told me that I was Dr. Blake's *trial run* before he got it right with her and that it was a shame he couldn't send me back like a bad meal at a restaurant. Then, while hiding in the teacher's lounge closet to finish my lunch in peace, I overheard Mr. Henderson report that the *Bad Blake* caused his angina—a statement that I'm sure can't be corroborated by his doctor. That was before I was sent to the guidance counselor for having the *audacity* to question the real-world relevance of iambic pentameter, which apparently makes me belligerent. Do you honestly believe that I care what any of them think of me, Henry?"

I didn't know what to say. I'd always known that school was tough for her. But hearing a list of indignities from a *single* day made me realize how much she didn't tell me—that every day was a shit day for her.

No wonder she came to me that night. The dread she must have felt over starting a new year and going through the torture all over again must've been terrible. And I made it worse.

Some friend I was.

There, in the greenhouse, she held up a finger, like a lightbulb had just blinked in her head. "Ah, I see it now… that's why everyone's calling me Flytrap all of a sudden." Her awkward, bleating laugh rumbled out. "Fly, as in Venus flytrap, and fly as in getting into the fly of your pants—double meaning. I get it."

"It's not funny, Venus," was all I could think of to say.

"I don't care what they think of me, Henry. I don't care what they call me. I. Don't. Care."

"I care. I care about *you*. When you've done something you regret toward a person you care about, you should apologize, even if they're not hurt. But I think you *are* hurt."

She winced. "I'm not hurt. But as is customary, I accept your apology. Feel better?"

"No."

"That's not my fault," she said in a huff. "All I want is to get through this year, so I can leave this place and never look back."

"Wait, I thought you loved this place," I said, faltering at this new vision of Venus no longer here. An ache arose in my chest, tightening my lungs. I slipped my hand into my pocket to have my inhaler at the ready. "Doesn't it matter to you that this is where we found each other and became friends? All the stories we share?"

"Of course. I'm not a robot. I have a fondness for us and our stories."

"A fondness, huh? Don't gush about it."

She softened, catching my sarcasm. "I like us. But this place has been slow torture for me. You'll leave, too, Henry. It's the natural progression of transitioning into adulthood."

"Maybe. But I won't leave *you*. Why have you been avoiding me?"

"That's the natural progression, too, and a rightful one. It's just like *The Breakfast Club*—you're a popular jock with friends and parties, while I'm the basket case. Everything is looking up for you with me out of the way."

"I NEVER wanted you out of the way," I said sternly.

"Well, I am."

"That's what you want?" I said after using my inhaler.

She supported her stoicism by folding her arms over her chest, but she didn't answer.

I stumbled over my words and latched onto the first excuse I could think of. "Okay. If this is goodbye, we should hug. It's, um, customary."

She groaned over my obvious manipulation, but opened her arms to me. It was a weak, obligatory embrace.

At first.

The pressure of a tight hold calms her. The first time she said so, we were eight, huddling in our handmade lean-to during a sudden storm. That's why she liked to sleep with me sometimes.

But then, I tightened my grip on her, burying my face in her neck, hoping that if I held on tight enough, maybe she'd relax into me. That, maybe she wouldn't leave. It felt like years passed before her arms finally flexed around my shoulders, holding me there. Her fingernails dug into my shoulder blades, almost hurting me while offering an assurance—Venus didn't want to say goodbye.

"I miss you." Her confession came out in the softest whisper. But that's all I needed to hear.

My locked arms edged lower until I lifted her. She laughed as I stared up at her, her hair drifting around her face like a curtain. Amber light from the stained glass windows flickered across her face as I spun us, sunlight and honey. "Don't miss me. Be with me. Let's pretend it's always summer for us."

"Okay, Henry."

But I disappointed her again. *Disappointed myself.* The ridicule followed her for weeks after, and twice, when my teammates teased me in the hallways over her, I acted like our encounter meant nothing. Once, I even denied we were friends to spare myself from their teasing. She never knew, and I never bothered apologizing.

I still hate myself for it.

By Christmas, my crushing shame forced me to stop caring what everyone else thought. To be more like Venus. To only care about her.

VENUS LOVE TRAP

Venus never "claimed" me or acted like a "normal" girlfriend, but I decided she was. She kept her distance at school, but I didn't. I sat with her at lunch again and sought her out in hallways and the library. She warmed up to the idea of us, slowly. For fear that she'd run, I didn't push for sex. But we held hands and kissed and spent every spare minute together.

And she started coming to my window again.

That was our best time... until *that* night when everything changed.

Now, lying in bed, my lungs still aching, I remember the last time I saw her before today, in the greenhouse, and her breathy confession that she loved me between kisses. *She loved me.* Those were words I never thought she'd say to me or anyone. And there they were, like music. Beautiful. Fleeting.

How could it have been true?

Seeing Venus has kicked up the dust of my subconscious. Memories long forgotten hang in the air, and another lands, making me ache—Uncle Jay and I examining arrowheads for his display case when I was fourteen.

"How's Rapunzel?"

I can't remember what I said in response, probably something about the garden we'd planted or how she sometimes snuck into my bedroom. Uncle Jay was cool with information like that.

"You love her, don't you?" I remember him asking.

"We're Antony and Cleopatra. Marie and Pierre Curie. Fitzgerald and—"

"I get it," he laughed.

"We love each other, but she doesn't know it yet."

"I bet she knows more than you think," he told me. "Just be there for her. As many times as she needs. The rest will fall into place."

I was *there*, but I wasn't there enough *for her*.

Is that why she left? Was it my fault?

I lay there for hours, floating between fuzzy conversations and blurred images, hoping to find the answers. Only I can't—not without Venus.

CHAPTER 10
Venus

I RACE HOME in an unrestrained panic, itching to create distance between us. I twist the wheel in my hands until my fingers throb and my rings pinch. I need the pain, want the pain, desperate for a distraction. I am livid and devastated, caught in an emotional tidal wave. Furious at my father. Sad for me. Desperately sorry for Henry. Embarrassed because I surely embarrassed him, especially if that redhead was his girlfriend... or wife.

I refuse to think about that.

This is why I hate emotions—they come on so inconveniently. They barge in, uninvited, unplanned, and unwanted, and seize control. A hostile takeover. Why couldn't I speak to him like a normal person instead of running away?

The look on his face... he *hates* me. Henry truly and utterly hates me.

Tears blur my vision as I turn onto our street and then down the dirt lane leading to the fairy house. Dust kicks up behind the tires as I barrel down the path and come to a jolting stop, crooked, in Dad's usual space. I slam the door shut and race up the deck.

Inside the house, I start grabbing things.

My journal from the kitchen table.

My pouch of pencils, pens, and markers.

My clothes, scattered on the floor.

I retrieve my hammock and blanket.

I'm haphazardly filling my suitcase when I hear the front door open.

It barely registers that someone has entered the house. I don't care. I keep stuffing items in, desperate to be on the next flight out of here, no matter where it takes me. On the plane, I'll make a plan when I can think, when I can breathe—

"Venus, are you okay?"

Ivy's soft voice makes my shoulders jerk. I don't look up. I don't say anything.

In my periphery, I see her move further into the room, but slowly, like I'm a feral animal she's afraid to approach.

"Venus, what're you doing?"

"Leave me alone, Ivy."

"Dad shouldn't have done that," she says. "You saw Henry? What happened?"

I groan, my fingernails digging into my palms as my hands fist. "Isn't it *nice* how you two are so close? That my business spreads through the household like a damn brushfire."

"You left *us*, Venus," she returns, keeping her calm tone like Dad would. "You're the one who rarely took our calls or answered our texts. You shut us out."

"No one wants me here!" My harsh tone mirrors the bitterness inside me and masks the sadness—more feelings I don't want. "Don't act like you weren't relieved that I wasn't around to embarrass you—what was it you told your friends? That I was only your *half*-sister? Please spare me the *sisterly* concern. You were both grateful to see the back of me. You didn't even want me here the other night."

"Of course, I did!" She plops onto the bed's edge with a defined slump. "The other night was meant to be about Gil and me. So, yes, the night became, *understandably*, about you, and that made me nervous... I *really* like him, Venus. And he has this annoyingly conventional family, and they're all extremely loving and close. I worried that ours would seem awkward to him. You know?"

My tense shoulders soften slightly. "Yes, I understand that feeling."

"But, you're right. I could've been a better sister back then. I *am* sorry. It's just sometimes you were..."

"*Difficult*. I get it," I fume, shoving more clothes into my bag.

"Smart, creative, adventurous, but yes, at times, difficult. And too direct. You told my best friend that you suspected her father was an alcoholic based on his driving skills in the carline."

"He was inconsistent and swervy."

"And remember, Connor, the boy I liked? You informed him that it wouldn't work out between us because he was too dumb for me."

"He was, Ivy."

"Okay, he was. But you shouldn't have said that. What if I wanted a dumb boy right then?" Her lips curl into a coy grin.

I smirk. "I hadn't considered that."

"I get that it was your way of watching out for me. But sometimes, your directness was… too direct. You didn't give anyone a chance."

Her words align with Dad's. *You didn't give them a chance to love you.* My anger relents behind consideration. Perhaps their observation is valid.

"*We* want you here. *I* want you here. I want us to be *full* sisters. But you have to give us a chance," she says. "You can't run at every little hiccup."

"A hiccup? It's more like a… brain aneurysm."

A light sigh slips from her. "Please, Venus. Tell me what happened with Henry."

Hearing her say his name again, so gently, shakes my emotions loose, like she's tipped over a jar of marbles. Tears plummet from my eyes suddenly and with such force that my knees buckle. Ivy catches me and pulls me close. I bury my face in her satin hair and inhale the scent of jasmine.

"He hates me," I blubber. "He hates me."

"He said that?"

"No, but…" I shake my head against her. "I. I. I can't be here anymore."

She rocks me against her, rubbing my back in small, consoling circles. "It's okay. Everything's okay."

But her words remind me of Henry, too, bringing both comfort and despair. I feel like I've charged straight into a storm, dodging lightning bolts all around me—seeing Henry, his anguish, Ivy's presence, Dad's trick, my sadness and loneliness now raw and stinging, all of this terrible vulnerability. Hit after hit after hit.

"Breathe," she whispers. "It's all okay… or it will be."

"How?"

She sighs against me. *We're still embracing?* The realization sneaks through my distress, but I don't pull away.

"Let's operate in facts. Shall we? The fact is…" she begins after a moment. "You shouldn't make any decisions about leaving while you're upset."

I nod into her shoulder and mumble, "Um, that's logical."

"Okay, we've got this. Do you trust me enough to try something?"

I nod again and relax away from her grasp.

"Deep breathing activates the parasympathetic nervous system, promoting relaxation. I call it Ins and Outs. Let's start there. In…"

She motions toward her deep inhale. Her chest rises, and her shoulders square. I doubt its efficacy, but desperate to stop the onslaught of tears, I follow her instructions.

"Out…" she breathes softly, watching me. "In…"

Several rounds of deep breathing later, the tension eases away.

"Tears have stopped… good," she offers a weak smile. "Now, let's add a muscle relaxation technique that I call Mighty Tighty, Loosey Goosey."

I groan over the silly name.

She smirks. "Don't judge. It works. I'm going to say a body part. Then, we're going to tense those muscles—only those muscles—and then relax them again. Let's start with our feet."

My toes curl in my boots as I follow her instructions. Tensing and releasing. Focusing on something other than my heart breaking all over again. We move up our bodies—feet, to calves, to knees, and so on up to our hands and shoulders. By the time we roll our necks, I feel centered.

"Now, close your eyes, and imagine something peaceful," she instructs. "It could be a place, a garden, a forest, anything that fills you and lets you breathe."

We stand in silence, breathing and imagining, and she whispers, "Where are you?"

"In a rainstorm. Thunder and lightning. Smells of wet pine and the sounds of battered leaves. The rough bark on the branches of our lean-to. Henry holding me tight," I respond dreamily, hypnotized by her soft voice.

"Hmm." She says it just like Dad.

"Where are you?" I breathe out curiously.

"The beach, gritty sand and salty air, warm skin and suntan lotion, and Gil, smiling beside me. I actually got him there recently. That was a feat. He has an anxiety disorder. He tries to hide it, but I know."

She takes another deep breath, places her hands on my shoulders, and slides them down my arms over my bracelets and rings to hold my hands. "Open your eyes. Feel better?"

"I do. Thank you."

She smiles. "He doesn't hate you, Venus. It was a surprise, that's all."

"How do you know?"

She drops my hands and holds up her phone. "Henry's business consultant, Marnie, is Gil's sister-in-law and my best friend. She's the reason I knew you needed me. She texted me as soon as you left."

I collapse to the bed's edge. "The redhead?"

"Isn't she adorable?" Ivy coos. "You'll have to come to a Tripp family game night and meet them all."

"Um, I thought she might've been *with* Henry. It was all so confusing. Is he okay? From his asthma attack?"

"Yes, he's fine. And Henry's single… since you're wondering."

Another tear slips loose, and I wipe it away. "All I do is hurt him."

"It's not your fault. Dad saw your journal and the notes to Henry. It's his twisted way of helping. He knew you wouldn't go on your own."

"For good reason. Henry doesn't want to see me."

Ivy's head tilts as she considers this. "He misses you, too."

"What? How would you know that?"

"He told Marnie. She told me. Insider knowledge is another perk of having friends. She's helping him revamp his uncle's curiosity museum, and you came up when they were discussing the garden. He's still angry about how you left. You devastated him. I heard he barely made it through his freshman year for all the partying, but he got his act together. He had to—"

"Dad didn't report that he was having a hard time—I asked."

She shrugs. "He was doing what was best for you at the time. You wanted space. He gave it to you."

"This is why he regrets sending me away."

"Yep. Well, partly. We also missed you, dummy." She starts folding my clothes from the pile on the suitcase. I follow suit, realizing the terrible mess I've made.

Ivy goes to the closet for hangers. "Dad had to explain it to Henry, remember? Poor guy. I never knew he was *that* hung up on you. He always seemed detached at school. The sex must've been amazing."

"We never had sex," I say weakly. "Well, we pleasured each other once. No penetration."

She stops fussing with my clothes to give me a disappointed stare. "Um, how romantic?"

I ignore her sarcasm. "I don't know what to do."

"Why not stay and see this through? For Dad? For me?"

I take another deep breath. "I'll fulfill my obligation."

"Good. That's a start." She reaches into the closet with a guffaw. "Ah, and you said you didn't own a dress."

Laughing, she holds up my prom dress. The tulle material swishes as she waves it through the air. "God, I loved this dress. I almost wore it to my senior prom, but I thought it might be bad luck. I did steal the shoes, though. Had to."

My fingers drift to the netting of the poofy skirt. It's a dreamy dress: dark pink with embedded sparkles, an A-line, ankle-length skirt, and a strapless corset top. Ivy helped me pick it out when I thought I could do it, when I thought I could be his girlfriend, his prom date, *his*.

His *burden*.

I flashback to high school, me sitting outside the guidance counselor's office while Dad met with her alone. The door was shut, creating a windowed barrier between me and their discussion. But the odd window that separated her office from where I sat was cracked open just enough to hear them—an oversight indicative of the gaping holes in my formal education, I thought. It was senior year. An oversized neanderthal named Brock, whose only usefulness appeared to be on a basketball court, had made unseemly and unwanted advances toward me in the art supply closet after school.

I handled it—it was not the first time a testosterone-driven, ego-inflated male had propositioned me, especially in private, where other classmates couldn't see. The matter should've been settled with my rejection, but he retaliated by circulating rumors. By the week's end, laughter and insults followed me wherever I went, and I became known for hand-jobs and blow-jobs. *A flytrap*.

That information wasn't discussed in the counselor's office—I never told anyone, not even Henry. Rather, I was in trouble for disrupting Mr. Henderson's English class when, upon discussing Kate Chopin's *The Awakening* and the word *rendezvous*, he said, "You know what that word means. Right, Venus?"

The class snickered at his obvious innuendo. That the rumors had reached the teachers wasn't a surprise. Nor was it shocking that Mr. Henderson would make his snide remark—he seized opportunities to "put me in my place," especially since it was clear from the start that I understood the English language and literature far better than he did.

I should've kept my head down and mouth shut.

But Henry looked devastated, slumping at his desk and tapping his pencil fiercely against his binder, enacting the system we devised in elementary school to help me curb my unwanted behaviors. Tapping meant I should ignore whatever was bothering me and refrain from reacting.

Only I couldn't.

"I know many words of French origin," I said, hands fisting under my desk. "*Enculé* is also relevant here. Do you know it?"

Mr. Henderson's bushy brow shot up as he snickered over his inappropriate joke. "What's that mean?"

"Loosely translated… motherfucker," I answered dutifully. "You're a motherfucker."

The class gasped and hooted while Mr. Henderson's face went beet-red. He pointed to the door while I gathered my things.

"Please, don't remove her," Dad said to my counselor. "She wants to be with Henry. That's what we arranged."

"Yes, Dr. Blake, I know. Your pressure to pair Venus with Henry is well known. He's a calming presence for her *sometimes*," she said, "but it's unfair to saddle him with that responsibility. Henry has a respectable GPA and is well-liked. He's the captain of the basketball team this year. He is well-acclimated, and she… isn't. For him, their friendship is a *burden*."

The dress waves in the air as Ivy shakes it out, bringing my attention back to her. "You should wear this to dinner next time. Christie would *love* it! The rest of your wardrobe is slightly atrocious."

"Do you remember Dad picking my school schedules?" I ask, dazed, still trying to capture the fuzzy memory.

"Yeah, of course," she says as if I should've known. "He wanted you with Henry, but it didn't always work out."

"I've only just remembered that."

"He'd argue with Maggie about it sometimes," she adds with a shrug.

Dad fought for me more often than I realized. Today's misadventure was another example.

"Are those your only shoes?"

She points to the hiking boots I'm wearing. I nod, taking the prom dress from her and laying it on the bed.

"Ugh, okay. I'm off Sunday," she says, glancing at her watch. For the first time, I realize she's in her nurse's scrubs. "I'll come over, and we'll deal with this wardrobe sitch. Okay?"

"I. I. I was wrong to leave Henry like that," I say. "Back then. I should've... explained. I wish I could've explained. To him. To all of you."

"I think I understand. You felt trapped, and you didn't know what else to do."

"Yes," I sputter with surprise.

"It scared you—almost losing him. Did you think losing you would be better?"

I gape at my sister, stunned that she figured me out. "Yes," I admit in a sigh. "Better for me. I needed a chance. I couldn't get that here."

"I understand. Then, this might be a second chance for all of us." Ivy's hand goes to my back in soft circles again as I hover over the useless dress. "You've been all over the world, done things I can't even imagine. No one is braver than you, Venus. You should lean into that more. Be brave for yourself. And for him, if you think he's worth it, huh?"

I nod weakly, and she smiles, but a glance at her watch causes her to wince.

"Sorry, sis. Gotta get back, but I'll see you Sunday. Deal?"

"Thanks, Ivy."

She leans up and gives me a smacking kiss on my cheek. "That's what sisters are for, and I'm determined to remind you."

Then, she leaves.

Sitting on my bed with the dress in my lap, I mull over her words. By typical standards, it seems brave to pick up a snake or sleep in a jungle. But those are things I understand, things that are easy for me. How brave am I really if I can't face who I am and what I've done? If all I do is run?

I remember Henry coming to the greenhouse, ashamed and upset about how he'd shared our intimacy with Brock and how the story spread, entangling me in it. I told Henry the truth—I didn't care. I didn't regret what we did, either. I would've been with him regardless of the aftermath, would've suffered through any assault on my character, would've forgiven him anything.

I only wonder if he could ever forgive me.

CHAPTER 11
Henry

I RUSH THROUGH THE MUSEUM, rehearsing what I might say to Venus in my head and worried that I might lose my nerve between here and the fairy house.

How do you calmly and reasonably demand an explanation from the woman who not only broke your heart but forever rendered it partially inoperable?

And if I manage to ask, will her answer hurt worse than not knowing?

Hours have passed since Venus left, but I'm still so consumed with thoughts of her that I don't notice the work still being done. Dot and Marnie pop up from the display case they're working on and stop me like a wall before I can slip through the hall to the main door.

"Henry, wait," Marnie says.

"I didn't realize you were still here. Sorry, I have to go out," I say.

"Yeah, you do," Dot smirks like she knows exactly where I'm headed.

"You'll want to see this first." Marnie hands me a hurried sketch that makes my heart skip a beat, and my lungs tighten.

The black-ink drawing shows Venus, perched on a barstool and staring into a drink at a docked tiki bar—a place I've seen not far from the museum. She appears to be waiting… waiting for me.

I read the message at the bottom.

If you want to talk, I'm here. Either way, I'm sorry, Henry.

"I caught her taping it to the door," Marnie says softly. "She was worried about causing another asthma attack."

"She seemed genuinely upset," Dot adds.

"So, what're you going to do?" Marnie asks slowly.

I take a deep breath. "Get some answers, I hope... Lock up for me?"

"Go get her, tiger," Dot says.

"Only don't be an angry tiger," Marnie adds. "Be a purring kitten. Listen to what she has to say, huh?"

I thank the ladies for their support and advice as I'm heading down the hall and out the door.

I've imagined seeing Venus again thousands of times. In my reunion fantasies, anger would rule, fueling my words. I'd accuse her of being exactly what my friends used to say—cold, calculating, and emotionless. How else could she have left me like that?

But when my eyes find her, glowing in the afternoon sun and in vivid color, like she might be a mirage, it's not anger that rules me. Not even close.

It's relief. I'm fucking relieved. *She's okay. I'm okay. We're together.*

She looks surprised that I showed. She slides off the stool and meets me at the boat's edge. Her lovely, tattooed arm reaches for me on the pier.

"Henry, I-I'm glad you're here." A weak smile emerges as she motions to the boat. "See? This way, I can't run. Come with me?"

I use the word *boat* generously here. It's a flat-bottomed floating dock with a bar, barstools, an outer railing, a grass hut overhead, and an almost laughable outboard motor.

Still, I take her hand and step aboard.

Finally, face-to-face with this confounding and devastating woman, ready to demand my answers and tell her exactly how shitty she made me feel, I do the fucking unthinkable.

The relief of her drives me straight into her arms.

Her breath hitches against my bearded cheek as I clasp her against me—I have to, to make sure she's real. I latch on to her, my hands roaming over exposed skin, rough fabric, and soft curls, unsure where to settle. Her hands lock around my midsection, bringing me closer.

"Henry," she whispers, her voice trembling.

"I can't believe it's you. Earlier, I panicked. Sorry."

"Me, too," she says. "It was my dad."

"I know."

"A misguided attempt to reunite us," she goes on, still pressed to me tightly. "Are you okay now?"

"I'm okay," I whisper.

I hesitate, dragging away from her slowly. I catch hints of rosemary in her hair and roses on her skin. Her glassy green eyes widen as she takes me in, and she smiles with what seems like relief, too.

"I've missed you," she whispers, her breath hitting my lips as I leave her.

I want to say it back, but I don't. How could she have missed me when she's the one who left?

Still, my fingers trace her as we pull apart—her bare shoulders, her arms, over her bracelets, and to her fingers. They mingle together, like old friends, as we soak each other up. Her sun-toasted skin, her softness, her tender smile, and the tears brimming in her eyes—this updated version of her, lovely, artsy, emotional, overlays Venus of the past. She's no longer the awkward, blank-faced girl from high school—the one no one understood but me. She's different, and somehow, still as perfect as I remember.

Her bold, green eyes watch me as mine travel to the cheeks I loved touching, the full, pink lips I loved kissing, and her dimpled chin that I often ran my finger over. Her hair is all over the place, held loosely by a scarf, but I love the way the tendrils dance around her face in the breezes.

Her former slenderness has transformed into etched, broad musculature across her arms and shoulders, as if she has filled out to her full form—capable and strong. The deep curves of her breasts draw my eye, as do the striking and detailed daisies over her heart. *Daisies are the friendliest flowers.*

My eyes trail the connecting tattoos, shamelessly ogling her like a museum piece I want to remember forever. They're *her* tattoos, *her* art—I recognize it at once. Her field journal sketches were so realistic that I expected the birds, bugs, and leaves to fly, crawl, or fall off the page.

The same is true for the ink on her body. My thumb runs boldly over the roses, peonies, and tangled vines along her arm, and her smile strengthens behind the distress in her brow, the worry in her eyes, and the nerves pulsing through her fidgeting fingers.

All of this from the woman I'd decided was cold and emotionless.

I release my hold on her, realizing that my touch has lingered too long.

Her hands fall to the dress she's wearing, fisting it in her palms. "It's my prom dress."

So focused on her, I barely noticed her clothes. A dress? The Venus I knew only wore a dress once—it didn't go well. That had been one of many things I'd been looking forward to with prom—Venus in a dress. She looks as elegant as I imagined she would—a sparkling, tempting package I want to touch, wonder over, and admire before giving in and tearing it open to ravish her properly.

"Um, why?" I manage to ask.

"I thought seeing me in something silly might," she says, almost breathlessly, "prevent your lungs from constricting."

"Silly isn't the word I'd use." Alternatives stream through my thoughts, far removed from *silly*. *Radiant, sexy, fucking gorgeous.* But I can't find my breath to say them.

She bends slightly, motioning to the worn, muddy hiking boots now peeking out from the pink layers.

A laugh rumbles from me, because, yes, it's a little silly to see a beautiful woman in a stunning dress while sporting old hiking boots.

"Ivy stole the shoes I bought to go with it," she explains. "I wanted to show you that I... I planned on prom. I wanted to go. To try."

"Then, what happened?"

"I want to explain..." Her voice trails off as she searches for words. "If you're willing to listen and I can calm down enough to... enough to... talk."

She hides her flexing fingers behind her back, bounces on her boots, and takes a deep breath. With so much tension and heartbreak between us, I feel the tension, too.

Though perhaps not as much as she does.

"I, um, have my inhaler *and* a backup, if it helps," I offer with a short smile.

She snort-laughs—a sound I never thought I'd hear again. "Good thinking."

She hesitates, as if finding her place in a book after losing her page.

"How about a drink?" I say, motioning to the bar.

"That's a good idea."

We perch on the awkward barstools. She moves what looks like water with lemon aside and orders a Vodka Cranberry from the pirate-esque bartender. I ask for a beer. The captain revs the weak motor and unties us from the dock. The bar tilts as the engine drives us toward the middle of the river.

"On a scale of one to ten, how safe do you think this boat is?"

"Three, at best. But don't worry. I'm an expert swimmer and hold an EMT-B certification. I studied and trained... *after*." She swallows hard at the word and looks away, as if embarrassed. "I won't let anything bad happen to you."

"I know. I didn't mean it that way." When it's clear that she's too nervous to start, I say, "I, um, I like your tattoos."

She swallows hard and manages a smile. "I like your beard. Very distinguished."

I graze it with my fingers in that thoughtful way I use when I need a dramatic pause with my students. "It helps to look less like the middle schoolers I teach."

Her brow quirks, and her green eyes flood with fresh emotion. "You did it? You're a teacher?"

"Yeah, history, geography, and government," I answer, surprised at her reaction. After what she went through with her education, I imagined she'd hate the idea.

Instead, she looks genuinely happy. "Your students are very lucky."

Coming from her, that's an incredible compliment. "I don't know if they'd agree, but, yeah, I love it."

The captain lights a cigarette and breathes out a heavy trail of smoke. I don't smell it yet, but I will.

"Sir? Excuse me, sir?" Venus's voice pulls me away from my beer. She repeats herself until he can't ignore her. "Could you please extinguish that? My friend is asthmatic."

He huffs. "We're outside."

Her eyes narrow in a challenge. "Yes, but he's sensitive, and so am I. Please?"

The irritated man grunts as he takes a long drag. He flicks his cigarette into the water, which makes Venus cringe, but she lets it go.

Her eyes shift from him to me and to her drink. She twiddles with her bracelets and thumbs the long, thick surface of the mood ring I gave her when we were kids. It had been in my grandmother's jewelry box, part of Mom's inheritance. Going through it, Mom held up the gigantic, gaudy ring and said, *"This looks like something Venus would like."* She also gave Venus a box of old scarves to *"tame that wild mane."* One of those scarves waves from her hair now, catching in the breeze. Vee's motherlessness brought out Mom's generous, sympathetic side. But only to a point that ended whenever Venus caused trouble for me.

That happened often.

"How's the family?" I ask when her nerves become apparent again. It's just like Vee to not bat an eye at confronting a large, gruff stranger, but be hesitant about opening up to me. If this were a classroom, I'd group her in the slow-to-warm-up category, requiring extra encouragement to speak.

"Ivy's in love with Gil," she reports. "She has a dog now, called Buster. She comforted me during a panic attack today, which speaks well for her skills as a registered nurse. She wants us to be sisters again. I'm not averse to the idea. It feels genuine, not like it did in school."

"School isn't a fair representation of the real world."

"Isn't it?" She fiddles mindlessly with her bracelets. "She's still the popular, confident, and pretty one. You're undoubtedly the same handsome nerd, friend to all that you always were. I'm still....the *difficult* one no one knows how to handle."

She smirks, but I don't find her words amusing.

"Fuck *handling* you. You didn't need handling. You needed to be loved, and I *loved* you. You left anyway," I snap.

Her eyes fall to the bar, and she bites her lip. "Yes. I-I couldn't handle me."

When she doesn't explain, I ask, "Why'd you come home?"

Her eyes pinch with my irritation. "Dad's fallen in love, too. Can you believe it? All that talk about love being inconvenient and unnecessary changed when he met the right person. He and Christie have gone on sabbatical. That left his summer teaching position open. He and Dr. Miner, my former mentor, conspired to have me replace him, and she fired me from our project, leaving me little choice. I feel rather manipulated, especially in light of today. I had no idea he was sending me to you."

I nod. "Yeah, I believe you."

"Thank you... How's your family? Maggie and Fred?"

"They're good, still at the old house. She's as anxious as ever, but Fred balances her out."

"Do you see your father?"

"Once a year at the Greene family reunion," I say. "He no longer smokes in front of me, thanks to you."

"Good. He shouldn't."

"He always asks the same three questions. How's Maggie? How's the Jeep? And how's that firecracker friend of yours?"

"I'm surprised he remembers or cares to ask."

"Well, not many twelve-year-olds would stand up to someone's dad."

"Someone had to. He belittled you and your mom, and he smoked around an asthmatic child. With my limited experience regarding typical family dynamics, even I knew he wasn't much of a father."

I can't argue.

"I'm a father," I say suddenly, like the gauge of my most important information has finally tipped into the red zone. "A dad. I have a son. Olly. Oliver Jay Greene. He's six."

Her entire demeanor lights up, and her eyes water with tears, like I've just shared the most perfect thing.

It *is* perfect to me. But that information isn't always well-received.

"No one's better suited to that honor than you." She swipes at a rogue tear. "I just hope you don't bore the poor child with history facts all the time."

I laugh. "Hey, even you liked my boring history facts sometimes. But he has broad interests. He may even lean toward the sciences. His mom's a doctor. We aren't together. She has him on weekends," I ramble, and the gauge of important information falls into the green zone again.

Our boat rocks against the wake of another as we travel underneath the bridge. Venus braces herself with the counter, but my hand goes up anyway, locking with hers. She smiles appreciatively as the waves settle again. The air is cooler under the bridge. Cars rumble over our heads, and suddenly, it doesn't feel like such a silly thing, being on this so-called boat on the river together.

"Feels like the lean-to," she says, staring up. "After the rain."

And it does have the cave-like quality we were once used to. I smile at the memory, but it fades fast under the weight of where we ended.

"Tell me why," I say as we emerge into the sunlight again. "I need to know why you left."

She nods, the sun catching her soft, green eyes, making them glow. "I was scared."

"Scared of *what*? You're not scared of anything."

"Not true. You *know* that's not true."

Her climbing in my window, curling against me, trembling—she's right. I'm probably the only one who saw through her fearlessness to the pain underneath. My anger retreats.

"I'm scared of many things," she goes on nervously. "Space travel freaks me out. I don't care for leeches, though I understand their purpose. Sinkholes and tar pits—"

"Venus—"

"*You*, Henry. *You* scared me. You *still* scare me."

"How? You used to say that I made you feel safe."

"You did... I-I-I nearly killed you, remember?"

"You might kill me today," I joke, motioning to the flat boat under us, but it falls flat against the weight of her sadness.

I grab her legs and spin her on the stool so she has no choice but to look at me. "Venus, please. I chose to be with you then. I'm choosing to be here now. We saved each other that night. It brought us together. For *always*. You told me you loved me. You bought the dress. You wanted to go to prom. Why didn't you?"

"I saw you coming through the path with your bouquet of daisies, the friendliest flower, just like from that movie," she says, smiling while tears slip, "and I couldn't do it. I couldn't do it to you."

"Do *what* to me?"

"Trap you," she breathes out.

The outboard motor pops and sputters as the captain curls into a wide U-turn, marking the halfway point. Pop Forty hits play on the speaker behind the bar, while the only other passengers—a couple in their fifties—dance awkwardly on the other side of the boat, mostly trying to keep their balance.

Despite the activity around us, our eyes stay locked on each other. Maybe I'm glaring at her. Anger, once again, pulses through me.

"You're the most intelligent, logical person I've ever known. You were my biggest advocate, my best friend, my fucking heart. You said you loved me. We had plans. Explain what I'm missing, Venus. Tell me what I don't understand. Because if I can't latch on to some understanding, some fucking peace over this, then when this boat docks, that's it. I never want to see you again."

CHAPTER 12
Venus

HIS WORDS HURT MORE than expected, even though I prepared myself for the worst outcomes.

That he'd be unkind.

That he wouldn't want to talk to me.

That nothing could be salvaged through his rightful hatred.

It's statistically improbable to retract a negative opinion once it's set. Anger and dislike form a concrete layer around the psyche, blocking change, and it takes a sledgehammer to break through it. It's a harsh truth that I know better than he does, better than most, probably. I never felt equipped with a sledgehammer to bust through the bad impressions, rumors, labels, or ill will toward me. I lacked the strength to wield it, even if I did. They were set in stone, unbreakable. I shouldn't expect this conversation with Henry to be any different.

But he's here. He showed. That alone suggests that hope exists, and it's far better than my prediction—me waiting on this boat all night until the captain gruffly asked me to leave with a, "He ain't comin', darlin'." Or some other southern colloquialism. Then, returning to my miserable life, consoled only by the fact that this time, he got to reject me.

He glares now, steaming over my vague and albeit simplistic explanation for what's desperately more complicated. Though it's the truth—I didn't want to trap him.

He's right to be angry—*I know that*—but how can I not feel validated by my decision to leave when his life, like Ivy's and Dad's, has only improved in my absence? He's a teacher, a business owner, and a father. He's shown kindness to me, despite his anger, by showing up and easing me into talking. When he held me, it felt like home—at least, how I think home should feel. He's everything I knew he would be and more.

The sunlight reflects off his glasses—no longer wire frames but thick, tortoiseshell ones that give him a more serious, grown-up look. His narrowed brown eyes appear lighter in the sun, golden like bourbon over ice. He's taller, broader, thinner in the face, and more confident in his style, but as handsome as always. Though I believe my brain would register him as attractive, no matter his appearance. His lopsided smile remains the same, but it's softer somehow, as if behind it he carries a deeper understanding and empathy.

I only hope that holds true.

I find myself sitting on this uncomfortable stool, in this ridiculous dress, on this absurd boat, falling in love with this man all over again at the *mere idea* of who he's become. The reality of him is likely to be my unmaking. *He's here. With me. Everything's okay.*

Only it isn't. Not yet. I must tell him the truth.

"I... I loved you, Henry." My voice shudders with emotion—it's overwhelming—but I remind myself that *this is it*. My last chance to talk to him, to tell him everything, and I can't hold back. "Still do... always will ..."

"Then, why?" he urges gently. "Talk to me."

"Um, senior year, many factors were converging for me at once—the end of a long and heinous nightmare, which I was still in, merged into this beautiful dream of us and a real future together. Despite my diatribes about romantic love being a farce, I'd wanted it to be true for us."

"It *was* true for us," he says quietly.

I grab the napkin under my drink and dab my nose and eyes. I take a deep breath, wanting so badly to dive into the water and be done with this conversation. It's too much.

But I can't do that to him. Not again.

"The love was there... yes. But do you know what it's like to love someone and be a constant disappointment to them? I didn't mean to, but I created problems for everyone who cared for me. Dad, Ivy, and especially you. All the times I got you in trouble with Maggie or at school—it may've seemed adventurous and fun at first, but even your view of me shifted in high school."

"I wanted to be *with* you," he cuts in with emphasis.

"You were embarrassed by me. If we'd stuck with the plan, it would've been... hard on you. Hard on us both."

His brow pinches with sympathy or irritation—I'm not sure which. "You don't know that. College would've been a new start for us. We had a plan."

I clear my throat and fixate on his light brown eyes. "Yes, you and me at UNC-Chapel Hill. I wanted to be with you. But it would've been more of the same, only worse, because instead of going home to my father, who understood me and gave me measured freedom, and Ivy, who at least tolerated me, I'd be sharing a dorm room with someone, probably like Ivy, except less forgiving and understanding. I'd be stuck in lecture halls, forced to take classes I didn't care about, to sit still, to keep quiet. I tried convincing myself that I could get through it with my head down and mouth shut—that had been my system, but it'd failed. Repeating the same faulty experiment seemed ludicrous and, honestly, I didn't have the capacity for it... even for you."

I sniffled, wiping my damp eyes. "I would've tried, though. I fully intended to try for you. But I remembered the countless times I embarrassed you in school, years of loneliness, ridicule, and separation, when you were with your friends and denied being mine. I was fully aware that I lived in two very separate existences then—a free and beautiful one, where I had you, and the other, where I didn't, and *one* of those was ending. I transferred that hurt and disappointment to us as adults, and I... I... couldn't do it."

I take a breath as he stares at me, transfixed and probably still angry.

"Prom night, I put on the dress, this dress," I say, fumbling with the tulle of the poofy skirt, "and looked in the mirror, hoping I could be *that* girl for you, *willing* myself to be *that* girl. I wanted to slip into normalcy, just like I did this dress, and become someone to make you *proud*. But no matter what I put on, it wouldn't make me any less of a burden for all the ways I continued to hurt you. Embarrassed you. Got you in trouble. Put you in the terrible position of having to choose between them and me—"

"I should've chosen you. That was my fault," he says, sounding regretful.

"No, it wasn't. You were right to distance yourself from me. That's what I wanted you to do. Just because I made myself an outcast didn't mean you needed to be. And... perhaps college would've been different. But then you almost *died* because of me. How could I trust in us when I couldn't trust myself with you? When I saw you coming down our path, I thought about what my therapist told me to ask when my impulses triggered: *Is this helpful, healthy, and safe?* And the answer was no—I was none of those things to you. I just kept hurting you, Henry. So, everything ultimately converged on one conclusion. *Loving you meant leaving you.* So, I begged Dad to turn you away, to lie, to say *anything* to make you leave. It's the most painful thing I've ever done. Even now, it hurts, and I'm ashamed that I couldn't talk to you. But two days later, I was on a plane, and for the first time in my life, I could breathe. I could finally *breathe.*"

His eyes close tightly, like he's disappointed, but then his arm wraps around my shoulders, and he pulls me to him across the barstools. My overflowing tension depletes in his arms, like he releases the pressure valve.

"I'm sorry," he whispers over and over. "I'm so sorry."

I don't know what to say—I never expected him to apologize to me.

"Why couldn't you talk to me then?" he asks softly. "You had all these... big feelings, and you didn't think I deserved to know?"

"Of course, you did. But I knew what you'd say. That everything was okay, or it would be—you'd make sure—and I'd believe you, despite the evidence against it, and I... I wouldn't be able to resist you, Henry." I shake my head, peeling away from his warm shoulder. "You deserved better, but I struggled to communicate emotions that I didn't understand. Still do. The only reason I'm able to now is because I've had a decade of therapy... and it's my last chance."

"A chance you wouldn't have bothered taking if not for your father," he huffs, rightly. "You *devastated* me, Venus. You can't convince me that it was for my own good."

"Wasn't it? The evidence suggests otherwise."

He cringes, but his head lowers in consideration, staring into the wood of the bar.

"It was the right thing for me, too. I needed what was helpful, healthy, and safe, and I couldn't find that without running away. I'm sorry for hurting you. I'll say it a million times if you need me to. But I don't regret leaving. It was best for you and everyone else."

"Losing you hurt everyone who cared about you—how could *that* be the best thing?"

"It's what everyone wanted, and what I needed to do. For them, for you, *and for me*." I shrug, feeling his disappointment like the too-hot sun on my bare skin, cutting into me, burning. "If it helps, it hasn't been easy for me. I've suffered several long-term effects of my decision."

"It doesn't help." He groans, like this is a sad consolation prize, but asks, "What effects?"

"I have no permanent residence and live out of a single backpack and carry-on suitcase. Some might consider that adventurous, but my therapist says it's a fear of commitment. She wants to write a journal article on me."

Henry cracks a smile at this. "That should please you, being studied."

A light smirk breaks through my emotional avalanche. "Well, it's one way to achieve scientific publication, though I won't receive any credit as a case study."

He fondles his beer bottle, looking contemplative. "Is that all?"

"Um, I've been called reckless. Dr. Broderick says that my lack of connection makes me take unnecessary risks, though I argue that someone has to, especially in the name of science and protecting the environment."

His head tilts in a half-shake, like this disappoints him. "You've always taken risks."

"My sister and father found their soulmates, and I didn't even know... not because they didn't want to tell me, but because I don't make time to listen."

"Anything else?" he asks, his tone softer.

"I am... lonely," I say, wishing my therapist could hear me now. Dr. Broderick would fall out of her posh chair to hear me admit it. "My sexual partners have been accommodating, but ineffectual at satisfying *that* need, though I can't fault them too much."

"How come?"

My cheeks flush. "Um, I have an annoying habit of saying *Henry* at the most intimate times."

Beer sprays over the bar at his choking sip. "Fuck me, sorry."

I hand him the napkin. "It's okay."

A rosy tint appears under his glasses—a look I like on him. He fumbles with his bottle as he cleans up the mess, nearly knocking it over. "Um, that's awkward. How did they react?"

I shrug. "My partners have been surprisingly forgiving at that stage in our engagement. I don't want to see them again, so it's a problem that resolves itself."

He gulps his beer like he doesn't know what to say.

"I have no one, Henry," I tell him, hoping that will lessen his resentment toward me.

"I never wanted any of that for you… I didn't realize you knew about me denying our friendship."

"I didn't live in a bubble."

"It was only once, not that it's any comfort. I hated myself for it. I felt horrible… I'm sorry, Vee."

"It's okay."

"How come you never said? You should've been pissed," he says.

I smirk, swishing the remains of my drink in the glass. "Everyone tells me how I *should* be. It's exhausting, and it flusters me. All I can say is that at the time, I was so grateful to have you that forgiveness was easy. Besides, given social hierarchies and school dynamics, I understood."

The boat jerks as the captain rams it against the dock. The happy couple nearly falls overboard, but laughs it off as they regain their balance.

We disembark the vessel. Henry takes my hand to help me onto the dock, and a spark flies up my arm, fizzing out somewhere around my heart. I know this is it—the last time we'll be together, but that's sadness I'll save for later.

In this moment, I feel lighter. The burden of carrying a thousand secrets lifts now that I've shared some with him, a result I didn't expect, though Dr. Broderick has argued as much for years. I consider extending the experiment to Ivy and Dad—to finally say everything I should have then.

For now, I twist to face Henry. Sunlight silhouettes his frame while a breeze ruffles through his hair. I expect him to stuff his hands in his pockets, glance around indifferently, and say something along the lines of "thanks" and "goodbye."

He does the first two things, but then says, "Have dinner with me?" he asks, running a hand down his beard. "I don't think this conversation is over."

"Okay, as long as you don't mind dining with a twenty-eight-year-old in a prom dress and hiking boots."

"I know a place where you'll fit right in," he grins, pointing to a cheery restaurant on the corner with a bright sign that reads, "Queens and Dreams Diner." I can't help but smile.

Chimes announce our arrival when Henry swings the door open to usher me inside. A jukebox glows in the corner, currently playing "Sweet Emotion" by Aerosmith. Bright red vinyl booths and barstools stand out against the black-and-white tiled floor. Neon signs beam against multi-colored walls, and light from metal pendants bounces off the touches of stainless steel along the tables. If happiness had a color palette, this would be it.

"It reminds me of summer," I say in a breath.

"I knew you'd love it," he says, smiling beside me.

"Henry!" A six-foot hostess wearing a fifties-style polka dot dress with a lacy crinoline peeking from the hem steps from behind the counter, her red-lipped smile widening as she takes us in. She snaps her fingers over her head, drawing more attention. "Girls, come here!"

And suddenly, we're surrounded by drag queens.

"Ooh, la, la, Cinderella grunge," she says, eyeing my outfit. "I love it!"

"What's the occasion, Henry?" a drag queen in a turquoise mermaid dress asks, linking onto his arm. "You on a date, for once?"

He looks sheepish, blushing again, but motions to me with formality when he says, "Ladies, meet Venus, an old friend."

"The goddess of love," one coos brightly.

"Venus, this is DeeDee," Henry says, motioning to the hostess.

She takes my hand in both of hers, her eyes drifting over me from head to boots. "Venus, finally."

I'm about to ask what she means when Henry diverts my attention. "Lucky Lucy's the mermaid—"

"I'm still waiting on my Aquaman," Lucy laughs, shaking my hand.

"And Sunny," Henry says.

"As in Sunny Side Up, but I'd say I'm over easy. Will you two be going hiking or dancing? I'm confused," says the waitress in a bright yellow, fitted dress suit.

"Wherever the night takes us, I suppose," I say.

They laugh, though I mean it.

"I love a girl who's prepared for anything," says Lucy, fondling loose strands of my long hair.

"Let's get you seated before Lucy starts fixing your hair," advises DeeDee, giving the mermaid a warning look.

She leads us to a booth in the back corner. I slide into the vinyl seat, my dress swishing as I go, and I can't remember the last time I felt pretty like this.

"Henry, you want the usual?" DeeDee asks.

"Yeah, thanks."

"I'll take his usual, too," I say, handing her the menu.

Her bright red lips edge into a flirty smile. "A girl who knows what she wants even if she doesn't know what it is… hmm." She saunters away.

My attention falls back to Henry, where I want it to be. Not on a menu. I shrug lightly. "They like my outfit."

"You're beautiful, Venus," he says, sounding defeated.

I'm about to thank him, as is customary after a compliment, but he leans forward, his expression turning serious.

"I need to say something. You've helped me understand your point of view, and I'm thankful for it, but I need you to understand mine."

I nod, nerves rising with his intensity. "I'm listening."

He hesitates, his eyes roaming toward the jukebox as the song switches to "Still Into You" by Paramore. "This was Uncle Jay's favorite place. He restored the jukebox—his grand opening gift to DeeDee. His own business was floundering, but he still invested in seeing hers succeed… He um, he died four months ago."

"Henry, I'm sorry," I offer, remembering the friendly man who nicknamed me Rapunzel for my long, blonde hair.

He fiddles with his silverware. "He struggled with his mental health, and instead of asking for help or even talking to us, he decided it'd be better to die, not to be a burden."

My heart seizes at the pain evident in his pinched lips and furrowed brow. His words slice through me, mirroring what I said to him on the boat.

"That's how it felt when you left, Venus. Like grief. Like life and love were ripped away from me without understanding why. It still feels that way."

Tears weigh down my lashes as I comprehend what he's telling me —that two people he's loved have believed themselves to be burdens and vanished from his life. Forced him to grieve. Left him with unanswered questions. I should apologize again, but I know it won't make any difference. That pain remains, nestled in like a burr, sharp on all sides. No apology will remove it.

"For me, too," I breathe, though he only shakes his head.

"But you weren't *abandoned*," he says. "I should've been a better friend to you. A better boyfriend. I took you for granted. I wasn't there for you, not the way you needed me. I knew you suffered, but not how much... maybe if I looked harder, paid more attention—"

"It wasn't your fault—"

"Letting you believe you were a *burden*? Yes, that's my fault." He leans against the booth and pulls his inhaler from his pocket.

"You didn't *know*, Henry. You couldn't have changed what you didn't *know*," I say.

"Then, why didn't you tell me? You always acted like *nothing* bothered you. You always said you were fine. You lied."

"No, I didn't lie. I don't lie. I *was* fine... with you. Don't you see? You were my only relief!"

DeeDee arrives with two frosty IPAs. "You two okay?" she asks, as he takes a quick puff off his inhaler.

"Fine," he manages shortly.

Her penciled eyebrow quirks, but she disappears into the dining room. Henry stares into his beer, his messy brown hair hitting the rim of his glasses and shadowing his thoughtful eyes. He doesn't seem angry anymore, but desperately sad, which might be worse.

"I kept my distance from you at school because, yeah, it was easier sometimes, but that's what I thought you wanted. That's what you said for me to do. I didn't realize things were... that bad for you. I'm sorry, Vee."

I lean forward, catching his eyes in mine. "Don't be sorry. You made it all better. Bearable. With you, I was... just Venus. Do you understand what that meant to me? It was everything to me, Henry. *Everything*."

I grab a napkin from the metal box on the table and dab my eyes, vaguely remembering how it felt to be myself without fear of judgment and missing that comfort and freedom. This conversation has probably been the most honest of my life. It hurts being this vulnerable, like I'm offering consent to be dissected on an examination table. *Ah, here's Venus's broken heart. Let's get that under the microscope and measure the cracks.* Henry was the only person I could trust to hold a scalpel to my inner workings, and even then, sometimes the scalpel would slip, nicking my heart. I ache to return to our weird and lovely relationship that no one understood but us, and now that pain surges in me, a flood of want, bursting through my carefully designed barriers. I want him to know me beyond being the woman who *devastated* him.

Devastated. I never thought I could hurt him like that.

When I left, I grieved. I feared the unknown. I lost my entire world, everyone, and everything I'd ever known. All those former pains shift behind a bigger one—*that I devastated Henry*. I trusted in his love for me then, but I suppose I expected him to dismiss it, the same way he did at school, or when we drifted into one of our long silences. Rather than grief, I imagined relief for him. Eventually.

Taking the scalpel to my inner workings means enduring another nick—I see how much I hurt him. His pain pours into me, saturating me, devastating me all over again.

A feeling that worsens when he says, "*You* were everything to me, Venus. I would've run with you if you'd let me. You and me, off on another adventure, like always."

His hand flies up to catch the tears slipping from his eyes, and I crumble into a quiet sob, imagining that missed adventure. I never considered the possibility that he'd run with me.

"That would've been… I wish I could've… I'm sorry, Henry. Feel whatever you need to feel about me. Hate me, resent me, never speak to me again, forgive me, forget me. But please know that it was love and desperation that made me run. Not you. You were and always will be the best part of me."

I guzzle my beer, needing relief. A break. A timeout. *Something.* The paralyzing tension inside clenches and growls at me as it grows.

"I never hated you. I wanted to. Hate would've been easier. But how could I? You taught me to climb trees, get dirty, and stand up against bullies and false claims," he says, his lop-sided smile returning like he needs the distraction.

I laugh, thinking of Frank the Frog and grateful for the relief.

"I just… missed you," he adds.

I nearly crumble again. "I missed you, too. I missed us, and I'm sorry."

He nods, a gentle smile on his face. "Thanks for helping me understand."

My bare shoulders bob in a weak shrug. "Only took me ten years."

"Better late than never."

Two heaping cheeseburgers arrive with a tower of fries. I can't help but chuckle over his exorbitant "usual." I dig in, suddenly ravenous and anxious for my tears to dry. Outside, streetlights pop on as the sun dips and fades behind the buildings, and I fixate on the traffic streaking by the window. I don't know what to say now that my heart lies dissected on the table between us. There are no conversational guidelines for moving on after such an emotional purge. Are there?

"Are you... okay?" he asks finally.

"Yes, fine, thank you."

"I'm, um, about to finish my Master's," he says. "In education with a specialty in AIG students."

"That's commendable."

He looks sheepish as his eyes narrow at me. "Commendable, huh? How many degrees do you have?"

"I have a doctorate in botany and two master's degrees in environmental science and art. The latter I did for fun. I may pursue another Master's in Art History soon—it'd be an easy addition to my resume. I'm also an EMT-B, a Mensa member, and a contributing member of several environmental organizations."

He laughs.

"Is that funny?" I ask, unsurely.

"No, Venus. You're amazing. It's just... I was trying to impress you."

A smirk curls up my cheek that he'd even *want* to impress me. "You want to help exceptional learners. I find that *very* impressive, Henry."

"You went from barely passing high school to stockpiling degrees," he says, twiddling with a fry. "What made the difference for you?"

"Freedom to learn as I pleased. Guided, virtual instruction and hands-on field work with my mentor," I explain. "Dad kept me in school because he feared I wouldn't socialize without it. Perhaps he had a valid point. Though ironically, all it did was reinforce my feelings of isolation. And I'm *still* socially awkward. It's funny that schools don't offer a class on socializing and connection, right?"

His brows perk as he considers the question.

But I go on, grateful to be talking about something other than my emotions. "Most students thrive with rules and routines—a system. But I performed better in classes where I was given trust and more freedom and had teachers who were willing and able to engage in discourse with me, without labeling me as belligerent for asking questions. The Socratic method, a forum of intellectual discussion and ideas, would've been my ideal when forced to learn with others. Self-guided study, if on my own."

I shove a fry in my mouth and reach for another. "Receiving my diagnosis and the Individualized Education Program helped me, and others, understand my ADHD. Understanding my high IQ and being raised on books and experimentation rather than TV and video games presented the greater challenge—many teachers couldn't relate to me. I was a difficult case—"

"I hate that word," he says, breaking my dialogue. "It's loaded with negative connotations and overused generally, especially with you. *Difficult.* Even you call yourself that now."

"What would you have called me?" I say, surprised that he noticed.

"Complex," he says, his earthy brown eyes meeting mine, "an intriguing opportunity. You deserved better."

"Thank you." Heat rises to my cheeks at his gentle acknowledgement.

He stares, nibbling the inside of his cheek in almost sad contemplation. It's a look I've seen before, like he doesn't know what to do with me.

"It wasn't all bad, Henry," I say. "I excelled in my art classes. I had the library, science labs, and… you."

His eyes slip over me with something softer, almost wanton, tracing the lines of my tattoos and pausing at my breasts. "Didn't you tell me that flowers are little more than lovely sex organs?"

A laugh emerges while my cheeks heat under his gaze. "So, you did listen to me?"

"*Always,*" he says. "You've covered yourself in lovely sex organs. What does that say about you?"

"Freud might have some theories. But they're not all sex organs. Fronds, foliage, and seeds, too. They all mean something to me, though." I motion to the daisies he can see peeking over the corset of my dress. "The heads of daisies aren't just one flower. They're made up of many tiny flowers. A whole world on each tiny flower head, all its friends and family in one place… no wonder Meg Ryan deemed it the friendliest flower in *You've Got Mail.*"

"Is that why you got that tattoo?"

"This was my first. I got it for you, to keep you close, even if we couldn't be."

His lips form a rigid line as his eyes lock on me, in an expression I can't gauge, but that makes my heart sputter and race in the fear that my admission hurts him further.

DeeDee arrives with the check, which I snatch before Henry can. I quickly pay with money from my phone case. When she returns for it, I tell her to keep the change and say, "Thanks for making me feel pretty."

"Oh, honey, you're gorgeous! Come back anytime you need the reminder," she gushes. "Hope you two enjoyed catching up."

I nod, tears circulating in my irises at the realization that it's over. She saunters off, carrying our dirty dishes, and my eyes return to Henry's, fixating on him because he's already staring.

"Thank you for listening to me," I say.

"Thanks for coming back and explaining."

I nod, desperately holding back tears over our looming end and not wanting to say goodbye. "I could install the garden, if you want. I mean, I could do it when you're not there or…"

He slips from the booth and reaches out to me. My hand falls into his as he helps me scoot out. The tips of our fingers linger together as he leads us through the brightly lit, friendly restaurant. We exit to the dark street, lightly peppered with people, and music thumping from a bar on the corner. He takes my hand, almost roughly, and pulls me along the sidewalk, away from the activity and toward the museum.

Under a streetlight on the Riverwalk, he suddenly stops, drops my hand, and pushes up his glasses, looking frustrated.

"Do you feel better?" he asks.

"Yes. Being with you always makes me feel better. It was good to explain. Do you feel better?"

His hand skates through his messy hair while he groans at the question. "No, Venus. I don't feel better. I feel fucking worse."

CHAPTER 13
Henry

MY GRUFF DECLARATION forces Venus to backstep, her hands fondling her bracelets with familiar agitation.

But she doesn't run.

She spilled her soul tonight, cut herself open, and laid herself, gutted, before me with honesty and vulnerability, feelings that, frankly, I came to believe her incapable of expressing. After she was gone, anger filled the gaping hole she left behind, crowding out what I once adored about her.

I forgot how loving she could be.

How funny.

How protective.

I forgot how hard she tried to contain her feelings so that they wouldn't betray her.

I forgot *her*.

Instead, my defenses kicked in, deeming her cold and heartless for leaving me.

She's neither cold nor heartless. She never was. I'm angry at myself for getting her so wrong, and pissed that she didn't give me a chance to get it right.

She stands under the lamplight, her eyes and dress sparkling, and I'm caught in this awful battle between wanting this to be over and never wanting it to end.

"Whatever you need to say to me," she says after a beat, "go ahead. Tell me."

"I'm not okay, Venus. I understand why you did it, but it still hurts. You say you're cursed because you fear commitment. I *crave* commitment, and can't have it. My relationships crash and burn because they aren't... well, they aren't *you*."

Her brow pinches with my confession. Maybe I shouldn't have said it, but it's the truth. And my last chance to say it.

She nods, encouraging me to continue even as her green eyes glint with building tears.

"... I've been with other people, obviously. I have a son I wouldn't trade for anything. I tried so hard to love his mother the way she deserved. I wanted us to be a family. That didn't work. No one has *worked*. Damn, Venus, you're the smart one. Why can't I let you go? *That's* what I should want. *That* would make it better."

"I understand." She nods, catching tears as soon as they slip from her eyes. "I feel it, too. It's because we're unfinished. We never even... that's the problem, Henry."

"How do we fix it?"

Her brows knit studiously as she considers the question, though I meant it rhetorically. There is no fixing us. We're the past. Not the future. With Olly, my career, and now the museum, my cast is set, and Venus would be the last woman on earth to mold herself to it, not that I'd want her to try.

It's like Dr. Blake told me when he found me passed out drunk in the greenhouse after she left, and I'd destroyed the remains of the herb garden we'd started in our corner bed. He sat with me, made me drink a lot of water, and said, *"Venus is a sunflower who believes she's a cactus. I'm sorry, son."*

Nothing he said then made sense to me.

Not that she'd left.

Not that she'd been struggling.

Not that it might be a long time before she returned.

And not that she didn't want to talk to me.

At that moment, I didn't give a fuck about sunflowers or cacti. All I wanted then was for her to sneak into my bedroom, curl against me, and apologize for prom by whispering, "My bad," from *Clueless. That* would've been enough for me.

But you can't *tell* someone what they are—I see it now. This unwitting sunflower bobs on her boots, looking desperate and believing she's too prickly to love, oblivious to how much I long for her. *Still*. She fiddles with her jewelry, one hand and then the other, and her cheeks flush with her rising nerves. How do you tell the most intelligent, confounding, beautiful, brave woman you've ever met that she let fear get in our way? That she didn't trust me? That *she* didn't give us a chance?

"I have an idea," she says, breathless.

Pages of memories flip through my thoughts, all the times those four words led us to something great, all the times they landed us in trouble. I wonder which it will be this time.

I have an idea… let's build a lean-to and test it in the storm.

I have an idea… let's start a controlled burn.

I have an idea… let's hide all of Dale's ashtrays.

I have an idea… let's—

"Let's fix it by finishing it."

"What do you mean?"

"One night together," she blurts, while her soft green eyes darken and flicker with hope. "We deserve a more satisfactory ending. We could get each other out of our systems and move on to an amicable closure. It would end some of the mystery and satiate this constant yearning for what might have been. We could stop idealizing each other. Or, better yet, we might discover that we aren't as compatible as we imagined, making our dissolution easier. It's *one* thing that we never did that we still could without adding complications."

"Since when is sex uncomplicated?"

She sighs softly. "Why does it have to be?"

"Says the girl who ran the two times we came close," I say with an unintentional scoff.

She slumps slightly, and perhaps it's unfair to bring up memories from so long ago.

But those two times are branded into me, too beautiful and upsetting to let go. *Big feelings* made her run the first time, when curiosity took our friendship to a new level.

She ran again later that year when we tailgated at the Fort Fisher Rock Wall. I'd hoped for a beautiful sunset, and the sky delivered with hazy shades of red, orange, blue, and purple. I wanted to ask her to the prom, but I got nervous and rambled on about the Corps of Engineers' construction of the rock wall in 1865 to improve river navigation.

This prompted her to tell me about the unforeseen environmental impacts, particularly the creation of the greatest salt marsh on the East Coast. She went on to elaborate on the algae, mosses, and vegetation along the banks.

My prom question quickly got away from me.

It evaded me again when we started making out.

With her straddling me on the tailgate, her long hair creating a curtain around our faces, I fit the question in between kisses. *"Go to prom with me. It's dressy and silly, I know... but I want to be dressy and silly with you. I want you by my side. Normal couple things, you know?"*

Breathless, she gaped at me, her eyes sparkling in the moonlight and her expression hopeful. But then, a shadow fell over her. *"I. I wanna see how far I can go. On the rocks."*

She ran away, thrusting us into *that* night like we were fated to be tested. A test we passed and failed at the same time.

"I promise, I won't run," she says now, eyes locked on mine. "Do you... I mean, would you... Do you find me desirable, Henry?"

"Yes, of course. But it's not that simple," I argue, growing more frustrated, if that's possible.

"I promise simplicity. No big feelings, no attachments, no more than one night."

"No, it's been an emotional day. We shouldn't be making decisions like this."

"This isn't me being impulsive." She glances at her feet.

"It's just one of your wilder ideas."

She shrugs lightly, her bracelets clattering as she moves. "Is it? Doesn't feel wild to me. Or impulsive. How can it be impulsive when it's what I've always wanted?"

Her words stun me, especially *always*, and I can't stop myself from saying, "It's what I've always wanted, too."

A tiny smile slips up her cheeks. "Then, what do you say?"

"I don't know what to say," I admit. "I don't think it's a good idea."

She steps forward, close enough that the tips of her boots and my sneakers meet. "Tell me to go, then. Tell me you never want to see me again, and I'll stay away forever."

I swallow a lump in my throat. "I'm not... I can't say that to you."

She inches closer, resting her hand on my chest. "Then, reject me at least. Push me away. Tell me you don't want me. Give me back some of the pain I've caused you."

"No," I say sternly. "We've hurt each other enough already."

"Then, let's make each other feel good for a change." Her fingertips graze my chest, even the softest touch making me ache for more.

"Fuck, Venus," I breathe out, hands slipping up her bare arms, unable to stop myself.

"We need this. It's one night to end so many others. One night to end the sleepless nights I still have, thinking of you. One night to end the agony of a thousand what-ifs. It would give us a final chapter to our story. That's all."

I long for a better end to our story, too. She's not the only one with sleepless nights and relentless what-ifs. Every second of wanting her, every moment we came close, every time I felt her absence—I have wanted Venus Blake since... *always*.

The first time I made her smile released butterflies in my stomach. Every smile since has done the same, a rare gift reserved only for me.

Latching onto her during the storm at eight years old felt like finding where I belonged. With her. Before I even understood *wanting*, I wanted her.

I have wanted her. Craved her. Yearned for her like breath in my lungs. And like my breath, I know what it's like to be without her.

Now she's offering herself up like a gift, wrapped in a prom dress—a gift I'm dying to unwrap. Eyes locked on mine, she leans closer, her chest heaving against her tight bodice, pressing against mine. Goosebumps erupt on her arms as my fingers slide up and down them, and I swear she gasps when I delicately graze her shoulder and the daisies on her upper breast. Her fingers curl over my shirt, pulling me tighter against her, and I'm sure she can feel my excitement through her clothes, even the full skirt of her dress. Her hand trembles over my heart and holds it there, perhaps waiting for me to move it. I clasp it in mine instead, pressing it to my racing heart.

I'm breathless, but in the best way. "This feels... like a game we can't win."

"Play anyway. Be with me, Henry." Her lips part in a breath that waves through a loose strand of her hair.

"One night." I breathe against her lips.

"One night," she returns, her fingers rising to the bristles on my cheekbones, and I swear I see starbursts in the dark green of her eyes, flickering like the sparkles on her dress, and I'm lost in them.

A heartbeat later, I'm lost in her lips, as I yank her against me. It's been too long. Too fucking long since I've kissed this woman. Held her. Touched her. My pleasure centers have been hibernating, and I didn't know it. Her hands glide over my chest, along my shoulders, and into my hair, dragging me closer. Her jewelry adds extra roughness to her movements, and it's as if each touch awakens the skin beneath.

"I've wanted you all this time," I mutter, biting her lip and flushed with all the things I want to do to her. "I don't know if we can handle what's about to happen."

She inhales sharply against me, her smile widening with her already-swollen lips. "I'm ready. Be whatever you want to be. Rough, demanding, anything. I can take it."

My lips curl. "How about I be Henry, and you be Venus, and we let this go wherever it takes us?"

She answers with a smiling kiss, latching onto my neck while I let my fingers dip into the seam along the top of her breasts, grazing a nipple.

She moans—a sound so sweet that I ache to hear it again and again.

I don't know how we make it the thirty yards to my front door without tripping on the uneven cobblestones or stumbling off a curb. But soon, I'm fumbling for my keys and pushing us inside. With one arm fixed around her waist as she licks my neck, I lock the door with the other, pull the shades, and push her against the counter. I lift her onto the edge and take in her wanton smile.

She tugs at my shirt, pulling me between her legs. "Tell me what you want, Henry. Tell me all the things you've ever wanted."

My fingers trace her collarbone and slip over the intricate daisies on her chest. "I want you out of this dress, as pretty as it is."

She tugs on the zipper hidden under her arm, loosening the bodice and revealing her bare breasts beneath. My chest constricts, not for lack of air but for wanting her. I trace the tight softness of her toned arms, along the veins of the ferns and ivy imprinted there, to her shoulder, down the slope of her breast, across the field of intricate daisies, and to the tantalizing tip of her perfect pink nipple.

A stream of *almosts* from our younger days skitter through my thoughts—her in my bed, in the Jeep, her in a bikini at the beach, us racing to the outdoor shower at the fairy house, stripping as we went, because she'd upset a beehive and we were desperate to get them off of us. I recall us in our underwear in the stream of the outdoor shower, checking each other for remaining bees and stings, and peeking at the dark outline of her nipples through her wet bra. Even in *that* nightmare, I wanted her. I've touched her breasts before, under her shirt, caught glimpses, but this is the first time I've *seen* her, the first time I've ever felt free to explore her the way I want.

"You're so fucking beautiful."

"I'm all for you, Henry." Her hands slip around my neck, dragging me to her mouth and kissing me so hard that my glasses crush against my eyes.

"I want to explore every inch of you." I bite her bottom lip and cup her breasts. "With my hands. With my tongue. Inside you."

She moans a breathy, "Yes, Henry," as my hand snakes under the layers of her dress, trying to find her. The fabric pools between us, but I reach lace. I run my fingers over the thin fabric.

Wanton delight surges in me as her eyes and head roll back simultaneously at my touch. She is wet and warm and hyper-responsive, trembling against me, as if each contact sends a jolt of heat through her and into me, stoking the fire inside me. I am achingly hard, pressed uncomfortably against my jeans, but I don't care. All I can think about is exploring her and making her come right here—she's so close already. I run my finger along the edge of her panties and slip them to the side, my thumb tracing up her center to land on her clit. She moans again, spreading her legs wider to welcome me.

I tug the scarf from her hair, letting it fall around her shoulders, and grip the back of her head. With my thumb rubbing circles on her clit and fingers curled and dipping inside her, our gazes lock—me watching her ecstasy and her doing nothing to hide it. It is the sexiest, most intimate thing I've ever done.

"Come for me," I tell her, "right here. On this counter. On my hand."

She cries out, her fingernails digging into my shoulders as I push deeper into her. Her legs wrap around my backside, her boots hitting my thighs. "Yes, Henry," she says, her eyes fixed on mine like she knows how much I want to see her face. My hand grips the back of her hair and tightens.

"Always say my name, Venus. No other name but mine ever again."

"Ruin me, Henry," she whispers against my lips.

Trembling, moaning, pulling, and pushing, but never breaking our intense but agonizing connection, she comes undone in my hand.

CHAPTER 14
Venus

I COME APART like a dandelion in a stiff wind, scattered and in pieces. He cradles me as I come down, hand laced in my hair and pressing his forehead to mine as my breathing slows and the tremors lessen.

Watching me. Waiting for me.

I have *never* climaxed like that before, full-bodied and explosive. I am sexually proficient and confident. I consider the activity a human necessity—food, water, shelter, sex—and I'm bold and greedy when it comes to meeting my needs. I've had plenty of satisfying partners, some less so, but always, *always*, I achieve climax. Orgasms are easy. It's illogical that this one feels different than the rest.

But it's Henry. And my orgasms of the past were mere rumbles compared to his demanding thunder.

This wasn't an exercise but a connection.

This wasn't clumsy or awkward, but intimate.

Henry wasn't the means to an end but the source. The creator. The composer. The artist. His intense gaze, the feel of his rough stubble against my skin, the delicious timbre of his voice, and the perfect pressure of his thumb. I imagine his fingerprint permanently branded there —that's his now, forever.

He holds me, savoring me and letting me savor it.

"You okay?" he whispers.

I answer by kissing him, all lips and tongue, and the gentle tickles of his beard against my cheeks and under my nose. His hands slide down me, along the back of my thighs, calves, until he tugs my boots to the floor. My phone falls, too. I don't care. I ease off the counter, pulling my dress down until it falls into a heap around my socked feet. My panties and socks follow, leaving me bare.

Henry's hungry eyes take me in by the soft light from the hallway. I don't feel the least bit modest about him seeing me. I want to expose myself to him. For him to see me. All of me.

He eyes my breasts, traces the artwork along my arms, and sees the large tattoo on my thigh—bursting sunflowers in yellow, burgundy, and gold for the ones we grew in the greenhouse that reached too high and ended up toppling over. *Sunflowers aren't like other flowers—they need more space to grow.* Leaves and vines swirl them together and trace around my leg to my calf and shin, where other favorites reside. Poppies, lavender, honeysuckle, and the fern that he has no idea belongs to him. His fingers slide down my arm, taking my hand, and he turns me around. My back is a botanical hodgepodge—the live oak I climbed often in the woods behind the fairy house, our lean-to, magnolia flowers, weeds, wildflowers, wild herbs, sweet pea, marigolds, and palmettos.

He traces the images with his finger, making my skin prickle with goosebumps. I wonder if he knows they're all memories. I wonder if he knows my body is our journal. His arm hooks around my waist, pulling me against him. I feel his hardness and ache to have him inside me.

His arm is wrapped over my breasts, his heavy breaths on my ear, and his tongue slips down my neck.

"Take me, Henry," I beg, my hand sliding over the bulge in his jeans. His lips curl against my shoulder.

"I can't decide how I want you next," he breathes on my skin.

"Then, let me choose," I mutter, knowing just what I want.

He growls, nuzzling my neck before biting me. "Upstairs."

I step from the dress heap on the floor, leaving it all behind, and follow where he leads me.

Holding hands, we weave through a maze of dark rooms to a staircase, occasionally glancing over his shoulder with boyish satisfaction at the sight of me. On a dimly lit landing, he pins me to the wall with untamed kisses as I wrap my legs around him and his hands skitter from my breasts to my thighs, gripping me tightly.

He carries me the rest of the way, barreling into a door at the top, out of breath but smiling.

"You okay?" I ask as he edges inside his apartment.

"Breathless for the right reasons," he grins.

We reach the foot of his bed, where he lets my legs drift slowly from his hands as he kisses me. Wild, frantic kisses, desperate and playful, like wildflowers in a field, spread wherever they wish to go. My feet find the floor, and I pull myself away just enough to gather the hem of his shirt. His smile falls slightly as I rid him of it. At first, I think it's shyness—it's been a decade since I've seen his chest, after all. Could Henry have what they call a *dad bod*?

No. Not a dad bod. *Not at all.* There's more substance to him than in high school, but pleasantly so, as if his muscles have become insulated with more muscles. Running my fingertips over his toned shoulders, rippled stomach, and patches of hair on his hard chest makes me ache to rid him of the rest of his clothes.

But I stop in a gasp when I see a tattoo over his heart, too. I trace the detailed lines of a bullfrog—not just any bullfrog. *Our* bullfrog. "It's Frank."

A small lamp in the corner casts a warm glow in his eyes, which have narrowed behind his glasses. He looks uncertain, almost sad.

"Why did you get this?" I can't help asking.

"I, um… I wanted to keep you close, too."

My eyes flicker from him to the frog and then back again. Despite the pain I caused him, he *wanted* to keep me close. Forever. A piece of me.

"I don't understand." My eyes drift to Frank's again, and in a moment of complete absurdity, I kiss him, thinking of that fairy tale about the princess who kisses the frog to turn him into her prince. It's a ridiculous story. No one should ever kiss a real frog—they're covered in bacteria and salmonella. Had I known that then, I wouldn't have let Henry touch it—we washed our hands vigorously after, regardless. But some part of me, the part that Henry has awakened, wants to harness any magic that might be out there for us.

That he did this with my drawing… my heart swells with love for him, new love layering on the old. It's as if loving Henry started as a penciled sketch that later became permanent, with inked lines that grew more prominent against a deliberate background, and finally filled in with color. Gorgeous colors. Blends of colors. Shadows. And light.

That picture takes hold in my mind, as so many have before, and I'm desperate for it to come to life. To give it all the color and attention it needs. To love him fully.

"It's just as I said." His thumbs wipe my tears on either side before he drops a finger on my lips. "Not now. We shouldn't talk about it now."

He's right—not now. But that it sounds like a promise to talk with me about it *sometime* fills me with something unexpected for us—hope. Beautiful, wretched, unfair hope.

His finger finds my chin and lifts my head until my damp eyes meet his. His boyish smile brings one of my own, and my body relaxes into it, especially when he says, "Come back to me, Venus. Be with me. Here. Now."

"I am," I assure him, pushing the rest away. "I promise I am."

His grin widens as his hands roam over me. I brush my face against his chest, closing my eyes to his scent. Mint and pine mix delightfully with his soap—the same as I remember.

"Kiss me, Venus," he whispers. "Kiss me and tell me what you want to do to me."

My face flushes just thinking about it, and with trembling fingers, I undo his pants. He kicks off his shoes, kisses me hard, and suddenly, we're at it again—full steam.

"I wanted to do it *then*," I say, breaking away just enough for him to hear me, "but couldn't find the courage."

"You? I don't believe—"

My hands slide under his boxers, squeezing his tight ass. "Sit down."

He obeys as I tug his briefs away, leaving him naked. I drop to my knees between his—me on the floor and him on the bed's edge—and run my fingers up his legs, watching him, watching me.

He is hard and thick and beautiful—I never expected to consider any genitalia, outside the plant kingdom, as beautiful. But he is. Long, lean, and so familiar behind the decade since the last time I touched him. His erection nestles against my breasts as he leans up to kiss me.

He nibbles my bottom lip. "Go slow," he says, pulling my hair aside and holding it out of the way. "Please, take your time with me, Venus."

He groans when my lips wrap around his tip, my tongue swirling as I explore him. A gentle rise and fall ensues, sometimes my mouth, sometimes my fingers, sometimes my breasts, and sometimes just my tongue, lapping the length of him. He leans back slightly, in a raspy growl, so that he can see me better. I tilt my head, eyes locking on his as I pleasure him. He almost looks pained by how good it feels, gasping, biting his lips, his brow pinching, his hands tightening on my hair. I slide my free hand up over his and squeeze, assuring him that it's okay to grip my head and tug on my hair. That I like the pressure. And with an expelled, "Fuuuccckk," his fingers tangle in my hair and pull harder.

It's strange how pleasure and pain often go together.

He tenses beneath me as I take him deeply in my mouth. And again. And again.

Though proficient in oral sex, I don't often offer it, unless I'm feeling generous. Sex is about me, about getting *mine*, and this typically isn't much of a turn on for me.

But here, now, I'm on fire over doing this to Henry. I want to taste him, to feel him hit the back of my throat. I want him to give me everything.

"Venus," he says in a shaky voice. "I'm close."

So, I pause, only long enough to tell him what he told me downstairs. "Come for me, Henry. Right here."

His hand tightens on my hair as I slide my tongue down him again. His hips press into me with delicious force, insisting that I take all of him. I match his rhythm and go deeper.

"Fuck, Venus." He trembles under me as his muscles flex. I feel him, ready to explode. My eyes find him in the beautiful chaos, and stay fixed as he cries out, filling my mouth until it spills out of the corners. I swallow and wipe my lips.

He falls back, sighing my name. "Venus. Ah, Venus."

I kiss his thighs and hips, making my way up him as he recovers. "My name..." I straddle his lap and tackle him against the bed in a flurry of kisses. "...will be the only one you'll say, too."

He laughs, wrapping his arms around me and flipping me over. Pinning me to the bed, he kisses my forehead, my nose, and then my lips. "Venus," he says again. "You're right. Damn, that was... unexpected."

"If it's to be one night, I want everything," I say between his peppering kisses.

"You'll have it." He caresses my nipple before lowering his head to kiss it. A moan escapes when I feel the light scrape of his teeth. But then he sits up, hovering over me, his eyes darting over every inch of me, like I'm a delicious buffet, and he can't decide what he wants first.

"I like you looking at me," I say, unable to remember the last time I felt this beautiful. This wanted.

"I like looking at you." He stares, running his fingers gently over me. "I've dreamed this a million times, but I never captured *you*. You're art, Venus. Fucking beautiful. Always have been, but now it's... it's..."

"Real," I finish, breathless and teary again.

"Real." He agrees, but our smiles dip simultaneously. *Real, but temporary. Only temporary.*

He takes my hand and brings it to his face, kissing my fingers one by one around my rings. He thumbs over the mood ring he gave me, and I wonder if he remembers it. He slips my bracelets off, setting them aside, and kisses the underside of my wrist. Softly, sweetly, teasingly, he moves along my arm. Then, he exchanges it for the other and does the same.

With my bracelets and his glasses on the bedside table, he returns to me, kissing my lips and nibbling my chin as he moves down the length of me. He watches me as he explores, lips, tongue, teeth, and I'm swept into the past again, memories that always make me smile whenever I latch onto them.

The first time I tapped on his bedroom window and the relief when he let me in.

In high school, when he pulled me behind the stacks in the library and kissed me against the sad romance section until we accidentally knocked over an entire row. *"They're just jealous of us,"* he said, smiling, as we set them right again. And I laughed because books don't get jealous, but it was a cute retort.

That night on the Jeep's tailgate, when we watched the most mesmerizing sunset between talk of engineering and environmental impacts. His anxiety over asking me to the prom was endearing, until those nerves transferred to me. *Normal couple things.* Normal seemed an impossible feat—for me, nothing had been. Not my family. Not my education. Not even us. *Normal* couldn't exist for us, not the way he wanted or deserved. *That* night proved it.

Come back to me, Venus. Be with me. Here. Now.

His lips trail across my stomach. His beard tickles my skin, and a moan escapes as his hands grip my thighs, forcefully pulling me to his mouth. I cry out, "Henry," when his tongue circles the same place he left his fingerprint.

"Be as loud as you want. It's just us here," he whispers, his breath hitting my clit enough to make me moan again. My back arches as arrows of delight seem to shoot from his hot tongue through the rest of me, hitting me in the loveliest places—the small of my back, the hollow of my throat, the tips of my toes, and the length of my spine.

But then, he stops. "I want to see you better."

He repositions us with me on top, my hands tight around the slats of the headboard, his face under me. Watching me. As I arch and writhe, and he undoes me all over again. The last orgasm was good—this is better. Stronger. Closer. Heart-stopping. Brain-rewiring. Muscle-memory reshaping around it. I won't be the same again.

I'm still trembling and calling out his name when he eases out from under me and says, "I love watching you come. God, I wish we could've done this all along."

Sadness swoops in again, but I shove it away. *Not now.* My hand goes to his rough cheek. "I need you inside me."

"Fuck, please," he says, leaning away to reach his bedside table, presumably for a condom.

I pull him back to me, draping my leg over his hip to hold him close. "Henry, wait. I want you bare… if you're comfortable with it. I haven't been with anyone since my last check, have an IUD, and I've never gone without a condom before."

He smirks, pushing hair away from my eyes. "I haven't been with anyone since I was last checked, either… If you're sure."

"Yes." I take his bottom lip in mine, sucking it gently. "Only with you."

"Only with you," he repeats, kissing me. "Nothing between us."

A moment later, we both cry out when he pushes into me. The remnants of my dying orgasm flare again with his thrust, like when we billowed hot embers to reignite our campfires back then—steady, strong breaths making it hotter and hotter. I lean up, kissing his chest from underneath him, and hear a gentle wheeze behind his quickening breaths. Worry spikes in me, but I don't want to draw attention to it.

"Henry, trade places with me," I say, and he readily agrees.

He rests against the headboard while I climb on top of him. I ride him deeply, but slowly, as he watches, his side-smile etched on his cheek. He grabs my thighs, guiding me, but when he sees that I'm doing fine on my own, his hands roam softly over my back, through my hair, across my chest, and then slide down my arms. His fingers intertwine with mine, locking us together.

"You feel so good, Venus," he says, breathless but no longer wheezing. "This is what I've always wanted. You and me, like this."

"Exactly like this." I battle the fresh tears cresting in my eyes. I want to tell him that I still love him, to cry over how good it is and how much I've missed him, to trap him inside me and never let go.

Instead, I hold his hands tightly, smile easily, and bring him in deeply until we both cry out. A hard pulse and a desperate moan from him, and I see it on his face, his exquisite pleasure. His eyes stay open, fixed on mine, as I come again, and he finishes with me.

I smile as he bites his bottom lip and relaxes inside me. "I love watching *you* come."

He growls and laughs, leaning up to kiss my nipple and tug me close. "Ah, that was… so fucking good."

With his head against my chest, I wrap my arms around his shoulders and rake a hand through his soft hair. I feel his heavy breaths on my skin as he tries to settle down.

"Let me get your inhaler."

He groans but releases me. I lean over the bed to the floor and slide his inhaler from his jeans pocket. He takes a quick puff and shakes his head, staring at the plastic and metal device in his hand.

"I don't usually need it this much," he tells me, as if ashamed.

"The air quality today is 61, moderate range," I report, lying on my side. "It's normal to have—"

"Venus, it's not the air quality. Not entirely. It's emotional these days. You run away with your big feelings. I can't breathe with mine."

"Then, you understand me." My words go unanswered, making me wonder if I said something wrong. I sit up, unsure what to do. "I'm sorry. Do you want me to go?"

He gives me a funny look. "You said one night—I want a *whole* night. I want to make you come as many times as you'll let me."

"Yes, please."

And, we do. We lay on his bed for a while, talking about nothing in particular and staying away from the two very different worlds awaiting us outside this room. We reminisce, good memories only, and we cuddle, listening to music and playing with each other's hair. We have sex again. And again. We raid his fridge and binge on juice boxes and apple slices. Then, I come undone for him again, and again, and again.

When it's very late, and we're very tired, we get comfortable on his bed. I roll on my side, staring out at the bridge lights through his window, and he curls up behind me, nesting perfectly against my body, just like we used to do. His arms tighten around me, giving me the pressure he knows I like and often need.

And all I can do is cry. He's done exactly as I asked—he ruined me.

CHAPTER 15
Henry

SHE TRIES TO HIDE IT, but I know she's crying. She makes no sound, only I feel the slight tremor of her sobs against my chest. I understand, but all I can do is hold her closer. Venus Blake is having big feelings.

So, am I.

Her vulnerability, her body, her beauty, everything about this night has been incredible. Mind-blowing, even. I never knew it could be *this* good. And she stayed, despite her feelings and the endless tugs by her impulse-prone puppeteer. She fought it all. For me.

That's how it's always been with us. She's the fighter. And until she left, I was the beneficiary of her wins. My long-held anger drifts away as I hold her. As is often the case with anger, it stemmed from a misunderstanding. I thought I was the blameless victim of her coldness and impulsivity. But her leaving was my fault, too. I pushed for us to go to UNC-Chapel Hill together. I believed, for once, that I'd be the hero who would save her at college by being the voice of reason when she needed it and holding her at night. I arrogantly thought that I'd be enough to turn college into a dream when the rest of her education had been a nightmare. I held myself in such fucking high esteem for it, too—taking her with me—when really, I just wanted her for myself and needed her to make me brave. I wasn't her hero—I was a selfish coward. God, she must've been under so much unbearable pressure. Pressure I caused.

I'm the asshole.

For trying to push her into the life I wanted, like everyone else had.

For failing to understand the *real* her.

But I want to. Not just what she's told me or what we've done, but *all* of her. I want to *understand* Venus Blake the way she understands the inner workings of flowers, to make up for not really knowing her then.

Only, my wants and feelings don't matter after tonight. She'll disappear once she's done with her obligatory summer. I'll resume my settled existence. And we'll both get to see if her experiment—and yes, it was an experiment—truly worked.

But I already know it hasn't. It's impossible to get her out of my system. Our confusing, frustrating, sad, and intoxicatingly beautiful night has only solidified what I already know—my heart belongs to Venus.

A gentle sob catches in her sigh, like she might be reaching the same conclusion, and my arms tighten. "It's okay. I'm here. We're together. Everything's okay," I whisper, like we used to when we were young.

But my words feel empty.

I want to roll her over and kiss her tears away. To clamp down on the tiniest bit of hope for us, like a flytrap would a bug. But there's no happy ending here. Not for the fly. Not for us.

So, maybe it's best to let the tears flow, I decide as one travels over my nose and into her hair.

She falls asleep—I can almost pinpoint the exact moment by the familiar gentleness in her breathing and the subtle, final release of her tension. It's like she melts against me. In her quiet, I find mine, slipping into a deep sleep.

When I wake, I feel ridiculously energized, like I've slept for days in mere hours. I think to stir her with soft kisses and engage in another round—I could never have enough of her—but she sleeps so peacefully that I don't want to disturb her. So, I slowly ease out from behind her with the same careful precision I use with Olly, and I close the door to the bedroom.

In the open living room and kitchen, I find Uncle Jay's wooden blue jay on my desk, atop the annotated paper from Mrs. Kwon. She was right—Buttercup's story isn't finished.

Or at least, I'm not finished with her.

My desk chair creaks when I fall into it, holding the bird, overrun with emotions, and flooded with our stories—stories that have taken on a whole new perspective after everything she purged last night.

I think of her falling from the tree and wonder, for the first time, if she'd been running from something that day as I had. I remember her hidden sadness, her stiff upper lip, the distance she kept, how she wouldn't hold my hand in the halls at school the few times I tried, how she said she was fine when she wasn't—I wonder, now, if she's been running this whole time.

Until last night. With me.

I switch on the desk lamp, move all my notes aside, and find a blank composition notebook in my desk drawer. My fingers slide over the black-and-white cover. Composition notebooks remind me of Venus. I set the bird on the edge of my desk, recalling what Uncle Jay said about being there for her as many times as she needed—a mission I failed. I long to capture everything about her and us into one place. I couldn't purge her from my system with sex, but perhaps I can through words, ink, and paper.

To get to the heart of us. The heart of her. And not for some damn book, but for me. To have her exist somewhere other than at the core of me.

To have something to hold on to when she's gone. Again.

And she *will* leave. She always leaves.

I reach for my favorite pen and start writing my earliest memories of her—the dirty girl in class, the tree-climber, the hero against bullies— and give every thought a place on the page just as she gives detailed lines to her drawings. Smiles find me through the stories. So, do tears, dripping onto the page and smearing the ink.

But it's fitting for us, as if love can't exist without pain. And I still ache for her. Even with her in my bed right now, with only a few feet and a wall between us.

An hour or so later, I look up to see gentle bands of sunshine creeping over buildings to hit the river outside my window. I feel satiated in a different way, that parts of our story have made it to paper, even if no one ever reads it but me. Though some stories are safe with Olly, there's more to us than childhood adventures, and I want to relive those memories, feel them, and see them from new angles. To discover our true history. My fingers crack and feel tight from effort. I stand, stretch, and make coffee.

I collect her things—her discarded clothes, scarf, boots, and phone from downstairs. I shake out her wrinkled dress and bring it to my face, inhaling her scent on it. She still uses rose-scented lotion. She smells like a botanist. I drape the dress over my leather chair to smooth out the wrinkles, and set her boots and phone beside it.

I resist the urge to rejoin her in bed—it's still early, and remembering what she said about sleepless nights, I want her to rest.

And I want to keep her here.

I have my coffee on the flat roof outside our apartment, presently cluttered with bikes and outdoor toys. The sun dances across the water, though the world remains dim and quiet. I love this time of morning.

On the Riverwalk below, I spot Derek walking his dog Pepper. I want to thank him for his kindness. However beautiful Venus is, I doubt she receives much positive attention, and DeeDee lavished it on her last night.

The open sign flickers on in the bakery window on the corner, and I imagine introducing Venus to their decadent cinnamon rolls—she loves sweets.

I rush inside, pull on sneakers, and grab my wallet and keys.

CHAPTER 16
Venus

MY EYES FLUTTER with the soft light coming through the window and a thud from somewhere. In a breath, it all comes back to me like a dream—I've never had a more perfect night. But the bed feels cold beside me. I sit up with a start and say, "Henry?"

He's not there.

I wander through his apartment wearing his t-shirt. His place has been recently painted, given the faded smell in the air, mingling with the scent of coffee. Sage green covers the bedroom, hall, and the adorable room across from Henry's, presumably Olly's. I peek in the open door to find a twin bed covered in superhero linens—no surprise, given Henry's underwear choices in elementary school. Toys and books fill the shelves. Hooks on the walls hold jackets, a cape, and a baseball glove. Library books form a wonky stack near the bed. I wonder if Maggie, a librarian, hand-picked them like she sometimes did for Henry and me. Colored pencils and markers are scattered across his desk. I step in to view his unfinished artwork—a rudimentary drawing of a man and a boy, both wearing glasses, staring up at a large tree with a woman standing on a high branch. She wears a mask and a billowing cape.

It reminds me of the day I helped Henry find his home.

But it's clearly a figment of young Olly's hero-laced imagination. I backstep from the room, feeling guilty for invading the child's personal space.

The living room, kitchen, and Henry's office space are painted a soft yellow. The open space is full of bright windows that showcase the outdoor roof space around it. The low rumble of air purifiers catches my attention—there's one at both ends of the room. Henry needs plants, though, and while the efficacy of indoor plants in improving air quality is widely debated, I still catalog a mental list of ones to bring him.

But the list dissolves into brain dust. He doesn't want plant advice from me. He doesn't want *anything* from me, except to let go and move on. To commit to someone else.

I won't linger. I just…

Unused camping equipment occupies the corner near the small dining table—an unpackaged tent, an air mattress, sleeping bags, a propane cooking stove, tools, cooking utensils, and an almost laughable assortment of contingency items, like a battery-operated radio, sunblocks in varying SPFs and application styles, bug sprays, and enough first aid to handle a small army. This all sits beside a converted tackle box with the words "Olly's Ouchy Kit" scrawled on an index card with "9-1-1."

That looks like Maggie's doing.

Regardless, I wonder what their plans are, and why these things haven't been used or even unpackaged yet. But it's not my business.

I feel like a trespasser, but I want to soak up as much of Henry as I can. It's my last chance to be *in* his life.

Action figures clutter the coffee table in the living room. He uses the same desk from his childhood bedroom with the ink stain on the left corner where one of my pens leaked over my hands and dribbled onto the surface—Maggie wasn't happy. It's crowded with papers and books, mostly historical tomes about local lore and legends. A carved blue jay seems to stare up at me from a composition book, which sits closed with a pen sticking out of it. I don't intrude, though a sneaky part of me wants to.

I turn from the desk, and my breath hitches at the framed prints over his red sofa. First, the black and white ink drawing I created of two crows squawking outside Henry's bedroom window one morning hangs in the middle. I recall sitting at his desk, watching them as he slept near me. When he woke up and came over to see what caught my interest, he laughed and said, *"Vee, two crows… It's an attempted murder."* I couldn't stop laughing because, technically, the group would need a party of three to be described as a murder.

I gave him the eight-by-ten drawing a few days later with *An Attempted Murder of Crows* written in delicate handwriting across the bottom. He handed it back to me. *"Vee, an artist is supposed to sign her work."*

I thought to debate him—I'm no artist. I'm a scientist. But his coy grin convinced me to let it go.

I lean closer to the framed drawing to see my scribbled *VB* in the bottom corner.

I'm stunned he kept it, let alone framed it. Stunned that it now hangs over his sofa along with two of my other artful gifts: the robin's nest with three eggs we found on a low-hanging branch when I finally got him to climb a live oak tree in the woods, and Frank the Frog, the inspiration for his tattoo.

Tears cloud my eyes as I remember his promise to keep Frank always—he did, twice over. Kept promises are a sign of love, not anger or disappointment. Regret swirls for the promises I couldn't keep to him.

A familiar current of unwanted energy courses through me, making my hands fist at my sides. I don't know how to feel about any of this—that my art hangs on his walls and is inked into his chest, that we shared such an incredible night, that I'm here at all. That he's not.

I turn toward his worn leather chair, with my dress hanging over the side, my underwear and socks neatly folded, my boots on the floor, and my phone tucked inside; my foggy understanding becomes clear.

One night meant *one night*. It's the morning. I need to leave.

I should commend him for avoiding an awkward and emotional goodbye. This is probably best. Still, as I scurry to get dressed, tug on my boots, and collect my jewelry from his bedside table, I feel disappointed not to have the morning with him, at least.

But that wasn't the agreement.

I make the bed and fold his shirt to leave neatly for him. But catching his clean, minty scent on it, I hold it to my face and reconsider. Would he miss it? I pull it over my dress, deciding that I deserve a treasure, since he has so many from me.

Walking through the apartment, I hunt for excuses not to go. What about the garden? What about a goodbye? What about that vague promise to talk *later* that he mentioned last night? But anything more would complicate what I promised would be simple. Last night's experiment can't work if I linger.

So, ignoring what my heart wants, I do what's best for us both and leave.

CHAPTER 17

Henry

I MEET Derek in the grassy patch near the bakery, where Pepper lazily roams as far as his leash will allow.

"Pepper's early-morning wake-up calls are going to be the death of me," Derek quips as I hand him a coffee from the bakery. "It's worse than having a baby."

My brow cocks at the comparison. "At least you don't have to change diapers."

"Yet," he counters with a laugh. "Pepper won't be young forever. Oh, but you might be if you keep having nights like that. Look at you."

Derek glances me over, waving his long fingernails over me like they might be giving me a body scan. "Oh, my… someone got lucky last night. Your reunion with Venus went very, very well."

A sheepish laugh rumbles from me. "You can't possibly know that."

His lips purse. "Honey, I know the difference between everyday Henry and the Henry who's just had his mind blown, partly because this is the first time I've seen him. Was it that good?"

I lean against the railing, trying to fight my flushing cheeks, but failing. "It was everything I've ever wanted."

"I can't say I'm surprised. Venus adores you—it was all over her perfect little face. And you adore her, too. The looks you were giving each other reminded me of my early days with Tyler—ah, that man still delights my very soul, even after twenty years. I never would've become DeeDee without him."

"What do you mean?"

Derek shrugs and twiddles the leash in his hands. "That's the best thing about love—the freedom to be whatever you want to be. Even if the world hates you, your soulmate stands by you. A blanket in the cold. An umbrella in the rain. A shelter in the storm. Love is freedom. If not for Tyler, I don't think I would've been brave enough to become DeeDee. I knew he'd love me whether I wore a suit or a dress, whether I failed or succeeded, or, hell, even if he had to call me by two different names depending on my outfit. He still fumbles that bit on occasion, but that's okay."

He laughs, and I join in with an appreciative chuckle. "What if someone believes she's a cactus when she's a sunflower?"

"Oh, that's a thoughtful question." Derek's hands find his hips. "I know Jay's version of things, but tell me, what's the story with you two?"

"Childhood best friends turned high school sweethearts turned... nothing. I wasn't there for her like I should've been, and she left when things got too hard."

"But she's back?"

"Temporarily, but she'll leave again."

"Why?"

"She's convinced everyone's better off without her. Cactus."

He nods, like he totally understands, though I can't imagine how.

"There's no future for us," I tell him. "It's complicated. Too much history. Too many obstacles. We agreed to one night only."

He scoffs. "Don't try to control the uncontrollable, Henry. Love isn't complicated. People are. If the love is strong enough, it'll bulldoze right through any complication. You have to want it and believe in each other badly enough."

Pepper yaps at his feet, as if bored with our conversation.

Derek rests a hand on my shoulder. "Just be delicate with her, help her see the sunflower behind the cactus. Then, and only then, she might feel safe enough to bloom."

I smile as he tugs Pepper away.

"Thanks for the cup of joe. Now, go to her," he says, walking backwards. "She might not like waking up in your bed alone."

Fuck, I hadn't thought of that.

I quickstep down the Riverwalk and cross the street to the museum, excited to see the look on Venus's face when she bites into the decadent cinnamon roll I got for her.

And then kissing the sweetness from her lips.

But Dr. Blake's Land Rover screeches to a stop at the corner before abruptly turning. She's already left.

"Damn it!" I yell, mainly at myself. I mope back to my apartment, feeling utterly foolish—*why didn't I leave her a note*—and more alone than ever now that she's gone.

But it could've been a relief for her. Venus is better at quick exits than goodbyes, and I would've tried to get her to stay. Still, I roam the apartment, berating myself for giving her the impression that I wanted her to leave.

The empty bed.

Her things gone.

The quiet apartment.

The sweets uneaten.

Our one chance at its abrupt end.

This isn't what I wanted. But it makes things easier.

I spot her scarf on the floor behind my leather chair and scoop it up like a treasure. The silky fabric molds to my hands as I bunch it in my grip. It's red with pink peonies bursting from its edges. Lovely and delicate, like her. I bring it to my face and inhale.

Rose from her lotion, and rosemary from her shampoo—*her*.

I plop to the edge of my leather chair, remembering Mom tying Venus's first scarf into her hair. Mom invited her over for Saturday morning pancakes. Venus's wild hair kept dipping into the syrup on her plate. Venus didn't care, but Mom snapped her fingers and said, *"Venus, wouldn't it be nice to have that hair out of your way?"* To which Venus perked up like it was a novel idea, and said, *"It would help when I do my experiments."*

Mom returned from her bedroom with a standard red bandana, swept Venus's hair back, and tied it into a headband, holding her hair behind her shoulders. Venus used the bandana every day after and practiced using it in new ways—in a top knot, half-tie, a ponytail, or even just around her neck until she needed it.

Noticing her loyalty to the gift, Mom eventually gave her alternatives—hand-me-downs from her closet and my grandmother's. Mom would pick up new ones at thrift stores and yard sales to gift to her.

Even when their relationship was strained, Mom collected gifts like these for Venus.

The one in my hand was my grandmother's. The edges are frayed. Ink stains one end. But it's just like Venus to have kept it. Just like her to still use it.

I inhale it again, wondering if it's okay to keep it, wondering how long I can go without washing my sheets or pillowcases to hold her scent there, wondering how long it will take for her to disappear from them, too.

Scarf wrapped in my hand, I return to the notebook on my desk, purging my thoughts onto the pages, the paper my new confessional. Then, when my fingers cramp and other tasks for the day call to me, I tuck the notebook and scarf into my bedside table drawer, determined to put her out of my mind.

For now.

CHAPTER 18

Henry

MARNIE, Marigold, and Dot arrive at lunchtime for our meeting to discuss the museum's progress. When she first presented her plan to turn Uncle Jay's campy curiosity museum into the Weird But True Museum in April, we thought it'd be a quick renovation—an updated design, a few new exhibits, an escape room add-on, and, of course, the upper garden.

But we've encountered problems ranging from termites to plumbing issues that have put us behind.

Today, though, there's only one setback concerning the group.

"So, what's the deal with the garden?" Dot asks. "We have the supplies. Want me to throw it together? I'm sure there's a YouTube—"

"No, it's a complicated process, and we don't have the plants, regardless," Marnie huffs, with one hand on her hip and the other hugging her Trapper Keeper. "I've left a message for Dr. Blake, but Ivy tells me he's traveling and won't be home for weeks. He purposefully left you in Venus's care. I'm so, so sorry, Henry."

Dot laughs. "Love-trapped, like I said."

"Have you recovered from yesterday, or are you still upset?" Marnie asks.

"I'm not upset." I motion to the spread I've arranged across the table—fruit, cheese, crackers, cookies, and lemonade. Marigold takes the bait, but the other two stare at me with scrutiny. "I'm fine."

"Yeah, how did the tiki bar reunion go, huh?" Dot tosses back a chunk of cheese, eyeing me suspiciously.

"We settled our differences," I inform vaguely.

They share a bewildered glance. "You don't seem pleased, though," Marnie points out.

"Yeah, what gives?" Dot asks while Marigold peers over her sketchbook. "Will she install the garden at least?"

The three perceptive women await an explanation. My shoulders slump under the heaviness I've felt since Venus left.

"Um, well," I start to say when a loud pound on the door interrupts. "I'll get it. Enjoy the snacks."

The man standing outside the front door wears a tattered t-shirt, worn blue jeans, old clown shoes, and a gap-toothed smile. "Henry? Is that you?"

"Yeah, I'm Henry Greene," I say, extending my hand.

He slings the leather strap of a rectangular black case over his shoulder to accept my handshake. He's in his fifties, bald with a beard, and with more tattoos than Venus, which says a lot. His tattoos are more traditional—skulls and swords stand out the most.

"Don't remember me, eh? It's been a while. I'm Eric the Sword-Swallower."

He pauses, like this information should register with me, but my brow pinches unsurely.

"Eric Massie. I was good friends with Jay. We used to hang out here at the museum. Last time I saw you, you were half this height. How'd you get so tall?"

"Um, growing up does that to you." A vague, misty recollection ghosts in my thoughts, but I can't latch on.

He points to the counter behind me and edges inside. "It's Jaybird! I carved that for him as a good luck charm. I'm handy with knives, you know." He picks up the blue jay sitting next to the register and gives it a toss between his hands.

Once again, I don't know how it got there, as it was on my desk upstairs this morning.

I shut the door and run a hand through my hair. "You've heard about Uncle Jay?"

His head droops in reverence. "I wish I'd been here. Been at sea with the cruise liners for a few years. I'm sorry for your loss. Jay was a good man—the best, really."

"Yeah, thanks," I say as he meanders around the entrance.

"He always spoke highly of you, the history buff, and your kid. He said Henry and Olly would rule his kingdom one day," Eric chuckles, motioning to the building around us. "Didn't know that day would come so soon. But the last time we spoke, he seemed off to me."

I gape at the emotional hit, hearing a stranger say that. "Really? How?"

His bony shoulders bob in a shrug. "He said he'd been tired, didn't feel like doing much. The Jay I knew never sat still long enough to have a dull moment. You know?"

"Um, yeah, I know." I think of his collection of concert tickets, the motorcycle we sold after he passed, and the ghost, alien, and monster-hunting adventures he'd tell us about at Sunday dinners, until he stopped coming. My regret sharpens for never questioning his excuses.

"When Jay slowed down, he spent too much time in his head," he says with insight that impresses and irritates me at once. But I start to remember him—an odd man in the corner behind the counter, leaning his chair back on two legs. He asked Mom on a date a week after she kicked Dale out, and I remember being relieved that she said no. He and Jay laughed a lot. Over beers. Over reruns. Over weird YouTube videos of hauntings and possessions. Over stories that often freaked me out as a kid, at least until I told them to Venus.

She would inevitably convince me that they were scientifically unsound—I appreciated that.

Still, I feel uneasy around him and troubled by our conversation. He either understood Jay's distress better than his own family, who were right here, or he's just saying he did, which makes him disingenuous. Either way, I'm not in the mood.

"Mr. Massie, it's been nice to talk, but—"

"I hear you're reopening the place soon. Mind if I take a look around for old time's sake?"

He doesn't wait for an answer, but heads to the main room through the short hall, where we're set up on a makeshift table and mismatched chairs between newly constructed displays and boxes of artifacts.

"Oh, hello, ladies." He bows dramatically.

"Guys, this is Eric Massie, a friend of Uncle Jay's," I say.

"Eric the Sword-Swallower," he says, shaking Marnie's hand.

"Eric the Sword-Swallower," he follows with Dot, who snorts.

"Eric the Sword-Swallower," he says to Marigold, who offers a brief wave instead of shaking his hand.

He salutes her before he helps himself to the snacks on the table.

"Sword-swallower, huh? Is that some kind of euphemism?" Dot questions.

"Ah, no. I swallow swords for a living." He hands them business cards from his shirt pocket. "I'm also a juggler, acrobat, and unicyclist. Jay used to let me perform here in the museum for tips. I was a big hit! I'd be happy to give a free demonstration."

"No!" My abrupt refusal surprises everyone, especially me. "I mean, sorry. I didn't mean for that to come out so harshly. It's just—"

"I understand, Henry. Not everyone can handle swordplay," Eric says. "I remember you were a bit squeamish."

"I'm not squeamish," I counter, pushing my glasses higher on my nose. "But we're in the middle of our meeting. So, if you don't mind—"

His hands go up submissively after he takes a handful of grapes from the platter. "Sorry, son. I didn't mean to intrude. Jay wanted me to check in on you and the place."

My eyes narrow. "I'm fine, but it's not a good time. It's been a strange few days, and we need to regroup."

"Looky here, Mr. Sword-Swallower," Dot says with authority. "Henry's got a full plate with this place, Olly, and losing his uncle. Besides, he's gone a bit bonkers over his first love showing up in town—"

"Venus is back?" he says, brightening. "Jay must be spinning tires on his Harley in heaven to hear that!"

"You know about Venus and me?" I ask.

"Jay thought you and Rapunzel would end up together," he says, surprising me again with Jay's nickname for her. "He told me you were lonely—that having a kid wasn't the same as having a companion. If only he could get Venus back, he said."

Marnie coos, "Aw, it's like he knew."

Dot nods. "Yep, he knew."

"No, he didn't. There's no getting back with Venus." I take a puff on my inhaler to fight the tight ache in my chest. "I never had her to begin with, and I don't want to talk about it."

Again, my words are stern and very unlike me.

But I'm bothered by Mr. Massie's persistence and inside knowledge. He's highlighting my pre-existing guilt over not being there for my uncle and, at the same time, rubbing it in that my uncle wasn't so oblivious about me. Jay not only noticed my loneliness, something I thought I hid well, but also worried about me, enough to mention it to *this* guy.

"Mr. Massie, may I show you what we have planned for the museum?" Marnie says with her usual chipperness, deflecting attention from my bad mood.

"Sure thing," he says, following Marnie to some of the more finished displays.

Dot's boots thud on the hardwood floor, and her wallet chain slaps against her dark jeans as she closes in on me. Her hair always makes me think of black licorice, which mirrors her personality—sweet but tough, and maybe not for everyone. But like Marnie, she understands people, and she's quickly become a good friend. "Henry, you okay? Your tension scale is registering about an eight."

"More like a nine," I admit.

She plants a hard slap on my back and says, "Your boxer briefs must be stuck high up there, huh? What's gotten in your craw?"

Marigold winces at the question, and, finding such talk distasteful, she retreats to Marnie's side.

"Don't know if I like that guy," I whisper.

"Marnie'll keep an eye on him. Let's chat in my office."

Her office is the back of her tricked-out work van, where she swings the doors open, sits, and pats the metal beside her. I follow suit because why not let this day get weirder? I've already unloaded my internal drama on Marnie. Why not do the same with my contractor?

Overhead, gray clouds circulate, and the humidity is near stifling. When I FaceTimed Olly this morning, he shared that his mom and Gregory, the fellow doctor she's seeing, were taking him out on Gregory's boat. I wonder if they took the impending weather into account. If he's wearing his life jacket. Ifs, all the ifs.

"So, you came to a truce with Venus?"

"I misunderstood the entire situation. I wasn't there for her, didn't *see* her," I breathe out. "And this guy shows up, reminding me that I didn't see Jay either."

"You saw what *he* wanted you to see," she says, surely. "I expect the same is true with Venus."

"What do you mean?"

"Well, you're a sweet dude. You're a great dad, always ten steps ahead of Olly, your students rave about you, and, whenever we're here, you pamper us with drinks and treats. You like taking care of people. I can't speak for Venus, but... " she says with a shrug, "Sometimes, people just want to be loved, Henry. Not helped. Not talked to or advised. Not taken care of. Loved."

Her words mix with Venus's from last night. "She left because she didn't want to be my burden. She didn't want me taking care of her. I get that now. But I don't think she wants love, either."

Dot scoffs. "Everyone wants love. *Everyone*, Henry. Anyone who says otherwise probably needs it more than most."

"I just spent the best night of my life with her. *That's* what we agreed to. It was her idea—one night together to let go and move on."

She laughs, like she's fully aware of the folly of our plan. "How's that working out for you?"

"She's been gone six hours, and I can't think of anything else. There's no future for us. I'm here. I have Olly. She'll leave at the end of the summer. There's no point in it. In us."

"No point? Dude! As smart as you are, you can be really dense, my guy. Fuck the agreement. Fuck what happened when you were kids. And fuck broken hearts—you already have those, anyway. You care about this woman, and she cares about you. Why not love her while you have the chance and let the future take care of itself?"

Pelicans squawk overhead. Tourists line up for the river cruises on the Riverwalk, and the tiki boat bobs hopefully in the water. It's another beautiful, though gray day in Wilmington. As I muddle through Dot's direct advice, she rises from the space beside me and stretches like she's crossed an invisible finish line.

"Thanks, Dot," I say sheepishly. "Maybe you're—"

The door pushes open, and Marnie ushers Mr. Massie outside. "We'll be in touch," she calls weakly down the sidewalk.

She turns, looking uncharacteristically bothered. "He volunteered an unsavory opinion about our new color scheme. I told him he had to go."

Dot snort-laughs. "Don't mess with Marnie's color scheme."

"Good. Thanks. Let's get back to work."

CHAPTER 19
Venus

"HOW COULD you do that to me? To *Henry*? The shock brought on an asthma attack." I fold my arms over my chest and glare at my father through the screen.

"Oh, heavens. Is he alright?"

"Yes, but he might not have been. He couldn't *breathe*, Dad."

"Hmm." He rubs the scruff of his chin. "His asthma is a variable I failed to take into account—for that, I do apologize. Ivy has already left a few angry messages."

"You shouldn't have meddled. Or forced us together. Or misled us. How did you think this would work?"

His brow quirks into a question. "I hypothesized a reunion would precipitate a rekindling of affection. I hoped you'd remember how much you loved each other."

My anger subsides. Having my father take action on my behalf, however misguided, is appreciated. His theory wasn't exactly wrong, though he misjudged the outcome.

I'm devastated, all over again.

Everything's worse now. I knew it would be—knew when I suggested my wild idea to Henry. The jagged cracks in my heart are now gushing wounds because I *know* what I gave up. I *know* what I've lost. I *know* how he tastes and feels and loves. I *know* how he lives, and that he's the incredible man I knew he would be. I *know* what I'll never have again.

I try not to use vague analogies, but it hurts like hell. Like deep, deep hell. I've loved as much as I'll ever love and been soul-linked to someone more than I ever will again.

"Venus, are you alright?"

My father's voice pulls me to the present, and I straighten my back. "No, but Henry and I have reached an understanding—"

"Oh, wonderful!" he perks up. "I knew you could—"

"We said our goodbyes properly this time. It's over."

Dad's shoulders droop two inches, and his brow crinkles with worry lines. "Hmm, I confess that I saw your latest field journal and your writings to Henry. I don't understand how you can hold that much love in your heart for someone and decide it's over. I don't believe it's over for you, Venus."

I shake my head. "Yes, it is. It has to be. Now."

Dad nods, his expression tired and disappointed—one I'm very accustomed to.

With an emptying sigh, I admit, "It's the normal couple things that hurt me, Dad."

"Normal couple things?"

"Henry's a teacher, father, and a business owner. He's settled and stable and deserves someone who's the same. Henry wants and needs normal couple things. I can't give him that. Never could."

"Hmm, one might argue that these so-called 'normal couple things' are unique to the couple. Look at Christie and me. We have normal couple things, but they're ours by design. I believe that everyone designs their own normal. Normal is what you decide it to be. Besides, why aim for normal when you can have extraordinary?"

I take a breath, wondering what that would look like for me. "Um, your thoughts are intriguing and worth consideration."

"Venus, it's been a decade. You don't know what Henry wants," he says, "but you should ask him. Better yet, ask yourself."

CHAPTER 20
Henry

MARNIE'S PHONE buzzes between the leftover bits of my snack tray and her open Trapper Keeper as we're finishing our meeting.

She answers it on speaker. "Hi, Dr. Blake. Thanks for returning my call."

"Yes, of course. I apologize for the shock of my switcheroo. That wasn't my intention."

"What *was* your intention?" I ask, leaning into the phone. "It's Henry, by the way."

"Oh, Henry, I was about to ask Marnie for your phone number to apologize to you directly," he says.

"We're in our bi-weekly museum meeting," Marnie explains, "with Dot and Marigold. It's good that you called. We need to figure out what to do about the garden."

"Ah, yes. Hello, everyone."

Dot and Marigold offer muted greetings before Dr. Blake speaks again.

"Might I have a word with you, Henry? In private?"

With Marnie's permission, I take her phone into the backroom with the obnoxiously frightening encased witch from *Hunter, The Return*. I turn my back on the creature to focus on our conversation.

"I'm here, Dr. Blake," I say, taking the phone off speaker and setting it against my ear.

"Henry, I'm sorry for the distress I caused," he begins. "Venus says you had an asthma attack."

"You spoke to her?"

"Oh, yes, you'll be pleased to know that she and her sister have given me a firm talking to about boundaries. But she *is* my daughter, so I don't apologize for interfering. Prompting your asthma, though—that is regrettable. I didn't expect that seeing her would cause such a reaction."

"Neither would I, but it's been a long time, and she and I... well, you know *us*."

He chuckles. "Yes, I do. She tells me you've reached an amicable parting of ways this time."

"Um, yeah, she came back later, and we talked."

"Hmm, any sparks left in the ol' matchbox for each other, then?"

A chuckle sputters out in surprise at the question. So much for his daughters' talks on interfering. "Sparks were never our problem, sir."

He laughs. "No, you two were more like a blazing fire, if all that sneaking around was any indication. You still haven't fixed my trellis."

"Oh, you knew about that?" I snicker lightly. "Thanks for not telling my mom."

"You needed each other more than you needed parental lectures on boundaries. You were always a steadying presence for her. She needed your support and friendship then. I only wonder... Hmm."

"What is it, Dr. Blake?"

"Well, I can't make this debacle any worse, I suppose," he says, more to himself than to me. "I love Venus. She's brilliant, creative, tenacious, and beautifully free-spirited."

In his pause, I say, "Yes, she's all those things."

"Stubborn and independent, too. She's never needed much."

He pauses again. "No, sir."

"But she's been all over the world, and she has yet to find where she belongs. She's lost, Henry, and if she is ever to find happiness, I believe she needs *you*. I only wonder... Do you need her?"

This time, I don't know how to fill the pause that follows. He says it kindly enough, but it's an intrusive question, and what good would it do to admit to him what I'd only concluded a few hours ago, that my heart belongs to her. Saying that aloud would lift the lid of Pandora's box and let hope slip out when there isn't any.

"It's not that simple," I say when the pause stretches too long. "We lead very different lives now—that's what *she* wanted. She'll leave again."

"Hmm, perhaps. Or perhaps she might find a reason to stay, a place where she belongs. Could there be a chance for Henry and Venus, part two?"

Through a frustrated sigh, I chuckle. "Perhaps I should join your daughters in reminding you not to interfere."

"That's fair," he says. "I regret the times I didn't interfere on her behalf. Or I interfered incorrectly, based on the advice of those who called her difficult and unteachable. I tried but failed to stop them from using words like that. It's quite startling how one word makes a difference, for good or ill."

Certain words followed Venus throughout her education. *Difficult, distracted,* and *belligerent* were common amongst teachers. But students had their own vocabulary for her, too, one that changed as we grew older. *Dirty, mean, fairy girl* eventually morphed into *crazy, annoying, know-it-all* until high school, when the words took a sharp turn, thanks to me.

"Now, I'm realizing that there were times when she needed my interference and didn't ask for it… or couldn't. I wish I could've helped her more," he says, his voice laced with regret. "This may be my last chance to interfere, Henry. There's already talk amongst our circles—a reforestation project in New Zealand is keen to have her on their team. She doesn't know that yet, but there she'd be practically cut off from us—"

"If that's what she wants, Dr. Blake…" I cut in, though my words lack conviction, considering the eight thousand miles and two oceans that would be between us.

"She doesn't know what she wants, Henry, and I say that with the deepest respect for her and her capabilities. She believes *we* don't *want* her, you see. If my interference quells that faulty belief, then I will barge right in. Wouldn't you?"

"I don't know," I answer honestly, remembering her racing away this morning. "We devastated each other once. We don't want that to happen again. Besides, neither of us can… change."

"Change is life's best-kept promise. Would you be content to lose her forever?"

I stumble over his question, unable to answer.

"Test her, then," he says after a long pause. "If there's any hope, you'll see it. Try some normal couple things. She doesn't think she's capable of normal things, but we know she is. Don't we?" He takes a long breath while I say nothing. "At the very least, let her install the garden. She'll do whatever you ask of her, Henry. You know that."

Would she? Still?

Her sobbing silently against my chest fills my thoughts, but is quickly snuffed out by Dr. Blake clearing his throat. "Thanks for listening, Henry. Whatever happens, you're a good egg."

His odd compliment makes me chuckle. "So, are you, Dr. Blake."

The call soon ends, and I try to put it out of my mind.

I don't have the time or energy to lose myself in thoughts of Venus.

But, I do anyway.

I can't stop.

And maybe, I don't want to.

CHAPTER 21
Venus

MY CLEARANCE RACK rescue mission has produced mixed results. I pick off the yellowed, brittle ends of a drooping tomato plant, hoping its energy will redirect to the healthier leaves. The yellow squash and cucumber plants face similar challenges, having been denied the nutrients needed for proper growth. Now embedded in nutrient-rich, composted soil, it may be too late. Still, I pluck the dried and withering parts, smiling as I remember young Henry calling them *baby pickles*, which I found amusing because, yes, they could've become pickles, one day, but only after they were cucumbers first. Not these, I decide, dropping the dead bits into the canvas tote hooked to my waist for scraps. The pepper plants slump, but there's hope in their tiny flowers. Their plastic identifiers claimed they were sweet green peppers (*Capsicum annuum*), but the dark center of the white flowers suggests otherwise—these are most certainly a spicier variety (*Capsicum chinense*). With my father's endless supply of extra-large popsicle sticks, I have labeled them correctly, hoping that restoring their proper variety will encourage them to become their true selves.

Thunder rumbles in the gray skies overhead. The humidity thickens as the pressure drops. I lift my chin, expecting raindrops to hit my face.

"*It's going to rain. We should go home, Venus,*" Henry's young voice echoes in my head. He usually played the unofficial weatherman of our friendship. *It's hot. It's cold. It's chilly. It's going to rain.* And I countered with reason. "It's just a little rain. It won't hurt us, Henry."

The weather proved me wrong. We were forced to crouch inside our newly constructed lean-to as the sky opened and lightning struck the ground so close that we screamed at the searing crack in the air and felt the jolt through the earth. He latched on to me, and I said, *"Tighter."*

The storm had been like many others in the summer—fierce and fast. By the time it drifted away, a tree had been splintered to dark spikes not twenty yards from our lean-to, and Henry was panting.

Two days later, he was diagnosed with bronchitis, likely brought on by the overexcitement, dampness, and the bloom of allergens that occur in the rain. Maggie blamed me. I blamed myself, too. The ten-page report I assigned myself on Henry's asthma did little to alleviate my guilt, but I like studying how things work. Or don't work.

Henry liked it, though. He said it taught him more about his condition than his pulmonologist. I wonder if he still has it. Tucked in a box or drawer. Another piece of me.

Now, I close my eyes to the heavy air, breathing it in. The breeze catches my hair, sending it around my face, and I still smell him on me. I imagine he's the breeze, sweeping over me, touching me.

The thunder rumbles again. I finish my work and deliver my scraps to the compost bin. I harvest a bulbously ripe beefsteak tomato, basil, and a green pepper from his overflowing beds, and retreat inside just as rain starts pelting the deck.

Ivy texts to confirm plans tomorrow—I try to look forward to shopping with my sister, rather than getting lost in thoughts of Henry. Tonight will be the hardest—I'm alone, fresh from Henry's arms with little to do.

Ivy will distract me tomorrow, and Dad's classes will engage me throughout the week.

If I can get through tonight, I'll be fine.

Or close to fine.

Fine adjacent.

Fine enough.

Though I'm not much of a planner, I create one for the evening. I force myself to shower, even though it means washing Henry away. I cry through it, but it has to be done.

Proud of this huge first step, I permit myself to wear his t-shirt afterward. I complete my evening ensemble with only panties and long socks, taking full advantage of the empty house. I wrap a cornflower-blue scarf around my head and tie it into a loose mermaid braid.

Then, I explore Dad's vinyl collection before deciding on Def Leppard's *Hysteria* album. "Love Bites" screeches through the surround sound because that's how I feel.

Music fills the empty house, making it feel warmer even as rain batters the windows and lightning and thunder play their game of tag.

I prepare a dinner just for me—another thing I haven't done in a while. I roast the veggies with olive oil, salt, and pepper, then drizzle them with fresh basil and mozzarella. I find crusty bread to go with my meal and a bottle of Pinot Noir to sip instead of my usual Vodka Cranberry. It feels nicer, somehow.

Then, I sit at the table with one of Christie's romance novels to read while I eat.

Perhaps romance isn't the best choice of reading material, but I suspect it will be too far-fetched to take seriously. It carries me through dinner, and when the kitchen is clean, I retreat to the living room, book in hand, where I curl up with a blanket on the couch like I used to. The story *is* outlandish, but very engaging. Even *I* want to discover how the treasure-seeking, swash-buckling pirate will win the heart of the beloved princess he accidentally saves from a witch when she's already betrothed to a powerful wizard who will protect her mother's kingdom.

It's the first romance I've read for pleasure, and the appeal isn't lost on me. Everyone wants to feel wanted.

"*Tell me what you want to do to me, Venus.*"

I close my eyes, tapping my forehead with the worn pages like it's a reset button. When that doesn't work, I lean back and stare at the skylights overhead. Rain splatters against them in sheets, and wind whips through the trees outside, creating an odd backdrop to the music. Huddling in our lean-to during the first storm we faced together helped us rely on each other through others. Too many to count or remember. But I wish I could relive each one, to have a collection of us like the classic romcoms in Maggie's basement to play whenever I want.

One for yesterday, too.

But a mental highlight reel hardly compares to the real thing or even keeps an accurate account. I already feel those memories slipping away, fading with time. Soon, I won't remember what amused him on the tiki boat, what his usual was at dinner, or the sweet words he said to me. I won't remember his touches or kisses, only that we had them. Only that we won't have them again.

Sadness envelopes me in a sudden wave. *I miss him.*

I *always* miss him. But it's sharper now, digging deeper, hollowing me out. The agony resurrects the parts of me I've worked so hard to numb. Feelings I don't want screech back to life like rusty gears in motion again, and I hate the rush of energy all of these conflicting mechanisms inspire.

I don't want this.

And yet, when it comes to Henry, I'd rather hurt than feel nothing. If I'm hurting, he's still with me.

The book slips to the floor as my hands grip my hair and tighten until it hurts. Impulsive energy gurgles and spits inside of me. I want the storm noise. I uncurl myself from the couch and switch off the record player without raising the needle. The spin slows with mumbled jargon before stopping.

Rain pounds on the roof through low growls of thunder. But it's not enough—I need to feel it.

To drench myself in it.

To run into it.

To trade one storm for another.

To let the rain extinguish the lit fuse burning inside me.

My socked feet slip on the hardwoods in my dash toward the door. I sling it open and rush into a black curtain of darkness and rain. I flee to the deck stairs, trip over my soaked socks, and fall straight into the arms of the man racing up to meet me.

With my arms locked around his shoulders, he lifts me by the waist from the step below. "I'm here. Everything's okay," he says against my ear. "Please, don't run."

"Henry," I sigh, relaxing against him.

He carries me to the front door and shuts us inside. When my damp socks squish against the wood floors, I stare up at him in desperate confusion. Did I conjure him from my deepest pain? Is he real? Or a fantasy?

I reach out, desperate for him not to be a dream. My fingers slide over his bearded cheek, and he leans into my touch, his lopsided smile emerging weakly. Water drips from the ends of his brown hair like tears. His dark t-shirt is soaked—it's unlike Henry to forget his raincoat. But when his eyes close to my affection, like it's exactly what he needed, I decide that he wasn't thinking about weather preparations.

Disheveled and worried, he looks as conflicted as I feel, and his grip on me tightens, like he's afraid I might disappear.

"It's not working." Raindrops speck his glasses, but not enough to prevent me from seeing his pupils blown wide, worry lines crinkling the corners of his eyes. "Your plan... It's not working."

"I know."

"It wasn't enough," he says.

"I know."

"One more night." His voice is strained, rough. "Please?"

"Yes, Henry. Yes." *He's here. He's really here. He's here for me.* His perfect lips curl in relief before his mouth meets mine—our kiss as unrelenting as the storm outside.

"Is that my shirt?" he asks at my lips, moving us further inside.

I pause our wild kisses to meet his eyes. "I'm keeping it."

"It's yours," he groans, looking me up and down. "Whatever you want is yours."

"You, Henry," I mutter, needily tugging his collar toward me before kissing him again. "After the shirt, just you."

An unsynchronized dance ensues as we kiss, touch, talk, and circle into the living room.

"I couldn't stop thinking about you," he whispers, biting my bottom lip and toying with my loose braid.

"Me, neither," I mutter breathlessly, finding the hem of his t-shirt and letting my hands wander underneath. "And the storm, too."

"The storm," he repeats with anguish, devouring my neck while his hands grip my ass. We stumble to the back of the couch, and he pins me against it. "It makes me think of us—our lean-to. I still get nervous with lightning."

"No matter where I am or what I'm doing, storms bring me back to you," I admit, ridding him of his damp shirt.

He traces my jawline with his finger, his eyes wide with delight. "I still dream of you sneaking in my window, even now when I'm three floors up."

A delighted chuckle escapes me as my fingers drag across his back. "I still can't fall asleep without imagining your arms wrapped around me."

His hands find my cheeks, and his thumbs sweep across them as his brown eyes delve into mine. A gentle crease forms at the bridge of his nose. "We might be in trouble here."

"I know," I say, as his forehead rests against mine and our noses nuzzle. My arms settle on his shoulders, and the hot breath between us fogs his glasses. I reach up, slip them off, and drop them onto the couch cushions behind me. Our gazes lock again. "Do you wish I hadn't come back?"

"No. Never." His quick answer brings relief, but his brow furrows again. "But you'll leave again."

"Yes," I breathe, knowing I don't belong here. Or anywhere. My transitory life has served me and everyone else well.

He nods against me. "So, you're you, and I'm me, and this will never be more than it is. What do we do?"

There's no suitable answer except to say, "We love each other now, and save the aftermath for tomorrow."

"Yeah," he says, kissing me again. "Tomorrow."

CHAPTER 22
Henry

TOMORROW COMES TOO SOON. Light crests the skylights over her bed, and a tear slips from my eye onto her pillow. That she's curled against my chest, asleep, makes no difference to my growing dread. It's only dawn and I'm in no rush to leave, but that time will come. Soon.

Tears didn't used to come so easily. I cried my heart out when she left the first time, but then, they dried up, as if my tear ducts shriveled into inoperability. Until Uncle Jay. Then, I cried in secret. For Mom's sake and Olly's, I had to join Fred in what I mentally referred to as the Fortress of Strength, handling the tasks that Mom couldn't manage, Olly shouldn't see, and no one wants.

It was a dark time, and even now, hope is only beginning to sneak in, but like the light through the multicolored panes in the Blakes' greenhouse, it feels muted. Weak and diluted. Not the bright beacon it should be.

Now, with Venus, tears come naturally. Tears over our history that I didn't fully understand, tears over my misplaced bitterness, and all the ways I let her down, tears over ten lost years and unfair what-ifs. If something, *anything* had been different, could we've had this? If I'd seen her pain and done something to make it better, would she have stayed?

And what would our lives be like if she had?

Our separation led to me having Olly—he makes the what-ifs pointless.

Even so, holding her like this is as close to perfect as I've ever come, and it's hard not to dream of possibilities a little.

We made the most of last night, like we were starved for each other. It felt like another decade had passed in merely a day since the last time we were together. The longing and relief had us against the couch, then the wall, and finally on the floor, right there in her family's living room.

The second time was different. She held my hand as she led me upstairs, and once there, we stood at the foot of her bed in this dazed and gentle fixation, exploring each other's scars, tattoos, curves, veins, everything. The slope of her nose, the puff of her cheeks, her sweetly determined chin, the goosebumps playing on her skin as I ran my fingers over the dark lines of her tattoos, and every other inch of her, mapping her for my memory. She did the same to me, and our kisses were slower and deeper for the tears behind them.

Now, lying here with her draped over me, arms locked to my torso, I will that tiny flower of hope to bloom. She's here. Love still exists between us. We have the summer. I think of what Dr. Blake said, that she doesn't believe we want her, and her admission that she thinks she's a burden. I now understand *why* she thinks that, but I want the chance to bring her through her faulty reasoning to the truth—I owe her that, at least.

And if I did prove that she's loved and wanted, would she stay?

I think of the day ahead, and reality chokes out any hope. Olly comes home at three. He'll rave about his weekend with Carly for a solid half-hour, a tradition that used to bother me—the whole fun parent versus the boring one. But I got over it the first time he got sick in her care, and wanted me to pick him up. That our kid preferred me for vomit duty secured my parental ego. With school out, our new schedule starts—me at UNCW and him at his summer day camp. We'll get everything ready for tomorrow. Then, we'll go to Mom and Fred's for dinner. Once home again, we'll start our bath and bedtime routine. When he's asleep, I'll write about her, probably starting with this weekend first, while it's fresh, and I won't stop until my fingers hurt. I'll stay up late, restless and frustrated, and inevitably drift off sometime in the middle of the night, imagining she's with me.

Like she is right now.

A sun band edges through the window, hitting the wall over her desk and reflecting off the glass jars shelved there. Her desk still looks as messy and full as it did the last time I saw it. Test tubes, beakers, and flasks line the walls. Plants tower over the shelves and hang down from the suspended baskets, lush and stretching. Her father must've cared for them in her absence.

I edge out from underneath her and silently tour the room.

A composition notebook is splayed open on the desk next to pens, pencils, and paints spilled from a pouch. It's thick with inked pages and captured treasures. It calls to me—a siren of art and beauty, her experiences without me.

Not *without* me—I discover with a quick inhale. My name corners the open page in thick, precise lettering with a comma after the Y, as if writing me a letter. The following text elaborates on the giant kelp forest she explored on a dive that day—words that make my mouth drop in awe and respect.

Venus goes on dives? But, of course, she does.

Macrocystis pyrifera isn't a plant, Henry. Don't be confused by its height, coloring, and overall aesthetic. It's algae, and quite miraculous in its growth rate of up to two feet per day, up to 160 feet overall.

She elaborates on its zoospores and sporophylls—words that have no place in my vocabulary—and I focus, instead, on the detailed image she's drawn—thick stalks, holding long, leafy blades with sea life filtering around it. It's beautiful, pulling me in with her thick strokes, blues, and greens.

Behind an asterisk at the bottom, she writes:

It's edible, but given your reaction to Maggie's seaweed snack that time, I doubt you'd like it.

A baffled smirk emerges as I fall into her desk chair and flip through the pages. I stop on an incredible humpback whale stretching across two pages, and the words:

Henry, I had a whale of a time!

She captures the whale's marks and lumps with such accuracy that it almost appears animated, ready to swim off the page. She tells me about the hauntingly lovely whale songs they heard one night, and they made her think of her father's records, specifically Pink Floyd's "Wish You Were Here."

We're just two lost souls swimming in a fish bowl, year after year

My lungs tighten—that's how it feels.

In the same breath, I imagine being there with her, on the ship, staring out at a black ocean under a star-filled sky, and hearing the ghostly melodies of whales. I picture slipping my hand around her, pulling her close, and her head resting on my shoulder while her hair plays in the wind.

It never happened, but it feels like it did. Like I was with her. She dreamed I was, anyway.

And just like that, this old love feels renewed and as deep as the seas she traveled over. She never let me go. She carried me with her.

Tears well in my eyes as I flip through more pages. Seabirds feature often, complete with detailed drawings and sample feathers taped in the corners.

On other pages, she draws what she sees through the microscope in the research vessel's lab, and explains polymers and the process of extracting microplastics from water, but she notes, rightly, in a corner that:

This may overshoot your interests, Henry, but I want you to know that my research is worthwhile and could help the environment on an expansive scale. I want you to be proud of me.

I gasp a little. I *am* proud of her—a feeling I wish I'd had when we were together. I wish I'd loved her boldly then, when I had the chance.

I flip to the last entry and find something different than the rest—an ink drawing of her, diving into the ocean. A vague representation of the ship looms behind her on the surface. She's kicking her feet, like she's trying to go deeper, trying to get away.

There is no note to me this time. Instead, she writes:

I can't accept what I cannot change.

A memory stirs. *"You must accept what you cannot change,"* her father said to her, his hand gently on her arm to calm her.

What was it?

The physical fitness test in sixth grade, I remember suddenly. We had to run a mile in gym class. I had a medical excuse to sit it out, but I didn't want to. I was slight, wore glasses, and had asthma—I was teased enough already.

Though out of breath by the first lap, I pushed on, despite my constricted lungs. That is, until Venus huffed, grabbed my arm, and dragged me into the woods, where we found a small creek and a downed tree. *"Rest and breathe,"* she ordered. *"Your lungs aren't prepared for that, Henry."*

"I know," I gasped, "but I want them to be."

"Gym class won't achieve that for you. Train on a regular, routine basis. Take on a sport. Basketball would suit you."

"You think I can play basketball?" I questioned with awe.

"You can do anything, Henry. Building your endurance might be challenging at first, but you can train your body just like anyone else. Your lungs will thank you for it. I'll help if you want."

Her help didn't happen because she got in trouble. Within an hour of our escape, we were in the principal's office with our parents.

"It's an illogical test, anyway, rating our unique bodies and physical abilities on the same scale," she'd argued. *"Henry is asthmatic. He shouldn't be judged on the same—"*

"Venus, stop being difficult," Principal Hecker admonished. *"You know the rules. You broke them. And you put a fellow student at risk."*

"At risk of what? Catching his breath?" she demanded.

That's when her father put his hand on her arm and said, *"You must accept what you cannot change."*

In the end, Venus received a month of after-school detention. I joined the basketball team and started running every day to build my endurance.

My fingers trace her image on the rumpled paper, latching on to hope again. She left, but she never left me. Her dad's right—*she believes we don't want her.*

"What are you doing?"

Her tone and suddenness startle me. The notebook falls onto the desk. I twist in the chair to face her. She sits upright on the bed, holding a sheet across her chest, hair wild, and green eyes puffy and bothered.

"You used to let me see your field journals," I say with a weak smile, suddenly aware that I've overstepped. "I thought I'd take a peek at your recent adventures."

She chews the inside of her bottom lip. "You should've asked first."

"You're right. I'm sorry." I return to bed and curl close, pulling her toward me, but she remains upright and covered. "Come here. Kiss me."

"You should go, Henry."

"It's early," I counter, kissing her tattoos up her arm. "It's Sunday. Olly doesn't get home until later. We have time."

She stays quiet, staring into the blankets between us like there's a universe there. I sit up, sliding her hair away from her neck and planting soft kisses along her collarbone.

When she doesn't respond, I whisper, "Remember that time you saved me from the mile run? I was so stubborn about it, but you stayed by my side. I never told you thank—"

"Henry." My name erupts from her lips with stern finality.

I lock eyes with her. "Venus?"

"I've given you all the time I can," she says, as coldly as an uncaring doctor trying to get to her next patient. "You have a life to get back to, and I have things to do."

She's shutting me out, like a beach house closing its shutters and sandbagging the entry points ahead of a hurricane. The same blank-faced, matter-of-fact persona that I remember from high school takes over—the one she used to shelter in when she needed to believe that she didn't care what others said or did to her.

Now, she wants to shut herself off from me behind *her* Fortress of Solitude, veiled in dark academia—the only real home she's known for the last decade.

"What things?" I challenge. "What has to be done at 6:30 in the morning?"

"My to-do list isn't your concern. I don't want to be rude," she tries again, "but—"

"But, that makes it easier, right?"

"I had fun. I hope you did, too. I'm glad to have apologized for my behavior and ended things on a more satisfactory note. But it's over. You shouldn't come here again." Her forced smile sends a cold blade through my heart, and her words twist it.

Then, she pulls away and flees, naked, into the bathroom, closing the door behind her.

Fun? Satisfactory? Her dismissive words don't even skim the surface of describing our time together this weekend. But I understand what she's doing. Her forced attitude makes leaving easier *for me*. I think of her wording—that *I* have a life to get back to, compared to her, who only has things to do.

She's right. I have a son, a family, a small business, and classes starting tomorrow. I have an excess of life to get back to, and she's giving me an out. It wouldn't surprise me if she stayed in the bathroom until she hears me leave—a backward version of her racing away at my place. Prolonging the goodbye would make it harder.

But it doesn't feel right.

I rise from the bed and find my scattered clothes throughout the house, putting them on as I come across them. I fold the throw blankets we used and make her bed. I rescue my shirt from the day before and drape it neatly on the back of her desk chair. I close her journal.

Yes, I'm lingering. Stalling. Uneasy about leaving this way.

I go to the bathroom door and tap it gently. "Venus?"

"Yes?"

"I'm ready to leave. Please, walk me out," I say. "It's customary to see guests out when they leave."

The door swings open, revealing an annoyed Venus in a silky kimono that hugs her curves and highlights the green in her eyes. Her hair is tied into a purple scarf, forming a thick knot on her head. She looks like an adorable grump.

She beelines down the stairs and to the front door, swinging it open with enough force to make her robe ripple in the wake of it. I stand in the doorway in front of her, making it impossible to close the door just yet. Her eyes bounce from the floor to the ceiling to anything but me.

"Venus," I say, catching her eyes in mine. "I did have fun. I won't return without your permission. But I need you to install the garden. Please."

Her tense shoulders fall just slightly. "Um, it'll have to be today."

"That's fine. Come whenever you're free," I say, sounding upbeat.

"It won't take long," she says, more to herself than to me. "An hour or two, tops."

"Okay." A beat passes in awkward silence before I reach out to her. "Hug me goodbye."

She groans in protest, but wraps her arms around my midsection and rests her head on my chest. I hold her there, tightening my grip until she relaxes. Her arms lock around my shoulders, pressing us closer.

"What if..." I say, holding her against my chest, "What if we tried being friends again?"

She breaks away from our tight-muscled grip and gives me a pained look that ends in a wry half-smile. "I never stopped being your friend... I have to go. Goodbye, Henry."

The door clicks shut behind me as I step outside. The warm morning sun hits me, but does nothing for the coldness of her parting words. I should be relieved to escape whatever this is without added complications.

Instead, I feel lost.

CHAPTER 23
Venus

"THE FIRST THING we need to do is take a proper inventory." Ivy stands in the middle of the bedroom, hands on her hips, eyes shifting between the open closet and the piles of clothes occupying parts of the floor like anthills. She spies my prom dress in a pink heap in the corner and gives me a coy look.

"You tried it on, didn't you?"

"Yes."

"Did you feel pretty?" she asks, even more coyly.

"Yes," I admit, thinking about how it sparkled under the sunshine on the tiki boat, how the queens gushed over it at the restaurant, the way Henry's eyes traveled over my exposed skin, and his delicious yearning when he got me out of it. "Yes, I felt very pretty."

"That's a big step for you," Ivy decides cheerfully. "Hold onto that feeling as we're putting together your wardrobe today. But before you get any ideas, you can't wear a prom dress to campus."

"My wardrobe is fine." I sit on the bed's edge, still in the silky kimono I found hanging in the bathroom this morning—left for me by Christie, I assume—and feeling all-around like a Grumpy Gus.

"It's not fine," Ivy says, holding up my cut-off jean shorts. "You can't teach college classes dressed like a slovenly student."

"My clothes are comfortable, durable, and shouldn't matter to anyone but me."

"Of course, your appearance matters." She plops onto the bed beside me. "You want to be taken seriously, don't you?"

"My extensive credentials will achieve that."

"What will people see first, Vee? Your clothes or extensive credentials?"

My shoulders slump. "Fine. What do you suggest?"

"Shopping. But first, I want to get a feel for your style… or at least, what it could be." She holds up a crocheted sweater from my exploded suitcase. "Do you like this?"

"Yes. I bought it from a local shop in Scotland. The clerk said it was hand-knit by an elderly neighbor."

"What about the colors? You like them?"

I eye the ambers, blues, and reds of the multicolored blocks. "Yes, they're nice."

"What about this?" She tugs a red, yellow, and white sarong from the bottom of my backpack.

"I bought that from a street market in Madagascar. I appreciated the versatility, and I needed something to wear over my bikini on beach days and at night for pig roasts. That one's torn, though. I was going to cut it into scarves."

She rolls her bright blue eyes, though I don't know why. "The colors?"

"They're pleasant enough."

She looks dissatisfied, but it fades behind curiosity when she holds out her hands for mine. She inspects them closely, focusing on my rings and bracelets.

"When I travel, I collect jewelry from local artisans, mementos that travel well and provide me with something to touch or twist or otherwise manipulate."

"Fancy fidget spinners," she giggles. "I get it."

Her finger traces the long, oval shape of my always-black mood ring. "You had this one long before you traveled."

"It was Henry's grandmother's. It's my favorite." I try to sound indifferent, but when Ivy's probing eyes find mine at the slightest tremor in my voice, I know I've failed.

"It's been a few days since Dad's trick," she says with a sympathetic tone. "Maybe you should try reaching out to him again."

"I did."

"What?" she blurts urgently. "What happened?"

"I apologized for everything. We came to an understanding. We had sex... five, no six times with penetration," I say for clarification. "We ended our relationship properly, and he left."

She looks dumbfounded, like I've just told her I'm a flat-earther and don't believe in global warming.

She gawks. "*Six times?*"

"With penetration. More if you count individual orgasms. Yes."

Her wide eyes and agape mouth are almost comical, especially when she says, "Wow! When you guys make up, you *really* make up. Hope you don't get a UTI."

I shrug lightly. "It'd be worth it."

Her surprise morphs into a smile. "The sex was *that* good?"

"Better than I can possibly describe. We are extremely compatible... sexually."

"Then, I'm confused. What do you mean you ended it?"

"Our compatibility stops with sex. Our lives are very different, and he expressed a desire to move on from me—that's what this weekend was about, purging the tension between us to bring closure to our past."

"Did you find closure?" she asks, brow triangulated on her forehead.

"I found..." My head spins in an exhaustive effort to find the right word, but I only come up with "comfort. And validation. Leaving was best. His life proves it. He has a son now. Did you know?"

She nods, though she still seems confused. "Yeah, but that shouldn't deter you if you want more—"

"I don't want more," I lie sternly.

She looks unconvinced. "Does he?"

"I didn't ask. But, yes. He wants a woman who will suit him, his son, and his life. He deserves normality and stability—things I can't provide."

"He *said* that to you?"

"He didn't have to. That was our arrangement, regardless. It's over."

Her hand goes to my arm. "Are you alright?"

"I'm always alright." When she doesn't seem convinced, I offer a redirection. "Have you figured it out yet? My style?"

She smiles lightly, like she understands the need for a subject change. "Boho pro—that's your new style. I know the perfect boutique to take you to. How about getting dressed while I clean up this mess?"

Ivy reaches for Henry's shirt, draped over my chair.

"No!" I shout, startling us both.

"What?"

"Just leave that one alone," I say softly. "Okay?"

"Okay." A delicate smile crosses her lips as she nods.

I grab clean clothes from the floor and head toward the bathroom.

"Practice your Ins and Outs while you're in there. Good energy in, and sad things out. Okay?"

I take a deep breath at her suggestion. "Okay."

When I return, my clothes have been sorted and the room tidied. Ivy sits at my desk, flipping through my field journal. I rush over, closing it in her hands.

"Why does everyone feel inclined to browse through my personal belongings?"

Her thin lips curve into a grin. "Because, dear sister, we so rarely have the opportunity. Lighten up. I won't hold any of your secrets against you, and—bonus—I'll keep them, too. Now, let's go."

She drives us to a boutique in Mayfair, specializing in coastal decor, artisan gifts, and, as she puts it, "Boho beautiful." It's a quaint shop that reminds me of similar boutiques I've patronized in coastal towns in England and France.

"Here's how this should go," she says, as we circle the store. "Point out anything that catches your eye, that you *really* like, and I'll build the outfits around your favs. Deal?"

"That sounds reasonable," I say, perusing a rack of tops.

"How do you feel about starting the job tomorrow?"

I hold out a sage green t-shirt with cuffed sleeves and hand it to her. "Anxious. I don't like classrooms."

"Well, whenever you feel butterflies, just practice your Ins and Outs. Don't think of it as a classroom. Visualize something more comfortable, like a coffee shop or campfire. Imagine you're talking to me or Henry."

I roll my eyes, wondering if she and Dad conspired with their teaching advice, too.

"Dad says you'll have office hours," she goes on, as I hand her cargo shorts that she quickly returns to the rack. "Are you worried about interactions?"

I huff, handing her a silk scarf with a blue and white French floral print. She smiles approvingly and matches it with a long denim skirt. "I'm always worried about interactions."

"Want some pointers?"

I consider her expertise in breathing exercises and say, "Yes."

"Okay, so, the first thing to do is smile," she says, demonstrating as if I don't know what a smile looks like. "Then, make conversation."

"About what?"

She shrugs. "It depends on the situation. If a student comes to Dad's office, then ask, 'How may I help you?' If it's in a more casual setting, ask 'What are you studying?' or 'What's your interest in botany?' or… better yet… point out something you like about the person. 'That's a lovely shirt,' for example."

I groan. This is too much already. "What if I don't like their shirt?"

"Then, find something you do like. Or forget looks. Try to connect personally. Let's practice," Ivy says, facing me. "Ask me something personal, something that shows you're interested in *me*."

"How many milliliters of morphine would it take to kill someone?"

She groans. "That's not personal. It's weird. I wouldn't answer such a question for multiple reasons."

I think again, scanning through our conversations for information. "Um, has Gil told you about his anxiety disorder yet?"

She lights up and slaps me playfully on the arm. "Much better. That ticks the box for a personal question and, double bonus, tells me you were listening the other day. Excellent."

"Listening is loving," I smirk.

"Alright, Dad!" She teases with a laugh.

I can't help but flash a short grin. "Well?"

"No, he hasn't," she sighs, as the store clerk appears to take her selections to a dressing room. "It'd be so much easier, but he's embarrassed, I suppose."

"Yes, he's embarrassed."

"I don't see why!" she retorts. "It's nothing to be embarrassed about, and I'm a nurse. I'm trained in handling anxious patients."

"He's not a patient, and he doesn't want to be handled. It's not his anxiety that worries him. It's *you*. You're entirely perfect in every conceivable way. He fears that you knowing about his perceived deficiencies might alter your opinion of him. You should be patient and let him come to you in his own time."

She gapes over a rack of summer dresses, seemingly stunned. But then, she smiles. "Careful, Venus. That almost sounded like sisterly advice."

A chuckle rumbles up from somewhere deep and forgotten, and I blush slightly. "I suppose it was."

"I'll take it," she giggles.

I spend an exorbitant amount of money at the store, but I've saved and can afford this rare splurge. Ivy insists I have enough outfits for the week, and she offers to coordinate them in my closet so that all I have to do is dress and go. We stop at a coffee shop for a late breakfast before going to a shoe store. Sensible flats, dressy sandals, and white sneakers complete the outfits. She insists on one last stop at a department store.

"Dad says you're sleeping in the hammock," she says, taking me to the bedding department.

"Yes, on some nights," I answer, sure I'll sleep there tonight. The bed won't be comfortable without Henry in it.

"A body pillow and weighted blanket might help." She heaves a soft lavender blanket into our cart.

"Perhaps," I say, willing to try anything.

"What else will make your stay with us better?" she asks, hands on hips and smile wide.

Her kindness is taking me slightly off guard. "I don't know. I've been living in ships, tents, and hostels. I'm not fussy—"

My eyes catch on a fuzzy lavender reading pillow, and I beeline for it. I take it into my arms like a lost friend, squeezing it tightly.

"I need this," I tell her, dumping it into a cart.

She giggles again. "That's the spirit."

We return home and lug our bounty upstairs. She coordinates the clothes into complete outfits, as promised. I take the tags off my new pillows and blanket, arranging them just so.

"Thank you. You've been extremely helpful."

"That's what sisters are for. Want to go to lunch?"

"Can't. I'm installing Henry's garden today, in one visit—not two as originally planned. The equipment is there, but I still have to harvest the plants from the outskirts of our garden, as Dad instructed." But fearing I've disappointed her, I add, "I would any other day."

She smiles, but it quickly turns to concern. "Is that a good idea? Seeing Henry so soon after your sex-fest? Won't it... hurt to be close to him now that it's over?"

I shrug. "I'm used to hurting over Henry. It's a task that needs to be done."

She places her dainty hand on my arm over my tattoos and squeezes gently. "You shouldn't *hurt* over Henry. You should either find a way to be together or move on to someone else."

I consider her options. "We can't be together, and there is no one else for me. But perhaps *he* can move on now. That's what I hope for him."

She groans. "You've always loved him. Plus, hot sex. You should hope for a chance with him rather than assuming you must live without him. Come on, genius. Work it out."

"Factoring in our careers, his child and the dynamics associated with parenthood and blended families, past disappointments and problems between us, as well as a myriad of other logistics... the probability of our finding happiness together is abysmally low."

She perks up. "So! There *is* a chance!"

I smirk, though she fails to see the big picture. It would go against her nature to view it realistically rather than idealistically. Or romantically.

She joins me in the garden where I collect healthy flytraps and pitcher plants—outliers in the expansive bog that won't thrive long term due to encroachment by other forest plants—and she assists. By that I mean, she holds the plastic tubs to carry the plants in, not that she gets her hands dirty. But any help is appreciated.

She talks nearly the entire time—about Gil, her work, Dad, and Christie—in a very stream-of-consciousness manner that is often difficult to follow. But I do my best.

Finally, we load the plastic bins into the Land Rover. I gather my fanny pack, carrying my additional tools and testers, and strap it over my jean shorts.

Ivy gives me a once-over. "Well, you won't win any hearts with that outfit, but you'll get the job done."

"That's the goal. Thanks for your help today. It was... nice."

She grins and bats her eyes in an overdramatic way that forces me to laugh. "Having a sister *is* nice, silly goose! Oh, before you go, I have an itty-bitty favor to ask."

"Go on."

"I'm pulling a few overnights this weekend at the hospital," she says. "Would you mind pet-sitting Buster? He doesn't mind his alone time during the day, but he needs a cuddler at night."

She gives me a pathetic puppy-dog face to drive home her plea.

"He's an angel, promise. I'd ask Gil, but Seagrove's an hour round-trip, so it's tricky to coordinate. Besides, I want to pop in on breaks for a cuddle, too."

Having never cared for an animal before, I'm reluctant. But the quiet house and expected lonely nights tip the balance in Buster's favor. How hard could it be? "Will you provide detailed written instructions on his care?"

"Absolutely! And I'll bring over all his favorite toys and treats. He'll adore getting to know his Auntie Vee."

"Fine. I accept."

She jumps, squeals, and hugs me at once. "Yay! You're going to have the best time together. Just don't go falling in love with him—I'll want him back."

"That won't be a problem," I assure her.

Finally overrun with what Ivy calls Good Sister Vibes, I leave for Henry's place.

CHAPTER 24

Henry

UNCLE JAY'S wooden blue jay stares at me with its black eyes that seem to bleed into the band around its chest. Its high head crest makes it look kingly, like it might be judging me or, at the very least, sizing me up. The last time I saw the bird was yesterday, when Mr. Massie pointed it out beside the cash register in the foyer. Now, it's on my desk atop my composition notebook.

Did I mindlessly bring it upstairs? I don't know, but I'm a grown man, a father, and far too old and busy to get the creeps.

Instead, I sit down, move it aside, and fill page after page of my new journal, pouring my heart out about Venus.

I never stopped being your friend, Henry.

Her words have inspired a flurry of memories and regrets. I stopped being her friend more times than I can count.

In third grade, when she came to school with her butt covered in mud. Everyone called her Mud-Butt, and though I didn't join in, I did nothing to stop it either.

In the sixth grade, when she announced her period to the entire class after our teacher refused to let her use the bathroom.

In ninth grade, when some girls slipped her a secret love note from a popular upperclassman. Venus confronted him in the cafeteria, and though she politely refused him, not knowing the letter was fake, he made fun of her in front of everyone. "I'd never *want someone like you*," he shouted. I didn't defend her.

Then, there was the flytrap debacle. And probably hundreds of small chinks in her armor that I don't know about, or was too selfish to notice, or too afraid to act on. She never stopped being my friend, but she should have.

The doorbell rouses me from my pity party. I race downstairs, taking two at a time, and end up needing my inhaler before I reach the door.

Venus stands on the other side, carrying a plastic tub of loose, leaning plants that serve as a barrier between us.

"I'm here to install the garden," she says, unnecessarily, "so, please direct me to the location, and I'll get started."

"Hi," I blurt with an awkward smile. "Are you okay?"

"Fine, thank you," she says, robotically, before adding, "Hi."

She offers a weak smile. My heart dips in my chest at how fast it fades.

"Um, come in. May I take that for you?" I ask, holding the door open.

"I've got it."

I lead her through the main museum to a wide staircase with a thick mahogany bannister that curls at the end, and red carpeting. Marnie insisted on keeping it this way for its antique vibe. Admittedly, it looks like something out of *Gone with the Wind*.

Pushing out the heavy door at the top, I introduce her to the cluttered space. "We installed lightweight wood tiles for a nicer look," I explain, motioning to our feet. "And the selfie sign." I point to the beautifully painted, rectangular sign along the outer wall, overlooking the river, that advertises the Weird But True Museum. "But we wanted to have the gardens installed before arranging anything else. So, pardon the mess."

She scans the unique outdoor sculptures Marnie has acquired, presently tucked into a corner, and the supplies to build a fairy garden. She bypasses that for the stack of gardening supplies and the large, plastic raised beds that Dr. Blake had delivered here.

"Water?" she asks.

"Over there." I point to the gray barrel along the edge of the building that's full from last night's storms.

"Good. I'll run some tests to confirm the pH and mineral content are correct. Rainwater is best. Never water them from the tap," she instructs.

"No tap for the traps. Got it," I chuckle, but she's unamused.

"I'll be creating two mini-bogs with moats to filter the water. You shouldn't need to do much once the garden is finished."

I nod. "Just the way I like it."

After a brief inspection of the materials, she sets her bin on the floor. "I'll retrieve the other bin from the Land Rover and get started."

"Can I help?" My words bubble up slowly through sudden, inexplicable nerves. "I could help, if you want."

"No need," she says blankly, "but thank you."

She edges around me for the door and flees down the stairs.

I don't know what to do with myself. I want to spend time with her, gathering up pieces of her before she's gone altogether. But I understand why she wants to keep her distance. I find work to do in the museum, close enough that she knows where I am, but not so close that I'm hovering.

She wears a teal scarf today, holding only half her hair. The rest waves lightly on her shoulders as she bounces down the steps ahead of me and soon returns with her second bin of plants. She doesn't look at me as she strides by, but keeps her eyes on the path ahead.

Her aloofness feels devastating. But I reason out my feelings with reality—I don't need the complication a relationship would bring, especially with a woman who won't stick around. *Focus on work*—that's what has helped before.

But it's not as effective this time.

Nearly two hours pass. Dot shows up, looking for her "little black tablet," which holds her schedule and supply lists for her projects. "If it's not here, I'm screwed," she announces, barging inside.

"I haven't seen it, but I'll help you look," I offer, glad for the distraction, but the doorbell chimes again.

Mr. Massie stands on the other side of the glass, holding his black case and looking determined. "I know you're busy, but I believe you *need* me, Henry."

"Need you for what?" I ask, trying not to sound annoyed.

"To help you run this place," he answers, like it's obvious. "I'll chat up the guests with my stunning personality and delight the masses with my sword swallowing routine while they view your incredible exhibits. I'll work for tips. You wouldn't have to—"

"No, Mr. Massie. No offense, but I don't want an act for the museum."

"But you haven't even seen it yet. Please? All I'm asking for is fifteen minutes. You'll be amazed. I promise."

My shoulders slump before jerking up again as items clatter to the floor inside. "I should help her."

"I'll come, too," he says, pushing through the door.

"Damn it!" Dot looks up from her frantic searching when we appear through the hallway. "I don't know what I've done with it. What did we do yesterday?" She scratches her black hair under her ball cap. Then, she snaps her fingers. "The witch!"

She flees into the inner room and returns, holding the tablet up like a trophy. "I set it down when I moved that display case in there on Friday... Oh, what's up, Eric the Sword-Swallower?"

"Hoping to show Henry my act," he says dramatically. "He's not too keen, though."

Dot slaps my shoulder. "What harm would it do? You know, except to his internal organs?"

"No Erics will be harmed in this production, but it might blow your mind," he quips, laughing.

Dot snort-laughs. "I'm game to have my mind blown. How 'bout it, Henry?"

"Um, well..." My refusal catches in my throat when Venus descends the stairs over Mr. Massie's shoulders. Her delicate fingers dance down the banister, and her hair flows like a golden cape behind her.

Dot leans closer. "Ah, I see what's gotten you so tongue-tied."

"It's Venus." Mr. Massie gawks like a cartoon character. He drops his case and falls to his knees, blocking her path. "Ah, Venus! Please say you remember me, or my heart will break into a billion pieces."

She tilts her head and quirks her brow. "Mr. Massie, hello."

"You remember him?" I blurt.

"He used to do so-called magic tricks with an invisible ball and a paper bag, remember?"

"You never fell for it," he laughs, taking her hand and holding it in both of his. "Still, it's a pleasure to see you again. You're lovelier than ever." He kisses her hand before jumping to his feet. "You're just in time to see my real act."

"What *real* act?"

He bows, like they're meeting for the first time. "Eric the Sword-Swallower, at your service."

"She's not interested, Mr. Massie," I say, annoyed by him and especially by that hand kiss.

"That's an erroneous assumption," Venus snaps, her green eyes wide and twinkling in a challenge. She turns her attention back to Mr. Massie. "You're a *genuine* sword-swallower?"

"Bona fide and verified," he coos. "I'm happy to show you, if Henry will allow it."

All eyes land on me, and I must relent. "Fine."

Mr. Massie grabs Venus's hand and escorts her to a bench against the wall. He motions for me to take the seat beside her. Then, he asks Dot, "Fancy being my assistant?"

"Does that mean I get to call 9-1-1?" she says.

"That won't be necessary," he says, unbuckling his case and opening it on the floor between them.

My arms fold over my chest as I prepare my thanks-but-no-thanks speech for when this is over.

"Why the reluctance?" Venus asks beside me as he gets ready.

"I'm trying to get away from the carnival vibe and turn it into something more authentic, historically, and locally. This guy might as well be a fake Elmo in Times Square," I whisper back. "I'm surprised you remember him."

Her shoulder brushes mine as she shrugs. "I *barely* remember, but Maggie didn't like him, and… he and I had that in common."

I side-eye her, adjusting my glasses. "You shouldn't have felt unliked by Mom or anyone. They didn't know you enough, didn't give you a chance to be liked. Truly, I'm sorry."

Astonishment flashes across her face for a nanosecond. "It's fine. That was the norm. You were the anomaly. They had valid reasons to dislike me, especially Maggie."

"You aren't unlikeable, Venus. Far from it. Mom was… is overprotective."

"She's right to be, and I don't blame her, even after—" Her lips clamp shut abruptly. "Sword swallowing is an ancient art—"

"Even after what?"

"Ladies and gentlemen, what you're about to see is not for the faint of heart," Mr. Massie announces loudly. "Never try this at home."

He goes on with his short, dramatic spiel while Venus leans closer, whispering in my ear. "Keep an open mind, Henry. I think you'll like this."

He asks Dot to test his swords, ranging in length from sixteen to twenty-four inches. I cringe when he licks the first blade, tilts his head back, and sends it down his gullet. He extracts it a moment later, seemingly unharmed. Then, he holds the longer blade in his hand, bringing it closer for us to inspect. I don't bother, but Venus picks it up and gives it a careful inspection.

"Impressive," she decides.

He returns to his act while my hands clench against my knees, and I consider reaching for my inhaler to stave off the shock of it.

Venus leans into my shoulder. "It's amazing, the discipline and control it requires. First, the swallower must learn to control his gag reflex, which is as much mental as it is physical. Then, he tilts his head to straighten the esophagus. A safe insertion is achieved through relaxation and focus and by allowing gravity to guide the blade into the esophageal tube—a very flexible structure that enables the blade to pass near the heart and lungs without notice. One wrong move and..."

"Getting tongue-tied has a new meaning?" I finish, leaning closer.

A rare grin appears on her face. "He'll be at a loss for words, that's certain."

"His real act will cut both ways," I quip, smirking.

She chuckles. "Like a hot knife through butter... *but the butter is his aorta.*"

"I don't think he's the sharpest tool in the drawer," I answer, only barely containing my laughter.

"Oh, that cliché cuts like a knife," she says, and we both lean into each other, snickering, like kids again.

Mr. Massie clears his throat. "Pardon me, but are you two paying attention?"

"Our apologies," Venus says. "We don't want to cross swords with you."

Dot cackles. He rolls his eyes, looking bothered that the gorgeous woman beside me has stolen his big performance. She sits more upright, restoring the gap between us, and I dislike the separation.

On the third and longest sword, he bends over and lets Dot gently push the blade down his throat. I'm amazed and appalled.

But Venus pops from her seat with applause when Mr. Massie bows. Dot joins in, and he blushes at the attention.

"I witnessed a performance in India," Venus tells me, sitting back down. "The art originated there. It takes years to perfect it, if one ever can, and only a few dozen people in the world can do it. It's not a carnival trick, Henry. It's an art."

"Do you think I should hire him?" I ask, arms still folded.

"I think… you have a sword swallower living here. What could be weirder or truer than that?"

She leaves me, disappearing into the short hallway and heading outside for whatever brought her downstairs in the first place. Mr. Massie sanitizes his blades, carefully returning them to his velvet-lined case. Dot plops into the seat beside me.

"Took my sage advice, I see," she says, her dark brow cocked high on her forehead.

"She's here to install the garden. That's all."

"That's not all. You just had the cutest *I-want-to-suck-your-face* moment with her," she says.

Venus strolls back into the museum, carrying a garden trowel. Her fanny pack bounces against her hips as she rushes by us for the stairs. I lean my elbows against my knees, trying not to watch her but failing.

Dot pats my back. "If I may offer one more piece of advice…"

"As if I can stop you."

"You'll want to hear this, Henry. It's not from me, but from a romance expert—my buddy, Jack Graham."

"The bestselling romance author? Fine. What would he say?"

"When it comes to love, always chase."

I consider her words—his words—and shake my head. "When I chase, she runs."

CHAPTER 25
Venus

THE GARDEN INSTALLATION takes longer than expected, and not just because of the pleasant diversion of a sword swallowing performance. Layering the peat moss, sand, perlite, pumice, lava rock, orchid bark, shredded bark, tree fern fiber, and rock wool between two large raised beds took time, as did filling the bogs with water from the rain barrel. I'd forgotten the work involved. The humidity is sweltering, and the sun bears down on me. But all that's left is the planting.

Perhaps I should have accepted his offer to help, but it's too late.

A professional wouldn't require help, and that's my shield—*professionalism*. I haven't dropped it once since arriving here, though perhaps I lowered it slightly during Mr. Massie's performance. It's hard to stay professional when Henry's being clever.

Or apologetic.

Back then, I was the apologetic one, forced to deliver half-hearted apologies whenever I made a mistake or acted on impulse. I don't think most children are required to apologize as much as I was. He certainly wasn't. Neither was Ivy. But they weren't *difficult*.

Still, it felt nice to hear an apology from him, like applying an ice pack to a swollen bruise. It numbed some inner pain that I've long ignored. Despite my actions, despite my mouth, despite my brain... I *wanted* to be liked.

By Maggie, especially. She was the closest to a mother I had. With Ivy's constant correspondence with hers, I longed for a similar connection. But her half-hearted affection only appeared in rare moments between the trouble she believed I caused. By the end, Maggie wanted all threads of connection between them and me severed permanently. I never blamed her. How could I? I nearly cost her Henry.

Practicing my Ins and Outs, I fix my hair off my shoulders and tie it in a messy bun with my scarf. Armed with garden gloves and my trowel, I plant the tall pitchers first to give the flytraps ample space up front, where they can best be admired.

"Sunflowers in the back and cherry tomatoes up front," I remember telling Henry when we planted one of our first gardens. *"That way, we can reach the tomatoes."* The first time we picked cherry tomatoes from the vine and popped them into our mouths, all warm and bursting, Henry beamed with delight. We'd grown the plants from seeds, cared for them, and finally reaped the juicy rewards. He'd been so proud that he picked a handful for Maggie and raced home for her to try them. Her reaction wasn't quite as amazed, but she was pleased.

It became the "Summer of the Tomato" for all the pizzas and salads we made with the bounty. The memory makes me smile, and I feel bad for this morning, when Henry tried to reminisce about that ridiculous physical fitness test, and I cut him off.

There's nothing wrong with keeping our memories, especially if they're all we have.

Movement catches my attention on the cobblestone street below. A Toyota hybrid pulls to a crooked stop in an illegal parking spot at the curb. The flashers blink on. *"My kid is better than yours,"* reads the lone bumper sticker on the rear end, which is both presumptuous and categorically untrue. The back door swings open, and a young boy escapes before the driver, a pretty brunette, exits to catch up with him.

Henry reaches him first, appearing just inside my line of vision from the sidewalk below. The boy races into his arms, and Henry lifts him, backpack and all, into a smiling hug.

Warmth blazes through me. This must be Olly. *Henry's son.*

I stare, paralyzed by an overwhelming joy for him, for them both, unable to look away, even though I need to battle back the emotional surge inside me.

Olly is adorable. He's Henry, in miniature. His head rests on Henry's shoulder, his messy brown hair blending perfectly with his father's.

They exchange words. As Olly speaks, he presses his glasses higher on his nose, just like Henry does. Henry fiddles with his hair, making him laugh.

The woman comes over, rolling a child-sized suitcase behind her. She is elegant, graceful, and smiling. She wears a floral sundress with sneakers—an outfit similar to what Ivy picked out for me today—and she rests her hand on Henry's arm as she speaks to him.

Unnecessary touching is a key indicator of attraction.

Olly slides down his father to take control of his rolling suitcase. His mother stops him with a demand for a final embrace. He obeys, waves goodbye, and takes Henry's hand in his free one. She rushes toward her vehicle, blowing kisses at Olly, Henry, or both, I don't know. I suspect both.

Waving goodbye, they stroll toward the building, talking nonstop, and disappear from my view.

My thoughts scatter amid wild wonders. I wonder what they're saying, what it's like to love and parent and be a part of something so precious. I wonder what it's like to pack his little suitcase, hold his hand, or pick him up and hold him close. To have a child's care, well-being, and love in your hands must be life's greatest adventure.

I wonder what it's like for someone to be *that* happy to see you.

Dread edges in soon and replaces my warm feelings. I don't belong here. Henry has a life, a family, that I have no business invading. I need to leave as soon as possible.

As my now jittery hands continue their work, I take measured solace in the fact that I'm nobody. Olly doesn't know me. As far as he's concerned, I'm another hired worker like Dot and Mr. Massie, here to do a job and leave. With any luck, Henry will sequester them both in their apartment so I can make a graceful exit without any awkward encounters or conversations.

I secure my shields, just in case. *I'm a professional.*

CHAPTER 26

Henry

THE FULL-BODIED RELIEF that happens when Olly returns home hits me instantly as we walk inside. Though I know Carly takes excellent care of him, I'm uncomfortable when he's not with me, like a constant tug-of-war between worry and letting go.

He gushes about his weekend until we run into Dot in the hallway.

"Golly, it's Olly!"

They enact their special handshake, slapping their hands together, backward and forward, bumping elbows, and then wiggling to end it, while he giggles and tries to get it right. Mostly, he does. She rustles his hair before holding up her tablet victoriously and saying her goodbyes.

"Dad, we had corndogs," he continues, "and watched *Spiderman*, and Mom wants to get a cat—"

He stops upon seeing Mr. Massie, who bows dramatically. "Olly! It's a pleasure to meet you. I'm Eric the Sword-Swallower."

Olly laughs. "That's funny."

Mr. Massie's smile lifts to me. "Henry, I thought we might talk? I know you're busy with this little tyke and Venus, but—"

"Venus? *THE* Venus?" His brown eyes enlarge to the size of golf balls, and his jaw drops.

"Um, yeah, the real Venus." I run a hand through my hair—I haven't prepared for this. "She's installing the garden on the roof."

I refuse to lie, but this is awkward. Wouldn't allowing them to meet break our no-attachments agreement? Olly's already attached to her through my stories, and Venus doesn't want to be attached to us.

But I think of what Dr. Blake said, that she doesn't know what she wants, and Dot's encouragement: *Why not love her while you have the chance and let the future take care of itself?*

"Dad! She's here?" he asks again, impatiently. His pleading eyes end any debate. This might be his only chance to meet her. After all my stories, how could I deny him?

"Could you wait here, Mr. Massie? I have to..."

He waves me off and plops onto the bench. "Take your time."

My son's cheeks puff with his hopeful smile.

I try to predict Venus's reaction. Will she run away? Is she already climbing down the fire escape? If she stays, will she be cold and aloof, ultimately hurting his feelings? *Test her, then. If there's any hope, you'll see it.*

I take his hand, leading him to the staircase. "I'm happy for you to meet her, but just remember, Venus isn't like other people."

He scoffs. "I know, Dad. That's what I love best about her."

Did he say *love*? Everything inside me sinks a little. I stop him on the stairs and crouch to his level. "I'm sure she'll love you, too, but it might be hard for you to tell that on the outside."

"Right," he says, rolling his eyes impatiently. "She's short on smiles but big on brains and feelings. I remember."

Olly pushes through the rooftop access door in front of me, almost tripping over his feet.

"Venus!" he shouts. "I've been *dying* to meet you!"

Shoving her gloves into her fanny pack, she turns—a deer caught in the headlights.

At first.

Olly races over, dumping his backpack and all but forcing her to meet him at his level. She goes to one knee just in time for him to crash into her arms.

And there it is, this sweet and elusive glimmer as she accepts his embrace—one I've rarely seen. Her hand falls against his back, ring-covered fingers spreading over him, and her eyes close as she tucks in her bottom lip, like she's tucking in her emotions, too. She nestles against his small shoulder. Her cheeks plump in an uncharacteristically wide and beautiful smile.

This is Venus, *happy*.

A sharp inhale makes my chest flutter at the sight of it. My heart catches in my throat—I never would've expected this. That Olly would be bold enough to hug a stranger or that Venus would be so gracious in her acceptance. Have I ever seen Venus hug anyone but me?

No—an answer that makes my emotions swell even more.

Olly pulls back, beaming at her. He grabs her arm, unabashedly touching and ogling her tattoos. "Aw, you're all painted. It's so pretty and cool. Dad didn't tell me about that."

Her eyes cut to mine. "You told him about me?"

"He's told me all your stories," Olly answers for me. "About climbing trees and Frank the Frog and ants in the pants and the gardens you planted and the adventures you went on—"

"Olly," I cut in, finally finding my voice to break his stream-of-consciousness. "He'll go on forever if you let him."

"I don't mind," she says, a little breathless.

"Did you really pick up a snake with your *bare* hands?" He cocks his head at her with scrutiny.

"Several times," she answers. "The last time, I became friends with a *Sanzinia madagascariensis* or a Malagasy tree boa in Madagascar."

Olly giggles. "You talk funny."

Venus's eyes catch mine over our shared memory—I said the same thing to her over our first lunch together in second grade.

A sad smile escapes her as she says, "So I've been told. Do you like snakes?"

"Eh, they're a bit scary," he admits with a light shrug.

"Well, some are very dangerous. You should never pick one up without knowing what type it is, if it's venomous, or if it seems nervous or unfriendly," she explains, "but snakes are often misunderstood… Oh, I have something you might like."

She holds up a finger and unzips her fanny pack. She digs inside the overstuffed bag until she pulls out what appears to be an ordinary brown rock.

"This reminds me not to be afraid," she says. "All creatures are treasures."

He raises his hands and his brow at once. "It's just a rock."

She flips the rock over. "No, it's a fossil."

My kid's head practically explodes with awe.

I step closer to see the soft, pale outline of a curled skeleton, small but embedded clearly in the stone. The snake's tiny skull reveals even tinier fangs. Olly runs his fingers over it, but only after she does.

"I named him Mango," she says, "after the Mangoky River where I found him."

"Aw, he's so cute," Olly coos, touching him again.

"Now, you've touched a snake, too," she says, flashing a soft smile.

Olly holds the stone up toward me. "Dad! I touched a snake!"

I barely manage a nod—I'm so shocked by the scene unfolding before me. Olly is his usual exuberant self times ten—that's typical. But Venus isn't what I thought she'd be at all.

Most adults act differently around children. They put on happy faces, explain things with simple words, and even use higher-pitched voices.

But Venus doesn't change for him, except to allow his affection. She stays herself unequivocally. And my affection for her grows more for it. She's passed the test easily, while I've made our situation harder.

I couldn't let Venus Blake go when I was angry. How will I let her go after this? What's to stop me from falling in love with this woman all over again?

A weird surge of protection and perhaps self-preservation overcomes me, forcing my hand on Olly's shoulder and squeezing him gently toward me. Away from her.

Venus stands, her green eyes landing on mine in guarded curiosity, as if wondering if she's done something wrong.

She hasn't, but this isn't what I expected. I'm not sure if it's even what I want. I've never seen my son so elated, and I'm with him every Christmas morning. Wouldn't it have been better for her to remain a mystery? A figment of his imagination?

Imaginary friends don't leave.

"That's great, Olly, but we should leave Venus alone to finish the garden." I manage, my mouth going dry. "Say goodbye to her and Mango."

Olly's face contorts from happy to devastated in a flash. "Dad, do I have to?"

"No, please keep Mango," she says, refusing to take it. "He's traveled all this way and needs a better home than my fanny pack."

Olly giggles before turning his pleading eyes on me.

"Thanks, Venus. That's kind," I say.

"Dad, can I help Venus with the garden? Pleeeaaasssse," he begs, clasping the fossil between praying hands.

Her eyes stay fixed on mine, her face expressionless, like she might be testing me, too.

"Um, okay, just for a few minutes. I need to talk to Mr. Massie downstairs, anyway." I meet Venus's eyes again. "Is this okay? Will you be alright?"

Disappointment outlines her face, like she's offended at my uncertainty, but she says, "Of course."

She points to the nearly empty bin of plants, showing Olly what's left to do. "We're planting *Dionaea muscipula* and *Sarracenia flava*—"

"Venus," I cut in, turning from the access door. "He's six. Maybe don't use Latin? It's too advanced for him."

Venus and Olly twist in my direction with highly offended, gaping stares. If looks could kill, I'd be dead twice over.

"Too advanced?" Venus begins to counter, but Olly chimes in with, "Dad, we got this."

Venus's brow cocks in a silent challenge.

Defeated, I back away and retreat to the museum.

CHAPTER 27
Venus

I CAN'T COMPREHEND the mental complexities of being a parent. The idea feels too beautiful and overwhelming to consider for long, like my brain might combust with the effort. In this regard, I'm certain that Henry knows best and infinitely more than I do.

But this interaction felt like a test. Henry looked anxious, leaving me alone with Olly. Does he genuinely think I'm incapable of basic care or even momentary engagement with a child?

Olly steps up onto the large planter I've turned over for him to use as a step stool and asks, "What can I do?"

"You are going to finish this garden." I hand him my gardening gloves. "Hands up, please."

He lifts his hands and giggles as I put on the gloves. They're too big, but they'll have to do. The last thing I want is to discover the hard way that he's allergic to peat moss or tree fern fiber. He smiles at me behind his floppy fingers, and I smile back.

It's hard to believe that only moments ago, I was terrified to meet him. Of course, my nerves were all but obliterated by the fact that he knew all about me. I still feel warm over his embrace, like it preheated the oven for our relationship, such as it will be. I don't know what to think about Henry sharing our stories with him. Flattered? Saddened? Annoyed? Proud? So, I file those wonderings away for later and refocus on the task at hand.

Olly is delighted to learn that the flytraps and pitcher plants rely on bugs for their food. He doesn't appear bored when I explain in full detail how their digestive systems work. He even asks thoughtful questions.

"How do bugs taste?"

"They're disturbingly crunchy, in my experience. I don't like them, but plants don't have taste buds like we do."

"Can flytraps eat people?"

"No, we're too large and complex for them."

"Do the bugs feel it when they're eaten?"

"Um, I don't think so."

"How do you know so much?"

"I read a lot."

"Dad says you're a brainiac," he says, giggling.

"Yes, I've been called that before. I don't like it."

"How come?"

"Brainiac sounds like maniac."

He giggles again, though I'm serious.

"Dad says you're not like other people."

My shoulders deflate over the possible meanings of such a remark to a child. Was it a warning? "I'm not. Neither are you. Everyone is different. Mango isn't the same as any other snake."

"Do you think Mango would like to sleep under my pillow?"

"Yes, I think Mango would enjoy that, if your father allows."

"Can Mango take baths with me?"

"Yes, if your father allows."

"Are plants afraid of the dark?"

"No, they need a break from the hot sun, just like we do. Besides, plants don't have eyes or fears."

"Are *you* afraid of the dark?"

I pause to consider his question. "I'm not afraid *of* the dark, but there have been times when I've been afraid *in* the dark. Do you understand the difference?"

He nods, pressing the sandy dirt around a lopsided flytrap. "I'm afraid of a lot of things. Dad says I need to be brave, like you."

An uneasy lump forms in my throat, and I'm unsure of what to do with that information. I've never considered myself brave for exploring nature—it's what I've always been taught to do. The other times that Henry considered me brave stemmed from my desire to help him and my need for his friendship. Having someone to be brave for makes all the difference.

"No, not like *me*. Be brave, like *you*. You have a brave heart, Olly. Look how you handled these carnivorous plants. Besides..." I ease Mango free from where he sticks out of Olly's pocket. "Mango needs you, now. Be brave for him, too. He won't be afraid of the dark as long as he has you."

Mango doesn't have fears or feel *anything* anymore—that's understood. And surely, a child as intelligent as Olly understands that while accepting the allegory I'm proposing.

"I used to be brave for your dad," I go further, "and it helped me be brave overall. Your dad was also brave for me."

"How?"

My shoulders bounce. "By being my friend when no one else would."

His brow quirks. "Because you're different?"

"I suppose so. But I'd rather be different, like Mango, than be another boring, old rock. Wouldn't you?"

Olly's cheeks puff into a big smile as he takes Mango into his hands and holds the rock up toward the newly finished garden. "Look, Mango. We did it."

The rooftop door swings open with a screech, and Henry bumbles onto the roof, as if hurried. He almost looks surprised to find us alive and well.

"Oh, well, Olly. Your father's back. I guess we can't rappel off the building now or set anything on fire," I say, locking eyes with Henry. Olly giggles, remarkably catching my sarcasm.

Henry's shoulders slump, and he sends a hand through his mussed hair. "I wasn't rushing to get back. I didn't want to impose on you. That's all."

I don't believe him, but I let it go. I help Olly off his planter perch and lean down to face him. "You understand that I was joking, correct? We don't rappel off buildings or set fires, not for fun."

"I know," he chuckles. "That wouldn't be safe for Mango, anyway."

"Precisely," I grin. "It's been a great pleasure to meet you, Olly."

"Wait, you're leaving?" he whines.

"The garden is finished. My work here is done."

"But I want to show you my bedroom, and my sword—"

"Play sword," Henry corrects.

"—and I went on a boat this weekend—"

"Olly, I'm sure Venus wants to hear all about it, but we have to go to Grandma and Grandpa's, remember?" he tries, softly.

"Can Venus come? Grandma won't mind," Olly says.

A sardonic laugh bubbles from me, but I stifle it quickly. Grandma would mind very much.

Henry looks almost desperately conflicted, not wanting to disappoint his son or offend me, so I do what I always do. I save him.

"Olly, it's a very considerate offer, but I have dinner plans." I gather my tools, piling them unceremoniously in the empty bins.

"Will you come back another time?" Olly asks.

"I will return to check on the garden," I say, "if that's acceptable."

"On a day that I'm here?" Olly pushes. "I go to Mom's on the weekends."

I meet eyes with Henry, who gives me an encouraging nod.

"I will arrange it with your father to make sure you're here, and I'll teach you everything you need to know about caring for our garden. Is that acceptable?"

"Very," Olly chirps and then salutes.

They walk me to the Land Rover, Henry toting a bin and Olly carrying my trowel. Once the items are inside, Olly latches onto my waist and squeezes tightly.

"We should be best friends and go on adventures like you and Dad did," he says, face crushed into my side.

Henry's brow quirks over the rims of his glasses, and he seems about to counter his son's request, but I say, "I'd like that," before he has the chance.

Because it's true, for Olly, but noncommittal for Henry's sake.

On the drive home, I'm fraught with mixed emotions. I replay the entire encounter, analyzing my words and actions to find faults that I didn't see at the moment.

I don't find any, though. Perhaps conferring with Ivy and Dr. Broderick might enlighten me.

Until then, I resist my insecurities and take some satisfaction in knowing that Olly and I got along so well. He was an inquisitive delight, and I excelled socially, for once.

My hands twist on the steering wheel as irritation slips in. Henry tells his son about our adventures, but warns him that I'm not like other people. Henry builds me up in Olly's mind, but is reluctant for us to spend time together. Henry knows I'm an adult, highly intellectual, and capable, and yet, he felt nervous leaving me alone with Olly. What does Henry think of me?

She's smart, but… Always with a but.

At home, I enact my dinner plans—spaghetti, Dad's jarred sauce, and veggies from the garden—feeling muddled and bothered. Henry doesn't want me in his life or Olly's. He only wants an idealized version of me that he can control and manipulate to teach lessons or be entertaining. I wouldn't be surprised if he uses me as a cautionary tale. *Venus is different than other people. She gets in trouble when she doesn't listen to her teachers or do her homework.* I'm nothing more than a bedtime story.

After dinner, I water the plants outside that need it, and as I wander through the garden, I see our old path through the woods. Henry's there, not a half mile from me, at Maggie's.

But for the first time, I have no desire to go there.

CHAPTER 28

Henry

"THE PROBLEM WITH SUNFLOWERS, *Henry, is that they need space to thrive. Vertically and horizontally. We never should've planted them here, with other plants, or in an enclosed space,*" Venus once said, pointing to our small garden bed in the greenhouse where the sunflowers wilted and sagged over the thriving tomato plants. "*They have thick, stubborn stalks that need support, and their big-headed blossoms require six to eight hours of direct sunlight a day. They need more than this place can give them, Henry. That's why they're dying. We killed them.*"

Crossing the campus to my first class, I rehash the words from my paper and sigh, considering Dr. Kwon's notes. *This is the heart of Buttercup's story. She needed more space to thrive.*

But does she still? I wonder.

That paper, Dr. Kwon's notes, and my nearly full composition notebook are safely secured in my messenger bag. Every spare moment I've had has been spent writing in it, as if Venus unleashed the dam holding my stories in. I can't stop them.

Inside the education building, I navigate the bright, crowded halls to my class, thankful that I'm familiar enough with the place to know where it is, as my head is elsewhere.

I want to apologize for yesterday. She was great with Olly. He couldn't stop talking about her, much to Mom's dismay at dinner. Still, I was awkward about their interaction, and Venus noticed. My reluctance had nothing to do with her taking care of Olly, despite her little joke about rappelling and starting fires. I *know* she's capable.

It's not her. It's me. I hesitate for the hurt that's to come. In only a few minutes, watching her with Olly, I started picturing the three of us together. *Really* together. I imagined a better life for us with Venus in it. One weekend with her makes me want a million more. I shouldn't entertain those ideas—it'll only hurt worse when she leaves again.

I take a seat near the window in class and glance across the pathway to the sciences building. I notice a woman with long, blonde hair bouncing up and down the stoop, repeatedly like a march. After a double-take, I realize that it's Venus.

She looks different. Professional. A long floral skirt billows around her tight calves, and the slit catches on her leg as she marches downward, revealing her sunflower tattoos on her thigh—*our* sunflowers, I realize sadly.

Her top seems molded to her every curve, and the cropped sleeves reveal her toned arms. Uncharacteristically mud-free, white sneakers replace her worn hiking boots. A canvas tote dangles from her arm. She fidgets with her rings and bracelets as she goes up and then down the stairs again. A blue and white scarf waves in her hair.

The woman who has no problem rappelling off mountainsides or picking up snakes is afraid to enter her father's classroom. I understand her anxiety, probably better than anyone.

I should help her. A kind, encouraging word might be all she needs to wrangle her confidence—I've seen it with students a thousand times. I grab my things, shoving them into my messenger bag, and I'm almost energized by the opportunity to do something for her.

But the professor enters the class with a loud greeting, and when I look back at the window, Venus has already gone inside.

CHAPTER 29
Venus

MY CHEST ACHES from the anxiety compressing it as I yank the heavy door open and enter the stadium-style lecture room. Light conversation ceases. Heads turn to see who's entered, but I don't make eye contact. I traverse the large stairs toward the opening in the middle, where a lone podium awaits.

I'm late. Sweat trickles down my neck, matting my hair to it. My stomach rumbles angrily because my nerves prevented me from eating breakfast. I practice my Ins and Outs, but my breath quivers on the release.

I slip in my new shoes on the last step, bumbling awkwardly and catching myself on the podium. The microphone catches my blunt curse.

"Fuck!" echoes throughout the room—a fitting start to this preposterous endeavor.

Finding no relief in the students' snickering, I breathe in deeply and straighten my shoulders. I take my position behind the podium and empty the contents of my bag, setting up my laptop and today's notes. The screen comes to life behind me, projecting today's itinerary over the extra-large whiteboard.

Finally, I glance up. Twenty-five faces scattered around the room stare back at me, waiting. A woman in the front row smiles encouragingly. The man behind her cocks his brow and smacks his chewing gum as he looks me over. Everyone is behind a screen, fingers at the ready.

The fluorescent lights hum overhead, and the faint smell of industrial cleaner mingles uncomfortably with my empty stomach.

Apart from the people in it, the room is boring and uninspiring. White walls meet gray floors and black seats with hideaway desks strung together, and I find myself inexplicably seeking out the color green, as if I need it to get through this.

My eyes land on the same woman in the front row. She wears a plain, forest green t-shirt.

I clear my throat, remembering Ivy's advice. "Um, nice shirt," I say to her.

She glances down to see what she's wearing. "Thanks," she says, like it's a question.

"Dude, are you the prof?" the man behind her asks bluntly, eyeing me in a way I don't appreciate. He reminds me of Brock from high school—tall, handsome, athletic, and arrogant. I look away from him and toward the other students.

"I'm Dr. Blake. My pronouns are she/her. This is Rare Plants of North Carolina, a special topics course, section PB 464. Is everyone in the correct classroom?" My voice betrays me, trembling with my words. I sound as nervous as I feel.

"Are *you* in the correct classroom?" the man laughs. "I thought Dr. Blake was a boring, old guy."

"Dr. *Richard* Blake is middle-aged, not old, and certainly not *boring*. But he isn't here. I'm teaching his class this summer. I'm his daughter, but I'm also a botanist and environmental scientist. So, don't call me dude."

The young man puts his hands up submissively. "No offense, and no complaints. You're easier on the eyes."

His wide grin makes me squirm, as do the dozens of eyes on me. I fiddle with my rings, sliding my finger over my mood ring.

"This isn't high school." Words I meant only for my inner monologue slip out and find the mic.

I clear my throat again, in and out, and consider my work with Dr. Broderick, how she stresses empowerment and finding my voice when I'm mistreated. "This isn't high school… and immature remarks like that won't be tolerated. Your name?"

He looks confused. "Brent Thomas."

"Mr. Thomas, I'm removing you from the class, and I will speak to your advisor. You may go."

The woman in the first row smiles. Someone else claps. He rises, mumbling and huffing and mouthing the word *bitch*. But he leaves.

Then, there were twenty-four.

"Anyone else care to offer commentary about my father or my appearance?"

Silence.

"Good. I trust that you have accessed the syllabus online and downloaded the materials," I say. "Let's begin with Dr. Blake's notes in part one."

My fingers shake as I move my cursor and prompt the material, which I read aloud, verbatim. By the time my phone chimes to indicate the class is over, nearly three hours later, I've read through three sections of materials, and four students are asleep.

Someone in the back row raises their hand.

"Yes?"

"So, is this how the class is going to be? You reading notes?"

"Um, well..." My voice trails off as the other students peer forward as if they have the same question. I should have elaborated with anecdotes or spoken on some of my research projects, but following the words on the screen kept me from racing out of here. Each sentence marked another moment closer to the end of class, and that was my goal—to make it to the end.

"I don't know."

"Is attendance mandatory?" someone calls out.

No one moves, awaiting my answer. I don't know what to say. I didn't take attendance at the start of class, as perhaps I should have. Making anything mandatory sounds brutal, reminding me of my fifth-grade teacher, Mrs. Harlow, who forced me to sit up front and take dictation of her lectures, word for word, even though I already knew the material. *"To keep you quiet,"* she said. My fingers would cramp after every class.

"No, nothing is mandatory," I say.

Everyone rises, and the room empties. In the quiet, I rest my head against the podium, knowing that I've failed to make a good impression.

But I stayed.

At noon, I exit the building, grateful for the sun on my face. I'm exhausted and irritated with myself. I've ridiculed so many teachers for being boring and failing to engage me. The last few hours have turned me into a hypocrite.

I slump and sigh. Tomorrow I'll have to do it all over again. It's going to be an intolerably long summer.

Looking up, I see Henry spilling out of the library across the green. He shoves a book in his messenger bag, adjusts his glasses, and heads toward the food court, exactly where I was going.

I imagine sharing a table with him and discussing our classes—he suggested resuming our friendship. Perhaps he'd share some teaching techniques to help me do a better job tomorrow. I step in his direction, relieved at the idea, but then stop abruptly when I recall his awkwardness and anxiety over my interaction with Olly.

Henry doesn't want me in his life. His suggestion of friendship was just Henry being Henry, a good guy who doesn't do one-night stands and eases his conscience by throwing words like *friends* around.

Hungry and alone, I retreat to my father's office. As expected, no one visits during office hours.

At home, I scarf down whatever I find quickly in the fridge—pickles, cheese slices, and a bunch of grapes. I lean against the sink, nibbling as I hold Christie's paperback close to my nose. The princess is imprisoned in a high tower "for her own protection" against the angry coven of witches determined to destroy her and ruin her plans to marry the warlock. She doesn't want to marry him either, but considers it her duty. The pirate who accidentally saved her once has set out to save her again, this time on purpose. He climbs up a rope fifty yards to reach the tower window—an impressive feat. She plays coy. "You're a rogue!" she whisper-yells when she could easily raise the alarm. She secretly hoped he'd show and save her from the life she knows she doesn't want, but feels she must accept.

I wonder if that's all that romance truly is—a bond that counters reason.

But I reserve judgment until I achieve a larger sampling of novels.

My phone buzzes in my pocket. With a pickle in one hand, I set the paperback down on my current page and slide my phone from my pocket with the other. A text alights my screen.

> How did your classes go? It must've been challenging to be back in a classroom.

A second text arrives as I read the first.

> It's Henry, btw. I got your number from Marnie, who got it from Ivy. I hope that's okay.

Is it? I don't know what to think or feel except surprise. I take a breath, mouth half-full with pickle.

> It's surprising, but not unwelcome. Hi, Henry.

> Hi, Venus.

I debate how to answer his original question. There's the truth—that my day could inspire a book entitled "How Not To Teach"—and there's a hundred vague dismissives that could satiate him without lying. *Fine. It's over and done. Could've been better.*

I huff. I don't want to lie and say it went well, but I also don't want to admit I failed, either. So, I compromise.

> It was a challenge, but not an insurmountable one. Tomorrow will be better.

It's a vague truth that must prove true, or I'll be on the next flight to anywhere else.

The teasing ellipsis appears and disappears, then reappears. And vanishes again. I consider Ivy's instructions and text him during the intermission.

> How were your classes?

The triple dots appear again before his text arrives.

> Good, thanks. A formality, really. I came across an intriguing book on local history in the library. Coastal Lore & Legends.

I access my library app and download the book. I read the synopsis and chuckle.

> This seems interesting. I've also been reading about pirates.

> Anything I might be interested in?

VENUS LOVE TRAP

I glance at the scantily clad pirate and princess on the cover of Christie's paperback and smirk.

> Probably not.

It's good research. The Graveyard of the Atlantic will be well-represented in the museum. I just acquired a shackle from Blackbeard's ship, the Queen Anne's Revenge.

> Impressive.

The mystical dots appear again, and I wait.

I'm sorry about yesterday.

> Could you be more specific?

I apologize for ambushing you with Olly. When he found out you were there, he had to meet you. It must've been a shock that he knew about you.

I consider his statement.

> Yes, but Olly is delightful. I'm honored that he knows about me.

Meeting you meant a lot to him. He talked about nothing else at dinner.

My eyebrow quirks.

> Maggie must've been thrilled.

She behaved. It's hard to argue with Olly's enthusiasm.

> It's nice having someone enthusiastic about me.

The ellipsis appears, vanishes, and reappears.

I'm also sorry if I seemed uncomfortable on the roof yesterday. I wasn't prepared for the two of you meeting or how well you got along. It brought out my protective side.

I groan and shake my head.

> Why? Were you concerned that I'd be unsafe or hurtful with him?

The ellipsis does its dance again. I bite into another pickle, awaiting his response. For his apology to matter, I must understand it. When the ellipsis disappears, I nearly set the phone down—this might take time for him to articulate.

But it rings in my hand, announcing Henry on FaceTime.

I jump and accept the call, forgetting the pickle hanging out of my mouth.

"No, Venus, that's not it at all. I..." he says sternly, forgoing a greeting. But eyeing my protruding pickle makes his eyes narrow before he manages a laugh. "Is that a pickle?"

I nod and bite off what I can chew before setting the rest down on the counter behind me. With puffy cheeks, I mumble, "I didn't expect you to FaceTime."

"Sorry, but I don't want you to think that, and I thought it'd be better to explain face to face. Is this okay?"

"Um, of course." A breeze tousles his earthy hair, and sunlight glints in his eyes behind his thick frames, reminding me of a *Cosmos atrosanguineus*, the chocolate cosmos—a beautiful, brown, and maroon-hued flower native to Mexico—especially with the blue sky behind him. "You're outside."

"On the balcony." He twists the phone to show me the river view. He turns it back on himself, flashing his lopsided smile as I wipe my lips with my hand. "Venus, I'd never think you'd be unsafe or hurtful with Olly. It wasn't you at all—you were great with him. It was me. I, um..."

He pushes his glasses up on his nose and shrugs. "I was worried about him getting too attached. Worried for me, too."

His chin droops while his eyes squint, and I feel his distress—it's a worry we share.

"I-I-I didn't mean to..." I swallow the thickness in my throat. "If you want me to stay away, I will."

"No, that's not what I want." His head shakes, and his smile returns. "I *was* worried, but... holding Frank the Frog also worried me, and that turned out okay."

He chuckles, and a smile appears in the little box holding my face, too. "Better than okay, Henry. We disproved a false claim and created a story to tell."

"An *illustrated* story, thanks to you," he adds, motioning to his heart. "Frank the Frog is Olly's favorite."

The emotion in my throat thickens again—a feeling that doesn't make sense scientifically but exists nonetheless.

"Have you told anyone that story?" he asks, looking curious as the breeze shifts his hair again.

"Um, no," I say, wondering who I would tell it to. Ivy would think it gross, while Dad would surely scold me for touching Frank without gloves. "I'm not—I don't—*tell* stories."

"Yeah, you do. You used to. You told Olly about Mango from Madagascar. You're just out of practice." His head tilts slightly, taking me in as I stumble over even more emotions, and a sexy smile graces his handsome face.

I consider how unpracticed I felt, socializing with Dad, Ivy, and their significant others. "Perhaps, that's true," I admit. "Practice makes perfect, or at least gets us close, as Dad would say."

Fearing our conversation might be coming to an end with his hesitation, I say, "But I'm glad that you shared about Frank. I like Olly. He, um, asks insightful questions, indicative of an above-average intelligence."

Henry nods and turns more serious when he says, "Venus, I'm glad you're home. I want you here."

I swallow another surge of emotions and manage a weak smile. "I… thank you."

"And, I'm not the only one. Olly spent his entire day at camp raving about you and Mango. Leave it to Venus Blake to save me from another boring summer, right?"

Laughter escapes me, and my cheeks heat under his gaze. "We saved each other, Henry."

Silence takes over again, and I search for something to say among the warm feelings he's elicited. He's glad I'm home. He wants me here. This entire conversation seems to bend our rules banning feelings and attachments.

"Olly's looking forward to his garden tutorial. I can't get him to do chores, but he'll consider your instructions his mission," he says, smirking.

"When would you like me to revisit?"

"Sunday afternoon, okay? I'll ask Carly to drop him off early."

"Yes, that's acceptable."

Henry's gentle eyes turn away, and tendrils of his hair dance on his head. I imagine standing beside him, leaning against his shoulder, and his arm wrapping around me. In my fantasy, we discuss the setting—he gives me historical facts about the USS North Carolina battleship in our view, and I counter with the impact of such a massive object on the waters it resides in. He breaks our engagement with a distraction—sweeping my hair out of my eyes, running his thumb over my cheek, kissing me—and my brain empties of all thoughts except one. *Henry.*

"He slept with Mango under his pillow last night," Henry says, breaking the spell.

Feelings stir again—ones I can't afford to entertain. "Um, I'm glad Mango has found a happy home."

CHAPTER 30
Venus

MY CLASS IMPROVES by the week's end because, by Friday, only two students attend, which is much less stressful than talking to twenty-five. Well, twenty-four now. Not that I am talking *to* them. It's more like talking *at* them. But as long as the information is delivered, I meet the criteria for this position.

I'm a terrible teacher. I'm not naturally charming or charismatic. Getting people to like me under everyday circumstances proves challenging—in a classroom setting, it becomes my personal hell.

Only, I don't *want* to be a terrible teacher, especially when the woman in the green t-shirt shows up every day regardless of how boring I am, as if she's waiting for the real Dr. Blake to appear. I'm passionate about the environment, and botany might as well be my religion. It's a hateful shame that I'm failing to get that across, especially to someone who seems equally excited about the subject.

The world needs more scientists. The world needs more female scientists.

She doesn't wear the same shirt every day, to be clear. And her name is Myla Rose, which, in my opinion, is very appropriate for a future botanist.

I've tried to insert amusing anecdotes into Dad's lectures and practice my storytelling, but it doesn't go well. It's like my mouth fills with rocks, and my stories sound choppy and incomplete. I keep office hours, but no one shows up, except for the occasional faculty member. Those interactions fare somewhat better, as I'm perfectly capable of pleasant conversation, but none return for a secondary engagement.

Ivy says it's my face, specifically my lack of suitable expressions. Smiles work wonders, she claims, and advises me to practice in front of a mirror. I tried, but it's weird. Since smiles don't come naturally for me, it's hard to remember and awkward to fit them in.

Plus, I'm not sleeping well, and tiredness often makes me grumpy. I've resorted to using the hammock. All the pillows and weighted blankets in the world wouldn't be a suitable substitute for Henry. At least in the hammock, I feel cradled, and I'm outside, which tricks me into believing I'm on a project, not mere miles from him.

Now that he has my number, Henry texts me frequently, usually sharing random tidbits about Olly and Mango or asking about my day. Sometimes, in the evenings, he'll start a text with…

> Remember when…

And share one of our stories, usually ending with a commentary on how much fun he had or how he misses those times. I enjoy his texts, but they also make me sad.

I answer, as is customary, but don't engage beyond polite responses. I don't know the protocol for reconnecting with Henry after we agreed to limits—no attachments, no big feelings, no more than one night, which we later amended to a weekend. So, when I see him on campus, my confusion about us prevents me from interacting with him. Dr. Broderick says avoidance is acceptable, *sometimes*.

"No! Not when it comes to Henry," Ivy retorts when I share this with her. Buster yaps, as if in agreement. "Venus, apply that logic that you love so much. He jumped through hurdles to get your number, and he's communicating with you every day. What does that indicate?"

I shrug. "Sympathy? Obligation? Boredom?"

"No, silly. *Henry wants more*," she says, poking my shoulder with her index finger at each word.

"More what?"

"More of you," she says, rolling her eyes like it's obvious. "How do you feel about that?"

"I feel like the subject of a cruel experiment," I say. "I *want* his attention, crave it, even, but I don't understand it. Henry almost refused sex over fears of complications, and yet, here he is, complicating us. I consider it... mixed signals."

"Then, make him clarify it. Ask him directly what his intentions are. But *don't* avoid him," she says, squeezing my biceps, like she wants her words to take hold. "You know you don't want to, and he doesn't want you to, either—facts."

I nod at my wise sister and fight an emotional surge with, "Fact—Buster has entirely too much luggage."

She laughs, glancing at the supplies she's lugged into the living room. It's Friday afternoon, and she's about to start her weekend shift at the hospital, leaving me in charge of Buster. His supplies consist of one oversized tote with his food, bowls, and snacks. He has two beds that he uses equally, depending on his mood, and a blanket. Another oversized tote holds toys, his leash, chew bones, a brush, and doggie shampoo, in case he makes a mess, Ivy explains. She provides two typed pages of instructions, which I read carefully. But beyond meal times and his potty schedule, it's mostly superfluous information like, "Be sure to tell him he's a good boy after he eats," and "When you brush him, call him a handsome devil and tickle his belly—he likes that."

Ivy looks nervous when it's finally time for her to leave. "If you have any questions or need anything, text me right away. I put Gil's number on the instructions, too. His brother's a vet, so if anything happens... I'm sure you've got this, though."

She says it as though she's trying to convince herself.

"Yes, Ivy. I'm perfectly capable of caring for another living thing and following instructions," I say with a slight edge to my voice.

She bobs on her clogs and steels her shoulders. "Of course, you are."

"I, um, I... if you need anything during your long shifts... food, extra clothes, um, reading material," I say awkwardly, "I can assist."

Her eyes widen with joyful surprise.

I shrug. "Don't look so shocked. I used to help you with things when you let me."

She nods. "I remember. Hair-braiding, reading, long division, fractions, and laundry. You mommed me all the time."

My brow scrunches. "I didn't mom you. I big-sistered you. Stop turning nouns into verbs. It's not right."

With a giggle, she says, "Forgive me, sis, and thanks. I'm prepared for long shifts like these. Usually, the only thing I might need besides sleep is a pep talk."

My brow scrunches, considering how I might help in that case. "I-I could try to assist."

"I might take you up on that." Shorter than me, she yanks me to her level, insisting on a hug. I allow it, though Buster barks.

When she pulls away, I'm surprised to find tears welling in her eyes. "You know, Venus, you are perfectly capable of so much more than you give yourself credit for, and not just big-sistering or pet-sitting. I mean, normal things. You might be different, but you're no less deserving of love and happiness than anyone else. Whatever you want from life, you should have it. Understand? Even if it's Henry…"

Her voice trails off, like she might be worried that she went too far, but she hasn't—evident in the fact that I latch on to her for a second embrace. Wanting Henry and *having* him have a near-zero probability of intersection, the latter of which feels impossible, but hearing her say that fills me with… good sister vibes. "Thank you," I whisper in her ear, which seems appropriate.

She smiles cheerily as we part. She eyes the black and white puppy staring up at us. "Now, get over here, Buster. Mommy has to go."

After giving Buster an excessive amount of affection, Ivy leaves.

Buster sits on the hardwood floor, staring up at me curiously. He tilts his head and perks his ears, as if awaiting my instructions. "Would you like to help me with the garden, Buster?"

He barks an affirmative.

I find his leash, attach it to his collar, and hook the other end onto my belt loop. Then, we get to work.

By Saturday morning, I decide that Buster is a nice distraction, despite the inevitable trouble he causes. With him around, I was forced to sleep in the bed, and he opted to join me rather than sleep in either of his. I managed a few solid hours with him curled against me. I awoke to him chewing on the laces of my hiking boots, which I'll have to replace. The laces, not the boots; I detest breaking in new hiking boots. He also barks at every little thing—the air conditioning clicking on, birds tweeting outside, a car horn in the distance—and it sounds like a question, "*What?*"

So, I answer him. I can't determine how much he understands, if anything. But he likes hearing me speak. He wags his tail and watches me intently. By Saturday afternoon, he seems conditioned to bark to get my attention, which tells me that he's a smart pup. I don't mind, even if I have to invent something to tell him.

Dr. Rob McCullum emails with an interview request for an assistant lead position on a reforestation and wetlands project at The Nature Conservancy in Aotearoa, New Zealand. It's a five-year project with housing—a private, furnished cottage. For once, I'd have my own residence, and I'd be out from under Dr. Miner's shadow. The idea energizes me.

I've always wanted to travel to New Zealand. I can't imagine a more promising position, and I grow excited as I research it. What could be better than getting lost in a foreign land of tall kauri and kohekohe forests and rainforests dominated by rumu, beech, tawa, matai, and rata, and surrounded by the ocean? I quickly agree to the interview, and Dr. McCullum arranges a video conference for Wednesday that fits my office hours.

I tell Buster everything, and he seems excited for me.

Sunday morning, Henry texts to confirm our meeting to check on the garden, and I quickly agree to be there at two. Nerves percolate all morning, but Buster is quick to distract me, and his presence puts me at ease. So, I bring him with me.

Olly greets me with unhindered enthusiasm, rushing into my arms like he did when we first met. He gushes over Buster, who barks and hops with excitement to have a new source of attention. He tugs on his leash, wrapped around my waist, and licks Olly's face as he pets him.

"Oh, Dad! It's a dog!" he says to Henry, who stands behind us, watching our floor display with his hands in his pockets.

"This is Buster. He's my sister's Border Collie. I'm pet-sitting." I glance at Henry. "Is this okay? I bathed him before we came over to reduce the dander and other allergens."

"Thanks, yeah. It's fine. Poor air quality, overexertion, and emotions are my downfall. Not pets." Henry cracks a smile when Buster jumps onto his feet and begs for his affection. Henry squats down, but loses his balance when Buster pushes into his arms.

"Buster, Henry didn't consent to that behavior," I chide, tugging on the leash.

Olly laughs and joins Buster on top of Henry's chest, making him groan in playful defense. With one hand tickling Olly and the other Buster, Henry regains control, sitting up. "That'll teach you to try to take me down."

Red-faced with laughter, Olly manages, "No, please, stop!"

Henry relents. Buster races to my side again, perhaps not wanting me to feel left out. I scoop him into my arms as I stand and straighten my dress.

"You look nice," Henry says as he rises and helps Olly up.

I didn't want to wear my usual cutoff jeans and t-shirt, so I opted for an airy summer dress that Ivy picked out for me last week.

"Thank you. Ivy has made it her mission to advance my wardrobe while I'm here," I explain.

His eyes skip over my bare arms and the exposed tattoos on my chest, and his smile falls behind whatever he's thinking.

"Let's go see the garden," he says, waving me through the hallway.

"Can I hold Buster's leash?" Olly asks.

I unfasten it from my waist and tie it around his. "Thank you. Buster would like that."

The museum has transformed significantly since I last visited. Henry stands by as I slowly move through the large room, taking it all in. New, freshly painted display cases line the walls, marked by retro-style lettering painted around them that divides the displays into sections.

Wilmington in Film showcases movie memorabilia from the numerous films and television shows produced in the area.

Claims to Fame features famous people born here.

Coastal Treasures features interesting finds, ranging from megalodon teeth to cannonballs.

True Tales showcases quirky stories, like an elephant named Topsy who escaped the circus and went on a two-day rampage through the city, and pictures of Wilmington's World's Largest Christmas Tree.

War Stories feature artifacts and articles from every war since the Revolutionary.

A Weird but True section boasts grainy photos, articles, and alleged proof of local ghosts, aliens, and creature lore, some of which were collected by Jay, an avid paranormalist. Henry has displayed his uncle's tools of the trade—an electromagnetic field meter, a spirit box, an electronic voice phenomenon recorder, an infrared thermometer, and night vision goggles.

A side room, still under construction, will become an escape room featuring local lore and history, Henry explains.

In the back, the words The Dark & Disturbing surround another entryway. "Some scary movie props, the Fort Fisher Mermaid, and an entire section about the Wilmington Massacre—I didn't want to cause little ones nightmares." He points to Olly over his head.

"Henry, it's exquisite. I could spend hours here, reading all the stories and placards."

"Thanks, yeah, it's amazing to see it finally coming together." He runs a hand through his hair. "We've gotten a lot accomplished. It's been a good distraction."

My eyes catch his, and he offers a weak smile.

"I've felt the same about Buster," I admit, as he and Olly loop around us and continue chasing each other around the museum. "I'm sorry if my return has... complicated your life."

"I'm not. I welcome the complication," he says.

"That appears evident, given the texting."

"Is texting okay?"

"It's..." Ivy's words about being direct keep circling through my mind. "Confusing. The boundaries we established are becoming blurred."

"I want them blurred." He nods and stuffs his hands in the pockets of his dark jeans. "Actually, I'd like to renegotiate. I meant what I said about us being friends, especially now that my son won't stop talking about you."

I nearly tear up at the idea of someone liking me *that* much.

"Am I complicating *your* life?" he asks, turning toward me.

"Being home is always complicated for me, but I'd rather have you in my life in some capacity than not at all, especially now that we've... cleared the air." My eyes cut to his.

"An asthma pun. I love it." Henry's cheeks turn rosy with my words, delighting me. "Yeah, I'm glad, too. Though if we ever must *clear the air* again, I wouldn't be disappointed, given our flawless and transcendent capabilities in that department." His pink cheeks bloom red with his innuendo.

A laugh rises from my core and tumbles through a surprised smile. "We were quite perfect with that. Weren't we?"

"Quite."

"Well, perhaps we should follow *your* advice in this regard," I say, butterflies filling my stomach with warm, fluttering wings.

"What advice was that?"

"How about I be Venus, and you be Henry, and we let this go wherever it takes us?"

His full lips widen into a delighted smile while his dark eyes seem to glow with the idea. "Agreed. It's summer, after all."

Now, I blush, recalling his words. *Let's pretend it's always summer for us.*

With a sheepish glance at his feet, his brown eyes return to mine. "I'd like that. I'd also like it if we'd stop avoiding each other on campus."

Embarrassment rushes over me, but seeing his coy grin reins it back. "You noticed?"

"It'd be impossible for me not to notice you, Venus."

Heat rises in me again. "Um, it would be nice to have a friend on campus."

His head tilts with scrutiny. "It's not going well?"

I consider dismissing his question with a vague response. But I recall Dr. Broderick's advice this week after telling her about my poor teaching performances: *"Practice gentle honesty with yourself and others, Venus. Don't be afraid to ask for help."*

"It's awful," I say, sighing heavily, like the information has been pounding at a locked door, desperate to be let free. "Attendance has dropped, and even the faithful ones have trouble staying awake. Dad's notes aren't stimulating without him here to mix in his stories. I get tongue-tied and nervous, so I read the notes he's provided without elaborating. The classroom has gray walls and humming lights, and being in there without color, without *green*, feels like wearing a hot, itchy sweater."

A full-bodied cringe wiggles over me as I explain. "The only way I get through the class is by focusing on the words I'm reading. My inability to do well makes me a hypocrite for all the teachers I've ridiculed over the years. It also breaks my heart because I love botany and want to do well for Dad. He'll be thoroughly disappointed when no one signs up for more of his special topics courses. It wouldn't surprise me if students change their majors out of the sciences altogether after suffering through it."

"Venus, take a breath," he says when I pause.

I'm surging with anxiety and twisting my bracelets and rings, so I do what he says. I shake out my fingers and inhale.

He steps closer, creating a warm pocket between us. "Listen to me. No one starts something new as an expert, not even you. It's your first week. Of course, you're nervous and finding your way. My first week of teaching, I muddled facts, forgot the name of the principal, calling him 'the monotone office guy' in front of the kids, and I led my class through the entire school in a fire drill because I'd been too busy decorating my classroom to bother learning where the nearest exit was. The monotone office guy told me that I was the first teacher in the school's history to fail a fire drill."

His confession makes me laugh.

"Lives could've been lost, Venus," he chuckles sheepishly, and his cheeks turn pink again.

"How did you improve?"

"I made connections. The more I got to know them, and they got to know me, the more comfortable I felt," he says. "Here's my advice for you. Stop using your father's notes. You know the material. You don't need notes, and they prevent you from making the class your own."

"But then, what do I do to fill the time?"

"Be authentically *you*. You were my best science teacher growing up," he says with a smile that sends tingles up my spine. "You can teach them, too, Vee. You don't have to smile or make small talk if you don't want to. You don't have to be anyone but yourself. Just share your love for botany the best way you know how to, and they'll respond."

His encouragement inspires strange reactions. My pulse quickens, my eyes water, and I think of art. When I want to understand and remember something, I draw a picture of it. But how could I apply that here?

Henry smiles as I consider his advice. "I'm proud of you. So is your father. Maybe it hasn't always been clear to you… or to us but we have faith in you. You should have faith in yourself, too."

"You are… that is…" My brain fails to connect the words for the emotion welling inside me, especially when his hand falls to my bicep for a gentle squeeze. My difficulty in expressing myself properly has led people to believe I don't have feelings or don't need the same support as others do. For a long time, I believed that, too. I still do, sometimes. But his support and encouragement help shift my thought process. I *want* to move forward.

"Let's meet for lunch tomorrow," he says. "We can discuss your class, and I have an idea I'd like your opinion on."

I'm about to agree when Olly rushes over with Buster panting beside him. "Is it time to go to the roof yet?"

Buster barks his typical, *"What?"*

"Lead the way," Henry answers, motioning for the stairs.

Olly and Buster rush ahead, but Henry lingers, taking my side as we move across the museum, and I feel dangerously optimistic.

CHAPTER 31
Henry

LETTING *her back into your life will only lead to heartache and disappointment. Why do that to yourself? Or to Olly?* Mom's words from Sunday night's dinner echo in my head as I watch Venus, Olly, and Buster on the rooftop.

This is why.

Venus delivers the garden's instructions, carefully describing the plants and how they function, but in a way that makes sense to a six-year-old, even when she uses scientific terminology. She says that the Venus flytraps' leaves look like faces, waiting for food, but that we shouldn't touch them. "It confuses them, like when something wakes you in the middle of the night, and you're tired the next day," she says. "When they've done their job for the plant, they turn black. That tells us it's time to prune or pick off the dead ones. It's like getting a haircut."

My son hangs on every word, and relates, bringing up times when he's been startled awake or gotten a haircut—he dislikes both, especially when hair stylists gush over his long locks and chubby cheeks. She reports that she also experiences difficulty with unwanted touching. And their bond thickens, like a tree that's gained yet another ring of age in its trunk.

The other night over dinner, he asked me what language Venus speaks. When I said Latin, he decided he'd learn it, "That way, I can talk funny with her." At the library, he checked out every age-appropriate botany book to "see what Venus does."

I've turned my son into a fanboy. I get it—I was the original Venus Blake fanboy. She drew me in with adventure and the unknown and kept me close by encouraging me, making me feel clever, and delighting me with her rarely seen smiles.

She's smiling now, naturally and easily.

It's almost comical that she asked me for teaching advice—she *knows* how to teach. It's her nerves and predispositions that prevent her. I'm honored that she sought my advice—she rarely used to.

But this enigmatic, beautiful woman isn't the Venus I knew, but a more refined, intentional version. She bravely prioritized her care, leaving home and the people she loved most to do it. Words I never thought I'd believe flash through my thoughts—*she was right to leave.* Leaving gave her what I couldn't—the freedom she needed.

It's like I told Marnie—sometimes, being alone is better. For a time, anyway.

I only wish I'd known. It breaks my heart more that she never felt safe enough to tell me—me, the one person she was supposed to feel safe with.

"What's spelunking?" Olly's voice catches my attention.

"It's exploring caves," she says, matter-of-factly.

"Where bats and bears live?"

She shrugs. "Yes, but I haven't encountered bears, only bats. Well, bats, beetles, spiders, cave crickets, and salamanders. Caves are an oasis for insects and other troglobites."

"Are they called that because they bite?"

She smiles. "No, but that's a funny joke."

Buster yaps at their feet as if in agreement.

I sigh—of course, she's been spelunking.

The tutorial soon ends. Olly relinquishes Buster's leash, and Venus affixes it around her waist again. Our typical Sunday to-do list beckons, and we're due at Mom's for our weekly dinner soon.

Even so, I hunt for reasons for her to stay. All weekend, I've forced myself to keep busy, hoping this unbearable longing for her might subside.

It hasn't. Her gentle patience with Olly. Her delicate smiles. The way the breeze flutters the scarf in her hair and catches her dress, pressing it to her curves. The teasing lines of her leg tattoos, vanishing under the hem of her dress. The others that I know are there and want to see again. Her belly button ring sticks out behind the thin fabric of her dress just enough to make me desperate to twiddle it with my tongue again.

Fuck.

She's going to destroy me all over again without even trying.

But it's hard to care.

"I'd like to bring Olly over to see the gardens," I say, breaking into their laughter as they walk ahead of me down the stairs.

She glances over her shoulder. "It's a public garden—"

"No, I mean *your* gardens, your dad's, and the greenhouse," I clarify, stepping in front of her. "I'd like Olly to see the fairy house."

It's an unfair request. I've put her on the spot, asking in front of her doting protégé.

On cue, Olly takes my side and puts his hands together in a prayer position. "Oh, please, Venus?"

When she reaches the bottom step, she opens her mouth as if about to address us together, but Buster's leash catches around her feet as he dashes toward the museum. Her feet get sandwiched together, and she loses her balance, falling into the nearest structure.

Me.

I could kiss that dog for giving me an excuse to touch her. Her hands go to my shoulders as I lean down, untying the leash from her waist and unraveling it from her feet. It slips from my grip. Buster takes off for whatever caught his attention, and Olly dashes after him.

"I'll get him," he says. "Buster, come here, boy!"

I stand slowly, letting my hand drift over her hip and lightly graze the belly button ring under my thumb. My eyes meet hers, and her irises have expanded to bright jade jewels.

Inches from her parted lips, I whisper, "I'm sorry. I shouldn't have asked like that. You can say no."

Her head tilts slightly, considering me, and a light smirk corners her lips. "What Henry wants…"

Her voice trails off, not that she needs to finish her sentence, and every cell in my body cries out for her. My fingers curl, digging into her side.

I am so fucked.

I groan. "No… what Venus wants."

Her smirk grows, like racy ideas are forming an itinerary, and I like imagining what that might include.

She brings her hand to my chest, resting it near my tattoo. She lightly fists the fabric of my t-shirt, but her brow creases with passing thoughts I cannot know. Still, she says, "Come for dinner Thursday at six."

"We'll be there," I say, my grin rising with hers.

Olly rushes over with Buster in tow. "Got him, but barely."

Our hands drop simultaneously, and I shift away from her. "Good job, Olly."

She thanks him and secures his tether to her waist with a firm, "Buster, friends stick together. Next time, come when you're called."

Buster listens intently, perking his ears, and barks in response, like he might be agreeing or saying he's sorry.

Olly giggles. "He's a good dog."

"Very good, until he chews up the laces of your hiking boots," she says.

"Oh, Buster," Olly coos, shaking his head like he's known this dog his entire life.

My hand rakes through my hair, worried that Olly'll start asking for a dog next.

"Will he be at the fairy house when we visit?" he questions without even knowing if she agreed.

"I don't know. If I do a good job, Ivy might let Buster visit again," Venus replies. "Maybe."

"A maybe isn't a no," he says cheerfully—words I say to him often.

She timidly moves toward the foyer as she says, "Buster and I better let you two get on with your day."

We walk her to the Land Rover, where she scoops Buster into her arms and allows Olly to pat him goodbye. I follow suit. Then, she gets into the driver's seat with Buster on her lap.

Olly and I stand there until she turns the corner at the stoplight.

"Dad, I want to go spelunking," Olly says.

"Yep, I bet."

"Can we bring Venus flowers when we go to the fairy house?"

"What? You know she's too old for you, right?"

He scoffs. "I don't like her like *that*, Dad. But I like her. And she likes flowers, so…"

"You're right. That's a nice idea. Olly, you know she won't be here long. You understand, right?"

"I know," he says with a carefree shrug. "She has more adventures to go on."

He says it like it's understood, and I realize that *I'm* the one who needs the reminder.

CHAPTER 32
Venus

"I WANT to start over with a new approach," I say to my class of two. Myla Rose looks skeptical, but she sits up, tapping her nails on her open laptop. My other loyal student, Jayden Jones, leans forward with a hopeful grin. Over the last week of classes, he has steadily moved from the back row to the seat right behind, but one space over from Myla, who sits in the same spot every day. He says something under his breath to her now, and she chuckles.

I clear my throat, nerves rising and stomach twisting into a knot, as I remember Henry's advice to teach as I like to learn, to be authentic, to forge connections. My bracelets jingle as I mess with them.

"I'm not a very good teacher." My mouth goes dry with the words. I slurp my water bottle while the duo eye me with skepticism, like they're unsure how to respond.

Ins and Outs.

"The fact that I don't like classrooms is one serious detriment," I say.

Their smirking faces encourage me to continue.

"For me, being in a classroom again resembles that annoying, needling sensation when a limb falls asleep from lack of circulation, and it hurts until the blood flows normally again."

They gape with raised brows, indicating I may have gone too far.

"So, for me to achieve proper circulation," I explain, "and you, a proper education, I need to teach as I like to learn and bring the outside in."

I leave the podium and approach the whiteboard, marker at the ready. At approximately five feet high and twenty feet wide, this is a much larger canvas than I'm used to. But I take another deep breath and calculate the necessary adjustments.

I start on the left side with a map of the Eastern Seaboard and draw in the features and relevant locations of our coastal plain. Midway through drawing in the details of inland swamps, I turn to my stunned, yet attentive students.

"Music would be appreciated," I say, "if either of you—"

"On it," Jayden says, swiping on his phone.

The room fills with an upbeat instrumental that makes me smile, and my markers move faster. I outline the endemic plants of each region, creating basic representations that highlight their features. The rare plants in North Carolina compose a thirty-page list, so I narrow the focus to endangered and threatened species by region, starting with those in the mountains.

I'm no longer in a classroom, but engaged in an activity that has calmed and inspired me a million times. I don't imagine Henry's here, but I recall him looking over my shoulder at my latest entry and whispering encouragement in my ear. *"That's so real, Venus! What's that part do? What's this thing? How does it work?"* And the tension of a classroom and students dissipates into *normalcy*. This is what I do. *I draw.*

Holding the marker empowers me to speak as I create, like a talking stick. I provide brief explanations for clarity. I even share that my father is allergic to most milkweeds, and incessant sneezing inhibits his ability to study them—a personal anecdote that I find amusing, even if no one else does.

I run out of space as I attempt to move east, and turning to my aghast students, I'm out of breath. Jayden quiets his music.

"It's a little rudimentary," I say.

"That's rudimentary?" Myla blurts.

Jayden laughs. "Dr. Blake, you're like a tattooed Bob Ross with your happy, little trees."

"Is that a compliment?"

They share a confused glance. "Um, yeah."

"Then, thank you." My phone alarm sounds, signaling the end of class. "Wow, we're done already. I hope you learned something today."

"I had no idea that North Carolina was so diverse," Myla says, pausing instead of jumping out of her seat as usual. "I recorded this to watch later. Is that okay?"

"Yes, of course. Please email with any questions about today's lesson," I say, reaching for the eraser.

"Here's a question," Myla says, "can you do that again tomorrow?"

My tension dissipates in a sigh. "Certainly. Have a nice day."

They exit the room, and I lean against the podium, practicing my Ins and Outs. *I did it.* I taught a class (albeit small) without boring them to death, *and* they learned something.

I'm elated, and a little pained. Forced to ignore the headache forming at my temples, I ogle my creation before erasing it. The result is vibrant and intricate, full of life, which is precisely what this classroom needed.

Board clean and lights off, now, I get to see Henry.

CHAPTER 33

Henry

VENUS SPILLS out of the Environmental Sciences Building and abruptly halts her rush when she finds me there, waiting for her. Her brow is pinched and smudged with dirt along the temples.

"Hey, how'd it go?" I ask with a smile, though my heart drops at the sight of her bothered expression.

Her mouth opens, but nothing comes out. The crease to her brow deepens, and she fidgets with her jewelry. She's on the step above me, putting us nearly at eye level. Her obvious distress makes me think that I'll need to give better advice, something more concrete and actionable than *be yourself*. "Whatever happened, we can—"

My cued-up platitudes fall to the wayside when she gives up on words and falls into my arms, silencing me with a warm, tight, full-bodied embrace.

"It was so much better," she whispers in my ear. "Thank you."

Her scarf tickles my cheek as I smile against her and wrap my hands around her back. "I knew you could do it."

People filter around us, the doors to the building screech open and thud shut, but neither of us lets go. Holding her brings a strange relief that I didn't know I needed. All the energy and angst of being a parent, teacher, student, and reluctant museum proprietor collapse at her feet like a house of cards finally folding. With her, I feel like I'm just Henry.

She tugs away slowly, letting her hands linger on my shoulders, and she looks confused. "I thought we were meeting at the food court."

"My class ended early, so I thought we could walk together. You have, um…" I motion toward the dark smudges on her face, and catching my meaning, she glances at her hands, which are also dirty.

"I was running late and didn't have time to wash my hands," she says, still looking anguished. "It's whiteboard marker residue—not the kindest medium. It's also given me a splitting headache from the fumes."

Her hands go to her temples again, but given the smudges, she reconsiders.

"Come with me." I take her hand and tug her to the nearest bench. A towering crepe myrtle showers us with tiny pink flowers, carried away by the breeze. I reach to wipe them off the seat, but she plops on top of them, uncaringly. Pink blossoms drift into her long hair while she closes her eyes, and damn, she looks so fucking pretty that it takes me a moment to remember why I dragged her over here.

I wipe the blossoms from my seat—Venus can pull off pink flowers in her hair or on her backside, but I'm not sure I can. I tug my messenger bag into my lap, flip it open, and rifle through my supplies.

"Drink this," I say, handing her my reusable water bottle. She peels her hazy green eyes open long enough to accept the bottle and take a sip. I pull out my arsenal.

Venus peeks curiously as I rummage through my collection. I hand her headache meds, and she swallows them in one gulp. Then, I open a package of hand wipes.

"Are you usually this prepared?" she asks weakly.

"I'm a father, a teacher, and my mother's son, so yeah. It's the side effect of always having to carry inhalers, I guess," I admit with a light shrug.

"So, it's not just to perpetuate the damsel in distress fantasy?" she asks, somewhat warily.

"Are you in distress? Because… I can't imagine that."

She snickers. "No, but this is, admittedly, unfamiliar territory for me. So, maybe I need a hero."

I grin, warmed by the thought that she might *let* me be her hero—if she ever needed one. "I'd like to be *that* guy for you."

"My hero?" she asks, amused.

"The one who has what you need, even if you rarely need anything. Hand, please," I say, like I do when I need to clean up Olly. She places her dirty hand into my outstretched one. I gently wipe it clean, and she closes her eyes again. I take my time, massaging her fingers and edging between her rings. When I replace the dirty wipe with a fresh one and repeat the process, I swear she moans at the touch.

I do the same for her smudged temples, bringing a sweet smile to her face as I lean in close to her.

"Thank you," she mutters softly through her full, pink lips, and it's a herculean effort not to brush them with mine for a gentle, teasing kiss.

"What Venus needs," I say instead, and her smile grows. "How about we rest here until you feel better?"

I slip my arm around her, and her head drifts to my shoulder. Her hair smells like her rosemary shampoo with a strange hint of markers. Her skin is achingly soft and sun-kissed, and she's warm, nestled into me. I feel grateful to have a reason to do this. Help her. Hold her. Be here for her.

I watch students pass, and people move in and out of the food court, academic buildings, and library, realizing I'm finally getting my wish—Venus and me, sharing a campus.

She drifts off, melting into me, and I rest my head against hers. With her in my arms, perfectly content and comfortable, I start imagining things I shouldn't—a second chance at things we never got to do—normal couple things, like Dr. Blake mentioned.

Dating, without limits or permissions or curfews.

Family outings, like beach days with her in a bikini, and Olly relishing her beach facts while I try to keep him sunblocked and hydrated.

Dinners with Mom and Fred, when keeping the peace between them is more amusing than frustrating, because they'd have to get along eventually.

Venus, telling Olly bedtime stories.

I imagine waking up with her beside me and grinning when we hear Olly racing down the hall to tell us it's waffle day.

A thousand cozy moments stream in my head in changing settings. Over burgers with Olly at Queens and Dreams. Watching TV under blankets on cold nights. In a tent in the rain. Anywhere and everywhere because we are all those places together.

Reality breaks in, an attempt to wreck my fantasies, but I don't let it. Maybe I won't get a thousand moments with Venus, but I have one now. *Right now.* I need to make the most of it.

I will my thoughts into hers like the flowers falling over our heads, wishful osmosis. *Venus, I want more with you. More time. More us. Please, want that, too.*

She startles awake with a gasp.

"It's okay. Everything's okay. I'm here," I whisper automatically. "Are you alright?"

She sits up, her eyes hazy with sleep. "I've kept you." She pulls her phone from her pocket, and her eyes go wide. "I'm sorry. I have office hours."

"I'll walk you," I say, before she rushes off, though it's only a few yards away. I speedwalk next to her, trying to keep up. "It's okay if you're a little late."

"I know. No one usually shows up. But, I want to be responsible."

My brows quirk at her sudden anxiety. "How's your head?"

"Better, thank you." She takes the stairs to the main door two at a time, like she's more interested in running away from me than making her office hours.

"Venus," I call from the bottom. She stops and turns around. "How about a redo tomorrow? You, me, and some very unhealthy cafeteria food?"

She softens in a sigh, but twists her bracelets. "Okay."

"Then, it's a date," I say, smirking as she rushes inside.

But I don't want to wait until tomorrow.

After visiting the food court and bookstore, I return to the Environmental Sciences Building and snake my way up to her father's office. No one's around. Most of the offices are closed, their lights off. But a dim light pours into the hallway. The door is ajar, so I peek inside.

Venus leans back in the desk chair, eyes closed, her feet crossed at the ankles and propped up on the corner of the desk. Her floral skirt has slipped up, revealing half of her thigh tattoo.

I knock gently. She bolts upright, sending her feet to the floor.

I grin when she looks my way. "Hey, I'm in desperate need of a botanist. I have this plant—Audrey II—and it prefers human blood. Is that normal?"

A coy smirk rises on her cheeks. "Oh, yes, very normal... if you're trapped in a musical."

"What do you recommend, Doctor?"

"Have you tried a blood bank?"

"Yeah, but it's a no-go. Apparently, they don't just hand out blood to anyone," I scoff.

She chuckles. "Do you have a list of enemies?"

"Don't we all?"

"Then, I suggest feeding Audrey II the people you don't like... after you break out in song, of course."

"I knew you'd know what to do, Doctor. May I come in?"

With a light giggle, she waves me inside, and I dare to close the door behind me.

"What are you really doing here?" she asks, as I tour Dr. Blake's cozy, bookish, and artful office.

I glance at her over my shoulder as I eye her artwork, framed and scattered along the bookshelves—pieces of her are everywhere.

"I couldn't wait until tomorrow." I set the little brown bag from the cafeteria down on her desk. "I brought you lunch."

She peers into the bag of wrapped sandwiches and chips. "Thank you."

"Oh, and this." I set a plastic bag down beside it.

She reaches inside and pulls out an extra-large pack of whiteboard markers—*low-odor* whiteboard markers. Her laughter makes my heart sing.

"Our best botanist can't have any more headaches," I tell her.

"Wow, you really are *that* guy," she says.

"For you, yes. As long as you let me." I remove the sandwich and chips from the paper bag and push them toward her. "Eat. It'll make you feel better."

Her shoulders bounce in a soft sigh as she unwraps the turkey and cheese.

My hands sink into my pockets as I lean against the door. "I want to say something."

"Okay," she mumbles, mouth full.

"I want the summer, Venus."

Her brow pinches as she catches my eye.

"I want the summer *with you*," I clarify. "And I don't mean just sex... Though, obviously, I want a lot of that too."

"Obviously," she says, her lips barely moving as she chews her food. "But why? What do you mean *exactly*?"

"A new experiment—you and me together as much as possible to prove or disprove the hypothesis that we belong with each other permanently. A fuck-it experiment," I say, thinking of Dot's colorful advice.

Her brow quirks. "A fuck-it experiment?"

"Yeah, fuck worries about the future or about heartbreak or all the what ifs. Fuck what anyone might say. Fuck holding back. Fuck it. Let's just be together now, while we can."

She nibbles her bottom lip. "Let's be Venus *and* Henry and see where it takes us?"

"Exactly. I didn't love you the way I should have then. I want a chance to do that now. In the end, you'll probably leave anyway—I *know*, and I don't care. I don't care if it wrecks us both. I'm wrecked already. But we wanted a better end, right? We can't have that without knowing we did all we could, knowing that we *tried*. This time, it's about *us*. Not our parents, or expectations, or all the other bullshit that kept coming between us. Only *us*. We have the summer, and I'd like to *try*. Will you let me, Venus?"

She looks stunned and says nothing for what feels like an eternity. I expect an argument, or, worse, her running for the door.

"As you said, it feels like a game we can't win."

My lungs tighten. "It's not *impossible* to win, though. Long-distance relationships can work. People do it all the time. Or you could stay."

"You *want* me to stay?" she asks, her voice pained and disbelieving. Her father's words stream into my head. *She believes* we *don't* want *her*.

"Venus, I don't want you to give up the life you want for me. But *if* it would make you happy to stay, yes, I want you to. I hate that I made you feel you had to leave in the first place."

"I-um, it wasn't *you*. It was everything." She swallows hard and pushes the food away.

"I know, but nothing should hold us back now. Fuck it."

She smirks. "Henry Greene not worried about the future? This is unprecedented."

"Only for you, Venus," I say, and her grin widens. "Is that a yes to loving each other while we have the chance and letting the future take care of itself?"

"Yes, Henry."

"Yes, you want to? Or yes, because I'm asking?" I clarify.

Her green orbs meet mine, narrowing slightly as her lips uptick in a grin. "Both… but mainly because I want to. Fuck it."

"Good. May I lock this door?"

"Yes," she says, looking curious.

The bolt slides into place. She keeps her eyes fixed on me as I cross the room and turn the corner of her desk. I roll her chair to face me and drop to my knees before her.

"May I touch you?" I whisper.

Her cheeks turn adorably pink, and the green in her eyes spreads with heat. "Yes."

My fingers dance across her calves, up to her knees, and push her pretty floral skirt up her thighs. I lean down, dragging my lips across her bright yellow, burgundy, and orange sunflowers. She relaxes, spreading her legs so I can nestle between them. I massage her thighs and hips, sliding her closer to me.

"Take my glasses off," I whisper, hands too busy to bother. She eases them from my face and sets them on the desk.

"What are we doing?" she asks, breathless and flushed.

"I'm being *that* guy, and you're letting me. Is that okay?"

She looks down at me, her brow still pinched, but a tiny grin coiling on her lips. She nods.

"Kiss me, Venus," I say, and she leans closer, her lips gently grazing mine. "Now, lean back."

Despite the heavy rise and fall of her chest, she relaxes into the chair while I push her skirt higher. "I like you in dresses," I say, smirking. "You're so damn pretty."

I run my fingers along her panties before hooking them and edging them aside. I lean in, taking several long, slow breaths against her, teasing her. Then, I dive my tongue into her wetness, taking one long swipe up her center, before gently sucking her clit. She cries out loudly, making us both laugh as she covers her mouth with her hand. I wedge my hands under her ass and yank her to the edge of the chair before easing her legs over my shoulders. The heels of her sneakers press into my back, and I love the pressure. I feel like a fucking madman over how desperate I am to make her come. Her hands rake through my hair, and she grabs on, pulling me even closer as my tongue teases and circles her clit. She writhes against me, arching her back and encouraging me.

"Henry," she moans behind her fingers. "You're ruining me, Henry."

Ruining us both, I think, but don't say. Ruining us for anyone else.

But I don't care. By summer's end, the only place she'll run is to me.

My tongue dips inside her before returning to her clit, working feverishly as she writhes beneath me. And then, she convulses almost wildly, making me brace her arms and hold her tightly. When her earthquake softens into tremors, I gently release my grip and exchange my licks for soft kisses, working my way from her mound to her inner thighs. She melts against me, moaning softly.

I ease her panties into place and trail kisses down her thighs as I adjust her skirt. She sits up, wrapping her arms around me. I nestle against her chest and hear her heartbeat thundering under my ear.

"Take me on the desk," she says, nearly panting.

"This was for you." I lay a kiss on her forehead as I stand. Her hand sweeps over the front of my pants, feeling my hardness. "Just for you."

I put my glasses back on and sit on the edge of her desk, crossing my legs at my ankles, trying to calm down. I grab the other sandwich from the bag and peel it open. I eat half of it in one bite, smiling over at her, all flushed and satisfied. She leans back in her chair, contemplating me like abnormal cells under a microscope.

"Are you sure you don't want to—"

"I'm sure," I cut in, grabbing one of the bags of chips and moving around the desk. I wrap my messenger bag around my shoulder, holding it up front to hide what's left of my erection, and head for the door. If I wait one more minute, it might be impossible to resist her. "Lunch tomorrow. Don't forget."

"I won't," she promises.

Then, I leave her.

CHAPTER 34
Venus

"I NEED MORE DRESSES," I tell Ivy when she answers my call. "Will you take me shopping again?"

"Girl, you know me. I'm always down for shopping," she answers, her voice giddy. "I'm off shift soon. I'll run home, change, check on Buster, and pick you up."

"Thank you," I sigh, shuffling into the fairy house. I race to complete the outdoor chores before Ivy arrives. I water my salvaged plants, glad to find them still thriving in their new home. I check the mini-bogs and additional garden beds in the greenhouse—all is well.

But when I traverse the acre-sized public garden, I discover two alarming problems. On the west end, a breakout of black spot, a disease that looks as it sounds, is spreading across the wilting leaves of a large patch of flytraps. To the east perimeter, the flytraps and pitcher plants are being ravaged by aphids, tiny, pesky little pests that twist and deform the leaves. I groan and stamp my feet at the annoying discoveries, upsetting an elderly couple taking a quiet stroll nearby.

An urgent search through Dad's shed produces Physan, the fungicide needed to control black spot. I mix it with water and return to that section for a liberal spraying. Dad is out of Orthene, which I need for the aphids. I make a mental note to stop by the same garden supply business that had the correct peat moss in the hopes that they will also carry the wettable powders best for flytraps.

Back inside the house, my shoulders slump as I change and wait for Ivy to arrive.

It's only been ten days since Dad left the gardens in my care, and I've failed my charge. Between this and my first week of lackluster teaching, he's bound to be doubly disappointed. It's as if problems follow me—or I create them—wherever I go.

"It's completely illogical to think that the aphids saw that there was a new girl in town and decided, *here's our chance, boys. Let's attack*," Ivy says, her manicured fingers twisting on the steering wheel as she drives us to the boutique. "*You* are not the problem, Venus. Nature is. Life is. That's the way things go."

I snort-laugh at her voice-acting aphids. "You're right. It's illogical. But I still feel bad."

"Don't feel bad. You'll teach those aphids not to mess with you, and you'll eradicate that black spot in no time. I'm *more* interested in why you need more dresses."

I turn to the passenger window, trying to hide the smile that creeps up my cheeks over memories of today. I'm still in shock over it, like perhaps I was high off marker fumes and hallucinated it—Henry's help, Henry's words, Henry's hands, Henry's tongue. An orgasm, *just* for me.

"I, um, just don't want to do laundry every five seconds," I say, "and you were right. My wardrobe needs help."

"Hmm, does this wardrobe revamp have to do with Henry?"

"Well, maybe Henry likes me in dresses, but so do I. They have their... conveniences."

Ivy pulls into a parking space in front of the store with a squeal of the tires and twists in her seat. "What conveniences, exactly?"

"Henry and I are spending the summer together," I redirect. "He wants a second chance, and he hopes I'll stay at the end of it."

"HENRY SAID THAT?" she yells.

"Yes."

Ivy bangs her hands against the steering wheel, but when that doesn't do enough for her excitement, she jumps out of the car and dances in the empty space beside her. She wiggles her hips and turns in a circle. Another snort-laugh bellows from me.

She waves me toward her. "Get over here, sister!"

I obey, deciding that it must be true—excitement is contagious. But maybe this is what sisters do—normal sister things. Sisters dance in parking lots.

She takes my hand and twirls me around, which is awkward because I'm taller than she is. Then, she tugs me to her for a weird dip that sends my hair flying backward to the concrete. Laughing, she pulls me up into a warm embrace.

"I love that," she whispers, holding on to me. "I love Henry for you. Do you think being with Henry for the summer will convince you to stay permanently?"

"I don't know," I say, honestly.

"Do you want to?"

"I want to... enjoy the summer," I answer cautiously.

Her head tilts, and her hands rest on her hips. "What are you so worried about? What's wrong with falling in love and living happily ever after?"

"Happily ever after doesn't exist for me. I hurt people, Ivy. I nearly killed Henry once. Remember?"

Her features soften. "It was an accident. Don't you know that?"

"An accident that *I* caused. I turned a sweet moment into a near-tragedy. I wasn't thinking."

"No one's *really* thinking at eighteen, but I understand how traumatic that was. You still don't trust yourself, but that was ages ago, and it wasn't your fault," she says gently. "It's normal to feel scared. Love *is* scary. Especially at the beginning, with the nerves and uncertainty. Those feelings will settle, though, and then it turns into the most amazing thing ever."

"It looks amazing on you," I admit, and she beams. "But it's an overwhelming prospect. I feel safer traipsing through jungles and hanging off the sides of mountains because, there, I can't hurt anyone else but me."

"I hate that you feel that way," she says, dragging her hand down my arm. "Because it hurts more when you're away from us."

"Thank you. It, um, it hurts me, too. I've missed you and Dad more than I expected. I'll take your advice under consideration."

"Excellent. That's a smart move." She loops her arm in mine, pulling me to the storefront. "For now, though, let's shop!"

I end up with six additional outfits plus accessories, including something Ivy says will be perfect for "date night." We stop by the nursery to pick up the pesticide. I avoid the plant clearance section, keeping my head down as I pay and return to Ivy in the car. Then, she takes me to an Asian fusion restaurant for dinner. It's tucked into the corner of a strip mall, but its facade is lined with gorgeous palms, Japanese myrtles, and bamboo plants, inviting us inside. We're seated in a side room with bright, spring green walls covered in gold-framed art, primarily portraits, some nude, and I can't stop staring at them.

"How is Gil? How's coupling going?" I say, piecing the questions together awkwardly.

She snickers at my attempt. "I'm so glad you asked. I want us to move in together. Rephrase—I want *him* to move in with *me*. My place is spacious, close to the hospital, and Buster has his backyard to play in. There's an extra office for Gil to set up all his monitors and desk toys—it's perfect."

"Have you asked him?"

Her shoulders sag. "Two things are holding me back. First, he's so close with his family. Like super-close. Game nights, dinners, soccer matches. Tripp Family Farm might as well be their compound for how often they're all together there. Gil still lives in his parents' basement, and I doubt that'll change without a damn good reason. That kind of closeness is beautiful but not what we're used to."

"Yes, but it's what we aspire to in some ways, I think. The closeness, not the dependency."

She nods. "Yes, good point. I believe Gil prefers Seagrove, and, honestly, I don't. It's too small, too quiet, and the only good shopping is at a quaint convenience store called the G&G. I *need* a decent mall, Vee."

"Given his nervousness in meeting Dad, and his inability to keep his hands or eyes off you at dinner, I believe he'd relocate."

She beams across the table. "Really? He couldn't keep his eyes off me?"

"It was sickening."

She giggles.

"What else holds you back?"

"His anxiety," she says. "Not that he has it, but that he won't tell me. I'm trying to be patient. But he posts activities with his family that make *me* anxious, like helping his brother, Grady, do medical procedures on cows and hanging out with gators at the G&G, but I can't get him to come to dinner on a whim or do something relaxing like paddleboarding. His anxiety seems to be keeping him from me and pushing him toward his family. So, if he can't trust me to help him with small challenges, then why should I expect him to trust me enough to live together?"

"May I make a suggestion?"

"Please," she gawks, sipping her wine.

"Plan a weekend away. Present the idea in a way no boyfriend could refuse. If he says no, then he will have to explain why, which may lead to him opening up about his anxiety. Likely, though, he'll say yes to make you happy, no matter how uncomfortable it makes him. If his symptoms arise, it'll force him to come clean, inevitably bringing you closer. Regardless, the forced proximity will allow you to explain your hope of moving in together. Time away will also test your compatibility and the strength of your partnership. If it's meant to be, it'll be a great weekend. If it's not, then you'll know. It's a win-win-win."

Her open-mouthed stare indicates surprise. "Venus! You're a genius!"

"Yes, I know."

"No, I mean... yes, but, ugh! That's the perfect idea!"

Our food arrives, interrupting her gushing. Once our meals are set and our wine refilled, she smiles across the table.

"I can't believe how much you've changed since high school," she says.

"I'm no longer a perpetual outcast full of teenage angst."

She chuckles. "No, I know. It's just... I wish we could've talked more then. I'm sorry if I made that hard on you. I know my friends weren't always nice to you."

I take a breath and wipe my mouth. "It's not your fault. I wasn't always nice, either. But I appreciate your apology and accept it on one condition."

"What's that?"

"That Buster stays with me while you're away."

She laughs, pointing her fork at me. "I told you not to fall in love with him."

"It's not love. It's mild admiration."

"Okay, deal," she says, looking skeptical but satisfied.

CHAPTER 35
Venus

DR. ROB MCCULLUM smiles broadly and greets me with a hearty, "Dr. Blake! What a pleasure to see you again!"

I lean toward my laptop, taking in his shaggy dark hair, scruffy face, and piercing blue eyes, but it's his kiwi accent that stirs my recollection. A smoky, low-lit pub in Oxford. Pints, fish and chips, and conversation that came naturally, for once. "The symposium on invasive species."

"Yes, and don't forget that tedious drivel on forest conservation."

A mild smirk arises, remembering the unfortunate speaker who turned an exciting topic into the driest lecture imaginable. "I struggle with public speaking, but still couldn't feel sympathetic."

"He did me a favor by sending us to the pub across the street," he says, his voice quieter. "That made it the best symposium I've ever attended. I've thought about you often."

A twinge of pleasure slips up my spine. We'd escaped the boring lecture at the same time, meeting at the back doors in the rain. We looked at each other, and, pleased with what we saw, he grinned as he said, "Buy you a pint?"

He held his jacket over our heads as we crossed the street and ducked into the busy pub. And kept his hand on my lower back as he guided me to a corner table. I enjoyed everything about that night—the stale air of the noisy bar, the glint in his eyes as he leaned closer to hear me, and, especially, spending time with someone who knew nothing of my *difficult* past. He saw me as a peer, an attractive peer, and I relished in feeling both equal and wanted under his gaze.

I was set to start the polymer project—my plane was scheduled to leave early the next morning. I discussed polymers while he impressed me with his work on flowering megaherbs. He was insightful and quite handsome, despite our age difference. Well past midnight, I remember his finger drifting over the top of my hand with an invitation to his hotel room.

If not for the plane I had to catch in mere hours, I would've said yes.

Now, my cheeks flush as he stares. He shifts into discussing the project, and, just like that night at the pub, I'm swept up in our conversation about New Zealand's conservation goals.

"I don't want you *on* the team," he says. "I want you to help me lead it, Dr. Blake."

"As your assistant?"

"No, partner. I'd be the cultural, geographical, and political leader. You'd handle the bulk of the scientific research and exploration. I know how New Zealand operates. I need someone who will take her on scientifically. You're my first choice."

My breath leaves my lungs in a puff. "Why me? There are others—"

"Yes, but you've done your due diligence. You've been Miner's puppet for too long, taking no credit for her *discoveries*, though, I bet, okra polymers was your idea—"

"Um, well..."

"Imagine what you can do without her, eh?"

My heart swells to a newfound capacity, taking in his praise. No one has ever valued my work so highly.

But then, I think of Henry—his encouragement to be authentically me in the classroom and the success he inspired. Not only are my students loving my new approach, but I look forward to teaching them. Even more, I love this new version of Henry and me. It's like I've been stuck, rereading paragraphs I didn't understand, until finally, we've turned the page, and the story makes sense, for the summer, anyway. We've spent the last two nights talking, and lunch yesterday was fun and engaging—as close as I've probably come to normal couple things.

"What do you think so far, Dr. Blake?" Dr. McCullum pulls me from my thoughts.

"Um, you should know that I-I..." I take a breath. "Dr. Miner fired me. I had an annoying habit of diving off the ship. I have ADHD and impulsivity issues related to that."

He scoffs, leaning back. "You had me worried for a sec. Learning differences are common, especially among the gifted. I'm dyslexic. Two on my team are autistic. None of that gets in the way of the work. Actually, playing to our strengths makes us a better team."

A huge weight lifts off my shoulders, imagining it—a place where I stand out for the right reasons.

I take a breath, meeting his eyes again. "The cottage would be entirely mine?"

"Yes."

"I don't have one, but if I wanted one, could I have a dog?"

"We have a local shelter full of them. Take your pick."

Our meeting continues well beyond the allotted one-hour time. He discusses the details of his five-year plan, and I'm impressed by the work and research he's already done. It will be a massive but thoroughly engaging project, with equal time spent in the lab and the field, as I prefer. He promises free time to explore New Zealand, which sounds ideal after the confinement and tight quarters of living at sea and the emotional overload of being at home.

A shadow moves under my closed door, prompting me to check the time. "Oh, Dr. McCullum, forgive me for taking so much of your time. I might have a student in need of my assistance, though."

"I've enjoyed our chat, Dr. Blake. Can I schedule another meeting for next week at the same time? Surely, you'll have more questions by then, and perhaps I'll squeeze more amenities from the Conservancy for you, make it impossible for you to resist."

"I'd like that."

"Speak to you then, but call me anytime. Cheers."

Closing my laptop, I feel immensely satisfied. I nailed the interview —a challenge for me—and the position is ideal. I can't wait to tell Henry. But my shoulders slump with the reality of thousands of miles and another five years away from my family. Away from Henry.

With a sigh, I rise from the desk, straighten my skirt, and move to the door to greet the shadow waiting behind it.

Henry leans against the opposite wall, bag hooked over his shoulder, his hands in his pockets, and a dizzyingly perfect smile on his handsome face. "Have time for me, Doctor?"

I match his coy grin. "Another plant emergency?"

"Nah, just wanted to see you. How'd the interview go?"

"I got the job, if I want it." I expect him to launch into questions to assess my interest and, perhaps, dissuade me from it.

"Of course you got it. You're brilliant and deserving. Sounds like future Vee has much to consider." He pushes off the wall and edges closer, slipping his hands around my waist. "Congratulations," he whispers before he kisses me.

His reaction relieves me, and not just because kissing Henry is always a pleasure. The decision feels *mine*. Safely in my hands without the need for him to offer feedback. Because it *is* my choice. And I already know what Henry wants.

In this moment, perhaps every moment, he wants me.

The kiss deepens in a breath as I yank him inside, shutting the door behind him.

CHAPTER 36

Henry

VENUS DRAGS me into the office, and thoughts of New Zealand are quickly forgotten. I allowed what I thought would be enough time for her interview to end before dropping by to see how it went. I didn't mean to eavesdrop, but it's hard not to listen to words like *New Zealand*, *5-year project*, and *call me anytime*.

I'm worried. If I thought there was even the tiniest hope that she'd stay, it's obliterated now. There's no way she'll turn down her dream job for us, and I wouldn't ask her to.

But damn, I wish she'd stay. I want her for more than a summer. I want her for always.

Still, I don't offer feedback on New Zealand, except to say the obvious—that it's an incredible offer, and she deserves incredible. I refuse to add pressure, or even hint that I don't want her to take it. One negative remark from me about the distance or anything else might dissuade her from an amazing opportunity. I want what's best for her, especially since her entire life until now has been about what's best for everyone else. She deserves to explore whatever jungle, mountainside, cave, ocean, or swamp her heart desires.

And I want to be *that* guy—*her* guy—supporting her every step.

That's what this summer is about. Us. Now. Me being there for her as many times as she needs. I don't want to make the same mistakes I made back then by designing a future for us that we weren't ready for and that wasn't right for her, for *us*.

If she stays, it needs to be because it's what *she* wants. Not what I want.

So, we set aside thoughts of the future for now.

The following afternoon, Olly bounces in his booster seat as I turn the Jeep into the dirt lane that leads to the fairy house. He's not used to taking treelined, dirt driveways, and laughs like this is a game and we're about to step into an enchanted forest.

I suppose we are—there is no place in Wilmington like this.

Sunset glows through the trees and over the house, creating shadows and dim corners. When the fairy house comes into view, Olly gasps with awe, as the place lives up to its name. The house *is* enchanting, from its triangular roof to its pops of blooms and greenery, to its endless string lights, which fill the dark pockets in a delightfully intentional way. The place glows and makes you wonder—is this a house in the woods or did the forest grow a house? Wood, glass, and light nestle amongst the trees and wild landscape as if nature intended it to exist there.

Olly unbuckles and slides out of the Jeep as soon as I park. "Come on, Dad."

From the passenger seat, I grab the bouquet that Olly and I picked out together—bold purple irises, delicate lavender, and, my favorite, brilliant sunflowers.

Venus appears almost goddess-like on the glittering front deck, all smiles and beauty. Buster looks up from her feet and yaps sharply.

"I told you—we're having guests for dinner. Olly and Henry are here," she says to him, in her level tone.

Olly stops abruptly and retreats to me, but only to grab the flowers. "Venus, look! We brought you these. It was my idea!"

Arms full, he bobbles up the stairs and thrusts the arrangement at her.

"*Helianthus annuus, lavandula,* and *Iris versicolor,*" she lists, admiring them.

"Latin!" he identifies triumphantly. "I call 'em flowers."

She smirks. "These are some of my favorites. Thank you."

"I knew you'd like them." He yanks his new treasure from his pocket and holds it up. "I brought Mango, too." Then, he drops to his knees to play with Buster.

I stroll up the steps behind him, catching Venus's green eyes in mine. Her soft smile makes me ache to touch her.

"Hi, Henry. I'm glad you're here." A lovely, rosy color shades her cheeks. "Thank you for breakfast and lunch."

"This'll make three meals together in one day," I point out with a cheesy grin. "Thanks for having us. Oh, and here. I thought you might need these."

She eyes the boot laces I picked up for her with surprised amusement. "I do. How thoughtful."

"No chewing on her new laces, Buster," Olly instructs with a laugh. Buster barks.

Venus ushers us inside. "Make yourselves at home," she says, heading to the galley kitchen.

Olly takes off with Buster, roaming shamelessly through all the rooms and then marching up to the loft. While he explores, I follow Venus into the side pantry off the kitchen, where she tries to reach a narrow metal pail on the upper shelf.

I wedge into the small space behind her. "Let me get that."

I only have a few inches on her, but it's just enough to grab the pail. She turns to face me, and we grin simultaneously at how close we are.

"Where's Olly?" she asks.

"Looking under your bed and going through your medicine cabinet upstairs."

"Good." Then, her hands slide up my chest and around my neck, dragging me closer for a greedy kiss. My entire body hums with the contact, and I sink into her touch.

"You've missed me," I accuse coyly.

Her brow pinches. "It defies logic. It's only been three hours since you kissed me goodbye. But yes, I've missed you."

"Best to go with those feelings, not try to reason them out," I smile before kissing her again.

"Campus walks, lunches… office hours," she says, breathless at my lips and blushing again, "are all nice, but for this experiment to work, we need more data. I need more time with you."

"That's what I want, too. Come over tomorrow for dinner and spend the weekend with me. I have a plan."

"What Henry wants…" she smirks, turning the corner out of the pantry as Olly rushes into the kitchen.

"Dad! You won't believe it!"

"Believe what?"

"She's got plants everywhere, Dad. And drawings. And a notebook full of pictures with your name on it."

"Olly, you shouldn't go through people's things," I say, using my stern voice.

"Dad, Venus doesn't mind," he says, as if he's known this woman all his life.

In a way, he has.

"I don't mind." Venus holds up the pail. "This is for the flowers. Want to help?"

Olly nods enthusiastically. Venus fills it with water and sets it on the table beside the flowers. He takes her side, following her lead as she unwraps them.

"Why do you write notes to Dad?"

Her perfect lips ease into a light smile. "He's my best friend. I take him wherever I go."

Olly's face pinches. "Can you start writing notes for me, too?"

"Notes? You'll get full letters with illustrations and treasures," she promises, "if I go away again."

My head spins over the word *if*.

"*If* that's okay," she adds, turning to me for parental permission.

"That's a great idea… *if* you go away again," I repeat—not to pressure her, but just to acknowledge her use of a hopeful *if*.

Her tiny smirk edges upwards. Olly plops flowers into the pail like she does. Before long, it's bursting with blooms.

"Beautiful. Thanks, Olly," she says. "Now, I need your help in the garden."

She hands him a wicker basket. "Let's go on that tour, and, while we're at it, we'll pick our dinner. We're having veggie pizzas."

Olly announces his approval, and they march ahead of me out the back door.

The gardens mesmerize him. He examines the flytraps and pitcher plants with an oversized magnifying glass that Venus provides—a scientific investigator. I take adorable pics of him peering up at me through the glass, big-eyed and smiling, and others of him, discovering nature with Venus. I share them in the family chat with Mom and Fred, hoping to defend Venus's return to our lives better than I did last weekend at dinner.

She squats in the dirt next to him when a ladybug lands on her finger, and he climbs into her lap with his magnifying glass to examine it more closely. "*Coccinellidae,*" she says, while he holds her hand and the red beetle moves up and down her ringed fingers. "Ladybug… but they aren't all ladies."

He laughs and leans his sweaty, tired head against her shoulders. I think to rescue her, but when her hand goes around his stomach, bracing him there, I realize that she doesn't mind.

"Funny name, then," Olly decides. "Your dad named you after the Venus flytraps?"

She slumps slightly. "Yes. He's the expert on them."

"You're lucky."

"You think so?" she questions, surprised.

He sits up to see her face. "He named you after his favorite thing, and it's the coolest plant ever!"

"Um, yes. You're right. I am lucky." Venus's brow quirks before she smiles, like she means it.

"I thought they'd be bigger, though," Olly admits.

She laughs, squeezing him gently to her. "Yes, they get that a lot."

As I take more pictures, my phone chimes twice in quick succession. A text from Fred:

> Adorable! Olly looks like he's learning a lot from Venus.

From Mom:

> Don't complain when Olly's covered in ticks and mosquito bites.

I tuck my phone away, determined to wear down Mom's antagonism the same way I do with bad attitudes in my classroom—with kind and gentle perseverance.

Venus leads us through the public garden to the private one. Olly twirls in the greenhouse's multicolored lights, prompting more pictures. And he insists on a "hammock ride" when he sees where Venus sometimes sleeps.

"Dad, can we do our first campout here? With Venus?" Olly asks as she swings him back and forth.

"This isn't a campground, son," I say.

"It's better. Here, we can practice, and we'll have Venus so that you won't be nervous," he answers.

That Olly understands my anxiety about camping shouldn't be a surprise. He's an insightful kid, and the fact that the camping equipment I was eager to buy still sits unused in our kitchen clearly indicates my second thoughts. He keeps asking when and where we're going, but I keep giving excuses.

Venus cuts me a curious look as if to say, *"Why would you be nervous about camping?"* And embarrassment tickles my cheeks.

We camped all the time growing up. In the early years, Mom would check on us nearly every hour, only to find us doing the same things we would inside the house, just in a tent or around a fire pit managed by Dr. Blake. Venus would draw, and I would read. Or we'd tell campfire stories—something I was good at, but Venus struggled to be dramatic. Dr. Blake took us to actual campsites when we were in middle school to further our outdoor education. With them, I always felt like the king of the woods.

Not anymore. And with Olly in tow, I lack the confidence.

"Sorry. My lectures on not inviting oneself haven't clicked in with Olly yet. Son, if you have an idea, share it with me. You're putting Venus on the spot."

"I don't mind," she says again, like it's her catchphrase when it comes to Olly. "But we can discuss it, if you'd like."

Olly takes that as a yes and runs happy circles around us with Buster yapping in tow.

"We'll see, Olly," I say, rustling my kid's sweaty head.

"We have enough veg for dinner," Venus decides, grabbing the basket of tomatoes, peppers, mushrooms, zucchini, spinach, basil, and broccoli—though, if my son eats broccoli, I'll buy a lottery ticket. "Let's go inside and make dinner."

Venus has apple juice for Olly, wine for us, and pre-made flatbreads with her father's homemade sauce for the pizzas. Olly is practically giddy about cooking dinner with her. She sets him up with a cutting board and a small knife, stressing the importance of being careful and watching what he's doing. Then, she gives him the mushrooms to chop. I offer to help, but she refuses, citing the small kitchen.

It's strange, being sidelined. Watching Olly clumsily handle a knife also primes my anxiety.

She hands me a glass of merlot and says, "Relax, Henry." And perhaps I am on edge.

Dinner is delicious. Prompted by Olly, she tells us about her adventures, which at first sound awkward until she relaxes into sharing them.

How lemurs attacked her camp in Madagascar, looking for food. Her favorite villages in England and Scotland. Octoberfest in Germany. Witnessing bioluminescence on the beaches of Puerto Rico. Experiencing her first storm at sea.

Her eyes find mine, assuring me that she thought of me.

"See? You tell great stories," I say.

She nods sheepishly. "Depends on the audience."

She and Buster walk us to the Jeep when it's time to go.

"I can't believe you still have this car," she says.

"I love this car. This was our first taste of freedom, you and me. Well, freedom beyond traipsing all over this place."

She nods, amused.

"Remember the first place you wanted me to drive you?" I ask.

She rolls her eyes. "The library."

"Yep. I've never been prouder," I say, remembering that day when I raced over, dangling the keys in front of her. *Dale gave me a Jeep. Can you believe it? Let's go somewhere. I'll take you anywhere you want.*

Olly grumbles, getting into his booster seat, and rubs his eyes. "Dad, can you hurry up?"

"He's tired." I shrug, standing at the driver's side door with Venus. "Thanks for a fun evening. We had a great time."

"Me, too."

With my back blocking Olly's view—not that he's looking—I lean down for a quick kiss. "Tomorrow night," I whisper.

"Tomorrow night," she repeats.

An awkward beat passes before she takes a step back, tugging Buster with her.

"Good night," she says before waving to my very sleepy son in the backseat.

That night, after Olly's abbreviated bedtime routine, I plan for the weekend. I'm desperate to spend time with her and provide irrefutable data that she's loved and wanted.

Once my plan is in place, I transcribe some impactful stories about Venus and me into a document and send the pages to Dr. Kwon. If something more comes of it, then I'll only go forward with Venus's approval.

But first, I wonder if Dr. Kwon will still find these new pages compelling enough for an entire book.

When I see Dr. Kwon waiting outside of my class the next day with an *I-told-you-so* expression, I have my answer.

"And you said you aren't a writer!" she beams, slapping my arm.

"The more I think about Vee—I mean, Buttercup—the more I believe her story should be told. What kind of historian would I be if I didn't document it?"

She nods, steering me through the crowd until we're outside the front entrance. "It's worth documenting. From what I gather, you believe Buttercup would've benefited from more autonomy, even in elementary school."

"She was used to reading, exploring, and studying on her own. I remember days when teachers sent her to the library as a punishment, and she loved it—spent the whole day with her nose in books. She never had trouble in her art classes, either—at least the ones she deemed *real* art classes."

Dr. Kwon chuckles. "So, no macaroni necklaces for her then?"

"No way. She called those *ugly wastes of food.*"

Students rush around us as we talk on the stoop outside. It's hot and humid, but a coastal breeze sweeps some of the heat away.

"I like Buttercup," Dr. Kwon says, "and so does my agent. I sent her your new notes, and I expect she'll request a meeting. What should I tell her?"

I push my glasses up on my nose, considering it. "Um, I'm open to a conversation, but I need to discuss it with Buttercup first."

Dr. Kwon's eyes widen. "I didn't realize you were still in communication with Buttercup. You sound so sad in your stories, like she's gone."

"She was," I explain, hands sliding into the pockets of my jeans, "but um…"

The heavy double doors of the Environmental Sciences Building screech open across the wide sidewalk. Venus pushes through as if desperate for air. Students follow, crowding her on both sides. She stops on the stoop, turns to face them, and engages in their discussion. She appears controlled, blankly responding, but she fiddles with her rings and bracelets, one hand over the other. I notice dark smudges on her fingers and on the side of her skirt where she must've wiped her hand during her art-fueled lesson. Mid-sentence, she glances my way, and the softest, sweetest smile perks up her lips upon seeing me. She must stumble over her sentence or stop talking altogether because her brow scrunches just enough to reveal that she's been knocked off her train of thought.

I fucking love it.

Everyone notices, especially when I grin and wave toward her.

She waves back, but it's the type of wave that says, *"Give me a minute, Henry."*

"Oh, my word!" Dr. Kwon pipes up slowly. "Venus Blake is Buttercup? I should've known. Dr. Blake used to come to me all the time about her struggles at school. Ah, the artwork, the IQ, the proximity... I can't believe it took me this long to put it together."

I answer with a light shrug, unable to take my eyes off of Venus as she talks with her students, at least until Dr. Kwon shoves her phone in my face.

"Buttercup's going viral. Did you know?"

Venus comes to life on the screen—it's a recording of her artful lessons. My eyes drift to the views, shocked to find *301k* and climbing.

"Look at this one from yesterday. It was meant to be a lesson on distributive patterns in the coastal plains, but she took her class outside and got sidetracked by explaining the importance and role of amphibians in healthy ecology."

Venus appears on her screen, teaching her class while straddling a ditch. Her skirt is hiked up her thigh to keep it out of the mud, and she's holding a skink. The striped lizard looks perfectly at home, perched on the back of her palm, as she explains the ecosystem of a ditch and compares it to that of a swamp.

"Admission inquiries have upticked since her students started posting. The school wants her to stay for another summer session. The marketing department has assigned a camera crew to record her classes. Isn't it fascinating, Henry? Has the so-called *worst* student become the best teacher overnight?"

"She's brilliant and can do anything. I'm not surprised. Does Venus know about this?"

"I'm sure she does," Dr. Kwon says. "What a perfect ending to your book, huh? It's practically writing itself."

My throat tightens, forcing me to use my inhaler. "I'll talk to her this weekend."

CHAPTER 37
Venus

I ARRIVE outside the museum five minutes before my date with Henry. Exiting the Land Rover, I straighten my dress. It's white linen, with a low-cut V neck, backless, and embroidered with an intricate blend of wildflowers in reds, yellows, and blues. Ivy called it a perfect date night dress—a happy coincidence since I didn't know I'd need it at the time. My tattoos are on full display, well, *almost*, and seem to match the dress. Strappy wedges complete the outfit—another purchase Ivy insisted on, though I don't need the extra height. With my hair done up in a pink scarf and braided into a bun, I feel well-put-together and, perhaps, close to normal.

Normal is what you decide it to be. My father's voice whispers through my thoughts.

Tonight's normal is dressy, according to Henry's instructions. He didn't elaborate but said he had a surprise.

Henry emerges from the museum's entrance as I cross the cobblestone path. I stop in my tracks, nearly stumbling on my wobbly heels. He races the ten feet to steady me, though I'm fine, just a little dumbstruck over how he looks.

He's wearing a dark blue suit that accentuates his earthy brown eyes and hair, making him look taller and broader overall. He's tamed his hair, trimmed his beard, and even his glasses appear shinier than usual. He's more handsome than ever, like he belongs in a grand ballroom with a princess hanging from his arm.

I may be reading too many of Christie's romances.

Henry-in-a-suit causes two conflicting ideas at once: first, that he should always wear suits no matter where he is or what he's doing, and, second, that I should remove his suit immediately. But slowly... I'd do it slowly. I think of telling him *that's what Venus wants*, but I refrain. *For now.*

"You okay?" he asks, hand on my elbow.

"You look exceptionally handsome in a suit, Henry. Like top notch. Stellar. A plus."

His lips curve into a delicious side-smile before he lowers for a soft kiss, gentle and sweet. "If I'm an A-plus, you get extra credit." He pulls away, admiring my dress. "You're perfect."

"Perfect?" I repeat, breathless over a word that's *never* been used to describe me. "That's, um... Your compliment is appreciated. Thank you, Henry."

He lifts his free hand, revealing a small arrangement of pale yellow and pink daisies with light purple freesia attached to a wristband. He slides it over my bracelets, and I lift it to catch the delicate, minty scent. The same arrangement sticks out of the breast pocket of his suit jacket.

"I-I... they're lovely."

"Go to prom with me?" he asks.

"Prom?" I repeat, having trouble forming words.

"Well, my version of it. A redo. Just for us." When I can't speak, his hands slip around my waist, pulling me close to him. "This time, no curfews, no annoying classmates, no chaperones, and no expectations. Tonight is whatever we want it to be."

I fight the swell of emotion constricting my throat. Our high school prom wouldn't have been a fun event for me, but a pressure cooker. Even preparing for it felt constricting, weighed down by what to wear, how to act, and if people would accept me. That, on top of worrying about our future. *His* future.

Similar fears threaten now. Our summer will end, and what will that mean for us? But I relax, thinking of Henry's words in Dad's office. *Fuck it.*

His forehead lands on mine, forging a soft, pressureless pocket between us. "Is that a yes?"

A breathy "yes" falls from my lips before he kisses them.

Slowly, he pulls away, extending his elbow for me. I loop my arm around his, and his free hand slides over mine, bringing me closer. *I'm the princess hanging on his arm.*

"Dinner first," he says.

A ten-minute stroll along the Riverwalk leads us to one of the city's tallest buildings. We take the elevator to a rooftop restaurant with water views on one side and the city skyline on the other. Henry has reserved a quiet table overlooking the water.

I order a Vodka Cranberry and the scallops. Henry orders an Old Fashioned with his steak and grilled oysters as an appetizer. We sip our drinks, watching the activity on the water. The tiki boat disembarks on a new journey, and our eyes meet as if we're both reliving the memory.

Henry slips his hand over mine across the table, lightly fiddling with the flowers on my wrist. "Tell me about how your classes went this week."

I light up over the subject matter. "Yesterday, we went on a ditch excursion, and today, we all brought boots and explored the turtle pond."

He chuckles. "I thought I saw you out there, wading in rubber boots."

"It's challenging in a dress. For the next outdoor class, I'm wearing my cargo pants. They're easier and have pockets. I don't think Ivy will mind."

"Probably not, especially if she sees you in action. You're becoming very popular. Have you seen the response on social media?"

"I'm not on social media, but, yes, I've heard about it."

"Your students have been posting your lessons. Hundreds of thousands of people are viewing them. Are you okay with that?"

I shrug lightly. "I've gone viral before. It's fine."

"You have?"

"Co-workers frequently post my interactions with wildlife or other encounters during excursions."

"You deserve the attention. But does it make you nervous?"

"I enjoy the positivity. It's a welcome change from how I'm usually perceived."

Henry's brow pinches, but he smiles when the oysters arrive, as if glad for the distraction.

When we're alone again, he leans closer. "I wish things had been better for you in school. I hurt you more than I helped you then. I wish I could change that."

"I wish I could've changed me. If I'd been more like everyone else, it would've been easier for us to be together."

"No, Venus," he says sternly. "If you'd been like everyone else, you wouldn't have been *my* Venus."

A light gasp falls from my lips at the idea of being *his*. Him, being mine. And the unique symbiosis we could have by merging our lives together. "*Your* Venus. I like that."

"Aren't I *your* Henry?" he challenges.

"Always. Even if…" I can't finish the sentence.

"I know." He reaches up, trailing his fingers along my cheek. "I wish I'd climbed out of the window with you during Mr. Henderson's English class. That guy was a fucking tool."

Laughter spurts from me, pushing back my sudden sadness. "Do you really?"

"Yes, and I wish we'd gone to the movies, not just watched them in my basement."

I smirk. "I wish I'd worn more dresses for you."

"I wish I'd stood up for you," he says more sternly.

"I wish I'd talked to you more about things that matter," I admit.

"I wish I'd listened, even when you weren't saying anything."

A smile crosses my lips, considering our many silences, not just moments but days, weeks, months, when we barely spoke—when I pushed him away, and he let me, while I wrongly decided that he was better off. Even in our absences, a quiet understanding existed between us, knowing we'd reconnect. Like the Venus flytraps, we'd enter dormant seasons before springing to life again.

Temporary. It's only temporary.

"Henry, this is the nicest date I've been on," I announce shakily, trying to stay in the present rather than let my thoughts carry me away from him and the beautiful night he's planned for us.

Henry looks curious. "Have you had many dates?"

Ditching the symposium with Dr. Rob McCullum comes to mind. It had the hallmarks of a good date—food, drinks, and engaging conversation with someone I would've enjoyed seeing again—but it probably doesn't count since it wasn't planned.

"Encounters, yes. Dates, no. I've been asked out often. The times I've said yes have taught me that potential partners like the look of me, but don't like *me*. Not that I put much effort into being liked. My goals were short-term only. Sex, Henry. Relationships don't work well with my career... not healthy ones, at least."

Henry winces at my words, and I fear I've misspoke.

He recovers with a sigh. "I doubt they disliked you, Venus. More likely, they were intimidated."

"Why?"

He gives me a funny look. "You're a beautiful genius who climbs mountains, goes spelunking, wrangles snakes, and lives out of a tent most of the time. Most egos probably couldn't take it."

"What about your ego?"

He shrugs and flashes his easy grin. "You inspire me. Always have. Besides, I know you *and* like you. It's too late for my ego to come into it."

Our meals arrive, and our server refreshes our drinks, and once we're alone again, I say, "Henry, are all topics open for discussion on this date? I don't want to broach an inappropriate subject for a prom redo."

"We can talk about anything you want. It's whatever we want it to be, remember?"

"Then, I'd like more information." I twist my linen napkin in my lap. "Tell me about Carly."

"Sure, okay. Umm..." He runs a hand through his hair and pushes up his glasses. "College was hard for me, at first. I partied too much and hooked up a lot. Carly and I were pretty good friends. She was ambitious, straightforward, and getting over a rough breakup. We bonded over that. She helped me get my act together. We both knew we weren't in love or anything. It was just... friendly and convenient. "

"But you wanted to love her?" I ask, remembering his words from the night of our reunion.

"Yes."

"Why?"

"For Olly. We almost didn't have him. An accidental pregnancy on the cusp of graduating, and with her about to enter medical school, the most reasonable option was termination. That's what she initially wanted, and I understood. Nothing should've stopped her from pursuing her education, and it was *her* decision."

"But? What happened?"

"I wanted to be a dad, Venus." His handsome smile returns in a flash. "Carly understood that even before I did. So she offered a partnership. She'd have the baby if I agreed to be his primary caregiver. I'll always be grateful to her for making that sacrifice."

I nod, my esteem for Carly rising.

"She loves Olly, and she's an amazing mom," he goes on. "We lived together during her residency and as she got settled into her career. We tried to be a traditional family for Olly. We couldn't make it work romantically, but it was good for us to be together then, to support her as she finished her education, and for Olly to see that his parents are partners and friends. When her residency was over, she picked Wilmington to stay close to us."

"I saw her from the roof the day I met Olly. She's quite beautiful."

His brow quirks. "I'm sure her boyfriend thinks so, too. It's nice to see her happy, and Olly likes him."

"How very amicable. Will she be equally supportive when you find someone?" I ask, remembering her unnecessarily touching Henry's arm and blowing kisses in his direction—two facts that fail to prove her as some nefarious feature in Henry's life—*I know*—but that increase my insecurities regardless.

For Henry and me to work beyond the summer, I'd be insinuating myself into a pre-existing family. It's hard enough to assimilate with *one* person, let alone his child, the mother of his child, and any other people of permanent significance. The prospect feels like agreeing to start a game without knowing the rules when the other players are ahead by a dozen turns. How would any outsider catch up? Or find a way to fit in without causing conflict or stress? I already know Maggie disapproves.

"Of course. She's already being supportive," he says. "It's not like she hasn't heard your name before. When I dropped him off earlier, she showed him a book she bought on fossils, so they could learn where Mango came from."

"Oh, good," I say, despite the anxiety rising within me. I'm suddenly fraught with confused feelings that clash with my reason. There is no evidence to suggest that being in Henry's life will create a conflict with Olly's mom, and she sounds like an exceptional person.

But I don't have an impressive resume when it comes to positive relationships. What if she doesn't like me? What if I bring confusion and tension to Olly's life? What if Carly is another version of Maggie, expecting me to mess up? To hurt Henry? To hurt Olly? And what if, like Maggie, she ends up being right?

Negative energy makes my leg bounce under the table and my

bracelets jingle with my tapping fingers. I lock my feet at my ankles, willing myself to calm down and stay put.

Henry takes my hands in his, running his thumbs over my pulse points. "Does Carly worry you?"

"Blended families acclimate to include new members all the time. Some might argue that they're more versatile and resilient in that way," I say, failing to sound casual. A sigh escapes. "But, yes, it worries me."

"I understand, but—" The flame from the small oil lamp between us flickers in his eyes before he shakes his head lightly. "You consider blending our families a possibility, then?"

My tension dissipates in his hopeful amusement. "One should consider all possibilities in an experiment."

"Then, consider this… I'm falling for you, Venus. I loved you before, but it's stronger, deeper, everything it should be this time. Stay or go—that won't change. You're already family to me. So, whatever you need, say it. What Venus wants, needs, hopes, fears, thinks, dreams, worries, imagines… I'm here for it all. And blending won't be a problem, not if Olly and I can help it."

My heart seizes in an emotional surge, starting with him and Olly becoming my valiant defenders and ending with Henry loving me, *always*. The idea of falling in love once seemed so ridiculous, but now I understand. It's weightless and heavy at once, freeing and desperate, beautiful and terrifying. How is one meant to handle such emotional conflict?

Words spill out of me to fill the awkward silence. "I-I-I, um, your feelings are valid and worth consideration."

His hands tighten on mine, releasing some of my tension. "Want to get out of here? There's somewhere else I want to take you."

Feeling breathless and antsy, I nod before he finishes his question. Henry takes care of the bill before reaching out to me. "Ready?"

I don't know, but I say, "Yes."

CHAPTER 38
Venus

THE QUEENS and Dreams Diner shines from a block away, its pink and yellow neon signs glowing across the darkened street like spilled tie-dye, so I'm surprised to find a CLOSED sign in the window as we approach.

"It's closed," I say, tugging on Henry's arm to stop him from opening the door.

"It's closed *for us*," he says, his lopsided grin urging me inside.

My confusion compounds as I step into the quiet restaurant. A silver disco ball spins overhead, reflecting the glow from the neon lights and candles on the long counter. Balloon structures occupy corners, and streamers, foil fringe, and paper lanterns hang from the ceiling, creating a pastel cloud overhead. Tables have been moved from the center of the dining room, leaving the checkerboard tile floor open.

The drag queens form a beaming huddle at the hostess station. A flash from Sunny's phone makes me blink—I can only imagine the gaping, tearful, wide-eyed expression she captured. And, as my eyes adjust to the darkness and the intermittent light, I see that the queens aren't the only ones there.

Dot catches my attention first as she twirls on a barstool, leaning close to an elegant woman with tattoos and a short haircut. Next to them, Marnie bounces with energy, hanging onto the guy next to her. She makes an *eep* sound, like she can't contain her excitement.

My heart rams in my chest when my eyes land on Ivy. Instant

comfort, warmth, good sister vibes—these feelings crash over me to see her, standing near the jukebox, giddy as she watches me, with Gil smiling beside her. An iPad hangs from his neck with Dad and Christie waving from the screen.

My eyes dart from the iPad to Ivy to Henry and back again as I try wrangling my big feelings.

"Welcome to Prom," DeeDee announces with a wide grin, and I gasp, a sharp inhale that everyone hears.

Henry eases his arm around me. "It wouldn't be a prom without other people, but I didn't want just anyone... These are *our* people."

A choking sob bubbles up my throat—*our* people. That feels almost as wonderful as the realization that, "You... you did all this... for me?"

The words barely come out, but Henry leans closer, holding onto me like he's afraid I might swoon. Given my rapid heartbeat and surging emotions, I could swoon. I brace myself against his shoulder.

"I wanted to give you something you'd remember forever," he says, looking sheepish and blushing under his glasses. "Something for us."

"I-I-I'm overwhelmed," I whisper to him, "but in a good way." I swipe away tears that clash with my smile. "I don't know what to say. What's the customary response to the most beautiful, romantic gesture anyone has ever done for you?"

"Just say you'll dance with me," Henry says before nodding to the queens.

"Yes, of course," I manage.

Lucy claps beside DeeDee as her arms open in a dramatic flourish, and the jukebox, aglow in soft yellows, blues, and pinks, hums over the speakers as a song starts to play—"Everything Has Changed" by Taylor Swift and Ed Sheeran.

Henry leads me to the center of the room and slips his hands around my waist. His fingers slide along my bare spine, bringing me closer, his touch calming me. My arms settle on his shoulders, careful of my wrist bouquet, and my thoughts spin—Henry says he's falling in love with me again, and the evidence is all around me. It is enchanting, overwhelming, and uniquely *us*. No romance novel could compete with this.

The other couples join us, offering greetings as they take their places around the makeshift dance floor.

Dot introduces her wife, Jaye, and says, "Nice shindig, Henry. Chasing's working out for you, eh?"

Henry smirks. "Always, right?"

Marnie spins in her partner's arms, facing us and leaning against him. He wraps his tattooed arms around her. "Henry and Venus, meet Grady, my husband," she says, giggling and tilting her chin toward him. "Gosh, I still love saying that."

He nuzzles her neck before smiling at us. "Nice to meet you. Best prom I've ever been to."

"Glad you and Marnie could join us," Henry says.

"You're Gil's brother," I say. "I see the resemblance."

He nods and glances at Ivy and Gil. "Yep, I'm betting our families will be seeing a lot more of each other."

"I concur," I say.

"It's so exciting," Marnie bubbles. "I can't wait for Ivy's bachelorette party—"

"Hold up," Grady cuts in, laughing. "Let's not get ahead of ourselves. No one's asked anyone about marriage yet."

Her smile widens. "It won't be long, Grady. We'll have to do something very special for her, huh, Vee?"

Usually, I wouldn't be pleased by event planning, but I don't mind in this case. If Ivy should choose to marry Gil, I'd like to be involved in the festivities. That's what sisters do, I'm learning—provide unsolicited fashion advice, dance in parking lots, and offer support in crises and festivities alike. As she's doing for me right now.

"Yes, I'd like that," I tell Marnie.

"Oh, Henry, it's a shame your folks couldn't make it," she adds.

Henry's eyes cut to mine. "Yeah, um, they were busy. Short notice."

His response sounds forced, and I wonder if they had plans or if Maggie didn't want to see me. Probably the latter, but I don't entertain the thought for long.

Ivy twirls across the dance floor, dragging Gil behind her, and she insists on an embrace, breaking between Henry and me and latching on to my neck. I don't mind.

"Isn't it so sweet and gorgeous, Vee? Marnie, DeeDee, and I did the decorating," she gushes. "It was Gil's idea to invite Dad and Christie."

Gil holds up the iPad secured around his neck.

"Oh, Venus and Henry... this is so... I can't... It's gorgeous... I can't... " Christie babbles, almost incoherently, and waves a hand over his face to dry his tears.

"Hmm, I believe Christie is trying to say we love you two, and we're glad you finally got your prom," Dad says. "As I like to say... one should always make time for dancing."

Christie coos and waves his hand again. "Always."

I want to speak. My mouth opens. But my words are inexplicably blocked by the lodge in my throat. It's not just that Henry has enacted this beautiful gesture for me. It's that they *all* have, that they're here to share it. I've been away from my family for years. Months would go by without speaking to them. I barely even know Christie. And yet, seeing them on the screen solidifies the fact that *I miss them. I've missed them all along.*

Ivy, Gil, Dad, Christie, and Henry stare at me, waiting, but I only choke on a sob.

"Um, now's a good time for dancing," Henry says, finally, as I lean into his shoulder, embarrassed at my inability to give a customary response. I should be thanking them for their attendance, complimenting Ivy's dress, and asking Dad and Christie about their travels—not emoting in silence.

"Good idea," Ivy says, before whispering, "Ins and outs. It's okay."

I nod as she takes Gil and his iPad away.

"Come here." Henry tugs me into our pocket again. Swaying to the music, his hands slipping up and down my back, and warmed by his breath on my cheek, I practice my breathing and slowly my surging emotions level out to a dull rumble.

Tucked against his shoulder, arms wrapped tightly around him, I finally manage to speak. "I-I'm happy, Henry."

"Then, we're even," he says, edging away enough to see my face.

"Is it strange that I wish Olly were here?" I ask.

"Not at all," he says, his smile growing. "He's your biggest fan, after all."

"I might be his, too." I swallow another lump in my throat. "I-I'm not *falling* in love with you, Henry."

His brow quirks curiously. "Are you sure?"

I nod, nuzzling my nose with his. "Loving you is a fixed constant. Unchangeable, regardless of any experiment."

"Let's stop calling it that," he says. "Let's be a fixed constant. You and me, together."

"I..." Reasons and worries crowd my thoughts, hindering my agreement. He makes it sound so simple, but it isn't.

His smile falls slightly at my hesitation. "Let's just dance for now."

Stricken speechless again, I only nod, but I'm grateful that once again, he's released the pressure.

We dance, slowly, closely, keeping the same pace even as the songs change. Hips pressed and swaying, legs mingling around each other, it feels delightfully like sex, only softer and sweeter.

He lets the silence linger, comforting me.

"I've never done this before," I whisper into the heart-shaped pocket between us.

He kisses my forehead while his fingers drift up and down my spine. "You'd think we would've tried it after watching *Dirty Dancing*."

I chuckle against him. "Or *Sixteen Candles*."

"Or *When Harry Met Sally*," he adds. "Mom's basement wasn't exactly a romantic venue."

"I don't know. I thought so. A few times."

"Which times?"

"Oh, the time you got creeped out by *The Blair Witch Project* and snuggled closer under the blanket," I chuckle.

"I wasn't creeped out. I *pretended*, so I'd have an excuse to get closer to you."

"Hmm, if you say so." I don't quite believe him, but I want to.

"What else?"

"When I fell asleep on your shoulder during *Dazed and Confused*."

His fingers tickle my back. "I played the movie a second time to keep you there longer."

"Did you? How sweet."

"I'm a sweet guy," he smirks. "What else?"

"*Never Been Kissed*. That prompted our first discussion on the use of absolutes," I remind him. "And our mutual desire not to end up kissless."

"That was our best basement moment. Remember how funny we were?"

The memory rushes in, making my cheeks heat against an unstoppable smile. "Oh, which part? Our lengthy discussion that led to agreeing to be each other's first kiss, deciding what kind of kiss it should be, or the act itself?"

"All of the above. Your argument for being each other's first kiss was very convincing."

"I believe you negotiated for a soft, slow kiss rather than a quick peck," I say. "*That* was the better plan."

He chuckles. "You insisted on no tongue, but then…"

My eyes widen. "I got a little carried away. You didn't seem to mind."

A delightful pink twinge appears beneath the rims of his glasses. "No, I didn't."

The same firecracker warmth spreads through me, just as it did then, and he leans down, softly, slowly, to recreate it.

"This is the best date I've ever had," I tell him when we part. "It's like you studied all of our favorite rom-coms to devise a plan for this evening."

"I just thought of what would be nice *for us*."

His words remind me of Dad's, about finding *our* normal. And suddenly, this is it—it's right here, all around me—and I imagine more for us, like tonight has opened a portal into an alternate universe that I didn't think could exist. A universe *with* Henry. The dried chrysalis of the past, holding my guilt and faulty notions about myself, is finally falling off my tired shoulders—a relief because I'm so sick of carrying it. Those mistakes, *that* night, shouldn't wreck us forever.

"It's perfect. Thank you, Henry."

"Us together—that's perfect, Vee."

After several songs, the other couples meander to the bar, and DeeDee announces a "Milkshake break!" We perch on barstools between the other couples and share a strawberry milkshake with two straws.

"How very Norman Rockwell," DeeDee gushes, leaning across the bar and beaming at us. "Jay would've loved this. With the jukebox playing, it feels like he's here."

Henry smiles. "Yeah, it does."

"Besides, he never said no to a party," DeeDee laughs, and Henry seems warmed by the memory.

Soon, Ivy declares Henry and me Prom King and Queen. She and Marnie adorn us with handmade crowns, gaudy and bejeweled but brilliant. We take pictures and act silly. We laugh over our guests' bad prom stories.

We pick songs on the jukebox, and everyone starts dancing, like we're in a musical. It's surreal and vivid, like stepping into a painting in a museum. The queens teach us to shag, barely, and by the end, we're hot and sweaty and laughing hysterically.

Somewhere in the midst of *our* night with *our* people, I imagine that I *could* stay. Here. Forever. That I could give up tents and wild rivers and mountainsides for something just as beautiful. Milkshakes, holding hands, camping in the backyard. I could buy a little house, get a dog, and have a job that keeps to regular business hours. I could be here for Ivy and Dad. But especially for Henry and Olly.

I could stay. I could be very *happy*.

It's the best night I've ever had. And for once in my life, I can't stop smiling.

CHAPTER 39
Henry

THE STREETS ARE quiet as we walk home, arms latched around each other like we can't bear to be apart. My last-minute prom came together perfectly, thanks to DeeDee and Ivy, especially. As soon as I shared my idea with them, they took over to make it happen. I'll never forget the look on Venus's face when we walked into the diner—blissful and beautiful, moved to tears.

Even now, she's smiling, like she can't stop.

I don't know what will happen with us. If the past has taught me anything, it's that the moment I believe I have it all figured out, everything changes a breath later. Despite our amazing night and the love we share, Venus has tough choices ahead. She'll decide our fate, and I sense those hesitations that I missed years ago. Behind her happiness, she is uneasy and unsure—anyone in her position would be—and I honestly can't say where she'll land.

But tonight I feel like I've restored some of what we lost then. I showed her that she's loved and wanted. And that's what I'll continue to do, as long as she lets me.

Closing the door to my apartment, my hand in hers, I blink and imagine thousands of versions of us arriving home like this—different clothes, different times of day, with Olly, with Ivy, carrying groceries. The home we're walking into changes too—a Christmas tree in the corner, a larger bookshelf, a dog, way more plants. She kisses me near the door, and I think this is where we'll kiss each other goodbye in the mornings and greet each other at sunsets. I think of her keys hanging beside mine on the rack and her mug next to mine on the counter. They're sweet and simple images I shouldn't let myself have, but I can't help it.

Tonight's been perfect, so I might as well let my mind drift to those perfect places while they're still in view.

In the bedroom, she takes her time, peeling me out of my jacket, her hands lingering on my shoulders and arms. The tie goes next, one delicate tug at a time, like she wants me in my suit for as long as she can stand it. Her fingers dance along the buttons of my shirt, and she leaves kisses along my chest as she undoes each one. She unfastens my belt slowly, eases my pants lower, and her eyes go wide as she explores me.

I remove her dress in less time, but nothing is hurried or frantic. It's slow and sweet and fucking sexy. My hands roam over her bare skin, loving how familiar she is to me now, kissing her sensitive places, enjoying her curves and her soft moans when I touch her just right.

I tug on the ends of her scarf, but we break into laughter when I create a knot. She teases it free, sending her gorgeous hair down like ribbons around her.

I take the scarf from her hand. It's long, pink, and silky-soft, like grass in the summer, tickling our ankles. I hold the delicate fabric between us, struck with a strange and sudden desire—it's a longing, desperate and powerful, to keep her here. To feel her surrender. "Um, I want to... would you let me..."

I shake my head, giving up on words that I'm too nervous to say. I take her hand, removing her jewelry before gently wrapping the silk around her wrist. I tie one end of the scarf in place, showing her what I mean.

Her irises widen to deep green, and she looks breathless, wanting, beautiful. "Yes, Henry."

The hitch in her voice reveals nerves and excitement—the same as I feel, attempting something I've never done before. But I long to feel her trust, to give her comfort and pleasure, to be adventurous.

She lies down on the bed, open for me. I place her tied wrist above her head, and loop the scarf over a notch on the headboard. My fingers trail down her suspended arm, across her breasts, and up her free hand, guiding it to meet the other. Secured into place, she gives her binding a downward tug and smiles her approval when it doesn't budge.

"Take me, Henry."

Hearing those words, seeing her like this—arms over her head, hands tied, her chest practically heaving for me to touch her, her pleasure at my mercy—I'm overrun with need, desperate to take her immediately.

I savor her instead. I touch the silk of her bindings before skirting my fingertips gently down her wrists and arms, making her cheeks flush red with heat. She's hyper-responsive, each touch inciting gasps and moans, as if the inability to use her hands has heightened her nerve endings.

She is fucking loving this.

I kiss and explore her, inch by inch. She's ticklish behind her knees. Touching the tip of her breast just a little makes her back arch. The more I tease her, the more her need builds until she's writhing under my hands and moaning my name.

When I kiss her thighs and settle between her legs, licking and teasing her clit, she wraps them around me, squeezing me against her tightly. I laugh at how frantic she is. Her sweet moans. Calling my name. Using her legs to insist I keep going. She's so turned on, so ready, that she comes for the first time in seconds.

So, I give her a few more. With my fingers. My mouth. Everything for her.

She cries out my name each time, and I'll never tire of the breathy, aching way she says it.

Her legs loosen off my back, and she says, "Let me have you inside me... please."

I satiate her with a deep kiss, and her legs slip around me, desperate for more. I'm still kissing her when I push inside her.

Still kissing while we moan at the same time over how damn tight and deep and perfect it feels.

Still kissing when I take her tied hands from off the post and hook them over my shoulders instead. Tying her to me.

"I need you closer," I whisper against her lips, and her arms clutch me. I lean back, bringing her with me.

And we're still kissing when she comes again, and I soon follow.

Arms linked around my neck, she collapses against me. "Henry, that was..."

"Yeah, it was."

She shivers against me, as if she's reliving her orgasm in echoes. "I've never done that."

"Me, neither. Never wanted to before," I say, kissing and nuzzling her neck. "Thanks for trusting me."

She leans up, catching my eyes in hers like she's surprised. "I-I do trust you. *Only* you."

"Mmm, I love it when you speak of me in absolutes."

She groans, but smirks. "*Only* with you."

I sit up, bringing her with me, and gently ease her arms over my head. She holds her tangled wrists between us, and I start to untie them.

"Henry, you will *always* be *that* guy for me. I will *never* forget tonight."

I smile at her declaration, but there's sadness behind it, creeping in. It feels like she's letting me down easy, and in the end, when she leaves again, she'll say, "At least we had prom." Our better ending is still an ending.

The scarf falls away, but I hold her hands tightly between us. "Go anywhere, Venus, but *stay* with me. Make *me* your fixed constant. I'm yours. Wherever your adventures take you. Okay?"

Her brow kinks with distress that I don't understand. If I'm her guy *always*, then agreeing to be with me regardless of her job or location should be a logical extension of her promise.

"I-I..."

Gently, I massage her wrists in case they might be sore, and wait for her to tell me what she's feeling.

With a light smile, she tugs her hands free from mine, and her fingertips trail down my chest. "Henry, I-I'm wilting."

"Wilting?"

"That's what a botanist says when she's tired."

"A joke? From Dr. Venus Blake? That's um... unexpected," I chuckle through the hurt I feel over her quick diversion.

"I have my moments," she says.

"Yeah, I know. Let's sleep then. I have a big day planned for us tomorrow," I say, trying to sound upbeat. I set her scarf on the bedside table, half-wondering if I should tie our wrists together to make sure she doesn't slip away in the night.

Once we're settled, I curl behind her, kissing her bare shoulder. I'm about to whisper goodnight when her voice, soft and unsure, cuts me off.

"You invited Maggie and Fred to prom?"

"Um, well, it's not exactly customary, parents at prom," I chuckle, "but yeah. When Ivy said Gil had a plan to bring your dad and Christie, I thought… anyway, it was short-notice."

"Maggie said she was busy?" Venus asks.

"Yeah, they couldn't make it."

"Do you… think that's true?"

I *know* it isn't true. Mom and Fred's Friday night plans haven't changed in years—home from work, dinner, and TV. It's what they do most nights. If they'd had real plans, I would've known. Not that I want to explain to Venus that Mom didn't want to attend because of her. *"I nearly lost you because of that girl. She broke your heart once. She'll do it again."*

I sigh into her shoulder before kissing it again. "Sorry, she's just… she'll come around."

She says nothing more, and I wish I could gauge her reaction. Venus loved my mom. I remember times when Ivy would receive packages from her surrogate, Marta, and instead of watching her sister gush over letters and Italian treats, Venus would grab my hand and say, *"Let's go see Maggie."* We'd find her in the kitchen, the garden, or washing the car, and Venus would find a way to join in without asking. At the time, I disliked it—the last thing I wanted to do with Venus was waste time on chores. Venus would insinuate herself awkwardly, grabbing the hose or the dish or whatever right out of Mom's hands. *"Venus, if you want to help, just ask,"* Mom would say before assigning her a task.

Mom enjoyed Venus, too. *In moderation.* A sweet montage of Mom giving her scarves, showing her how to braid her hair, trying on jewelry, and teaching her to cook flips through my thoughts. Mom would bake her a cake on her birthday and put presents for her from Santa under the tree, though Venus never believed in *"magical absurdities."* Still, Mom treated her like the daughter she never had, *until* she viewed Venus as a threat to the son she did.

I can't imagine I'd be too happy with any friend of Olly's causing him trouble like Venus did for me. And the night at the Fort Fisher Rock Wall that nearly cost us both our lives was traumatic for Mom, too. I'm trying to be understanding, especially since she's struggling with the loss of Jay.

But Mom needs to get over her problems with Venus.

The next morning, we drive to Seagrove for a six-mile hike around the lake. It's nothing like the wild excursions she's used to, but she loves it anyway, and I'm glad I took Marnie's suggestion. There's nothing more beautiful than Venus in the outdoors—it's where she thrives and relaxes, where she feels most at home.

Venus picks wildflowers along the way, tucking them into her hair, and educates me on the mosses, mushrooms, and ferns we encounter along the dirt path. We take diversions around the lake bank and into the dense pine trees.

She climbs a spindly and widely-stretched live oak tree and stands hero-like, twenty feet up. I take pictures to show Olly later.

She beams as she says, "Henry, it's just like old times."

She climbs down, and I greet her with a wild kiss. "Not *exactly* like old times," I grin, and she laughs.

At a rickety old dock, she strips down to her blue bikini and jumps in. Once I'm convinced that she's scared away any gators in the vicinity, I get in, too. She pretzels me with her legs and warms me with kisses.

"I'm having so much fun," she says between our lips.

"Oh, yeah?" I dunk her in the murky water. She emerges aghast and ready for retaliation. A back-and-forth game ensues until we fall into kissing again.

Later, over hot dogs at a retro convenience store called the G&G, she offers to host our first campout at the fairy house. "I'm pet-sitting Buster next weekend. Do you think you could get Olly for the weekend, too?"

"I'm sure Carly wouldn't mind swapping some nights."

She smiles as I wipe mustard from the corner of her mouth.

"I'll talk to Mom, too," I say. "Don't feel bad about them not coming to prom, okay? Mom just needs time."

Venus nods. "Maggie liked me once. She could again, if she'll let go of her negativity bias."

"What do you mean?"

"She once confessed that my standing up to Dale about his smoking helped convince her to do the same. She never told you that?"

"Um, no."

I recall Venus's directness with my father vividly. *"You shouldn't smoke close to Henry or in the house at all,"* she told him, before rattling off facts about the dangers of secondhand smoke and particulates. It made me cringe and cheer at once, like so many times in school when she defended me or herself despite the conflict and negative attention it caused.

My hand brushes through my hair. "I didn't know that. Why wouldn't she've told me?"

"That's the negativity bias in effect. Most people have a negativity bias—it's not just Maggie. It's a psychological tendency to dwell on the negative and give bad experiences more importance. It's like how you might remember a bad day more than an average or good one. It's difficult for Maggie to see beyond the ways I've hurt you, Henry. She remembers the worst of me."

"That'll change. I promise." I lean forward, planting my elbows on the edge of the picnic table. "She's done the same with Uncle Jay, holding on to her guilt and pain over his death instead of just... remembering him. She can't even talk about him."

I expect Venus to launch into her spiel about the stages of grief, but instead, she nods and slips her hand over mine on the table. "I'm sorry for Maggie. It must be devastating to lose a sibling... and an uncle. If it helps, talk to me about him."

Over hot dogs and soft drinks, I spill dozens of good memories, along with the bad, like her permission has lifted the ban Mom put in place. It's as cathartic as writing about Venus, allowing me to see his life and our stories from different angles. Sharing Jay with Venus also feels like making the memories last longer and giving them a new life, just as it does when I tell Olly our stories.

After our adventures in Seagrove, we return to Wilmington. At the fairy house, I help her tend to the gardens while she talks about New Zealand.

"You don't have to choose between me and New Zealand, Venus," I say, reiterating what I tried to express to her last night. "We'll make it work if that's what you want."

"I don't know what I want," she returns flatly, reminding me of her father, who said the same thing during our call.

"That's how I felt when Jay left me the museum. I didn't want the place. I was angry at him, overwhelmed by the aftermath, and I already had too much going on to take on a business. I felt so out of my depth that I put it on the market, ready to be done with it."

She nods. "It does seem like a massive undertaking. What changed?"

"DeeDee asked, 'What's the rush, Henry? The decision will wait for you.' So, I waited for the right answer to come to me instead of chasing it. Taking the pressure off helped. I spent time in the place with Jay's things and brainstormed possibilities without worrying over the details. I loved watching Olly get excited over arrowheads, old coins, and pirate lore. I talked to people, sought advice, and was surprised that Olly wasn't the only one excited about it. Instead of being worn down by Jay's death, I started to feel uplifted by good memories. Then, I read about Marnie. She'd transformed several small businesses into amazing successes, including the G&G. When she agreed to the project, everything fell into place. Besides, selling is always something I could do later, but I can't take it back once it's done. I'd rather take a chance now than regret it later."

"That does put a different perspective on your decision," she says in a troubled sigh as she picks weeds from an eclectic garden of flowers, vegetables, and herbs outside of the greenhouse.

"The place might fail, but I won't regret trying. That's all Jay would've wanted from me. You'll figure out what's best for you, and everything will fall into place."

She stops tinkering with the garden and nods. "Thank you for the advice, Henry. I'll take it under consideration."

"No problem," I say, taking over the hose. "I've been meaning to talk to you. I need your advice, too."

She perks up. "I'd be honored to advise you."

The entire story about my paper, "The Problem with Sunflowers," Dr. Kwon, and her book proposal gushes from me in that excited, easy way that I remember talking to her as a kid. She listens intently as we work through the garden. She snickers over my pen name for her—Buttercup. And at the end of my spiel, she faces me, hands on her hips, and nibbles her bottom lip.

"What do you think?" I urge her finally.

A soft smile edges her lips, relieving my sudden nerves. "I think... that's a book I'd like to read."

CHAPTER 40
Venus

THOUGH HENRY INVITES me to their weekly dinner at Maggie's on Sunday, I decline. After our beautiful weekend, I need to prepare for classes tomorrow, and I don't want to surprise Maggie until Henry has had time to talk to her—she wouldn't appreciate it.

Henry shows up around dinner time, anyway. When I greet him and Olly at the Jeep, he hands over a black-and-white composition notebook with papers tucked inside. "I wanted you to have this. My notes, our stories, what I remember, anyway. I've been writing like crazy since you came back."

"On paper?" I gawk slightly. "A laptop would be more efficient, Henry."

He shrugs, his lopsided smile playing at his lips. "I like pen and paper—probably the influence of someone's field journals."

I smirk. I let the pages fly under my thumb—he's filled the notebook with words in thick, black ink, and his heavy hand has caused the paper to ripple. Words jump out as I flutter through it—*education, difficult, hallways, pedagogy, Shakespeare, trees, Darwin*—and I'm nervous, but excited.

"It's only fair that you get *my* field notes for once, right?" he says. "I can't wait to hear what you think."

So, that evening, I set aside Christie's latest paperback for Henry's notes, finding them to be even more romantic.

Big feelings swell and bloom over his pages, like his words are raindrops aerating the soil to allow room for the roots to expand and get what they need. This is what *I* need—to know Henry loved me through it all, even when he didn't know how to show it. Or when I didn't let him.

He compares me to the sunflowers we attempted to grow in our raised bed. That experiment failed miserably. Sunflowers need three feet in circumference and at least eight feet in height to thrive. They had neither in our small, overcrowded bed in the greenhouse. Nor did they have sufficient light.

It was a losing battle, especially against the tomato plants that took over the garden and crowded out the sunflowers.

Their stalks were thin, their blooms small, and eventually they slumped over from a lack of nutrients. Henry and I had a funeral for them over the compost bin.

He describes that event, too, by writing:

> Buttercup felt that loss the way other kids might feel in losing a pet. Everyone thought of her as this emotionless robot, but the opposite was true. Buttercup knew more than most people and felt more, too. Her big feelings clashed with her big brain, leading her to one erroneous conclusion—that she was a burden, impossible to love. It's like her father told me after she left: She's a sunflower who believes she's a cactus.

Everything he writes creates big feelings—the stories make me laugh, feel sad, and cry. But they also resonate and bring me to some alarming truths—he's absolutely right. I felt trapped, where I couldn't thrive, forcing my frustration and negative self-talk, until I believed a lie.

Dad loved me. Ivy loved me. Henry loved me. Even Maggie loved me in her own way. I think.

Why didn't *I* believe it? Why didn't *I* love myself?

I don't put the notebook down until the middle of the night, and even then, I can't sleep.

I leave the house early, but instead of driving to the campus for work, I go to Henry's.

It's barely 7:30 when I park outside the museum. Nerves arise as I sit there, twisting the steering wheel and practicing my Ins and Outs. It's probably rude to come over without asking first, especially so early. I fear that Henry might not like the intrusion.

But I must see him. As I slam the door shut to the Land Rover, the museum door opens. Henry and Olly spill out—Henry with his messenger bag strapped over his chest and carrying an extra-large travel mug, and Olly bouncing on his sneakers with his backpack and lunchbox—ready for school and camp. They don't see me at first, but carry on with an animated conversation as Henry locks the door. He runs a hand through his hair while Olly pushes his glasses up his nose. Then, Henry extends his hand, and Olly automatically takes it.

It may be the most adorable thing I've ever seen.

They look up at once, see me standing there, and flash me identical lopsided grins.

I stand corrected—*that's* the most adorable thing I've ever seen.

"Venus!" Olly booms, glancing both ways and then rushing across the cobblestone street. He latches onto my side. "Dad showed me the picture of you climbing that tree. That was awesome!"

"Thanks," I say. "Um, good morning, Henry."

He leans in and kisses me on my cheek. He smells like coffee and soap, a pleasing combination. "Good morning. Everything okay?"

"I hope you don't mind the intrusion, but—"

"Dad, it's Derek and Pepper," Olly says, pointing to a man walking his dog on a grassy area nearby. "Can I say hello?"

"Yeah, sure," Henry says with a light wave to their friend. "That's Derek. You met him as DeeDee."

I wave enthusiastically and call out, "Thank you for prom!"

"Anytime," he waves back.

Returning my attention to Henry, the words I want to say jumble in my head.

Henry glances at my wiggling fingers and says, "You're not intruding, Venus. You're always welcome... Is something wrong?"

"I read your notes about us," I manage, fighting back the emotional surge over his stories—our stories. "There were so many times growing up that I felt alone, like no one saw me. But *you* did—more than I truly understood. And not just when we were together, building lean-tos or planting sunflowers. You *saw* me, Henry. My anxiety, my frustration, my hurt. The stories prove it."

His head shakes, and his smile falls. "I saw you, but I did nothing. The stories only prove all the ways I let you down."

"No, you didn't let me down. I mean it. I never wanted you to join my fights or save me. I would've hated you coming to my rescue. Gosh, Maggie would've banned me permanently. Where would I've been then? I would've been friendless, hopeless, *and* difficult. I don't want you to regret it... I want you to... I just..."

My words fail me as energy pulses through me.

He sets down his things, freeing his arms to slip them around me. "So, you have big feelings, and you ran to me? If I didn't know any better, I'd call that romantic."

Tension slips away in a breath as I nestle against him. "Not romantic. Necessary. I wanted to tell you right away that you're an excellent writer, very insightful, and that I believe people could benefit from our experiences."

His forehead presses gently to mine. "If you want me to write it, I will."

"I want us to tell the *full* story, Henry," I say, letting another burden fall from my shoulders and crash at our feet. "You thought I was brave for speaking my mind, but there were times when I said nothing, and I should have. To Dad. To Ivy. To you. I shouldn't have suffered the way I did in school—I don't blame myself for it, but I regret my silence. I regret not telling Dad. I thought making it harder on me made it easier on everyone else. That wasn't true. I don't want to run from that anymore. I want my family to understand. I want my story told. And I want you to tell it."

He nods through the concern evident on his face. "We'll tell it together—"

"Dad! Look!" Olly calls as he dances around with Pepper chasing him.

"Um, I should... let you get on with your morning."

"Please, don't go. We're going to the same place. Let's go together," he says.

I accept his offer, and a rather blissful routine develops over the subsequent days—me, Henry, and Olly meeting each morning and going to our destinations together. We share dinners, either at his place or at the fairy house, and we talk about our days, and in quiet moments, stories from our past. It feels like an existence we were meant to live, that's been waiting for us until we were ready to accept it.

I invite him and Dr. Kwon to visit my classroom on Thursday—a crowded event already, with twenty-four students and other guests from around campus. I must shoo visitors from Myla and Jayden's usual seats, as they have become my assistants. Dr. Kwon and Henry slip into the back of the class at the start.

His lopsided smile brings one of my own—full and wide—as if there's no one else in the room.

"Is she smiling?" I hear Myla whisper to Jayden, which jolts me out of it.

"We have traveled across North Carolina, ecologically speaking, examining the rarest species, their environments, and conservation efforts, and today, we finally arrive at the coastal plain and the state's rare taxa of carnivorous plants to which I am... personally connected."

Laughter waves across the audience, though I don't know what's funny.

"Next week, we'll examine these plants in person before our final exam." Nerves rise as I turn to the whiteboard. I grab a marker from the metal tray, knocking another over.

Jayden holds up his phone. "What'll it be today, Dr. Blake?"

I take a cleansing breath. "Something upbeat. Thank you, Jayden."

An energetic song soon thumps through his portable speaker. Catching Henry's eyes once more, an exchange of smiles moves me forward.

I succeed in focusing on science rather than Henry—a feat I've all but mastered over the last decade, but it proves more challenging with him in the room. The class passes expeditiously, with a few slight diversions when my students ask questions. My phone chirps its usual end-of-class warning, and, upon turning around to ask if there are any questions, my audience breaks into unsolicited applause.

"Class is over," I say, my voice raised above the noise and putting a swift end to it.

My students chuckle, as if I'm being weird. I probably am, but I don't like the attention.

I grab two erasers to clean the board, but I'm bombarded with people who want to discuss the lesson. Myla and Jayden relieve me of the erasers and clean the board. Amid the questions and accolades, Henry moves beside me and leans in to whisper, "Incredible class, Dr. Blake," before introducing me to Dr. Kwon, who shares her excitement for the class and Henry's future book. Considering my abysmal teaching performance at the start of this experiment, it feels satisfying to hear such praise, especially from another educator.

Even better, it's pleasing to hear it with Henry beside me.

After class, I retreat to Dad's office and prepare for another meeting with Dr. McCullum. He's emailed me about dogs in their local shelter and the housing they're providing—a stunning cottage nestled into a lush garden with a wrap-around porch. A stained-glass cutout in the front door reminds me of the greenhouse. I've never had my own place before, and though I'm still debating my future, it's difficult not to picture myself there.

Even so, I take Henry's advice—to stop chasing an answer and wait for it to present itself. I have a little more time before summer classes end, Dad returns, and my sojourn here is over—I might as well use it. Besides, I appreciate that freeing myself mentally has allowed me to be more present with Henry and Olly.

At the correct time, Dr. McCullum blinks to life on-screen. He's in the same leather desk chair with bookshelves behind him as last time, but he's moved the camera to catch his companion, a cheerful-looking yellow Labrador with sparkling eyes and a studded, pink collar that reads *Daisy Duke*.

"No fair, Dr. McCullum," I say with a disapproving look.

He feigns innocence. "What? I went to the shelter to take pics for you, and ended up falling for her. Do you blame me?"

"I don't," I say sheepishly. "But you can't woo me with potential pets."

"But she has a sister, Calamity Jane," he says, grinning. "Looks just like her."

My shoulders slump, and his devious expression relents.

"Then, how can I woo you? Tell me," he says, his voice lower.

I want to answer him with a definitive list, but all I can think of is being at sea, staring into the murky, choppy water, desperate to dive in. And then, that moment, when I hit the surface, and everything falls away.

That's what New Zealand would be. Another ship. Another ocean. Another escape. This time, with a dog, a cottage, and a partner who values me as a scientist. I'm drawn to that life. It's what I've wanted. It's what I'm used to.

I'm not used to this existence with Henry, regardless of how much I want it.

I feel lost. And for once, feeling lost isn't welcome.

"You should know that I am considering other offers, and that the decision has become... complicated."

"Uh-oh, glad Daisy's here to help me persuade you, then," he quips before gauging my seriousness. He leans toward the camera. "Of course you're considering other offers, Dr. Blake. I'd be shocked if you weren't. But I'd guess that none will offer you the large-scale environmental impact of the difference you can make here."

I can't argue his point, especially when he elaborates on their Blue Carbon Initiative and their alliance with Project River Recovery—just two of many impactful undertakings this position will afford me.

"You said in your email that I have another week to decide?" I clarify.

"Yes, ideally, we'd like you here and acclimated in early August," he answers, petting Daisy.

I promise to have my answer the following week, if not sooner. Dr. McCullum stifles his clear disappointment with a gregarious smile. "If there's anything we can do to win you over, let me know."

Daisy Duke gives an approving bark before we end the call.

CHAPTER 41

Venus

"THE APHIDS ARE BACK," I say with irritation. "I've applied several applications of the pesticide, and they refuse to care."

"Hmm, perhaps rain washed it away before it could be entirely effective," Dad says calmly. "When at first you don't succeed—"

"Try again. I know."

"Venus, I sense some distress." He peers into his laptop camera, as if he might reach through it and feel my forehead for a fever. He's sitting on a rustic picnic table outside a quaint pub in Oxford. It's late afternoon there. Sunset casts its golden glow through the weeping willow trees behind him and reflects an amber hue from his half-drunk pint. Wren and Christie wander along the banks of the River Thames behind him. My Friday morning call began with Dad and Christie introducing Wren, Christie's daughter, before gushing over Henry's romantic gesture, a discussion that strangely diverted into the deliciousness of fish and chips and mushy peas. Though I don't care much for the delicacy, it made me long for travel again.

I didn't engage in much conversation with Wren, though she's intriguing, or Christie, because, frankly, I don't feel like talking. I want a solution to my problem—that's all.

"Tell me what's wrong," he implores me.

I groan. "If I don't contain the aphids, they could spread through the entire garden."

He shakes his head. "Apply once this afternoon and once more in the morning—that should do the trick. Now, tell me what's *really* wrong."

My eyes narrow. "I-I-I can't be trusted to make good decisions."

"I trust you completely." He looks offended, his bushy blond and gray eyebrows pinch behind his glasses as his head pulls back. "You're taking excellent care of the garden. What do you mean?"

"I suppose I mean that I don't trust *myself*." My head lands against the table with a thump. "I don't know what to do, Dad."

"Hmm, explain your dilemma, and I'll offer my opinion, if you want it," he urges.

I think about Henry's advice and nod. "Henry is permanently affixed here, and I've been offered an incredible opportunity in New Zealand. Accepting it means five more years away, and though Henry says we'll make it work, it's too great a distance for that to be feasible. He doesn't want me to give up the job for him, but I don't want to be like Dr. Miner with a FaceTime family."

"Then what *do* you want, Venus?" he asks, rubbing his chin.

"I want… to make a good decision that doesn't hurt anyone, that's fair to me *and* those I love," I say with frustration, "unlike last time. I want an end to this pressure that *doesn't* make me run."

"Do you feel like running?"

"Yes, most of the time." I huff, fiddling with my jewelry.

A dog barks and chases a frisbee behind him, and I realize that perhaps this isn't the appropriate time to bring my father into my relationship conundrum. Perhaps Ivy should've been my go-to resource.

"It's just…" I go on anyway. "I left Henry once. He had these plans and expectations for us that I knew I couldn't live up to—not then."

"And now?" he pushes.

"Now, I fear disappointing him again. What if I stay, and the novelty of being with me wears off? Or we shift into a dormant season, like we used to do when we were teenagers? Don't misunderstand—this summer with Henry has been the best of my life. He's been attentive, loving, and the sex is incredible…"

"Um, well…" Dad looks perplexed.

"But how can I make a decision based on such a small sampling? How do I trust it to last? And how do I take such a risk, considering the collateral damage I might cause, not just to Henry but to Olly, too? I feel like I'm in one of Christie's romance novels, living page to page in a beautiful story that will fall apart when it becomes clear that I don't belong here."

"Why don't you belong there?"

I shrug. "I've never belonged anywhere."

"That's a false statement," he says. "You belong with us—your family."

As if cued, Christie turns toward the camera from twenty yards away and gives me an exuberant wave.

My forehead scrunches as I wave back. "It is nice having… people."

"Leaving Henry behind is an experiment that you've already performed, and it failed. Ten years apart didn't stop you and Henry from caring about each other. When it comes to love lasting forever, that's fairly compelling evidence in your favor."

"True."

"Venus, if you hold on to what you love, you have a greater chance of keeping it."

I can't fault his logic.

"You belong with Henry," Dad says slowly to heighten the impact. "Whether that's here together or with you abroad, that's only for you to decide. I'm tickled hibiscus pink to learn that staying is a possibility." He grins, looking sheepish as he pushes his wire frames up on his nose.

"Henry wants me to. It would be more ideal and I… I don't know."

"If you stay, stay for yourself, Venus. It should be what *you* want. But I promise—we'd all love to have you."

"Thanks, Dad. I, um… I want to amend my answer to your previous question about regrets."

"Oh?" He looks surprised. "What's your regret, then?"

"I regret not asking for your advice more often. You're an excellent father. In the near future, I'd like to discuss the past to bring us both a better understanding, if that's agreeable."

His lips part in a stunned gaze. "Um, why yes, of course… and Venus, you're an excellent daughter. I trust that you were right to leave us, that you made the best choice, especially for yourself. But home is here, whenever you want it."

"Thank you." A light smile grazes my lips as emotion builds underneath. "Tell Christie and Wren, thanks for letting me interrupt your pub night."

"Interrupt anytime," Dad says. "Oh, and Saturday's the big campout, correct?"

"Yes, me, Henry, and Olly in the backyard. I'm looking forward to it."

"It's a good reason to put big decisions aside for a bit of fun. Memories won't make themselves. Just beware the coyotes and mind your campfire."

"Yes, Dad. I know," I say, rolling my eyes.

"Sending your dad a few pictures would also be appreciated."

"Hmm, I'll think about it," I say with a smile. We soon end the call, and I feel better.

CHAPTER 42
Henry

"WOW. THAT'S A LOT OF GEAR," Venus says, hands on her hips as she eyes my overloaded trunk. "How long are you staying? A month? A year?"

Olly chuckles beside her. "I wish."

"Better to have it and not need it than to need it and not have it," I say, fighting embarrassment.

"As long as you can carry it," she grins before laying her hand gently on Olly's shoulder. "I'm pet-sitting Buster for the weekend. He's inside, if you wish to say hello."

Olly gawks and bolts for the fairy house.

Venus's light smile turns in my direction as I take a hit off my inhaler. Her brow creases in the middle. "The air quality is poor today. Controlled burns over the river. Are you sure we should do this tonight?"

I inhale deeply and motion to the cross-body bag around my chest. "Yep. I've got every asthma medication known to man, and I've got you. I'll be fine."

Her smirk grows. "We can always retreat to the house. You'll tell me, right?"

"I promise." I smile, leaning over to kiss her cheek.

She blushes, glancing over her shoulder to see that Olly isn't watching. I hook my hand around her waist and tug her closer. "Don't worry. I've talked to Olly about us."

"You did? What did you say?"

"The truth. That we're more than friends—we always have been—and that we're spending time together while you're here. He knows you might leave for more adventures, and he understands."

She relaxes in my arms. "I don't know what to say."

"No need to say anything." My forehead rests against hers. "I had to tell him something. I can't go a whole campout without touching you."

Her cheeks turn adorably pink. "I think I want to stay." She blurts her declaration so quickly that it sounds like one word with syllables tumbling over each other.

"That's... We'd love that. I'd love that." Relief spreads through me like an ocean breeze on a sweltering day, and I try to hold it in. But my lips magnetize to hers, and overjoyed in our embrace, I lift her off her feet.

She laughs, her hair dangling around us.

"Dad!" Olly rushes from the house with Buster, leashed and tied to his waist. "Buster wants to help set up camp."

Buster barks as if to say, *"Yep."*

I set her down, but my hands stay fixed on her sides like I can't let go. "Sounds good. Grab whatever you can carry."

Venus leads us to the outskirts of her father's garden, where tall pines and scraggly live oaks take over, and she's outlined a path into the woods with solar lights wedged into the ground to see at night.

When we can no longer see the fairy house, she stops beneath a familiar live oak tree, sprawled and imposing with its thick, low branches and drapes of Spanish moss. She stands in front of it with her hands on her hips.

"Look familiar?" she asks.

"Absolutely. Olly, this is the tree Venus fell out of the day we met."

"It's also where we built the lean-to that sheltered us in that storm. Do you know that story, Olly?" she asks.

He nods with a wide-eyed expression before he pushes his glasses up further on his nose. "Oh, yeah. Dad said he was terrified."

"Not *terrified*," I correct as Venus gives me an amused look. "Concerned."

"I was also very *concerned*," she admits, "but we got through it together."

Olly drops his backpack and runs around the tree with Buster.

Venus has already prepped the area. A wheelbarrow of bricks, sand,

and firewood sits away from the tree to build a fire pit. The ground has been raked free of rocks and sticks to make way for our tent. She's even slung her hammock between two smaller trees nearby.

We set up the tent first—a six-person, domed mega-tent. It has windows, a ventilated peaked ceiling, a shaded porch with banners, and I can stand up in it.

"Wow, that's a tent," she says. "Are you expecting guests?"

"Hey, this isn't one of your minimalistic expeditions. I want space to move around, and a little luxury," I defend lightly. "Even you'll be impressed by how comfortable we are... Only two or three more trips to the Jeep, and we'll be all set."

She looks amused but says nothing.

An hour or so later, we plop into our camping chairs to survey our hard work. The fire pit is ready for when darkness falls. We have coolers full of drinks and snacks. The camping stove is set up. A trash bag hangs off a low tree branch. The flashlights and lanterns are ready. And music plays gently from the portable radio. The shade from the live oak and the tent's porch, where our chairs reside, creates an oasis in the summer heat. Still, I look forward to the cooler evening and the three of us telling stories around a campfire.

Venus looks up from her field journal. "So, what do you two adventurers want to do first?"

Olly rattles off a long list, and they eventually decide on a hike. We spend hours exploring the property around the fairy house, just like Venus and I used to do as kids. Venus shows him bugs, lizards, and birds through binoculars and magnifying glasses. They touch lumpy moss and discuss the veins in leaves. We jump over muddy creeks, examine downed trees, collect samples for Olly's new field journal—a gift from Venus—and construct a lean-to near the campsite.

We are sweaty and dirty when it's done, but we have so much fun that no one seems to care.

When the sun starts falling behind the tall, slender pines, we rest in our camp chairs.

"I'm hungry, and so is Buster," Olly says.

"Let's pillage the garden and grab supplies from the house," Venus says. "We could make hot dogs—"

"No, I have dinner covered," I say.

"What's for dinner, Dad?" Olly throws Buster a stick, which he immediately retrieves.

"We're expected at Grandma and Grandpa's," I say, glancing over at Venus. "If that's okay."

Venus automatically fondles the sage-green scarf wrapped around her head and laced through her bulky side braid. She forces a smile, though I can tell she's already nervous. I wonder if my plan is a mistake—getting the family together tonight—especially after Venus's declaration. It's been all I could think about during our adventures. The three of us together, not just for the summer, but always. It's been hard not to imagine family trips, holidays, Venus in my bed every night. *She thinks she wants to stay.*

I only hope Mom doesn't mess it up.

"Yay, can we bring Buster?" Olly asks.

"Of course," I say.

"Um, let's grab the basket and clip some flowers to take to Maggie," Venus says, putting her notebook aside. "And perhaps a nice bottle of wine?"

"Sounds perfect."

After touring the garden for the prettiest blooms for Mom's bouquet, we retreat to the fairy house to get cleaned up. Venus arranges the flowers into a pile and ties them together with a string. She places them into a basket with a mason jar and a bottle of wine from her father's collection.

Then she turns to me. "Should I change into something more… normal? A dress?"

Her words resurrect a memory from third grade. I recall her wild hair, overalls, rubber boots, and dirty t-shirts being a constant topic of mean-spirited discussion among the other girls in our class, with their hairbows, dresses, and sparkly shoes. On one of our walks home, I finally asked Venus, *"Why don't you wear normal clothes?"*

I didn't care what she wore. I only thought that stating the obvious might help her fit in better.

But the next day, she showed up in one of Ivy's dresses, which was too small for her, and she spent the day inadvertently flashing her underwear because she wasn't used to bending or climbing in a dress. And it was impossible for Venus not to climb something.

The end result—she was made fun of even more. And I felt bad for encouraging her to change.

"No," I say, slipping my hands around her waist. "You look great."

"Does she know I'm coming?" she asks, leaning into me.

"Yeah, don't worry. She'll be fine."

She takes a deep breath. "Okay, Henry."

Olly bounds out of the bathroom, his hands still damp from washing them. "Ready! Let's go!"

We exit the rear of the house, Olly and Buster bounding down the deck steps ahead of us.

"Where's the trail, Dad?"

Venus and I share a quick smile before she shows him the overgrown cut in the woods. The path isn't as defined as it once was, but it hasn't disappeared, either. We push through stretching branches, around wiry oaks, and through what we used to call the "tall soldiers," a patch of slender pines surrounded by huge fallen cones that I deemed discarded cannonballs.

"Remember when Maggie would send us out here to collect pinecones for her Christmas decorations?" Venus asks.

I slide my free hand in hers, locking them together tightly. "Yep, you always instigated a pinecone fight."

"You insisted on acting out historical battles, remember?"

"Absolutely, with sticks, forts, and pinecones," I chuckle. "You always went off-script, though."

She smirks. "I only implemented better strategies."

Olly's the first to see the tall shrubs and exterior fence that mark home. He races around the side of the house, yelling in victory. "We're here! We made it! Grandma! Gramps! I brought Buster!"

Venus tugs my hand and stops us at the corner where no one can see. I set the basket down to give her my full attention. "Are you okay?"

She takes a deep breath. She drops my hand and fiddles with her bracelets. "She's the closest thing to a mom I've ever had, you know. I-I want her to be happy to see me."

My heart sinks with her rising anxiety. I can't imagine what that's like for her.

"I want you here. Olly wants you here. Buster and Fred want you here. Mom will, too. She's outnumbered."

"Can we have a signal? Like we had in middle school? The pencil tapping? Remember?"

"Yeah, I remember."

"Something that tells me when to… be quiet?" she asks, a little breathless.

"No, you don't need that anymore. I don't want you to be quiet.

How about we have a different signal? To assure you, not change you. One that says that everything's okay?"

Her nerves vanish behind a gentle smile. "I'd like that."

I take her hand, place it on my heart, and hold it there. "This time, whenever you see me touch my chest over Frank the Frog, you'll know everything is okay... and that Frank and I love you and think you're perfect."

She snort-laughs. "I don't know if Frank would concur, but yes, I like that. Thank you."

"If it helps, she's probably more nervous than you are."

"I don't wish her anxiety, but, yes, that helps." She smooths out her t-shirt and jeans, fiddles with her braid, and takes another deep breath. I hold out my hand, and she takes it.

Around the corner, we step through the gate and into the backyard. Fred mans a smoking grill filled with burgers and hot dogs. Olly guzzles lemonade while Buster yaps at his feet. Mom steps out from the sliding glass door with a stack of plates and a small bowl on top.

"Olly, Buster's thirsty, too. How about pouring him some water in this?" she says, handing him the bowl.

The gate door shuts behind us, catching everyone's attention, except for Olly's. He snatches the bowl and races to the outdoor sink.

Mom's brown eyes run over us, hesitating at our locked hands. I narrow my eyes at her, and she smiles lightly. Fred makes it to us first, tongs in hand.

"Venus, our brilliant world traveler, is back from saving the world! Great to see you," he says with his usual top-notch enthusiasm. "Love the ink, honey. Absolutely gorgeous."

"I have fifteen tattoos," she reports awkwardly, "all my designs. And, yes, it's lovely to see you, too, Fred."

Mom moseys over slowly, tucking her hands behind her back like she doesn't know what to do with them. "It's been a long time," she says, barely making eye contact.

I reach for my inhaler and take a quick puff. "Mom—"

"Maggie." In a surprise move, Venus steps forward and forces an embrace that lingers until Mom gives in. "I-I'm happy to see you. Thanks for having me over."

"You, too," Mom says, glaring at me over Venus's shoulder.

I give her my sternest look. *Be nice*, I mouth. Convincing Mom to host tonight wasn't difficult—not with Fred's help. But over coffee the other afternoon, she explained, "The last time I saw her, it was over a hospital bed with *you* in it, Henry. Then, she left, and you fell apart. I nearly lost you *twice*. You want a second chance with her, and I get it—you two have always had a sweet, if not challenging, connection. So, I'll host the dinner, put on a smile, and make potato salad. But I know her. *You* know her. Chances are, she'll leave you behind and destruction in her wake. She makes me anxious for you and for Olly."

I argued, of course. I explained why Venus left in the first place and fought for Mom to let go of the past and be pro-Venus for my sake *and* Olly's.

Now, spotting Mom's pinched brow and pursed lips as Venus embraces her, I wonder if anything I said mattered. It sweeps me back to high school, and the stories Venus has slowly shared with me—the mistreatment she endured, more than I knew—and anger charges through me as I lump my own mother into that category.

Venus releases her from the awkward hug, but pulling away, Mom's eyes finally reach Venus's face. A real smile emerges from behind the forced one as she takes her in, and relief softens my anger.

"That's my mother's scarf," she says, surprised, running her fingers along Venus's loose braid. "She wore that to our wedding with her sage suit. Remember Fred?"

Fred nods. "Oh, yes. She looked pretty in it."

"I can't believe you still have it." Mom traces the top, where Venus has it tied as a headband.

"I have most of them. I wear them every day." Venus smiles weakly, looking unsure. "I, um, lost the pink plaid one in Borneo, though. I used the teal polka-dotted one to tie off a gaping arm wound I received in a beech forest in the Carpathian Mountains. The blood stains rendered it unsalvageable."

Venus's expression contorts in apology.

Mom gapes into a breathy laugh. "Oh, Venus. That's okay. It's nice that you could use them, even for wound care."

Venus lifts her shirt sleeve and twists her tattooed arm to show Mom the raised scar. "Ten stitches."

"Adventure comes with risks," Mom sighs, her brow pinching again.

"Damn, Carpathian Mountains? Borneo?" Fred shakes his head. "Isn't that something?"

"I go where the plants are," Venus says with a light shrug and a smirk. "Everywhere."

Mom takes her hand, ogling her rings. "Mom's mood ring, too?"

"I believe it's onyx. It's never changed color, but I love it."

"I can't believe you still have it," Mom says.

"I've learned to take home with me... The scarves, the ring, my notes to Henry in my field journal—they're home to me," Venus explains, and I think my heart might burst over her sweetness and honesty.

"Well, that's very nice," Mom says, appearing moved despite herself.

Venus takes the basket from my hand and offers it to Mom. "Are roses still your favorite? I brought the best ones."

"They're... yes, my favorite," Mom says.

"And wine," Venus adds.

"Good thinking," Fred chuckles when Mom says nothing. "I'll get this baby open. Come, sit down, and tell us about your adventures."

When Venus glances over her shoulder at me, I put my hand fully over my heart.

The evening passes with good food and light conversation, fluctuating between the grand opening of the museum next weekend and Venus's travels. As dinner winds down, darkness takes over, and Olly asks to return to camp. I tell him to go inside for the bathroom and to clean up.

"Well, it's been a great evening," Fred says. "I'm proud of you two for mending your fences and reconnecting after all this time. It's a joy to see you together again."

"It's only temporary. Henry says you're moving to New Zealand?" Mom says.

"Mom, I said she had *an offer* in New Zealand. She hasn't decided yet. So relax."

"I'm relaxed, Henry," she says, her high-pitched voice refuting her claim.

"Venus..." Fred sits up in his seat, breaking the glare between Mom and me, and clears his throat. "New Zealand sounds exciting."

Venus twists her napkin under the table. I reach over, resting my hand over hers. "Staying is also an appealing option. I haven't made a final decision yet. New Zealand is a great opportunity, but in light of the new offer, I don't—"

"What new offer?" I cut in.

"UNCW offered me a permanent teaching position," she says. "They want me to teach more special topics classes across two disciplines—environmental sciences and art."

"Art, too? That's incredible."

She shrugs. "I have advanced degrees in both concentrations. I'd have an office next to Dad's and all the art supplies I could ever want. That's what they said, anyway. It's a lofty promise, though."

"Wow, congratulations," I gush, incredibly proud of her.

"Yeah, congrats, honey," Fred says. "Henry showed us your teaching videos. I'm not surprised they're trying to win your heart with art supplies."

"It's a great reason to stay," Mom says weakly.

"Henry and Olly are the best reasons to stay, and reason enough, truly," she says dryly, and I squeeze her hands tighter. "But a career that matches my qualifications and experience is important to me, and those are scarce around here. I-I don't know if I want to be a teacher."

When silence takes over, she glances in my direction, a worried crease between her brow. My hand falls on my heart again, and her smile returns with my secret assurance.

CHAPTER 43
Venus

MY INTERACTIONS with Maggie felt strained, but to her, I'm a catalyst that causes Henry pain. She'll need more data to counteract what history has supported—data that only time will provide.

But tonight was a start. The tension vanishes when it's the three of us again, snaking our way through the woods with flashlights.

After we return to the campsite, Olly and Buster pile leaves, twigs, and logs in the brick circle of our fire pit.

"Is it time for s'mores and stories yet?" he asks while Buster yaps his usual, *"What?"*

When I have the fire blazing, we make gooey s'mores while Henry tells us about the Cape Fear's "Gentleman Pirate," Stede Bonnet, and his associate, Blackbeard's, final battle.

He then tells us watered-down versions of ghost stories about the Battleship North Carolina, Bellamy Mansion, and Thalian Hall, until Olly says, "Dad, tell us about the elephant again."

So, he shares about Topsy the escaped elephant instead. And Frank the Frog.

He is excellent at storytelling, which I imagine also makes him a great teacher. We giggle over owls above our heads, bats zipping by, and fireflies dancing through the trees. We talk about the nearly full moon and lie on our backs to gaze at the constellations.

Then, when Olly gets tired, we put out the fire, clean up our snacks, and get ready for bed. I go to my hammock, but Olly rubs his eyes, tugs on Buster's leash, and says, "Venus, sleep with us."

My eyes meet Henry's and find his easy side-smile. "There's plenty of room."

"That, there is, if you're sure it's okay."

Their urging expressions are identical, making me chuckle. We kick our shoes off at the door, and they lead the way into the spacious Greene family tent. Buster and Olly settle on the right, curled to each other. Henry unzips his sleeping bag, laying it out flat for the two of us to climb onto. Then he pulls an extra blanket over us and nestles against me.

It's surreal and all-consuming, the perfection of it, that we're camping together like a real family. This could be *my* family. I could be with Henry like I've always wanted.

Olly's lips pucker with a sudden snore, waking Buster with a sleepy yap.

A giggle rumbles through me, and Henry does the same against my back. His hand slips up to my lips, gently covering them and chuckling as he says, "Shhh" in my ear.

Olly and Buster go still and peaceful again.

I twist around to face Henry, still holding in my laugh. "He gets that from you."

"I don't snore," Henry refutes under his breath.

"Oh, yes, you do. Only you're not *quite* as cute when you do it." My smile stretches across my cheeks as I tease him.

Henry feigns offense.

"But you're still cute," I whisper with a shrug.

"Cute, huh? I prefer other adjectives."

"Like?" I urge, leaning up to kiss him again.

"Like handsome, hot," he says with another kiss, "sexy…"

"You want me to objectify you?" I clarify.

"Absolutely," he whispers back.

"But there's more to you than that, Henry," I say quietly, running my fingertips over his t-shirt.

"Oh, yeah? Tell me, then. I want to know everything you're thinking."

"I also think you're… kind and funny and patient and a very good father and… good for me. Thank you for tonight."

He takes my hand and places it over his heart. "Thank you for handling her so well. I'm sorry for how she was—"

"Don't be. She's just afraid that I'll hurt you again."

He sits up slightly, resting his head on his hand as he stares at me. "I can't wait to prove her wrong. Do you still think you want to stay?"

"I-I want to, yes." His fingers graze my temple, as if prodding my thoughts free. "I think... I could get used to this. It feels like home. Maybe for the first time. I've fallen for your son, too."

"Yeah, he's irresistible." He laughs and tears up at once. "I'd love for you to be here, but I meant what I said. Go anywhere you want, Venus, but *stay* with me. With us. A fixed constant. Okay?"

"Okay," I smile, as he nestles closer on our shared pillow. He locks our hands between us, and for the first time in our history, Henry and I fall asleep facing each other, holding hands, me dreaming of thousands of nights just like this.

CHAPTER 44

Henry

FALLING asleep with my hand wrapped around Venus's, her face the last thing I see before drifting off, may go down as one of my favorite memories of all time. With Olly close to us, his occasional snore brings another comfort. My two favorite people, the family I've always wanted.

Sleep comes easily, especially with Venus's assurances whispering through my thoughts. That she wants to stay. That she's fallen for me again. Fallen for Olly.

Falling.

I'm not sure what wakes me first—Venus's body jerking in alert and rising from our bed or my son's muffled, pained cry in the distance.

Venus races from the tent, calling for him, as I register that he's not here. His sleeping bag is a rumpled, empty mess beside ours. My heart rams mercilessly in my chest as my hand scatters across the space in a desperate search for my glasses.

I scurry from the tent to the sound of Buster barking, Olly moaning, and Venus saying, "Olly! Look at me!"

Around the bloated trunk of our tree, I find them. Buster barks and spins like he doesn't know what to do. Olly sits in the dirt at the base of the tree, blood slathered over his pained face.

I slide next to him, pulling him into my lap as Venus looks him over. His glasses lie broken beside me. Blood from a gash along his hairline covers his forehead and drips down his cheek.

"I wanted to climb," he says weakly.

Venus squeezes his hands, eyes wide as she says, "Look at me. We're here. Don't worry. I need to examine you."

"Olly, tell us what hurts."

"My arm. My head." He makes eye contact with her, but he squints to see her clearly.

"There's a lot of blood, and blood is scary, but you're okay," she assures him calmly.

He nods as she examines the cut on his forehead.

"Two inches, superficial laceration, some dizziness," she reports, her voice even-toned. She glances at the tree branch overhead. "Your head hit an exposed root, and your arm..."

Olly cries and whimpers as she tries to move it gently.

"... Appears to be fractured. I know it hurts," she says, her expression softening as she bops his nose.

"I'm okay," Olly says weakly, though it's clear he isn't.

Her eyes land on mine. "It'll be okay. I promise. His airways are clear, breathing sounds good, and his circulation seems unencumbered. His eyes look fine, and he is coherent enough to follow my instructions. His head wound is probably superficial, though he may be concussed, and the arm is a concern. He'll need an X-ray."

I nod, remembering her EMT-B certification and feeling grateful that she's here regardless. Her calm authority comforts Olly and me at once —a stark relief against the pure terror of the moment. My head spins with what-ifs, but somehow, Venus battles them back.

She unravels the scarf from her hair and pulls another from her pocket. "Henry, use this to apply gentle pressure to his head."

I angle Olly against one arm while I tend to his gash with the other. "It's okay, son. We've got you."

Venus secures his bent arm in a makeshift sling, and he tucks it close to his chest. "Try not to move it."

"I can't move it," he cries, his tears wetting my shirt along with his blood. I'm devastated for him, pained for him, and pissed at myself for not waking when he left the tent. "I just wanted to climb the tree. I thought I could be like Venus."

He buries his head against me like he's embarrassed. Venus glances at me, her brow pinched, and I can almost see the guilt settling on her shoulders.

"It's not your fault," I say sternly to them both. "It was an accident."

She doesn't look convinced. She grabs Buster's leash. "Okay, Olly. Ready for a short drive?"

He shrugs and winces with the movement.

"Henry, if you'll carry him to the Jeep, I'll meet you there," she says, tugging Buster toward the house. "Oh, and keep him talking."

I rise, gently scooping him into my arms as I go. Cradling him to my chest with as little movement as possible, I say, "I know it hurts, but you'll be alright.... How about telling me your favorite things about camping?"

Following the solar lights that mark the trail, I make my way through camp. It's barely sunrise, gray with sun peeking through.

"S'mores," he says, looking slightly loopy against my chest. "Sleeping in the tent with Buster…"

"Yeah, that was nice. Buster's a good dog," I say, snaking my way through the garden. "What else?"

He smiles against my chest. "Your stories… and Venus."

I reach the Jeep at the same time as Venus. Buster barks from inside the house. My med bag hangs across her chest—I hadn't even thought about my inhalers—and she has my keys in her hand. She opens the back door, and I ease Olly into his booster seat.

"Ride with him," she instructs. "It's best if he doesn't fall asleep."

Venus closes the door once I'm inside and settles in the driver's seat. She peeks at us in the rearview mirror as she drives away from the fairy house, kicking up dry dirt along the path.

"Do you remember that time when you had the flu, and you had to get an IV?" I ask Olly.

"It was awful," he breathes out.

"But you felt better, right?"

"Yeah," he answers.

"We're going to the hospital so you can feel better."

"Okay," Olly says. "I feel bad."

"How bad? What do you mean?" I ask.

"Like… like… I ruined the campout," he says through muffled tears. "I'm sorry, Dad."

"No! You didn't ruin anything," I assure him with a smile. "That's the thing about campouts. Anything can happen. Right, Venus?"

"That's exactly right. Everything will be okay," she says. "We're together. We know what to do. You'll be fine."

Traffic is thankfully light this early on a Sunday morning. She navigates the few miles to the hospital and pulls up directly to the emergency department's front doors. She helps me get Olly out of the truck and starts to follow us inside, leaving the Jeep with its doors open.

A security guard stops us at the door.

"Can't park there, ma'am," he says gruffly.

Venus leaves us to deal with the car, and I rush inside with Olly. A few people are scattered in the oversized waiting room, but a nurse assesses the severity of Olly's injuries and takes us through to the emergency department. I carefully set him on a bed in a small, curtained-off section of the ER as the nurse asks questions and enters information into the computer. When the doctor arrives and begins his exam, I peek outside the curtain to find Venus.

She's at reception, looking slightly wild with her loose hair and distressed expression. I wave her in our direction. She meets me just outside the curtain with a sigh of relief, her hand circling my elbow.

"Is he okay?" she asks.

"Of course, he is. Thanks to you. He's with the doctor now."

A shuddering breath escapes her, as if the morning's events are just now catching up to her and shaking her free of her steady calmness.

I lead her inside the curtained section. Olly sits upright on a bed. Her bloody scarf lies unraveled beside him.

"Nasty cut you got there," the doctor says genially.

Olly nods, looking weepy.

Venus hesitates near the curtain, but I pull her along with me to the bed.

"How'd it happen?" the doctor asks.

"I was showing Buster, the dog, how to climb a tree," Olly says, almost proudly. "But I fell. We were camping."

The doctor chuckles. "An excellent pastime. I take my family camping every fall when the leaves start changing. We don't climb trees, though."

Olly's shoulders slump. "Yeah, I shouldn't have done it."

"Whatcha got there?" the doctor points to Olly's closed hand. He loosens his tight grip to reveal Mango.

"It's a fossil. Venus gave it to me. It's a snake named Mango," Olly answers with a smile.

"Cool," the doctor says.

He performs a neurological exam, testing Olly's vision, balance, and coherence.

Finally, the doctor turns to us with a wide smile. "Relax, Mom and Dad. The head wound is superficial…"

Venus's eyes meet mine with relief and uncertainty. She expects me to correct him, but I don't. She is his mom right now, and a damn good one, too. My smile grows with hers, like she knows what I'm thinking.

"We need an X-ray of that arm, though."

"Will it hurt?" Olly says, nervously.

"It's just a picture," I say, lightly rustling his hair.

"I'll tend to the wound first," the doctor says. "A popsicle will help. What's your favorite flavor?"

"Um, cherry," he whimpers.

"Coming right up," the doctor says, rising from his stool.

"Thanks, Doc," I say as he leaves. My hand slips around Venus's waist. "Will you stay with him for a minute? I need to make some calls."

She nods weakly, though she looks unsure—I don't know if it's over worries about Olly or this gigantic, sink or swim, shove into parenting.

All I know for sure is how I feel—impressed, comforted, and even more in love with her.

With a short peck on her forehead, I whisper, "Everything's okay."

Then, I step into the hallway to let his mom and grandmother know what's happened.

CHAPTER 45

Venus

MY FEARS and anxieties dissipate under Henry's soft gaze as he kisses my forehead. *Everything's okay.* He steps out of the curtained room just as the doctor returns with a cherry popsicle wrapped in a paper towel. Olly is pleased and distracted.

He arranges his tray to prepare for the sutures. He cleans and flushes the wound with saline and then applies a numbing cream.

"Mom, mind coming over here?" the doctor says, pointing to the opposite side of the bed. "Olly might need you."

I don't bother correcting him—Henry didn't the first time he made the error. I decide to act as a surrogate in Carly's absence, hoping she wouldn't mind. I sit on the bed behind Olly, and he leans against me like I'm his reading pillow.

"Will it hurt?" he asks weepily, handing me his popsicle trash. I toss it in the nearest receptacle and wipe the drippings from his mouth.

"Yes," I answer, "but it's nothing you can't handle. The doctor must close the wound to stop the bleeding and promote healing."

"Will I have a scar?"

"Maybe."

"Just like you. That'd be cool," he says.

"Yes, scars are cool. But getting them isn't fun. Next time you want to climb a tree, ask me to spot you. Okay?"

"Okay, sorry, Venus."

"Accidents happen. Don't apologize."

"Do you think Dad'll let me go camping again?"

"Yes, of course," I assure him.

"Okay, this'll hurt a bit," the doctor warns. "Hold on to Mango, and, um, Venus."

Olly presses his weight against me and closes his eyes. He whimpers as the doctor works, but stays still and brave. I imagine this is what having a child is like—a constant tug-of-war between love and fear. I understand Henry better now, with all of his worries and what-ifs. I feel them, too. I hate that Olly's in pain, but at the same time, I tear up over how well he's taking it and the adventurous, curious spirit that landed him here, all his brilliance and potential and tender-heartedness. I barely know Olly, but I love him—love that physically hurts in this moment, hurts when he hurts.

The evidence is overwhelming that he and Henry are my family—one I can't be thousands of miles away from.

"That should do it," the doctor announces. "You're my bravest patient today, Olly. Good job."

Olly's tension releases in a heavy sigh. The curtain screeches across the top rail, and a woman enters. Blue scrubs, a white jacket, and a beaming smile that appears surprised at the sight of me.

"Mom!" Olly calls out.

"Oh, Dr. Miller," our doctor says, "Is this *your* Olly?"

"My one and only," she says, repositioning the curtain and approaching the bed. Her hands slip into the pockets of her doctor's coat as she assesses the situation.

"Um, it's nice to meet you. I'm Venus," I say, fixed in place by Olly and unsure what else to say or do.

"Hi, I'm Carly," she says, her smile widening when her eyes meet Olly's. "What happened, bud?"

He groans. "Fell out of a tree."

Her hand falls to her hip. "What were you doing in a tree?"

"Climbing it."

"Why would you do that?" she asks, her tone friendly but high-pitched.

"I dunno. I wanted to show Buster I could climb a tree, just like Venus. She does it *all* the time, Mom."

She glances from him to me, and I blurt, "It's my fault. As the guide, I should've given him a detailed list of dos and don'ts for our campout. I-I'm sorry."

"Accidents happen," Carly says, graciously. "Bumps, bruises, and breaks are a part of growing up, right, bud?"

"I guess," he huffs.

"We're lucky it wasn't worse," she adds, mussing his hair.

A dark curtain falls over the relief I felt only moments ago. It could've been worse. Not just worse, but devastating.

Our doctor rises from his stool. "The next stop on your hospital tour is the imaging department, Olly. Have you ever ridden in a wheelchair before?"

"Uh, no."

"I'll take him," Carly says.

Henry reenters, his brow twinged with worry. He slips his phone into his pocket and runs a hand through his unruly hair. "Everything okay in here?"

Olly sits up, holding his hand out toward Henry. I take that as my cue that my surrogate-parent position has ended, so I rise, giving Henry more space. The room feels crowded and stuffy.

"Glad you two have met," Henry says awkwardly. "Sorry, it's under these circumstances. Carly, I didn't think you'd get here so fast."

"I was in the on-call room. I took an extra shift since you were on your campout."

"Mom, it was so fun," Olly perks up. "We had s'mores and campfire stories and—"

"I want you to tell me all about it, bud," she cuts in, "but let me get that wheelchair. We need to take a picture of your poor arm."

Trapped in the corner, I stay put until Olly's wheeled off to the imaging department. Henry lingers behind with me.

"Sorry that you met Carly without me," he says. "You okay?"

"Fine." I pull his medicine bag over my head and hand it to him. "Um, I'll just be in the waiting room."

"Venus, no. Come with me to imaging," he says, tossing the bag over his shoulder.

"I don't want Olly to feel… conflicted. He needs you and Carly right now. Besides, I noticed a snack machine. He'll be hungry when he gets back, and he should have something in his stomach to buffer the pain meds."

Henry's brow pinches unsurely.

"It's okay," I say. "I'll be just outside."

"Alright," he nods finally. "Thanks, Venus."

We head in opposite directions. I fiddle with my rings as I retrace my steps to the main lobby.

This is my fault. I'm responsible for Olly getting hurt. He's hurt because of me. It could've been worse.

I'm overcome with sudden, sharp regret. Henry and Olly wanted me to keep them safe on their first campout. I should've told Olly not to wander without us, not to climb trees, not to be like me.

I practice my Ins and Outs, fighting against the unfair energy surging within me, telling me to run. I've promised Henry to supply snacks—a task I latch onto to keep me from racing out the sliding doors. I can do that, at least.

The lobby is slightly busier than when we first entered. I navigate the chairs and the people for the vending machines in the corner, contemplating the options. Once I have a packet of gummy bears and a cold soda in hand, I search for a salty option. But it's hard to think.

I notice Olly's blood smeared on my trembling fingers between my rings and under my nails. My heart races, imagining his sneakers slipping from under him, the small branch he held onto breaking, and his head and arm smacking against the protruding root. I picture the fracture in his arm, his small bones breaking, his tears and cries.

Maggie's words from *that* horrible night long ago stream into my desperate imaginings. *All Venus ever does is hurt Henry.* A sob escapes me—it's true for Henry *and* Olly now.

Logic tells me that Olly's okay, accidents happen, and his body will heal with time. But the mark will remain, hiding under skin and muscle, etched into his bone. He will *always* have it.

And I'll know it's there—another mark against me, wrecking my confidence and proving that I don't belong with them.

I belong alone.

My hand shakes as I type in the final code for a bag of chips. Gathering the items in my arms, I turn to see Maggie and Fred rushing into the lobby. Her brown hair is pulled into a messy ponytail at the nape of her neck. She's not wearing any makeup, and her wrinkled jeans and barely tied sneakers reveal that Henry's call surely pulled her from bed. Her hands twist around the strap of her purse, hanging diagonally over her chest.

She looks panicked, hurting for Olly and Henry. My agony compounds, especially when her eyes catch mine and narrow with disappointment. Her expression repeats what she used to say when I was a child. *Accidents happen... especially around you, Venus.*

Tears spill as my frustration rises. I feel like a child again, begging Maggie for time with Henry after getting him in trouble or causing him asthmatic distress.

Always at a disadvantage.

Always on the outside.

Always hurting.

Her arms fold as I approach—armor against the invasive species threatening her family.

"Venus, everything okay?" Fred asks, his lined brow etched with concern. "Henry said Olly's fine. What's upset you, honey?"

"I-I..." I should apologize, shoulder the blame as I did with Carly. Perhaps if I explain it properly, we'll all find comfort in the present facts rather than dwelling on past mistakes. Fact—Olly is a human with freewill, which he exercised this morning. Fact—I would never have permitted or encouraged him to climb a tree without an adult present. Fact—Henry and Olly don't hold me accountable for his mistake.

But logic fails under the crushing weight of Maggie's disapproval—she looks anxious and exhausted, as if my return is akin to a prison sentence and she has to spend more decades worrying about her son and grandson in my presence.

"I knew something like this would happen," she says, almost under her breath.

"Mags," Fred says softly, flashing surprise at her. "It's not Venus's fault."

But it is.

The daggers of guilt and shame cut deeper, twisting at the hilts. *This is Venus. She's brilliant but...*

I push the snacks and drink into Fred's hands.

"Olly's getting an X-ray. Caloric intake will, um, alleviate gastrointestinal discomfort from the pain medicine," I say through gasping sobs. "I-I have to go."

I twist on my boots and race through the double doors.

"Venus?" Fred calls, but I don't stop.

I don't breathe again until I make it to the Jeep.

CHAPTER 46

Henry

THE X-RAY TAKES FOREVER. Once the doctor confirms a fracture, we accompany Olly back to the ER to be fitted for a cast. His pain meds kick in, making him tired and grumpy. I amuse him with funny animal videos as he's being treated. Carly gets called back to work. I text Venus to meet us in the ER, but she doesn't respond.

Mom and Fred rush in as the nurse dictates our instructions—rest, hydration, and keeping the head wound clean as we watch for any further signs of distress like headaches and nausea. The next twenty-four hours might as well be a waiting game to get to the finish line of "he's fine." But I feel confident that he's okay. The nurse leaves with a promise to return with the final paperwork.

Fred dumps snacks on the bed and pops the top on a soda. Olly gulps the rare treat and rips open the gummy bears.

"Where's Venus?" I ask.

Mom forces an awkward smile for Olly's sake, but her brow pinches. "She left."

"Left?" I repeat dully.

"You know how she is." She tilts her head, transmitting weak sympathy through her stare. "She handed over the snacks and said she had to go."

Olly decapitates a gummy bear. "What? Why?"

Mom wedges herself on the bed's edge with a shrug. "It's a mystery."

Fred scratches his messy hair. "She seemed upset."

A sinking, desperate feeling rises in my gut as I duck out of the curtained room. "I'll be back."

The double doors slide open as I rush toward them. I step into the bright sun and scan the parking lot for the Jeep. When I don't see it, I call her.

No answer.

I call again.

No answer.

After a string of pleading texts, she doesn't reply, and I'm still texting when Fred, Mom, and Olly appear through the doors.

"We're all done," Fred announces genially. "Everything okay, Henry?"

"No, she's not answering." My head spins with disbelief and confusion. *Did she really leave us here? After everything?* I replay our last conversation—she seemed alright, though perhaps a little unsettled by everything that happened. Who wouldn't be?

"Good thing we're here, since you need a ride home," Mom says snidely.

Her cold remark irks me. "Did something happen? Did you say something, Mom?"

Her hands raise in defense. "She was upset *before* we got there."

"That's true, and she couldn't tell us why." Fred's hand lands on my back. "Don't worry about it, Henry. She's got your Jeep. She won't get far."

"Let's go back to our house for ice cream, huh?" Mom says, expertly changing the subject. "Ice cream always helps me feel better."

"Yeah," Olly answers weakly. His green cast makes his arm look twice the size. Judging by the gray bands under his eyes, he's exhausted. I need to get him home, so we can begin his recovery where we're most comfortable.

But I need to see Venus.

"Can I have Rocky Road?" Olly asks.

"That can be arranged," Fred says, slipping an arm around me. "We'll watch Olly while you find out what's going on. How's that?"

I nod, though my lungs constrict with the resurrection of familiar pains, like old wounds reopened and freshly gushing. She wouldn't leave us without a reason. Maybe she just got scared—seeing Olly like that scared me, too. Whatever has happened, I want to be there for her, helping her through it. I plan to take the path to the fairy house, talk to Vee, pack up our gear, and get my Jeep while Mom and Fred watch Olly.

But my plan unravels like a pulled thread when we reach the driveway. The Jeep is already here, loaded with our gear.

"Dang, Venus must've moved like lightning to do all that so fast," Fred says. "Kind of her, though."

I exit the car as soon as it's in park, and go to mine. The keys sit on the front seat. I open the trunk and find our supplies neatly packed and organized. She didn't do this on impulse.

"Shit, this is bad," I mumble under my breath. I'm crushed with fears—me showing up at the fairy house to find her gone, my calls and texts going unanswered, and her father eventually explaining that my sunflower prefers her life as a cactus, that it's easier, that I only made her feel trapped.

"Come on, Olly. Let's find your backup pair of glasses," Fred says. "They're probably in the junk drawer next to the ketchup packets."

"I'll grab the ice cream," Mom says, following behind them.

"Mom?"

She turns on the first step while Fred and Olly disappear inside.

"Did you say something to her?" I ask again.

Her arms fold, and her shoulders sag. Her brow scrunches with regret. "Um, she was already upset, Henry… but I'm sorry, it just came out."

"What came out?"

"I said… I knew something like this would happen."

"You *knew* this would happen? She felt terrible about Olly, and you made her feel worse?" I snap, anger surging inside me. "You're so grief-stricken about Jay, so worried that you pushed him away. But you're doing the same thing to Venus. If you make me choose between you and Venus, I'll pick her every fucking time."

Her feet shuffle backward as she stares, stunned and near tears over my harshness. Her hand trembles as she brings it to her mouth. "Henry…"

"I have to go." I wave a dismissive hand toward her and race around the fence line. I don't stop running until the rear deck of the fairy house comes into view. Buster yaps at the sliding glass doors as I approach. It's a relief, knowing that Venus wouldn't shirk her pet-sitting responsibilities. She *must* be here.

Knocking doesn't produce her, though. I move to the front and spot the Land Rover in the drive. I ring the bell.

No answer.

I consider climbing the trellis to the upper deck and Venus's bedroom, like I did when we were teens. The broken slat reminds me that I'm not a teenager anymore, and falling off her trellis wouldn't help anything.

Buster barks and bounces at the sliding glass doors. I try the handle, and it slides open.

"Venus!" I call into the silence. I traverse the stairs, calling her name.

I don't find her, but bags are strewn on her bed—one open suitcase and a heavy-duty backpack, half-packed. Piles of t-shirts, shorts, and cargo pants lie beside the open luggage.

In the open closet, her new wardrobe hangs neatly, but her dresses, skirts, and blouses are pushed back with her prom dress, as if she doesn't need them anymore.

She's leaving them behind. Leaving us behind.

But, she hasn't left yet.

CHAPTER 47
Henry

THE SHARP SMACK of the greenhouse door brings a startled gasp from within. I edge around the messy tables and bubbling bogs and find Venus in the middle. She's camped out on a blanket, lying on her back, and staring into the glowing mosaic overhead. Her hair is splayed around her. Her boots are kicked off to the side. She holds a tumbler against her stomach, of ice and presumably vodka, as the bottle sits nearby, like she plans to make a day of it. It clinks against her belly button ring as she begrudgingly makes space for me beside her in the narrow alley between plants.

She isn't crying or upset, at least not at a glance. She holds up her glass and says, "When the afternoon sun hits it just right, it creates a rainbow. Remember?"

"Yeah, but is that why you're here? Or are you hiding from me? We should talk."

"Actually, it's not a rainbow. It's an optical prism. The flat surface refracts the light, and the combined colors form what appears to be a rainbow. However, if the light combines with the mist produced by Christie's watering system, a real rainbow is possible."

"That's not what I meant by talking."

"I don't want to talk," she says before breaking the short silence a moment later with, "Is Olly okay?"

Her question reminds me to check my phone. I haven't missed any calls or messages, but I turn up the volume just in case. "He's at my parents' and eating his weight in ice cream. He picked green for his cast for you and the garden... He's a kid. He made a mistake. Accidents happen."

"Yes, especially around me," Venus returns quietly. She sits up to gulp her drink, which she promptly refills.

Her words circulate through dimly lit hallways in my memories—Mom used to say that to her, snidely, off-handedly, half-joking and half-serious. "Venus, whatever Mom said doesn't matter."

"All Venus ever does is hurt Henry," she says, almost robotically. "Those were her words to Dad *that* night. Today felt like being dragged through it again. I still can't... I'll never get over *that* night."

My hands fist as my anger toward Mom sharpens, especially with Venus's resigned voice. The battle she faced then becomes clearer—her trying to be *that* girl for me, saying yes to our future, our prom, even buying the dress, while Mom's words broke her heart and twisted her hopes into the dirt.

"I ran from you—*you*, the safest place I've ever known—because I couldn't tell you how I felt—"

"You ran because you felt trapped," I correct gently.

The memory takes hold with the word *trapped*. Our lovely night together, Venus and I on the tailgate, stargazing and making out. Then, her entire demeanor shifted at the mention of prom and doing normal couple things, like she was overwhelmed with the future I'd mapped for us. I remember her nerves, her bracelets jingling as she twiddled them, and finally that uneasy, desperate look on her face—the same look she has right now.

"I knew it wasn't safe to run out on those rocks, knew you'd chase me," she says, like she's reliving the memory with me. "It was reckless. Stupid and reckless."

"It was a mistake. You were eighteen."

"It was careless impulsivity. I-I slipped and fell in." Her trembling hand lifts to her head, rubbing her temple like she still feels the impact from the rock she hit on her way into the water. The same impact Olly felt today.

"It was an accident. It could've happened to anyone."

She gasps like she can't breathe, like the dark sea is swallowing her again. "No, not anyone," she says between labored breaths. "Anyone else would've stayed with you, would've been grateful and excited about prom, college, and a life together. I-I ruined it, ruined us, almost lost you."

"I jumped in after you—it was my choice, and I'd do it again."

"You nearly died!" she yells.

A chill creeps up my spine, remembering the dive into the inky water, unable to see, and my frantic search. I still feel her cold fingertips grazing mine, so gently, before I grabbed onto her with urgent force. And the relief I felt when I had her against my chest.

"I think that's why I jumped into the ocean so many times aboard that ship," she confesses. "I wanted you to find me again."

She's crying now, and my chest constricts with the memory.

Latching onto her.

Dragging her to the surface.

The agonizingly slow swim to shore with one arm wrapped around her.

On the beach, she found her breath again, while I lost mine in the exertion of it. Wheezing, panicking, gasping for air that I couldn't find —*that I'm losing now*—and still, nothing mattered except saving her.

"You should've let me drown," she says. "Sometimes, I wish you had."

"Never wish that again." My voice is harsh, raspy. I reach into my pocket for my inhaler, and my lungs open in a breath. "Never, Venus."

I remember her frantic search for my inhaler that I lost, saving her, choking for air, and her yelling, *"Breathe, Henry. Just breathe!"*

She sets her drink down and pulls her knees to her chest, tightening herself into a ball. "I can't help it. You saved me, but you almost died. Holding you in my arms on that beach, begging you to breathe. I honestly didn't think you'd—"

"But I did. We both did." I sit up, meeting her where she is. My hands travel to her cheeks, and I thumb away her tears. "That night, I got a chance to do for you what you'd done for me *all along*. *I* saved *you*. It was the first time I felt truly brave, and the irony is, I never could've done it if you hadn't shown me how, time and time again. It made me the man I am. *You* made me the man I am. It's why I tell Olly all of our old stories, and one day, I'll tell him that one, too. It's because I want him to be brave. Brave like Venus. Brave like me, too."

A gasping sob blubbers from her as she curls against my chest. "But Henry... this isn't how it should be. And today, with Olly, dredged it up again."

"Stop," I order. "You aren't to blame for that night or today. I don't regret *that* night. Not one minute. When you slipped and disappeared into the water, I didn't think twice about diving in after you. *That's* how much I loved you. And when you held me on the beach, trying to get me to breathe again, I felt how much you loved me. Our love was tested, and we passed."

"Until I failed." Our breaths mingle in our tiny pocket, and more tears escape when she whispers, "I was so scared that I'd lose you, Henry. I'm still scared, like I'm always on that beach, begging you to breathe. Don't you see? I don't want to hurt you or Olly, but it's inevitable. Today proves it—"

"No, today proves that you belong with us. You did everything right."

"I can't go through this again. As much as I love you, I can't," she says, as if she's stopped listening to me. "I can't be what you need me to be. I can't be what Olly needs. She's right—all I do is hurt you—"

"No, she's not right—"

"It doesn't matter. Even if she's wrong, I can't exist in this place, in this family, where I'm to blame when something goes wrong, where I'm expected to cause problems, to be difficult, to run. I survived that once—I won't put myself through it again. Not even for you, Henry."

My lungs constrict again, agonizing over her pain because I get it. She *shouldn't* have to live like that. I wanted a second chance for us, a better existence, not a repeat of the past with her playing defense and suffering through it for me.

"You're right. I don't want that for you, either. I'm asking you to trust me. Today was rough—I get it. But you're *still* here, and today, *that* night, they shouldn't decide forever." I sit up and grab her hand between us. "I trust that you love me. I trust that you love Olly. I trust you to do what's right for you, *even if* that means leaving. But you don't have to leave *me*. Don't let *today* decide for you."

"I won't let today decide," she says finally. "I won't do anything *today*."

I bring her hands up to my mouth and plant tiny kisses on her knuckles. "Thank you."

That she's willing and able to put her turmoil aside fills me with relief—relief that's quickly extinguished when she says, "But..."

Her voice trails as little beams of green and amber light flicker across her face. Her tears catch the light and make her cheeks sparkle. "But you said I'd get my answer if I stopped chasing it... and I have. I will accept New Zealand."

"That's fine. We can—"

"No, Henry. We can't." She barely gets the words out before her head hangs, and a soft sob escapes her. "I love you, Henry... but it's the life I'm used to, the one I'm most comfortable living. That's where I feel accepted and valued. It's where I'm safe. And where everyone's safe from me. It's what I want. I can't be there with a family here, missing me and living with disappointment because I'm absent. That's not a good life—not for you or Olly. You both need someone who's... here."

Her words feel acidic, burning through me, eating away at my hope. Only I can't argue because she's right. Separating again, missing each other, trying to make our family work over texts and calls would be difficult for all of us, including Olly. We'd be divided with all that stands laughably between us—miles, mountains, oceans, people, entire worlds blocking our path to each other.

Every cell in my body screams in protest, every muscle aches, every old loneliness returns with renewed sharpness and agony. It's the past, overtaking me again, only this time *with* her rather than without.

If she'd given me the chance back then, I would've talked her out of leaving. Begged her. Argued. Pressured her into what *I* wanted. Promised her that I'd make everything okay.

But how can I do that now? She'd been right to leave then. It was her way of saving us, and she ended up saving herself. Finding herself. Doing all the incredible things she wanted. I can't make her stay now. I can't make her choose me or us. Not over herself. Not over what she wants. I can't ask her to accept a half-life, hoping that Olly and I can make up the difference. I can't ask her to give up her adventurous, comfortable world for an unfair one.

And she refuses to ask me to settle for a half-life with her, either. So, I can't argue.

I can only... my head falls against her shoulder—cry.

"I'd go with you, if I could," I sob into her. "Follow you anywhere."

"I know." She scoots toward me on the blanket, wrapping her hands around my neck to tug me closer. "I thought I could stay. I wanted to. But outside of you and me... and us and Olly... I don't belong, like I'm trying to fit into a life that's not mine. Yours. Dad's. Even Ivy's."

"I know. It's okay. If it doesn't feel like home, then it isn't," I say, running my hands over her wet cheeks, and hating how hurt she is.

Hating how hard this is for her—the pressure of deciding, feeling torn between us and the life she knows, and shouldering the aftermath of her choice. Even *that's* unfair to her. "I'm sorry. I wanted to be *that* guy, helping you through this, but all I've done is make this harder for you."

"No. You are *that* guy for me. *Always*," she says, her fingers running through my beard as she smiles. "This summer has been the best of my life, and I'll carry it with me wherever I go. I don't regret anything, not one second."

A smile breaks through my sadness. "Me, neither."

Her lips meet mine in a desperate plea. The sweetness of the alcohol mixes with salty tears, and my tongue plunges into her mouth, needing more. In a breath, we're intertwined, on our knees, bodies pressed, hands everywhere, but lips together. Each kiss full-on, feeling like the last.

She tugs on the button of my jeans and slips her hand inside, stroking me. Her firm, confident grip reminds me of the first time she touched me, and how I came over her delicate hand. And then, how she came against mine. I take all those perfect memories—the ones of just her and me—and seal them between us now, in our wild affection. Our first kiss, and every first between us. First love and last. I leave her lips only long enough to pull her shirt over her head. My hands dig into her shorts, squeezing her ass and pressing her closer.

"Henry," she whispers against my lips as she pushes my jeans down my hips. Her lips part like she wants to say more, but she can't find the words.

"Shhh, everything's okay. I'm here. We're together."

The words force more tears that mingle with hers when I kiss her again.

I unhook her bra, and she frees me of my shirt. Sunlight beams in from the stained glass, specking her beautiful skin in purple, blue, and pink bands. My lips slide down her neck, across her collarbone, teasing and tasting her. I lay her gently on the blanket, careful of the hard surface underneath, and devour her with my mouth—the curves of her breasts, the valley between them, her tight stomach, and her sensitive belly button ring. She whispers my name again, and I know I'll hear her in my dreams.

I rid her of the rest of her clothes, and take in her gorgeous body under the streams of light. She smiles up at me, and a tear slips from her eye. I kiss it away before letting my tongue travel the length of her.

Lower and lower still, until I wrap her legs around my shoulders and take her—desperate to have her in my mouth, all tongue, lips, and fingers, until I don't know what I'm doing anymore. My motions are wild, frantic. I'm lost in her. Devouring her. More hysteria than concentration. It's almost a surprise when her hand rakes through my hair, and she comes wildly, screaming my name.

For a strange second, I think of her next lover, hearing my name instead of theirs. Fuck him. Fuck them all. She'll always be mine.

Tears fall with the thought.

Her hand moves to my cock, lining me up to her entrance, but I pause, hovering over her, motionless, stunned at how tragically beautiful she looks beneath me. Her hands cup my ass, pulling me in, nudging me inside. And when my will finally breaks, I cry out, "Venus," as I slam into her. I grind into her, locking her to me to ease the friction. It feels good—she always feels good—but I'm desperate to be deeper, to have her closer.

I flip us over, position her in my lap, and bring her close to my chest. She takes what she needs, understanding that I want more connection. She watches me watch her. Softly kissing her perfect lips. Sharing the taste of her on my tongue. Catching the scent of campfire still in her hair, mixing with the gentle rose of her skin—burned roses—and still, I capture everything about this moment, sealing it into my memory. My fingers drift up and down her back as she rides me. Our connection is so strong and all-consuming—heads touching, chests locked, arms and fingers intertwined, and her thighs bringing me in—that we aren't two people. We're one, about to be split apart again.

My soulmate wants me. I want her. But we can't be together. The fucking unfairness nearly ruins this. But her hands drift across my beard, and she says, "Come back to me, Henry."

With a relentless kiss, I do.

She sweeps my tears away as I kiss hers, and I soak in her love and comfort. I try holding back, savoring this and the familiar comfort between us, but it feels too damn good. I come, bringing her with me, until our hot arousal pools between us and we curl into each other.

Ecstasy soon gives way to sobs, and we're crying into each other's shoulders again.

"I'm sorry," she whispers, a tremor in her voice.

"Don't be," I say, running a hand over her head to hold her closer. "It wouldn't be us without big feelings."

Through a ragged breath, she chuckles. "And *they* used to say I was emotionless."

"I remember. *They* never knew you."

"No. They didn't realize... I saved all my feelings for you." She sighs against me, fingers trailing over my back. "I'll never love like this again."

My chest tightens, and that loneliness, sharp and bitter, resurges in me. "What's your rule about using absolutes?"

She pulls away to see me better. Her brow furrows in anguish. "I won't, Henry."

"I won't either," I say in a breath, "not like this. You're the heart of me, Venus."

"And you're mine." She latches on to me again. "I'm sorry. I hate hurting you again."

"Even a day with you is worth a lifetime of hurt. I'll be okay. I promise," I assure her, desperate to take away her pain. "You'll be okay, too. We won't have this, but...but love will find you."

She moves away from me, pulling the end of the blanket over herself as I speak. I tug on my underwear and shirt.

"When the pain softens, and you're resigned to a life alone," I go on, pulling on my jeans. "It'll sneak up on you gently so as not to scare you. He'll be unattached like you, free to follow you anywhere, dazzled by your brain and body without needing much else. He'll be *easy*."

I stand, reaching out to her. She takes my hand, and I lift her from her blanket. I use the blanket's corner to clean off her inner thigh, wiping me away.

Then, I dress her, bending down to put on her panties as I talk, and wretched emotions keep coursing through me.

"You'll give in, little by little, sharing pieces of you, only just enough," I say, hooking her bra. "Not right away, but eventually, you'll decide—*this is love*. A watered-down and murky version, but *love enough*, anyway. Companionable. Practical. Pleasant. And you'll relax into him the way you can't with me. I know you, and he only knows what you want him to see. That'll make him feel safe. But how safe is he, really? I'll still be the one you think about every night, the one you want in a storm.... You'll still be the one *I* think about."

Her shirt falls over her head, and I tug it across her chest. Her glassy, green eyes land on mine, pained.

"Henry, please..."

I shrug, trying to knock the hurt from my shoulders. "It's true. You know it. I know it—I lived it once already. But know this, Venus. No matter where you are, how far you are, who you're with, or how long it's been—I'll love you still. And I'll always be here, hoping you'll climb into my window. Hoping you need *me*. Hoping that... you finally feel safe enough to come home."

My hand goes to my chest and rests over Frank the Frog, a last effort to assure her that everything's okay.

Even though it isn't.

I clear my throat to keep it from closing and take a pull on my inhaler. "I have to get back to Olly."

She nods, and another tear slips. I don't want to leave her like this. But I can't handle any more, either.

"Promise me..." I thumb new tears away, hating that I can't pull myself together. "Promise you won't leave without saying goodbye. Not this time. Please."

"I won't. I promise."

With a kiss to seal her words between us, I head toward the door.

But I hesitate before exiting. I twist to see her, standing there in her t-shirt and panties, tears specking her cheeks and colors streaming all around her. She's so fucking sad and beautiful that it feels like death to leave her.

"Venus, thanks for what you did for Olly today," I say, clearing my throat and finding strength from somewhere. "You were exactly what he needed. What I needed, too."

A weak half-smile appears. "Tell Olly he's brave."

The door thwacks shut behind me.

Rushing away from the greenhouse feels like half my body is tearing away from me, inch by painful inch. Hurt leeches through my pores with the sweat now emanating in the summer heat and spills in the tears that I can't seem to stop. In the middle of the tall soldiers, I rest against a tree, catching my breath and pulling myself together as best as I can for Olly's sake.

I can't believe I've lost her.

Spilling into Mom's backyard, the grief hits me again—that's the last time I'll take that path. I take a breath, steeling myself behind the Fortress of Strength, like I did after Jay died.

Olly sits under a blanket between Mom and Fred on the couch. He looks heart-wrenchingly pathetic with his gauzed head, last year's glasses, his thick green cast, and an exhausted twinge under his huge, round eyes.

"Olly, let's go home," I say, sounding curt but not meaning to.

He nods weakly and shoves the blanket away.

"Everything alright, Henry?" Fred asks, his bushy brow pinched with concern.

I glance at Mom, and anger resurfaces. "No, but Mom should be happy."

"Henry, I'm sorry," she whines. "What can I—"

"Nothing," I snap, still reeling over her words to Venus—today and *that* night. But I don't have the energy to deal with Mom now. "Olly, don't bother with your shoes."

I reach down, lifting him with one arm until he's latched to my side. His head falls to my shoulder. I grab his shoes and tote him to the Jeep.

Fred follows, edging around me to open Olly's door. I tuck my tired, hurt son into his booster seat and click the harness into place. I tussle his hair. "Venus said to tell you you're brave."

"Venus said that?" His eyes widen, like she's permitted him to be impressed with himself.

"Yep. Ready for home?"

"Yeah," he mutters, squeezing Mango in his hand. "Is Venus coming too?"

The question makes my heart seize in my chest. I can't answer.

Instead, I shut the door and turn toward Fred. "Thanks."

"Hey, Henry, um, it'll be alright."

"No, it won't, but we'll get by. Like always." I nearly tear up at the word.

Then, we go home.

CHAPTER 48
Venus

"VENUS! WHAT'RE YOU DOING?" Ivy's voice splits through a chaotic dream involving cloning research and Henry. Buster rouses beside me with a weak, *"What?"*

"Sleeping," I mutter begrudgingly when my sister plops on the bed beside me.

"No, I mean, why aren't you in class right now? It's after nine," she reports urgently.

I sit up, my head throbbing enough to elicit regret. Buster hops over me to tackle her, making the bed shake. I rub my temple. "I called in sick. Canceled my class. It's allowed."

"Oh," Ivy says, calmer now. Her cold hand finds my forehead. "Are you sick?"

"Sick on love and vodka." A summary of yesterday crowds my thoughts, bringing the pain with it. Longing burns through me like a controlled fire, clearing the brush for the raw earth underneath. I ache for Henry. The despair I feel seems illogical when I try to analyze it. How can I miss him so sharply when I was with him only yesterday?

But love is illogical.

Beautiful, terrible, and illogical.

Feelings, good and bad, rarely equate with reason. The pain of his absence isn't only for the present, but made sharper for the future and the prospect of returning to a life without him. Without Olly. The thought suffocates me.

I deliberated for hours last night. I treated myself like a specimen and examined every part, looking for hope. Perhaps I'd find some unknown predisposition for domesticity, hiding in my corners. Or devise a brainwashing scheme for Maggie. Or discover a need to settle into a stable career. Or maternal instincts. Or Ivy-like charisma. Or general normalcy, hidden in boxes in my mental attic. Then, I could pull out the necessary tools to make this work, to make others see me as I am—not just a grown-up version of my former difficult self, but also as someone who would keep the two boys I love most safe and sound, as much as it's in my power to do so. Then, I could take those empty boxes, fill them with the past, all the shame, blame, guilt, and other negativities inside them, and hide them from my consciousness.

I was quite tipsy by that point.

But that's what this summer's experiment was about, me trying to belong—and it failed. Again.

I lay back down, curling into my plethora of oversized pillows, hoping to fall back asleep, the only place to find relief.

Ivy slaps my ass. "Get up!"

"Owwww!" I whine.

"I'll fix you my hangover cure." She stands with her hands on her hips. "Take a shower. We have to get moving and grooving. Dad's arriving at the airport in…" She checks her watch. "One hour."

"What? Why? He's not due back for another week."

She shrugs. "All I know is that Christie texted us… Where's your phone?"

I glance around. "Don't know."

She groans with irritation. "Anyway, he said that Dad's arriving and asked if we could pick him up. So, shower. *Now*. Come on, Buster."

He yaps and follows her out of the loft bedroom.

Ivy's hangover cure is toast, two pain pills, and an iced coffee mixed with coconut milk, which she has thoughtfully put into an oversized travel mug. She pushes everything toward me when I come downstairs. She gives me a once-over, not bothering to hide her dissatisfaction.

"All those beautiful clothes we got you, and this is what you're wearing?"

A glance down at my usual t-shirt, shorts, and boots causes a huff. "What? It's the airport, not a date. I want to be comfortable, and I don't need those clothes anymore."

She groans. "You're regressing and don't think for a second I didn't notice the half-packed bags on your floor. What's going on?"

I shove toast into my mouth instead of answering.

She holds up a finger. "Hold that thought... You can spill the tea in the car. Let's go."

Perhaps it's the coffee or pain pills kicking in, but in the twenty-minute drive to the airport, I spill about the campout, Olly's injury, acting as a parental surrogate at the hospital, meeting Carly, Maggie's words, and the greenhouse. I tell her my plan to accept New Zealand and list the extensive benefits of that decision, reminding myself of them as well.

She grunts, pulling into a parking space at the airport. "Why do you have to go thousands of miles away to change the world? Why can't you do that right here?"

I'm about to answer, but she bangs her hands on the steering wheel. "And screw Henry and Maggie. What about us? Dad and me? We just got you back, and we want you here. Can't that be enough?"

I gape as my sister—the same sister who once described me to her friends as being *barely related*—tears up over the prospect of me leaving. She grabs a tissue from the center console, groans again, and checks her watch.

"We have to go," she says, but stepping out of her car, her phone rings. She answers with a chipper, "Hi, this is Ivy."

I meet her at the front of her car, and we slowly start to snake our way through the expansive parking lot. "Oh, hey... yeah, it's fine that Marnie passed along my number..."

She holds the phone out between us and puts it on speaker.

"She's not answering her phone. She cancelled her class." Henry's voice is bothered, rushed, but it's a relief to hear it. "I shouldn't have left her alone yesterday. We were both upset, but Olly needed me. I need to make sure she's okay—"

"Henry, it's okay. Her phone's MIA, but she's fine," Ivy chimes in while I shake my head to indicate that I don't want to talk to him. "She, um, got a little carried away on Vodka Cranberries and took a sick day."

The sliding doors open, and we're hit by cool air and background noise. An announcement chimes over the loudspeakers, reporting a flight delay.

"Ivy? Did I hear the word *flight*? Are you at the airport?" Henry blasts through the phone. "Is Venus there?"

"Um, yes, but no. Don't freak out. She's not running, Henry. I promise," Ivy says. "But she can't see you right now. She needs... I don't know what she needs, but maybe time?"

"She's taking the New Zealand job. Did she tell you?"

"Um, yeah. I'm not happy about it, either. But she hasn't done anything *yet*."

I roll my eyes at my hopeful sister, knowing I won't change my mind.

There's a brief silence before Henry sighs. "I understand why she wants New Zealand. It's unfair to ask her to settle for anything less. It's just... I love her. I've always loved her. I'll go on loving her wherever she is. Maybe it's selfish—tell me if it is, Ivy—but fuck it... I want her here with *me*."

His words are stern and decisive, sending an electric charge up my spine. Ivy gives me a sympathetic look while I shake my head, unable to hold these weighted emotions right now.

"Venus doesn't hurt me or Olly—she makes us happy. We *want* her in our lives. She must know that."

"Your mom isn't the only one living in the past," Ivy tells him, "but she's wrestling with the facts, too. You know how she is, Henry. Big feelings freak her out, and she's trying to ignore them so that she can complete an exhaustive mental analysis before reaching a sound and logical conclusion to her dilemma. She says she can't accomplish that around you and Olly. It's too *difficult*."

He groans. "I hate that fucking word." The line gets noisy for a moment—it's Henry using his inhaler.

"You okay?" Ivy asks.

"No," he growls in a scratchy exhale. "I'm not okay. I don't want Venus *reasoning* this out. I want her to trust her feelings. To trust *me*—"

My hand goes to the silky pink scarf in my hair, and how freeing it felt to let him have control, to love me as he wanted, to trust him.

"—Please, Ivy. Tell her I won't give up on her. Tell her yesterday wasn't goodbye. I'll come there. I'll leave right now. You don't have to tell her. I'll just show up."

"No! Don't do that. I'd break the fundamental laws of sisterhood if I betrayed her wishes like that. Sorry, Henry. But I promise to talk to her, and she won't be alone."

"Good. But wait, Ivy. Please, tell her... everything's okay. It's only a storm—we should hold each other through it," he says, his words choppy. "It'll pass. And I'll still be here, wanting her. *Always.*"

Ivy's eyes go as wide as golf balls as she glares at me over Henry's sweet words. My eyes shut tightly, sealing the emotions inside me.

A short pause later, Ivy says, "I'll tell her," before the call ends. She slips her phone into her pocket, points to Dad's arriving gate, and drags me through the airport.

I watch the exit gates, where the flight from London via DC has just landed, and passengers should emerge at any moment. The airport isn't busy, but the buzzing glow of bright lights and the occasional drone of the speakers unsettle me, even more than I already am.

"Gil's agreed to move in," she says, breaking through the noise and inner angst. "You were right. Getting away together loosened him up, and he spilled the beans about his anxiety, prompting me to pop the question. He said he'd take me over Seagrove any day."

A weak smile emerges. "Excellent. That's a very positive outcome."

Movement from the hall's end catches my attention, but it's only staff shifting through the corridor.

"What Henry's mom said isn't his fault, you know," Ivy says.

"I know. Henry hasn't done anything wrong. He's done everything right, actually."

"Then, why not talk to him?" she asks, her voice soft and sweet.

I take a breath. "We've talked already. What more is there to say?"

Ivy groans again. "That you love him, and New Zealand isn't what you want. You're a sad sack in hiking boots—a ten on the pain chart. You thought you'd turned a corner into their family, and now, you're scared and bullying yourself into believing you don't belong. But it's not true, Venus."

"I don't intentionally hurt anyone, but it happens around me," I retort. "The facts are indisputable."

"Forget these so-called facts. They're circumstantial. You could argue that people are hurt around me, too," she says, smirking.

"You work at a hospital."

"Right, *circumstantial*. Henry says you should trust your feelings. I agree with him."

"I know you're keeping your promise to Henry, but I don't want to talk. I'm not upset or emotional. I'm controlling my impulses. I'm handling this perfectly well. I'm fine. Absolutely fine… and when I leave again, I'll be absolutely fine then, too. It's what's best. For everyone."

Ivy appears like she might argue, but the heavy double doors swing open, and the area floods with people, distracting us both. Dad emerges through the crowd, beelining around families and couples toward us. From his wrinkled khakis, plain collared shirt, and tousled blonde and gray hair, he looks the same as always.

But my heart rate upticks anyway, and I find myself bobbing on my boots, back and forth, in anticipation.

Ivy reaches him first, meeting him halfway. She latches her arms around his shoulders for her excessive show of affection—she's always been a self-proclaimed hugger. He pats her back, and they share friendly greetings.

When his grayish-green eyes land on me, his gentle smile unlocks the pent-up tension of the last twenty-four hours. All at once, my feelings converge. I recall the fear I felt when I saw Olly hurt, the relief I felt with every question he answered, and the pride I took in how well he handled his emergency room visit. I remember Henry calling me *family*, and the blissful comfort of sharing the tent with them. The agony returns, too. Maggie's disappointment and the raw, aching truth in her words. The all-encompassing beauty and devastation with Henry in the greenhouse. I am helplessly saturated with feelings. Utterly soaked. Lost in a storm.

"What brings you home early, Dad?" Ivy asks.

He answers with a simple, "Venus," smiling gently as he says it.

Hearing my name unlocks the drawbridge, freeing everything inside. I crumble into his arms. That he would cut his trip short for *me*, like he knew instinctively that I needed him, makes it true. I *need* him. And Ivy. And all the love and support they're willing to give me. I *need* my family.

He holds me there in silence as the world shuffles, rolls, and patters around us, and I do the unthinkable. I cry into my father's shoulder.

"Oh, you guys," Ivy coos, latching her arms around us both and crying, too.

"My amazing daughters," Dad says, with one of us occupying each of his shoulders. "It's good to be home."

CHAPTER 49

Henry

THE LOUD BUZZ of the museum's antique doorbell has me racing down the stairs two at a time. The last forty-eight hours have been hectic and exhausting. Between taking care of Olly, finishing the museum for the launch party on Friday night, and turning in the final papers for my two classes, I've been overwhelmed.

But most of all, I've been worried about Venus.

Texting with Ivy has brought some comfort—Dr. Blake has returned, Ivy's been staying at the fairy house for extra support, and despite what she said, Venus hasn't accepted the New Zealand position yet.

Last night, Venus finally texted to ask how Olly was doing. She didn't communicate long, but she texted that she loved us both before saying goodnight.

So, I hoped it might be her at the door, overrun with big feelings and desperate to see us.

But it's Mom. She applies a weak smile when I appear in the foyer, looking nervous but determined. It's a surprise to see her here. It's the first time she's been to the museum since Jay died. I've invited her several times—when I wanted her advice regarding my inheritance, when Fred and I hoped she'd help sort his things, and when Olly and I moved into the apartment upstairs.

But every time I asked, she'd grow anxious and, even if she wanted to help, she'd finally be forced to admit that she couldn't. She got as far as the parking lot once before panic took over. This is where Jay lived, where his dreams never quite reached his expectations, and where he left us. She feels responsible for the brother she couldn't save.

I push the glass door open, unsure what to do. "Mom, you're here."

She takes a deep breath, seeming to force her nerves to retreat. "No choice. I need to see you."

"Look, Olly'll be up soon. I have a lot to do. Why are you here?" I ask, leaning against the doorframe.

"You were right," she says firmly. "I owe you an apology that's... been a long time coming."

"It's Venus you should be apologizing to," I say, folding my arms over my chest.

"Yes, and I will... but I need to talk to you first. Please."

Anguish brims in her brown eyes, and her hands tighten around each other, like she fears I'll turn her away.

"Fine, but I need to be close to Olly. You'll have to come inside, up to the apartment," I say, assuming she'll refuse.

But she nods and moves into the foyer as I step aside. She glances around the room, surely taking in the changes. It must look like an entirely new place to her. She doesn't comment, though, as if limiting herself to only what she came here to do.

Until she sees the wooden bluejay on the counter. I try remembering the last place I saw it, but give up caring when a warm smile cuts through her anxiety.

She takes it in her hands and says, "Jay used to toss it my way whenever I felt anxious. 'Hold on to Jaybird. He's lucky.' It seemed so silly, but it helped."

"Hold onto him now if you want."

She nods appreciatively. "Lead the way."

Upstairs, I peek in on Olly, relieved to find him still asleep. I've kept him home from camp since the accident. Perhaps I'm overcautious, but his aches and the pain meds have taken a lot out of him. I didn't want to push him.

I return to the kitchen to find Mom pouring herself a cup of coffee from the pot I made earlier. Over her first sip, she motions to the cluttered mess scattered over my kitchen table. "What's all this?"

Shifting the papers so she can sit down, I say, "Research. A list of all flights to New Zealand over the next six months, info on expediting Olly's passport, rentals near Venus's new job, how my health insurance works overseas, school calendars, Carly's calendar... I've spoken to her about taking some long trips with Olly, and she thinks it'd be great for his education. She may even come with us sometimes. Venus prefers facts, so I plan to present her with as many as I can, to show her that we can make this work."

Mom squeezes the bluejay in her fist as she sits down. "I'm sorry for the damage I've done, Henry. I don't know if it's possible to repair it. But I promise, I'll try."

"She overheard you *that* night in the hospital, telling Dr. Blake that all she ever does is hurt me. You let a scared eighteen-year-old girl who nearly lost her best friend believe that she was a burden, unworthy of us, and then you made her feel that way all over again on Sunday. I don't think there's any coming back from that."

Her fingers shift over her mug, and tears spill from her eyes. "I have no excuse… only an explanation. If you'll hear it."

I stand opposite her, folding my arms over my chest, unsure if I want to. Her only saving grace right now is that she showed up here, the one place I feared she'd never come again, in the hopes of a reconciliation. That tells me she's trying. So, I nod, allowing her to continue.

"Venus did for you what I couldn't," she says, her voice strained. "She protected you from bullies at school. She protected you from Dale. She even helped you with your asthma, in the long term anyway. The truth is… if it weren't for Venus, I may not have had the courage to leave Dale. And I loved her for all of it. *I loved her*, Henry. Still do… But I resented her, too. At eight years old, Venus Blake bumbled into our lives, held up a mirror, and showed me exactly where I'd gone wrong… and I couldn't stand it. So, whenever she got you in trouble or got you sick, I latched on to the problems until they became all I could see—that's what my therapist says."

"The negativity bias," I breathe out, remembering Venus's words.

"Yeah, and that first night in the hospital, after nearly losing you, I-I stopped seeing her as the child I loved, but the villain who hurt you, and… I suppose, in a way, it turned me into a villain, too. I am desperately sorry, Henry. So sorry that even if you send me away and stay angry at me forever, I will *never* stop trying to fix it."

She takes a breath, swiping at tears that have created black smudges under her mascara. I hand her a tissue from the box nearby, and she smiles lightly.

"Grandma? Why're you crying?" Olly says from the hallway leading to our bedrooms. He holds Mango in his cast hand while he rubs his eyes with the other.

She chuckles through her distress. "Olly, I'm just sad because I miss Venus. I, um, haven't talked to her since the hospital, and I hope she's okay."

He wobbles over to her, edging into her lap. "Me, too."

"Here, I brought you something." She sets down the wooden bluejay to pull something out of her purse. It's a framed picture of Venus and me from our senior year, when things were good between us. I'm laughing, and she's giving me a coy grin, like I've just said something funny.

Olly giggles over it. "They look different."

"They were younger," Mom says. "I thought you might hang it up with all of your superhero posters."

"Oh, cool." He hops off Mom's lap, flies Mango around the room, and carries the frame to his bedroom.

"He's feeling better," she quips before her eyes find mine again. "Tell me, Henry. What can I do?"

What-ifs swarm me with her question. What if Mom hadn't said those words to Dr. Blake? What if she'd been a mom to Venus all the time, even when she was upset? Would Venus have stayed then? Now?

I also remember how hard it must've been for Mom—Dale bullied her, too—and she was constantly on high alert over worries about me. She was a single parent, even when she was married to Dale, the primary source of our family's income, and was constantly summoned by school nurses or administrators over me... and Venus.

Olly is blissfully low-maintenance by comparison.

I refuse to make the same mistake with Mom that I did with Venus the first time she left—assigning blame and holding on to anger. Venus wouldn't want that, regardless.

"Um, I don't know what to do. She's still here. Dr. Blake and Ivy are with her. But she doesn't want to see me. I made her promise not to leave without saying goodbye, but I don't know... she's distancing herself, making it easier for her to leave when the time comes. She's trying to protect us. She believes leaving is the best thing she can do for us. How can I convince her she's wrong when she's believed it for so long?" I shift in my chair, feeling uneasy just talking about it. I smirk sheepishly. "After prom, I'm tapped out on big, romantic gestures."

Mom's brow cinches in the middle. "Venus doesn't need romance, and if anyone needs to give her a grand gesture, it should be me. I'll speak to her."

"I don't think that's a good—"

"Henry, trust me. I'm the one who's messed up. I should be the one to fix it. Besides, I can't make it any worse, right?"

"That doesn't fill me with overwhelming confidence, Mom."

She stands, slinging her purse onto her shoulder and gathering my messy papers into one stack. "There are a few things I need to take to her, so I'll deliver your research as well." She holds up one of the leftover invitations that Marnie made for the museum's launch party that must've gotten mixed in. "I'll deliver this, too. She *must* respond to an invitation. Right?"

I smile. "Well, that would be customary."

CHAPTER 50
Venus

DAD and I stand on the front deck of the fairy house, staring at the crowd of future botanists and environmental scientists from the special topics course on rare plants. I planned it weeks ago, unaware that Dad would be here or that I would be a mess, held together only by my scarf, boots, and overalls. For once, I almost blend in. Everyone wears boots and gardening gloves. They carry their own field journals. They eye us with hopeful anticipation—today, it's their turn to get their hands dirty.

I'm excited for them.

For me, too. It's a pleasant diversion. I need to accept the New Zealand position, but every time I sit down at my laptop, my fingers freeze after typing *'Dear Dr. McCullum'*. Perhaps it's the word *dear* that hinders me. Though an acceptable salutation, it feels disingenuous. He is not dear to me. Only a few people in the world are, and those people are here. Not New Zealand. Not at the other end of an email.

Myla Rose looks up from her clipboard. "Everyone's here, Dr. Blake."

"Thank you," Dad and I say together, though she was talking to me.

We share a bemused glance before he clears his throat. "Apologies, Venus."

"No need to apologize," I say, before announcing, "To avoid confusion, please refer to my father as Dr. Blake, and to me as Venus for today."

Myla smiles, bouncing on her boots. "Yes, Venus."

"Today, you'll assist with routine maintenance of the gardens," I continue before my father, and I take turns describing their duties. "During the second hour, we will be harvesting flytraps and pitcher plants for the on-campus garden installation that we'll build during class time tomorrow... Your challenge for today is to study flytraps in various stages, and to identify invasive species or any other threats."

The crowd disperses at my instruction, spreading into the garden or congregating around the baskets and tools I've laid out.

Dad gives me a surprised look. "A campus garden?"

I shrug. "A raised, circular garden near the turtle pond. It will be called the Blake Bog. It'll be similar to the installations at the Raleigh Botanical Garden. The campus should have carnivorous gardens. Don't you think?"

"Why yes! Of course! How did that come about?"

I shrug lightly. "Administrators are surprisingly amenable toward requests from faculty who've gone viral in a positive way."

"Does that mean you're still considering their offer?" he asks, leaning closer. "You said you were accepting New Zealand."

"I will. I am. Soon. I've neither accepted nor rejected anything yet, but teaching holds the least appeal. I want to be in the field, doing the work that brings about real, large-scale environmental impact."

Dad nudges my shoulder softly as we survey the area—students fan out amongst the wild and lush bog, edging carefully between growth on the pavers and bending to examine the flytraps nestled near the ground.

"Look what you've done here. In my experience, the biggest impact comes from small acts and concentrated effort. As long as there's dirt under your boots, you can make a difference." A gentle hand lands on my back consolingly. "Perhaps your decision will come easier without hefting the *entire* world on your shoulders, hmm?"

A sigh escapes with my tentative nod. Dad's words bring some consolation, especially in view of the twenty-four bodies in our domain, excited and respectful about the world they're observing. There's more hope here than I ever had with Dr. Miner, especially at sea. A glance at my dirty boots makes me smile—I didn't have the earth underfoot there, either.

"Excuse me, Venus," Myla says, timidly approaching the deck with Jayden behind her. "Jayden had a great idea."

I manage a weak smile at my most loyal students. "I'd like to hear it."

"Me, too," Dad says.

Myla gives Jayden an encouraging smile, and he says, "Um, so I was on my 5k at Long Leaf park this morning, and thought, why isn't there a carni-garden there?"

Dad and I share a glance while we mentally translate his question.

"Is that what we're calling them now?" Dad asks.

"No, but expanding carnivorous gardens to the parks department is an intriguing proposition," I say.

Dad rubs his chin. "Perhaps we could create more natural habitats to combat those being destroyed by development."

"We should explore this further," I say.

"Can Jayden and I come up with a proposal for it?" Myla asks with excitement. "We'd love to research it together."

"By all means. Perhaps we… I mean, you and Dr. Blake can meet next week." I turn to Dad with a questioning look, realizing I shouldn't make plans. I'll probably be on a plane by then.

Dad agrees to the meeting, and once a time is established, the students disperse into the carnivorous field. He gives me a look as if this proves his earlier point. I shrug lightly, and we separate, infiltrating the garden on either side to assist students in their endeavors.

But my thoughts are elsewhere.

Two nights ago, after my dramatic display at the airport, Dad, Ivy, and I returned with Buster to the fairy house, where we initiated what Ivy called a "self-care slumber party." We ordered takeout, dished about our boyfriends, and performed beauty rituals that even Dad participated in. Ivy took selfies of us on the couch, our faces covered in clay masks that she claimed would "detoxify" our skin *and* our bad feelings.

My bad feelings remained, at least until I purged my innermost thoughts and feelings about Henry and my future. We bonded over glossy fingernail polish, scented lotions, and the sweet validation I didn't know that I needed. My family understands my conflict and has stressed the importance of exercising patience with myself in making such an impactful decision.

My inability to type my acceptance letter proves I'm reluctant about New Zealand. I keep thinking of Henry's words. *Everything's okay. It's just a storm. It'll pass.* But what will pass exactly? My discomfort with choosing New Zealand, missing Henry, Maggie's disapproval, or the need to escape back to my former existence? Will I get to New Zealand

and discover I've made a colossal mistake? Would I realize the same if I stay?

The pressure to decide mounts, making me perpetually nervous and uneasy.

How can I leave?

How can I not leave?

How can I stay? How can I go?

The class concludes three hours later, but students linger in the gardens, continuing their work and enjoying the beautiful day. I watch them from the deck, in case they have more questions, but as they mill about, a car snakes up the dirt driveway, parking diagonally between a Braxton pear tree and a longleaf pine.

I'm not pleased to see Maggie. She wears a cornflower blue dress and sensible shoes—her office-wear as if she's on her lunch break from the library. Reading glasses are hooked to her collar. She retrieves a box from the backseat, hefting it awkwardly in her arms.

She makes her way to us on the deck, looking apprehensive. She leans the box against the bottom railing of the deck's steps. A weak smile emerges as she motions to the students. "Um, what's going on here?"

"A special topics course on the rare plants of North Carolina," I answer.

"*You* are not enrolled," Dad says with a surprising snap to his voice. "I *don't* mean to be *rude*, but you're *not* welcome."

I gape at my father, who, to my knowledge, has never raised his voice in his life. His face is flushed with anger on my behalf.

"Dad," I gasp. "Thank you."

He sterns his stance. "Of course."

My shock compounds when Maggie puts her hands up delicately and says, "Please. I only want a moment with Venus. To apologize."

Dad's questioning brow matches mine when we look at each other, and a whole wordless conversation occurs between us:

Hmm, are you alright with this scenario?

I don't know, but I want to hear what she has to say.

I'm curious, as well. Would you like me to stay for moral support or leave for privacy?

She might be more forthcoming in your absence. Besides, you could make tea.

"I'll put on the kettle," he says aloud, with an uncharacteristic huff, before turning toward the house.

My attention returns to Maggie, who stands nervously at the foot of the stairs. I motion to the settee on the deck. She reminds me of a skittish intern about to explore a cave for the first time after admitting a predilection for claustrophobia.

"Are Henry and Olly alright?" I ask as we sit down.

"Olly's fine. They're headed to the optometrist to replace his glasses. Henry's kept him out of camp this week as a precaution."

I nod and hesitate. "And Henry?"

Her head tilts as she shrugs and tears well in her eyes. "You're the love of his life, Venus… so, he's miserable, thinking you won't be in it. That's what happens when soulmates aren't together as they should be—misery. He's desperately afraid that he's losing you again."

Her words surprise me. I used to believe that the concept of soulmates, as frequently depicted in the rom-coms Henry made me watch, was a failing in their storylines. Attraction, sure. Chemistry, yes. But a mystical, almost magical connection that forges two people together for life, regardless of any other? That gave me doubts. More likely, I believed that couples in love subconsciously weighed the pros and cons, mentally measured the long-term likability of their partners, and latched on to their most compatible mate. More science than mysticism.

But that's not Henry and me. We're a terrible match on paper, but we yearn for each other anyway. Our long separation should've destroyed any existing bond, but it didn't. Even now, I struggle to do what used to be so easy—booking a flight and getting lost *somewhere*, because wherever that is will be too far from him.

It's evidence that soulmates exist, and Henry is surely mine. Even Maggie sees it.

"But if you believe that," I say, "then why…"

"I reacted out of fear, Venus. Olly's accident wasn't your fault… neither was Henry's back then. My remarks were cruel and unfounded, and I only said them because I was upset. I apologize if you felt you had to run because of me. It kills me to think that I caused you and my son heartbreak. Then and now."

My irritation retreats, but I don't know how to respond. I don't blame Maggie for our heartbreak the first time—that was inevitable. We weren't ready for each other then. Our solo adventures were necessary based on the results. Along with my travels and education, I gained self-acceptance and confidence. Henry got his education and Olly. It was meant to be.

But it's difficult to accept her apology when she's always mattered so much to me, and I've only ever disappointed her.

"I have a rotten tendency to misplace blame when I'm upset... or scared. Henry's everything to me. Trying to protect him brought out the worst in me. I'm sorry you became a target," she goes on, tears collecting on her eyelashes. "I'm working on it in therapy, but it's obvious that I don't handle my emotions well. I think that's why Jay... well, he couldn't talk to me."

"Jay's struggles weren't your fault, Maggie."

Her brow pinches, but a weak smile emerges. "Thanks for saying that. I don't expect you to forgive me, Venus. I hope you do, but that takes time. For now, just know that... I've always loved you as a daughter. *Truly*, I have. And I'd love to have you as a daughter again now, if you'll let me."

Pesky tears threaten my eyes now, too. She digs into her bag for a tissue pack, hands me one, and takes another for herself, reminding me of Henry and his arsenal. "Why do I bother with mascara? Oh, and... I brought you supporting evidence."

"Really?"

"You love evidence, right?" She smiles. "I pulled these out of the closet the other day, and thought you should see."

The front door opens, and Dad steps out awkwardly with a tea tray. He sets it on the table between us with a loud clatter, smiling at me and giving Maggie a huff of disapproval.

"The cookies are for Venus," he warns her, though it still sounds nice somehow.

"Richard, I'm sorry for the trouble I've caused Venus and your family," she says, resting her hand over his on the tray. "I hope you'll forgive me one day."

"Hmm," Dad says, glancing from her to me and back again, unsurely. "Well, that's up to Venus."

"Thanks for the tea. Will you join us? I, um... You should see this, too," Maggie says, motioning to her box.

I offer him a reassuring nod, and he says, "I shall fetch another cup then."

Maggie sifts through the nondescript brown box, first handing me a clunky file folder. "Henry wanted me to pass that along. He's been busy."

I flip through the pages of calendars, dates, flight schedules, and miscellaneous information ranging from New Zealand food costs to interesting tourist destinations.

Dad returns with his cup and serves the tea. The scents of ginger and lemon fill the air, instantly comforting me as I take in the information.

"What is this, exactly?" I finally ask.

Maggie grins. "Henry's worked it out with Carly. Should you go to New Zealand, Henry and Olly will be there, too, as much as they can be, anyway. If you'll have them..."

"I-I..." Words fail me.

"He wants you to know that he'll do whatever it takes to make it work," she adds softly.

Tears crest my eyelids, falling onto Olly's school schedule, as I imagine the three of us traveling together, not just to New Zealand, but everywhere. My mind maps out milestones in Olly's education—me teaching him Spanish, French, and Latin; currencies and customs; the scientific method; art and music; and advising him on his first experiment. And Henry... kissing him under waterfalls, on trains, in museums, in the rain. I'm overrun with so many fantastical dreams that the tea splashes in my trembling hand.

"Here's what I wanted to show you," Maggie says after a long pause. On top of Henry's plans, she sets a green scrapbook with worn corners and flips to the first page. It features Henry in kindergarten—his school portrait, class picture, report cards, and samples of his school work. It's striking how much Olly resembles him.

She turns the page, revealing more of the same, and I smile over his clumsy handwriting and oversized grin. His first-grade year is featured next. But when the page flips to second grade, I gasp.

It's me—my school portrait—right next to Henry's. A copy of my report card is posted beside his with a message from my teacher requesting a parent-teacher conference. I vaguely remember running home through the woods with Henry on report card day, and him proudly handing it over to her in expectation of treats for his good grades. Her voice echoes in my thoughts, *"Venus, your turn. Let's see it."* She'd read it over, brow raised, before saying, *"You're brilliant enough to do better, but it's a good effort,"* and handing me treats, too. She must've made a copy while Henry and I gorged on cupcakes or chocolate cookies.

Page after page, I'm showcased almost as much as Henry. Pictures of us playing are wedged between drawings I gave her and homework she saved. The elementary school essays we wrote every fall on what we did during summer vacation mirror each other both on the page and in the narratives.

This summer, Venus and I....

This summer, Henry and I...

Tears slip from my eyes over our history, collected and preserved, and how desperately I want more. More pictures. More momentos. More Henry and me.

"Hmm, this is… lovely, Maggie," Dad says, scratching his head. "I was never much of a scrapbooker."

She shrugs, eyes fixed on me and my ceaseless tears. "Well, I'm a librarian. Documentation and collecting make me happy. You and Henry were inseparable back then. It wouldn't be *his* scrapbook without you."

Third-grade me had wild hair, but the following year, it was braided. Maggie taught me how. By fourth grade, I wore scarves and bandanas and clunky costume jewelry that she gave me to *"Give my hands something to do."*

The icy numbness I've been trying to achieve to accept New Zealand and plan my departure thaws as warmth spreads through me. Maggie *must* love me. And like me, she struggles with big feelings, too.

"I kept them through high school." She lifts the other albums from the box—there are five more, thick, with pages peeking from their edges. "You should keep them… take your time. There's a lot to see."

My brow cocks as I look up at her. "You'll leave them with me? Here?"

"Of course," she says. "I brought Olly's scrapbook, too. I thought you might want to—"

Her voice stops at the screech of my chair as I stand. She's handing me the best moments of my childhood—memories she saved and cherished. *And Olly's, too?* Overwhelmed by these beautiful books and her trust in letting me hold onto them, I fist my hands, energy surging. They stare at me, wide-eyed and stilled, like I might explode.

It feels like that.

I race inside. The door slams behind me. I climb the stairs, taking two at a time, and rummage through my open and overstuffed backpack. When I have what I need, I thump down the steps and bang through the door.

Dad and Maggie look perplexed by my urgency, but their expressions change to surprise when I hand over an item that I treasure—my passport.

"My collateral against your loan," I say. "I'll exchange your scrapbooks for my passport... when I'm ready. If that's acceptable."

She tugs the passport from my hand, looking baffled over my gesture. I wonder if my action seems weird to her, but it's my way of thanking her and comforting Henry.

"Hmm, it's customary to secure an arrangement between borrowers and lenders with something of similar value," Dad says, validating me.

"That's fair. Thank you," she says, tucking my ability to travel in her purse. "May I let Henry hold on to it, though, for safekeeping?"

I swallow the lump in my throat. "That would be acceptable... My job decision is still pending. I have much to consider. But I promised Henry I wouldn't leave without saying goodbye. This assures it."

"Whatever your answer, Venus, it has to work for *you*... But perhaps you're ready for a new adventure."

"New Zealand?" I ask.

"No... What's scarier or more exciting than love and parenthood?"

Dad laughs. "Isn't that the truth?"

"I'd better get going." She rises from her seat, but digs through her purse again. She pulls out a postcard-sized paper and pushes it to me. "Your invitation to the museum's launch party. Bring the whole family. Henry wanted to make it official."

Dad reaches the invitation first and answers for us. "It'd be an honor to celebrate Henry's achievement with him. We'll be there."

She steps toward the deck railing, but turns and smiles back at me. "Oh, and Venus... the rest of that box is filled with scarves. I never stopped collecting them for you."

CHAPTER 51
Henry

"I THOUGHT this was supposed to be an *intimate* gathering?" I ask Marnie as crowds gather outside the museum, twenty minutes before our private launch party.

"Um, yes. But then we invited Jay's biker friends, and the queens from Queens and Dreams—"

"Well, they *are* catering," I cut in, running a hand through my hair.

"Don't forget the contributors," Dot chimes in. "Like my wife and Jack Graham. You *had* to invite them."

"And their families," Marnie says.

"Oh, and I couldn't leave out the ghost hunters club," Eric says. "Or the alien geeks. Or the conspiracy podcasters, Beyond the Truth."

"That's debatable," I huff.

"Who do you think'll put this place on the map, huh?" Eric argues.

"Well, there's the local TV station and that journalist, Cleo Spire. She did that piece about my business in February. I'm still getting calls from it," Marnie says, tapping her pen against the guest list in her Trapper Keeper. "We *need* the free publicity."

"Hell, is that a guy wearing an alien costume?"

Everyone peers out the window around me.

"Yep, that's Ken, president of We Are Not Alone," Eric reports. "You wanted weird, right?"

"Don't stress out, Henry," Dot says with a stern pat on my back. "It's not a party without a guy in an alien costume."

My shoulders tense as I take a quick puff off my inhaler.

"Sorry, Henry. We got overzealous with the invites," Marnie says, face scrunched. "The good news is that so many people are excited and invested in your success. Right?"

"Right," I say, though nerves rise under my shirt collar. It's been a difficult week with everything converging at once—Olly's injury, courses ending, this place opening, and Venus leaving. My best saving grace has been Mom, ironically. When she showed up with Venus's passport in her hand, my fear that I'd never see her again abated, along with my anger at Mom. I even hugged her.

But Venus's silence tells me she's still conflicted. Whether about us, the job, or both, I don't know. She asked for time to think, and I've respected that, though I'm desperate to see her.

As if reading my mind, Marnie asks, "Any word from Venus?"

"No, not yet."

"Buck up, Buttercup," Dot says, making me smile. "She'll be here, and she'll love what you've done."

"Nothing like last-minute changes to keep us on our toes," Marnie says, her tone somewhat strained. "But everything's ready—I think."

Her attention turns to the window as the crowd continues to congregate outside.

"Dot, could you help with traffic control?" I suggest watching cars circling the block.

"Aye, aye," she says, rushing outside.

"And Eric—"

"Yes, boss?"

"Entertain the early birds at the door?"

"Okie dokie," he salutes before grabbing his sword case.

"I'll do one last round of checks before the doors open," Marnie says, disappearing down the hall.

I take another puff of my inhaler, my lungs feeling heavy and tightening with each breath. The wooden bluejay catches my eye—it's perched beside the register. I scoop it into my hand.

"Well, Jay, this is it. What do you think?" A heavy sigh escapes. "Will she show?"

A light tapping at the glass door makes my shoulders pop. Mom, Fred, and Olly stand on the other side, peering in through the glare. I slip the bird into my jacket pocket and let them in.

"It's a bit chaotic out there," Mom says as they come inside. "That's a good sign."

Fred's in a button-down, tucked in, with dark jeans, which is about as dressy as I've ever seen him. He pats my back, "Congrats, Henry. It'll be a big hit if that crowd's any indication."

"Dad, Grandma says there's going to be cake." Olly wears khaki pants with a grass stain on the knee and a green collared shirt that matches his green cast, which he's already gotten used to wearing—he pretends he's got one Hulk arm. He musses his brushed hair and pushes up his glasses, awaiting my confirmation.

"Cake *and* Venus flytrap cookies," I report with a grin.

"Real food first, Olly," Mom says. She wears a green satin dress, soft and friendly, and her nerves seem contained, though her brown eyes land on Jay's memorial, her brow perking as she takes in our work—she helped me finish it. A graffiti-style blue jay wearing a black leather jacket serves as a backdrop for frames and shadowboxes, highlighting everything Jay, from his military service to the museum and how it's changed over the years, to family pictures, concerts, hobbies, and trips. It doesn't represent a life lost, but a life lived.

I slip my arm around Mom as she takes it in. "You okay?"

"It's perfect, Henry. I'm happy to celebrate with you. Happy to celebrate Jay, too… Any sign of Venus?"

"No, not yet."

"She'll be here," Mom says unwaveringly.

Her words restore my confidence.

Soon, the doors open. Marnie and Eric greet guests in the lobby and funnel them into the museum, where Mom, Olly, and I invite them to explore the displays and enjoy the food and drinks. Led by DeeDee, the diner queens circulate with hors d'oeuvres and drinks that sparkle under the ambient lighting. Their sequined dresses sparkle, too, giving the open room a brilliant, colorful glow. The museum soon fills with guests, delighting in lore, legends, and treasures. I overhear phrases that fill me with pride:

Wow, I never knew that happened here.

It's incredible to think that this is true.

Who knew this small town could be so interesting?

The historian in me—the *teacher* in me—finds instant reward in their amazement, just as I do in my classroom on good days. My hand rests on the bluejay in my pocket, knowing Jay would be proud to see it.

But it's not perfect.

I move to the elegant staircase and perch on the fourth step. From here, I can see almost everything in the main room—each carefully constructed section, the entry to the room of darker displays, the small buffet along the wall, and the new escape room, presently hidden under a curtain with one of Marigold's signs: *coming soon*. The quiet artist stands with her boyfriend near the entry, seemingly happy to be apart from the crowd. Marnie and Grady mingle close by, smiling and holding hands. Dot stands with her wife, Jaye, beside her contribution—early artwork from her graphic novels. I spot Jack Graham and his wife, Rowan, laughing with the man in the alien costume and the reporter, Cleo Spire, next to Jack's donations—his latest manuscript, lovingly and thoroughly annotated by his wife, the English teacher and our district's current teacher of the year.

Carly and her boyfriend Gregory follow Olly as he gives them a tour of the place, while Mom and Fred watch in amusement, probably saying something about his endless excitement.

In the last half hour, I've been introduced to Lena and Ben Wright of Saddletree Farm and Café, where *Hunter, The Return* was filmed. They not only provided the movie memorabilia, but Lena also baked and personally delivered a three-tier Wilmington-themed cake with ships, mermaids, fossils, flytraps, and pirates that Marnie had ordered for the occasion. Lena fiddles with her gorgeous centerpiece while her stoic, but attentive husband puts his arms around her and leads her away to enjoy the party.

Delilah Duffy-Teague, the bookstore owner and Mystery Maven of Tipee Island, rests her head on her husband, Sam's, shoulder as they ogle the leather starfish notebook and magnifying glass necklace she contributed—mementos from the cases she's solved. Her half-smile makes me wonder if she misses it. Sam urges her over to meet Jack Graham, and the book lover immediately gushes over his romance novels.

Movement near the entry hallway catches my attention. Dr. Blake and his partner enter. Dr. Blake seems as calm and relaxed as always, while Christie gushes and coos, waving a pink handkerchief in the air. Ivy and Gil follow behind them, holding hands and gravitating toward Marnie and Grady. With bated breath, I watch for Venus to enter next, but when Ivy catches my eye with a sympathetic, I-don't-know shrug, my hope deflates.

Everywhere I turn, I see signs of loving relationships—the automatic touches, familiar smiles, and knowing looks. Normal couple things, I think with a measure of sadness. As perfect as all of this is, it's incomplete. I ache for the woman who completes me.

"Dad! Is it time to cut the cake yet?" Olly asks, dashing across the room. Mom and Fred scurry behind him, barely keeping up. He barrels into my arms as I lean down. I lift him as I stand, and he rests on my shoulder, tucking his cumbersome cast to his chest. The time will come when he'll no longer want to be held like this, and he'll be too big for it, anyway, another thought that comes with a measure of sadness. But I'm grateful it's not tonight.

"We'll have cake soon," I say.

"Wow. You can see everything from up here."

"He's a tad overstimulated," Mom says.

"Aren't we all?" Fred returns with a laugh.

"Want to help me do the toast?" I ask Olly.

"Yeah, Dad!" he agrees with unhindered enthusiasm that would be the same no matter what I asked.

"Go with Grandma to get your champagne," I tell him, setting him down.

He smirks. "You mean grape juice, don't you?"

I tussle his hair. "I can't trick you."

He races off with Mom and Fred while I notify DeeDee and Marnie. DeeDee and her team spread out amongst the guests, armed with glasses of champagne.

Marnie gives me a concerned look. "Are you sure? We could wait a smidge longer."

"Nah, it's fine. Everyone wants cake. Let them eat cake," I say, resigned but still glancing at the hall entry.

"Oh, a Marie Antoinette reference... I'm not sure that'll bring us good luck," she notes.

"Actually, there's no evidence she said that. It was a cliché attributed to her after her death," I say sheepishly.

Marnie gives me a half-amused and half-sympathetic look. "Want me to check the parking lot, just in case?"

I glance at my phone. No messages. Even knowing that her passport is safely stashed away offers little comfort now. I wonder where she is, what she's thinking, if she's okay. If she wants to run. "Willing Venus to appear doesn't work—I've tried it for years. We're already behind schedule."

"What about the escape room?"

"I'll, um… adjust the speech. We won't unveil it tonight."

Marnie nods. "Okay, then. I'll grab the microphone and signal you when everything's in place."

The elegant staircase acts as a stage for Olly and me. He dutifully stands beside me, holding his crystal tumbler of grape juice, as I test the microphone Marnie hands me. With one last glance at the empty hallway, I swallow my nerves and begin… without her.

"Welcome and thanks for joining us tonight to celebrate the Weird But True Wilmington Museum."

Applause echoes throughout the building.

I introduce Olly, Mom and Fred, and the team that so diligently helped me make this place happen, offering my thanks for their support. Marnie tears up over my words and leans comfortably against Grady as the crowd cheers.

While the noise dies down, I glance to the hallway—still empty—and fight back my mixed feelings over this proud, but imperfect moment. Suddenly, I wish I'd waited for her just a little longer, but with a room full of expectant faces now staring at me, I must go on. *You must go on.* Dr. Blake's words swim in my head—it's what he said to me in the greenhouse after explaining that my sunflower believes she's a cactus. Does she still believe that? The hurt and confusion resurface, too, jumbling my thoughts. I glance at Mom, and she gives me an encouraging smile.

"Um, Uncle Jay started this place with a dream to bring together everything he loves… history, mystery, curiosity, and people. That dream took a few detours over the years. Mom and I weren't too happy with its gator and serpentarium era… or with the serial killers…"

Laughs.

"… But we always understood the vision. Jay taught me to love the past and question the present. He showed me how to spot a fake ghost-sighting video and what pirates' treasure really looks like. We'd talk about alien theories for hours, which always felt way more interesting than anything taught in school. He told me scary stories, against my mom's wishes, which Venus—"

My voice catches on her name, and my thoughts skip, like the needle bumping over a scratch on a record. "Um, Venus…"

My eyes drift to my feet, trying to piece together what I meant to say. But my thoughts get lost in her, and fears over why she isn't here. I went a decade without her, and yet, all that yearning stacks up, tightening my chest, and this moment becomes the hardest. She belongs here. With me. With us.

Someone clears their throat, and I blink, returning to the present. A crowded room. Jay's museum. My speech.

"Um, sorry. What I meant to say was," I say, looking up, "Vee—"

Her name sticks for a third time, only because my sore eyes find hers. Her gentle smile locks with mine as she slips into the crowd from the side hallway—a breeze, filtering between guests.

"Venus…" Her name falls from my lips, this time with relief, and echoes over the loudspeakers. The crowd turns toward her, shifting to let her through. She looks incandescently beautiful. She's wearing her dusty pink prom dress, this time with proper shoes, and every move she makes sparkles under the twinkling lights. My favorite scarf waves through her hair, filling me with heat as I remember it tied to her wrists. Her sweet surrender. Her with me.

"Um, hi…" I mutter, rather forgetting the crowd.

"Henry, forgive me for being late," she says, fiddling with her rings and bracelets. "I-I had a dilemma."

My brow pinches. "Dilemma?"

"I couldn't decide what to wear," she says, unsurely.

Laughs.

"Happens to me all the time! You look gorgeous!" DeeDee slips beside her, taking her arm, and escorting her to the stairs next to Olly and me. My son automatically slips his hand into hers. My tension dissipates in a breath. Now, everything is as it should be.

Blushing and grinning to the point that my face hurts, I force my attention on the crowd. "Um, where was I?"

"Scary stories!" someone calls out.

"Right, Jay's scary stories that would've caused nightmares and sleepless nights, if not for Venus refuting them with scientific counter-evidence, making me feel better. *Temporarily*. Until Jay would tell me the next one…"

Laughs.

"He encouraged me to find the stories behind objects, oddities, and people, and then to go deeper to see the stories *behind* those stories. What are we without our stories?"

I take a breath, my throat closing up with emotion, until my eyes land on Venus. She smiles softly, and it's just enough to take the edge off my nerves and pull back the tears threatening to fall.

"He taught me to be there for the people I love as often as they need me... To live and love fully. Rebuilding his dream has helped us grieve him, but it's also been a celebration of his life. That's what he wanted this place to be—a celebration of life, all that's weird and true."

I hold up the glass in my hand.

"So, here's to Jay, forever in our hearts."

The crowd clinks glasses and toasts, "To Jay!"

My glass gently meets Olly's and then Venus's. I lean closer, kissing her cheek and breathing her in. "You just made tonight perfect."

A coy smile curls over her lips, but before she can respond, I hold up the mic. "One more thing before we cut into the most gorgeous cake I've ever seen..."

Lena beams from the audience.

"...the unveiling of our newest and most puzzling addition, our escape room!"

Marnie and Dot remove the curtain in one swift pull, revealing the door behind it. The crowd gasps, taking in the intricately designed Venus flytraps circling the door.

"The Botanist's Study, inspired by my favorite botanist, Dr. Venus Blake, to thank her for yet another perfect summer," I grin with a glance at Venus. She's practically aglow with surprise and anticipation, especially when Marnie swings the door open, revealing the room inside. Even at this distance, it reminds me of what Venus might one day have: its plants, scientific tools, a backlit work table, an art easel, bookshelves, and field journals.

Venus gasps beside me. "Henry, it's... I... I thought it was supposed to center around local lore and history."

"It's *our* lore... *our* history." I lean closer to Venus. "Want to try it?"

"Henry, it's... I... yes," she manages, looking almost giddy.

Into the mic, I say, "The escape room has yet to be tested. So, guests are welcome to enjoy cake and cookies while Venus attempts to free herself from the room that she inspired."

Olly races toward DeeDee for cake. I take Venus's hand and lead her across the museum.

CHAPTER 52
Henry

THE PLAN WAS for Venus to test the escape room first—alone. I wanted her to take her time, marveling over the room's thoughtful design, the plants and artifacts, and the clues and puzzles that I lovingly created with her in mind. The challenge blends our two loves—botany and history.

I made the room all about us. Our favorite movie posters line the walls between botanical prints and some of her drawings. A TV tucked in the corner plays the opening number from *Little Shop of Horrors*. The shelves are filled with books from our childhood—history, art, and science. Lab coats, gardening aprons, and scarves hang from a coatrack. Plants take up every space in planters, jars, and hanging from the ceiling. Paints, scientific tools, journals, and flowers, *so many flowers*, clutter the backlit counter, as if she'd been working there, engrossed in a thousand things at once. An art book lies open on the desk, displaying Van Gogh's *Sunflowers*.

Turns out, I wasn't tapped out on romantic gestures after all. I doubt I'll ever be when it comes to her.

But ten minutes into her seclusion, and with the crowd distracted by drinks, cake, and Eric's more family-friendly juggling routine, I can no longer stand it.

Escape room doors aren't actually locked—that would break all sorts of laws and codes—so when no one's looking, I slip inside.

Venus sits on the edge of the cluttered desk, her face buried in her hands. *Crying.* Her sadness turns me inside out, guts me. My best intentions fizzle into hopelessness, seeing her like this.

This isn't what I wanted for her. Not tonight. Not ever. Yet, I'm the cause of it. She's leaving, and I've made her even more heartbroken over it.

The antique key and the wooden lockbox that ends the game sit beside her. Inside the box, winners find a code that, once entered into the iPad perched by the door, declares their success with lights and music.

Tonight, though, that box holds her passport and a note.

Venus,

 You've always been my favorite adventure. Now, we're family—you, me, and Olly.
 Wherever you go, I'll chase.
 Whatever you need, I'll give.
 Whenever you're ready, home will be here, waiting.

        Love ALWAYS,
         Henry

She holds both in her lap as she sobs—my big romantic gesture has only made our reality harder to accept. I go to her, crossing the room in two long strides, and run my hands up her exposed arms.

"I'm sorry," I whisper as she reaches out to me. She tugs me close, opening her legs for me to nestle against her thighs. "I didn't mean to… I thought… I'm sorry, Vee."

Tears speck my eyes as I realize—it's the greenhouse all over again. I've prolonged the agony, made it sharper, forced her into a long, devastating goodbye when her way would've been easier. Home should be a sanctuary, not a trap. And perhaps the only place for Venus to feel free is out there, lost, away from us.

I lean into her, nuzzling her nose and resting my forehead against hers. Our hot breaths mingle, and her damp cheeks catch against my beard. "It's too much," I whisper. "I'm sorry. I didn't mean to make it harder for you."

"No, Henry, no. You haven't," she cries, her hands rising to my neck, as if she needs me close. "I love it. It's... *us*."

It *was* us. My brow pinches with the thought of her boarding a plane, taking off, leaving us behind. Tears slip from my eyes as she studies me. I want to ask her when she leaves, to calculate how much time we have left, but fearing the answer, all I can get out is, "When?"

"I'm not leaving, Henry," she says softly.

I sputter a breathless, "What?"

Her eyes find mine, though our breaths fog my glasses. "I'm not leaving. Not leaving you and Olly."

A guarded smile emerges as my hands grip her soft cheeks. "But you're crying?"

"You and Olly, this room, your note—I couldn't help it," she mutters. "I'm crying because I'm happy."

"You're not leaving?" I ask again, sure I must not be hearing her right.

"I'm not leaving," she says, slower this time. She pushes the passport against my chest. "Keep it. Put it with yours and Olly's because the next trip we take will be together."

I tuck her passport into my jacket pocket and collapse against her, blubbering with happiness and relief. With anyone else, I'd be embarrassed—the king of the ugly cry.

But it's *her*.

Brilliant, bold, beautiful, *her*.

Brave and vulnerable, *her*.

My absolute, my fixed constant, *her*.

My best friend, *her*.

Partner, soulmate, *her*.

And she loves me just as I am.

The same way I love *her*.

Tears, big feelings, and all.

She swipes her palms over my wet cheeks as I do the same to her, and laughter breaks through. Venus has never made me feel bad about anything, certainly not something as natural as tears. But joy zips through me at the thought that from now on, all those big emotions, hers and mine, we'll experience together. *It's okay. You're with me. Everything'll be okay.*

"I've never been happier," I mumble softly.

"Me, neither," she says, her voice catching on emotion, too. Unable to hold back any longer, I kiss her, and she laughs at the urgency of it. Over and over, kissing her. I can barely stop to ask her what she means. "So, you're staying?"

"We've been apart too much already, Henry," she says. "And with Olly at this optimal stage of his development and scientific education, I don't want to waste another minute."

More kissing.

"But what about your work? New Zealand?"

"That's also why I was late," she says breathlessly before kissing me again. "Renegotiating with Dr. McCullum. I wanted to accept New Zealand, but I couldn't without some changes."

More kissing. "What changes?"

"I'm *consulting* on the New Zealand project. It'll mostly be remote, but I'll spend a few weeks there in August to get the team started. I want you and Olly to go with me."

"To New Zealand? This summer?"

Her brow crinkles. "It's short notice, I know, but according to the detailed plan you outlined, it's possible if you can leave the museum. It *truly* is magnificent, Henry. I'm so proud of you."

A smile peeks through my incessant kissing. "Thanks, and yes, we'll go wherever, whenever you want. I'll speak to Carly, and I've made Eric the Sword-Swallower, Eric the manager. It's too much for me, and Jay would've wanted me to have help."

"Help is good," she says, her brow pinched as if trying to come up with something more eloquent, though she said it perfectly.

More kissing.

"Oh, there's more," she says. "I've agreed to teach special topics courses at UNCW and assist Dad with his research part-time, so I can pursue my art, too. A textbook company has reached out about hiring me for illustrations."

"That's amazing. You're amazing." My lips crush hers in yet another desperate kiss. "I love this plan. I love that you want us with you. It's fucking perfect."

She pulls away, smiling coyly. "It's me being Venus and you being Henry, and us, finally getting to love each other like we've always wanted."

"Finally." I take her hands in mine, bring them between us, and kiss her fingers. "Venus, look! Your ring!"

Her damp eyes widen as she takes in the long, oval surface of my grandmother's ring, now an unmistakable blue. Bright and serene, like the perfect summer sky.

"I-I don't understand," she gawks. "It's not onyx."

"No, it's a mood ring," I remind her.

"Mood rings use thermochromic liquid crystals that change according to body heat and blood flow. The crystals absorb energy, causing a molecular color change. Why would it change now? After all this time?"

I can't contain my sappy grin. "Because you're happy."

Her brow pinches with scrutiny, her eyes fluctuating between me and the ring, and I sense the scientific argument that's building in her head.

"Trust it. Don't reason it out," I say with a laugh before kissing her again. "I bet it stays that color from now on."

"Highly unlikely, scientifically," she says, "but anything's possible with you."

I kiss her again. "I like the sound of that. Maybe it's blue because you're being so damn romantic. Staying with us."

"Not romantic. Pragmatic," she corrects. "I'd be too distracted to work and make incredible scientific discoveries without you and Olly close at hand."

"Yeah, right," I say, with playful sarcasm. "Us being together—it's for science."

"The world needs me at my best," she says. "Olly, too—"

As if whispering his name summoned him, a low pound on the door is followed by, "Dad? Venus?"

I laugh against her. "Think we can pull ourselves together enough to get back out there?"

She tugs my glasses from my face and wipes the smeared lenses with my tie. "I hope so. There's cake."

"Just a sec, Olly," I call before kissing her again.

She straightens the knot in my tie while I sweep out the wrinkles in her dress.

"How long did it take you?" I ask, realizing that the escape room test will need a result.

Her coy smirk gives me pause. "Eight minutes."

"Damn, only eight?"

"It's very enjoyable, Henry. I predict it will take the average group with limited prior knowledge about forty minutes, especially given the obvious conflicts and debates typical of a group endeavor. That's ideal, I think."

My eyes narrow at her as we move toward the door. "You think so?"

"The oleander clue and the Tar Heel reference were especially clever. Oh, and I love the movie and the posters."

"*Little Shop of Horrors* and *You've Got Mail*, just for you."

Stopping at the door, she twists around again, seeming to examine every small detail. "I love it. It's perfect... but perhaps it's best not to tell them that it only took me eight minutes. It might make them think it's too easy."

I reach for the door handle, but hesitate. "Yeah, but you *are* a genius."

She nods. "True. Let's say it took fifteen."

"Ready to escape?" I ask with a grin.

"With you, I think I'm ready for anything," she says, taking my hand in hers.

I open the door, and Olly practically falls inside and launches into an excited report of the evening's highlights for Venus, who listens attentively and asks thoughtful questions as he leads us to the cake.

Venus

EPILOGUE

"SO, YOU'RE STAYING? FOR *REAL*?" Ivy says, her blue eyes bright with excitement but also suspicion.

"Yes, I'll still travel for work and pleasure, but Wilmington will serve as home base," I explain to the group assembled around the rear deck of the fairy house. The fans Christie installed swirl overhead, taking the edge off the humidity. The solar-powered twinkle lights pop on across the backyard, over the garden paths, inside the greenhouse, and along the deck. Everyone smiles, as if marking the start of a pleasant evening.

"That's wonderful news, sweetheart," Fred says, squeezing Maggie closer by the shoulders. "Ain't it, Mags?"

"Wonderful," she repeats with an easy smile on her face.

"Good thing we upgraded that mattress up there," Christie says.

"We're delighted to have you," Dad says.

"Oh, I'm not staying *here*. I mean, for now, yes. Thank you. But not for long."

"Are you moving in with me and Olly?" Henry perks up, his lopsided smile widening with the idea. "We'd love—"

"No, I'm not doing that either, but thank you for the offer." The group stares expectantly, awaiting my explanation. "I have money saved. I want a house with a yard and a garden. I want a greenhouse, an art room, a study, and a porch." I turn to Henry, locked at my side, and hope he's not disappointed. "Your apartment is very nice, but it simply won't accommodate me. Oh, and I want a dog."

"AHHHHHHH! Buster's getting a cousin?" Ivy yells, rousing the dog at her feet. He yaps his usual *"what"* as if he missed my big announcement.

"Don't worry, Henry. I'll invest in air purifiers so you and Olly will be comfortable staying with me, because I want you to stay frequently. I'm thinking Olly's room should have an archaeological theme, but I'm open to discussion."

"A dog? My own room?" Olly recaps, abruptly stopping his race around the deck with Mango flying through the air. "Can we get one just like Buster? Can I have a bunk bed? Can we paint stars on the ceiling?"

"Maybe, maybe, and yes," I answer.

Satisfied, he flies Mango around the deck again, this time with Buster in tow.

"Ivy, will you accompany Olly and me to pick out my new pet, since you're more experienced?" I say.

She bounces on her sparkly sandals, the ruffles in her skirt swaying, before she takes my hand and spins me around like we did in the parking lot. "I'd be happy to! We can take our dogs to Grady for check-ups and spa days—"

The doorbell interrupts her dancing.

"Oh, speaking of the Tripp family, that's Gil." She rushes along the deck to greet him at the front door.

Christie rounds the group with wine, refilling our glasses. He wears a green scarf around his neck that reminds me of my collection. He leans in to whisper, "He's a dreamboat, Vee. I'm so happy for you."

"Me, too. I'm glad you came home early, Christie."

He waves his free hand with a flourish. "Well, I missed your dad, and I was jealous about your self-care slumber party. Besides, Wren wanted to travel to Scotland for a druid ceremony, anyway. But she predicted that you'd find your *true escape* before she left—she's always been somewhat of a soothsayer. It won't surprise her, but she'll be thrilled that you've ended up with your fern guy after all!"

"Fern guy?" Henry asks, as Ivy returns to the deck with Gil behind her.

"Oh, no! I mean, was I not supposed to say?" Christie's eyes dart from Henry to me. "Me and my big mouth."

Ivy rushes over, her brow peaked. "You didn't tell him?"

Henry twists in my direction. "Tell me what?"

"I discovered a new species of fern and named it after you."

"What?" he gapes.

I point to the spindly fern with brown flowers, like dandelion heads, wrapping my calf and moving up my leg. "Henry's fern."

He looks aghast. "You named a fern after me?"

"Yes."

"That *you* discovered?"

"It's not uncommon for a botanist to discover a new variety. About thirty percent of—"

Henry kisses me—hands to my face, lips pressed on mine, his tongue taking a gentle dip into my mouth. I laugh, returning his affection amid the hoots and claps of our observers.

"On that note, I'll grab the lasagna," Christie says.

"I'll get the salad. I love eating alfresco," Maggie says, following him inside.

The crowd disperses to arrange our dinner. But Henry stays with me.

"You've been holding out on me. That's so fucking romantic," he whispers at my lips.

"Oh, no. Not romantic. Practical," I counter. "The plant needed identification."

He chuckles. "I've turned you into a romantic. You're *romancing* me."

"No, I'm not. Romance is a construct of novels and rom-coms. It's not real."

"Then how do you explain the weak feeling in my knees and the butterflies in my stomach? What would you call it?"

"Medical distress?" I try, not wanting to give him complete satisfaction. Still, I feel my cheeks turning pink with his attention. I love this game we play.

"The only *distress* I'm feeling is how long I have to wait to get you naked again," he says in my ear before nibbling my earlobe. "Will you stay at mine tonight?"

My lips part to say yes, but Ivy bursts through the sliding glass doors with more wine and the crowd following behind her, and announces, "Gil and I are moving in together," as if she can no longer contain the news.

A second round of excitement and well-wishes commences. Christie claps while Dad says, "Wonderful news!"

Henry offers his congratulations while sneaking sexy glances at me.

We settle around the table, heaping our plates with lasagna, salad, and bread over our excited conversations.

I've never seen our family this animated and happy for each other. Growing up, it always felt like an every-person-for-themselves existence, each in our separate corners. I recall Ivy's distress over us and what she called our "weirdness." *Why can't we go to football games? Or have a TV? Or get our nails done, like normal people?* To which Dad, rubbing his chin, pushed up his glasses, and said, *"Hmm. Why would we want to be normal people, Ivy?"*

Trying to be "normal" is rather miserable. Whenever I tried, I only wanted to escape the straitjacket confines of it. Even Ivy, with her team of friends, found herself disappointed by trying to fit in and live up to societal ideals. In the end, those friends scattered like dried leaves. Now she has the friends she chooses rather than the ones she had to work to keep, and her roots. Us.

Now, I like our roots. If I had a second chance at growing up, I'd choose more of us embracing our weirdness *together* rather than fighting it apart. Weird, but true to ourselves and each other.

Around this table now, that's what we're doing. Our significant others have taken our loose strings and tugged them all together, knotting and binding us. As Henry leans close like he can't drift too far away, I bask in the beauty of our tightly knit pocket. I'm warm, safe, loved, perfectly myself, and exquisitely happy. And that's not vagueness or my subconscious claiming an elusive and ultimately impossible happily-ever-after.

It's a simple fact. One that is conveniently corroborated by my delightfully blue mood ring.

"So, what happened to your arm?" Gil asks Olly as he struggles to grip his fork with his obtrusive cast.

"It was awesome!" Olly gushes. "I climbed up a gigantic tree, super high. I could see over the tent, and in a bird's nest, and..."

Nerves rise as Olly explains his misadventure with such enthusiasm. Images of him climbing a tree again, only to fall and break his other arm, fill me with angst.

"...the bark was rough. Next time, I'll—"

"But Olly." My gentle interruption happens simultaneously with Henry's, saying the same thing.

We lock eyes, and feeling like I've overstepped, I say, "Sorry. Please," and motion for him to go on.

He laughs. "No, go ahead. It'll mean more coming from you."

With a smirk, I address Olly. "Remember our talk about tree-climbing?"

Olly's lopsided smile appears. "That I shouldn't do it without you?"

"Exactly. We'll start smaller next time with safety measures in place... and only when you're healed. Adventures are fun, but only if they're safe."

"Okay, Venus," Olly says with only slightly less excitement.

Satisfied that he's heeded my reminder, I take a breath and glance at the rest of the table. Everyone stares at me, surprised.

Well, except for Christie, who tears up and waves a scarf to dry his eyes. "What a sweet teaching moment."

"Hmm, well said, Venus," Dad quips while the others smile warmly.

Henry's hand slides over my thigh under the table. "I couldn't have said it better."

Warmth spreads through me as I bask in their approval and the sweet realization that this is where I belong, with my family.

Fall in love with my backlist and other characters from *Venus Love Trap*:

For a disastrous meet-cute... Marnie and Grady (and Christie, Ivy, and Gil) in *Every Chance After*

To *always chase*... Jack and Rowan in *Yes No Maybe*

For love and reinvention at the worst time... Lena and Ben (and Dot) in *One Thing Better* and *Every Good Thing*

For bookshop mysteries & second chances... Delilah and Sam in *The Delilah Duffy Mystery Series*

Help others find their next great read by leaving a rating or review for *Venus Love Trap*. Find links to Goodreads and others using the QR code below.

You'll also find access to all my books (including signed copies with swag), and BONUS CONTENT. Rejoin Venus and Henry one summer later, free for subscribers, & get a sneak peek at *The Holiday Haters*, coming 2026!

bio.site/authorjessicasherry

From the Author

First of all, THANK YOU FOR READING *Venus Love Trap*! There are so many beautiful books out there—the competition for your time and shelf space is fierce. Taking a chance on an independently published title champions the underdogs of the industry. Your support keeps me writing and makes this arduous publishing journey worth it. So, THANK YOU.

Venus Love Trap is my tenth novel! Ten books have taught me not to try this alone. It's a team effort to create quality books that readers love and deserve, and I'm lucky to have an exceptional one.

Thanks to Sam Palencia of Ink and Laurel (@inkandlaurel) for this stunning cover. I dreamed up Venus and Henry and that incredible greenhouse, but you brought that dream to life.

Thanks to my trusted alpha readers, Joe, Jenny, and Tabitha—you always help me get to the heart of the story. Thanks to my insightful beta readers, Mai Lagdameo and Kristina Grigaityte, for helping with all the fine details. Extra special thanks go to Jenny Austin, my friend and professional editor, for her detailed notes, extra passes, brainstorming sessions, and endless patience.

Thank you, Fozi (@fozireads), for creating social media buzz for *Venus Love Trap* and all my books. Thanks to Good Girls PR and the ARC team for reading, reviewing, and promoting *Venus Love Trap*. This launch has been the best ever thanks to your help!

And back to Jenny… When planning my next book last year, Jenny said to me, *"Did you know there's a carnivorous garden near your house?"* I had no idea about this uniquely beautiful garden, tucked between a school and a neighborhood, not two miles away. Visiting the Stanley Rehder Carnivorous Plant Garden at Piney Ridge Nature Preserve instantly inspired me—nature often does. Though *Venus Love Trap* isn't connected to the Rehder family, I'm grateful to them for preserving and educating us on carnivorous plants—one delightfully weird feature of Wilmington. There's no A-frame fairy house at the inspo garden, but when I visit, I see it there, along with Venus, Henry, and Olly, playing and exploring. So, thank you, Jenny, for telling me about this hidden gem, for encouraging me to write a STEM FMC, and for your constant inspiration!

Finally, Joe... After this book, I feel a bit tapped out on romantic gestures. Just kidding—there's always romance left over for you, even after thirty years. Every book I write is for you, for us, for our future. Not only do you inspire them by being *that guy* for me, but I write them with you in my heart, hoping to give you all the feels, hoping to make you proud. Thanks for partnering with me on another beautiful story, and I hope that this is our year, that those numbers you watch so diligently, skyrocket.

Big Hugs,

Jessica Sherry

www.ingramcontent.com/pod-product-compliance
Lightning Source LLC
LaVergne TN
LVHW091702070526
838199LV00050B/2252